PRAISE F
P

MW01483809

Publisher's Weekly: "Known primarily as a bestselling humorist, Greenburg here essays crime fiction for the second time. A race-against-death closing segment will have readers turning pages as fast as they can."

New York Times Book Review: "Mr. Greenburg writes an engrossing tale filled with black humor and psychologically interesting characters. Great grisly fun."

Chicago Tribune: "Greenburg's chief skill is his ability to blend comedy, horror and tragedy in the same situation."

San Francisco Chronicle: "Greenburg weaves in enough plot twists and street-tough legalese to make these pages nearly turn by themselves."

Houston Chronicle: "The authenticity of *Exes* grabs you, and the gory reality may give you nightmares. Greenburg's talent for blending psychodrama and mystery pays off in a blockbuster thriller."

New York Newsday: "It is the atmosphere of authenticity, reminiscent of Ed McBain's 87th Precinct police procedural novels, that gives *Exes* its impact."

Boston Globe: "Dan Greenburg creates a police thriller that reads as realistic as anything Joseph Wambaugh ever produced. It's alternately absorbing, sad and funny."

FEAR
ITSELF

ALSO BY DAN GREENBURG

FEAR ITSELF

THE MAX SEGAL SERIES
BOOK THREE

DAN GREENBURG

THOMAS & MERCER

The characters and events portrayed in this book are fictitious. Any similarity to real persons, living or dead, is coincidental and not intended by the author.

Text copyright ©2013 by Dan Greenburg
All rights reserved.

No part of this book may be reproduced, or stored in a retrieval system, or transmitted in any form or by any means, electronic, mechanical, photocopying, recording, or otherwise, without express written permission of the publisher.

Published by Thomas & Mercer, Seattle

www.apub.com

ISBN-13: 9781477848951
ISBN-10: 1477848959

Cover design by Cyanotype Book Architects

Library of Congress Control Number: 2013910734

Printed in the United States of America

ACKNOWLEDGMENTS

For technical assistance in the writing of this book I am indebted to:

The detectives and officers of Manhattan Homicide North, NYPD

The detectives and senior officers of Queens Homicide Squad, NYPD, especially Det. Maryann Herbert

Lt. Edward "Fast Eddie" Mamet, former commanding officer, 9th precinct, NYPD

Raymond Pitt, PhD, police psychologist, NYPD, emeritus professor of sociology, John Jay College of Criminal Justice, City University of New York

Dr. Michael M. Baden, former Chief Medical Examiner, City of New York

Dr. Lawrence Kobilinsky, Associate Professor of Biology and Immunology, John Jay College of Criminal Justice, City University of New York

John Bergman, prison psychodrama therapist

Michael Marcum, former warden, San Francisco County Jail #7, former Assistant Sheriff, San Francisco County

The warden, correctional officers, and inmates of the Northwest State Correctional Facility, St. Albans, Vermont

Brian Bilodeau, Case Work Supervisor, Northwest State Correctional Facility, St. Albans, Vermont

Jack Bush, PhD, specialist in prison reform

I would like to express special thanks to Dr. Elizabeth A. Sharpless, the New York psychologist who steered me to my most valuable research in the treatment of phobias.

For information on gambling I'm indebted to longtime Las Vegas resident and even longer-time friend Marv Rubin.

I'm also deeply grateful to my editors, Alison Dasho, Larry Kirshbaum, Andrew Bartlett, Terry Goodman, and Kevin Smith, and also to Phil Burgess for their outstanding contributions.

CHAPTER 1

AT FIRST IT looked like suicide.

Detective Max Segal saw the emergency service vehicles and the red and amber lights winking in the steamy August evening and, although he was off duty and so exhausted it felt as though his clothes weighed about eighty pounds, he figured they might need help and pulled up and parked in a loading zone.

Max was smack in the middle of a divorce which had taken away both his beloved eight-year-old son and his ability to digest food. What little energy he had left tonight was sapped by heat and humidity, either of which had to be higher than the IQs of the goremongers who now clotted the flow of traffic.

Max made his way through them to the uniformed sergeant who appeared to be in charge. Because the sergeant wasn't anyone he knew, Max took out his gold NYPD detective's shield in its worn leather case and flashed it at him.

"Whatta we got here, sarge?" asked Max, blotting perspiration from his eyes and hairline with a folded handkerchief.

"Young female come off the roof," said the sergeant. "Off the twentieth-story roof."

"Jumper?"

"Yeah," said the sergeant. "You from the one-fourteen?"

"No," said Max. "From Queens Homicide."

"*Homicide,*" said the sergeant. "This here ain't no homicide."

"I just got off duty," said Max. "Happened to be passing by. Thought I'd stop and see if there was anything I could do."

1

"Check with the one-fourteen," said the sergeant, "but no way this here's a homicide."

"Right," said Max. "You have an ID on the deceased?"

"One Virginia Morales," said the sergeant, checking his notepad.

"What shape's she in?" Max asked.

"Not great," said the sergeant. He looked a little queasy. "The body must of cartwheeled. About halfway down she hit the railing of this terrace and just . . . come apart."

"She came apart?" Max repeated, not quite understanding what he was being told.

"When I got here it looked like the first officer on the scene had strung up a piece of red tape, like crime scene tape, to keep people away," said the sergeant. He shook his head. "It wasn't red tape."

"What was it?" asked Max, instantly sorry he'd asked.

"If you don't believe you got like thirty-six feet of intestine inside you," said the sergeant, "I could show you otherwise."

"Jesus," Max breathed.

"Part of her stayed up on the terrace," said the sergeant, suddenly needing to talk about it. "Emergency Service had to go up there and retrieve it. The rest come down. The way she hit that railing just unwrapped the intestine and stretched it right out on the bushes in front of the building." He held out his hands, about a yard apart. "Looked like a red tape. A red ribbon."

"Okay," said Max, making a mental note to avoid such questions in the future.

"I don't know," said the sergeant, shaking his head again. "You're supposed to show professionalism, you know, and like it doesn't bother you, but . . . boy." He took a deep breath and then let his lungs collapse like bagpipes.

"I know what you mean," said Max sympathetically, aware he'd now be obliged to view what was left of the body himself and that the image would imprint itself upon his retinas and invade his dreams for months to come. "Who caught the case?"

"See the young guy over there?" said the sergeant, pointing. "With the droopy mustache, the ponytail, and the earrings?"

"Yeah?"

"Name's DaVinci," said the sergeant. "He's with the one-fourteen. Talk to him if you like, but this sure as shit ain't no homicide."

"Right," said Max.

Max pushed his way over to the young guy with the droopy mustache, the ponytail, and the earrings, who was taking notes in a little spiral-bound notebook, trying to interview a distraught middle-aged woman wearing a flowered caftan.

There was no love lost between homicide detectives, who had an average of fifteen years on the job, and precinct detectives, who could now get gold shields after only a year as undercover narcs. Max, who'd gotten his own shield at the unlikely age of twenty-five and had to endure more than the routine teasing given rookies, found to his dismay that at age thirty-seven he no longer identified with young detectives. He still wasn't sure what he thought about earrings on both ears for men and had always felt ponytails looked best on teenage girls and ponies.

"I mean I don't understand it," said the woman in the flowered caftan, shaking her head, "I just spoke to Virginia this morning."

"What about?" asked DaVinci, notebook open and pencil poised.

"About Mrs. Ramos," said the woman. "Our neighbor in 2D?"

"Yeah . . ."

"Mrs. Ramos is a chain smoker," said the woman, "and the walls are so thin in our building, the smoke seeps into all the apartments on the floor. They've already proven that secondhand smoke is as dangerous to you as asbestos, did you know that?"

"So?" said DaVinci. He was a smoker himself and didn't need to hear any more about secondhand smoke.

"So," said the woman, "why would you be upset about second-hand smoke if you were planning to kill yourself?"

"Did Miss Morales seem at all depressed or despondent?" asked DaVinci.

"Only about Mrs. Ramos and the smoke," said the woman.

"Well, thanks for your help," said DaVinci, slapping his notebook shut.

"How ya doin'?" said Max to DaVinci by way of greeting, flashing his shield.

DaVinci looked up, noted Max's shield, but did not otherwise acknowledge the senior detective's presence.

"I understand you caught the case," said Max, trying again, a little ticked at the apparent slight, but determined to give the kid the benefit of the doubt.

"The fuck are *you*?" asked DaVinci.

Max took a deep breath. "Detective Max Segal. Queens Homicide."

"*Homicide*," said DaVinci. "This ain't no fucking *homicide*."

"So I've been told," said Max, heating up fast, stepping toward the younger cop. "Look, I'm off duty, I happened to be passing by, and I thought I'd stop and see if you needed help, okay?"

"Well, we *don't*, asshole," said DaVinci, pushing Max away with a hand on the chest. "So go home or back to Homicide or to shul, but get the fuck out of my face, Hymie."

The unexpressed rage that Max had been sitting on for months suddenly cracked out of its shell. Without thinking what he was doing, Max grabbed a finger of the hand on his chest and bent it sharply back, hearing a satisfying crack. DaVinci cried out—a high, embarrassingly girlish sound—but Max gripped the doubtlessly broken appendage like a bench vise and stepped within an inch of the younger cop's face.

"If you *ever* touch my person again, or if you *ever* disparage my religion again, *ever*," Max hissed, "I promise you I will break off

4

every single one of your fingers and ram them up your fucking nose. Do you understand me?"

DaVinci stared at Max, pop-eyed and in pain, unable to speak.

"If you understand me," said Max quietly, slowly, and distinctly, bending the finger back farther, causing DaVinci to inhale sharply, "please signify by saying 'Yes.'"

"Yes," whispered DaVinci.

"Thank you," said Max and released the finger.

DaVinci, the woman in the caftan, and everyone else took several steps backward.

Max returned to the sergeant. Inside Max's shirt a light drizzle had begun to fall.

"The ME been here yet?" Max asked.

"Not yet," said the sergeant.

After a preliminary examination of the body, the medical examiner would classify the death as a suicide or, if there were any doubt in his mind, a CUPPI—Cause Unknown, Pending Police Investigation. Unless Max were able to find evidence of foul play.

"I'm going to take a look inside," said Max.

"Whatever," said the sergeant.

Max walked into the lobby of the apartment building and flashed his shield at the doorman. There was a desk and two large potted trees with obviously plastic leaves. The lobby was deliciously air conditioned and Max was tempted to stop and chat, if only for the chance to cool off.

"How long ago this happen?" Max asked.

"About an hour," said the doorman. "Give or take."

"You on duty at the time?"

The doorman shook his head. He was short and stocky, with very black hair, dark skin, and Eastern European features. His uniform had been made for somebody tall and skinny.

"I was on a break," said the doorman.

5

"Who was on duty when you were on your break?" Max asked.

"The porter."

"What's his name?"

"Surtees," said the doorman.

"Where's Surtees now?"

"Went home."

"What's your name?"

"Khatchatoorian," said the doorman.

"Mr. Khatchatoorian, did you know Miss Morales fairly well?" The doorman shrugged. "Just to say good morning, good evening, that type of thing."

"She seem depressed to you of late?"

"How the hell would I know that?" asked the doorman, irrationally annoyed.

"Have the police been up to her apartment since she died?" Max asked.

"Not that I know."

"What apartment she live in?"

"2E."

"You got a key?"

The doorman thought this over a moment, then gave Max the key.

Max realized his motivation had changed from merely helping out his fellow officers to finding evidence the death was a homicide and proving DaVinci wrong. Was proving DaVinci wrong a good reason to initiate a homicide investigation? Maybe not, but the guy was sure one unpleasant sonofabitch.

Max knew why DaVinci felt strongly about keeping this case a suicide. Precinct detectives were under pressure to maintain a high clearance rate or batting average of solved cases. If this one remained a suicide, it didn't endanger the clearance rate. The ME, however, had no clearance rate to worry about. All he had to do was move a certain number of bodies across the autopsy tables every year, but it was more embarrassing for him to have a death he ruled a suicide turn out to be a homicide than to have a homicide turn out to be a suicide. So if there were any doubt, the ME would be inclined to classify this one as a homicide. Homicides tended not to get solved and this one would screw up the precinct detective squad's clearance rate.

Although the deceased's apartment was only one flight up, Max took the airless self-service elevator, too tired to walk. Sweat stood out in pimples along his hairline and under his shirt. He mopped his face with his handkerchief and alighted on the second floor. As he slipped the key in the lock of the door marked 2E and was about to grasp the doorknob and step inside the dead woman's apartment, he had a sudden thought: If Virginia Morales *wasn't* a suicide, then poking about in her apartment before the Crime Scene Unit took pictures and dusted for prints would contaminate the scene. On the other hand, if he *didn't* poke around in there and find something suspicious, Crime Scene would never have any reason to come here at all.

He took out his handkerchief again, wrapped it around the doorknob, turned the key, and entered Virginia Morales's apartment.

A narrow hallway with religious pictures on the wall. Jesus, the Virgin Mary, and a few other folks wearing halos and beatific expressions whom Max couldn't immediately place. An exercise bike opposite a large screen TV in the living room. Did suicides work out on exercise bikes?

In the bedroom, on the wall above the bed, a Mexican sombrero, a large wooden crucifix, and a framed photograph of what must be the extended Morales family. On the bed a dozen teddy bears of all sizes and colors, arranged as if posing for a class photo, the smallest ones in front. Max had the uneasy feeling he always got when in the homes of the recently deceased: a terrible invasion of privacy.

On the kitchen counter a box of Familia, an egg timer in the shape of an egg, a ceramic cookie jar in the shape of an orange tabby cat, and a bunch of bananas about to turn into banana bread. Familia was a health-food cereal, the bananas an exercise enthusiast's source of potassium. Would an exercise and health-food enthusiast be a candidate for suicide?

On the refrigerator door, several scraps of paper held in place by magnets shaped like miniature pizzas, hamburgers, and hot dogs. On the scraps of paper, telephone numbers, directions to a restaurant in TriBeCa, a schedule of masses at a local church. Are religious people serious candidates for suicide?

In none of the rooms of Virginia Morales's apartment could Max find anything resembling a suicide note.

He took out his cell phone and snapped photos of all the phone numbers on the refrigerator door, pocketed the address book he found on a small desk in the living room, then let himself out of the apartment, grasping the knob of the front door again with his handkerchief.

He paused before the door of the adjacent apartment, noted the name Ramos on the nameplate, and then knocked. After a moment, a woman's voice, husky with whiskey, cigarettes, or both, called out, "Who's there?"

"Police, Mrs. Ramos," said Max, holding his shield up to the peephole. "I wonder if I can ask you a few questions about your neighbor, Virginia Morales?"

The door was unlocked and pulled inward. In the doorway stood a short, stout, squinting Hispanic woman with a lit cigarette wedged in the corner of her mouth. The smoke from the cigarette rose directly into the woman's eyes, which was doubtlessly what was making her squint, but this did not appear to bother her.

"She dead?" said Mrs. Ramos.

"Yes, ma'am," said Max.

"Good," said Mrs. Ramos. "Bitch never gave me a minute's peace."

"You had altercations with the deceased?" Max asked. Mrs. Ramos didn't invite Max into her apartment, so he remained in the hallway. He took out a small spiral notebook like DaVinci's and began to scribble illegible notes with a Scripto pencil.

"Not a day passed she didn't give me some shit about second-hand smoke giving her lung cancer," said Mrs. Ramos. "Cancer this, cancer that—I never heard so much cancer in my life. If my smoking's giving *her* cancer, what the hell's it giving *me?*"

"Pardon me?"

"If *I'm* not worried about cancer, and I'm the one sucking on the goddamned cigarette," she said, "what the hell's *she* got to worry about?"

She took a crumpled tissue out of her pocket and hocked a huge glob of phlegm into it.

"Tell me, Mrs. Ramos," said Max, "when was the last time you saw Miss Morales?"

"When did I *see* her?"

"Yes."

"Not for, oh, three months," she replied.

"I thought you said not a day passed she didn't give you some shit about secondhand smoke," said Max.

"She didn't have to *see* me to give me shit," said Mrs. Ramos. "She put letters in my mailbox, she stuck notes under my door, she yelled through the wall—these walls are so thin she didn't even *have* to yell. She coulda whispered."

"But you didn't actually see her for the last three months?" Max asked.

"Three, four, I don't know," she said. "Tell me something."

"What?"

"She was so worried about cancer, why wasn't she worried about walking off the roof?"

———

Max took the elevator up to the twentieth floor, got off, and walked to the end of the hall. He opened the door to the stairwell and walked up another flight of steps to the roof. A warning on the door expressly forbade exit to the roof: EMERGENCY EXIT ONLY. KEEP OUT. ALL PERSONS ARE FORBIDDEN FROM EXITING ONTO THIS ROOF FOR ANY PURPOSE WHATSOEVER UNDER PENALTY OF LAW. He pushed the door open.

There was a slight breeze out on the roof. Max pulled the back of his shirt away from the spot between his shoulder blades where it had stuck.

A four-foot-high brick parapet lined the perimeter. A system of air-conditioning ducts erupted from the tar paper, then ran for several yards along the parapet before plunging back into the roof. A thicket of TV antennas sprouted from a buttress at the back. A series of gigantic round turbines, the size of 727 jet engines, whirred ominously on all sides.

Max strode to the parapet. Taking out a small black high-intensity flashlight, he walked slowly along the roof, playing the beam of the flashlight over the tar paper surface till he got to the front of the building where the death had occurred. He didn't know what he was looking for. He knew he wasn't finding it.

On a sudden whim, he placed both hands on the parapet, boosted himself onto it, stood up slowly, and looked down on the assemblage of emergency personnel and equipment on the street and on the railing of the balcony where Virginia Morales had hit and come apart and on the pieces of the body that were now covered with plastic tarps.

For an instant he had a dizzying urge to fling himself forward and go hurtling downward like Virginia Morales, screaming and flailing, the pavement rushing upward at thirty-two feet per second per second to smash his head like a pumpkin, squash his body to jelly, or have the railing of the balcony split him in two and stretch his intestines out on the bushes below like red tape.

The moment passed.

Very, very carefully Max climbed down from the parapet and, with great relief, felt his feet come once more into contact with the solidity of the tar paper roof.

He was trembling and weak. What the hell had he just experienced? A long-dormant urge to self-destruct? Was he in such agony over his divorce, the loss of his son, and his current financial difficulties that he subconsciously wished to die? He had never understood suicides, had never been able to imagine why anyone who was not terminally ill and in excruciating pain would ever choose death voluntarily. He still felt that way.

He walked shakily back to the entrance of the building, descended the stairs to the top floor, and took the elevator down to the lobby.

"Find what you were looking for?" asked the doorman.

Max shook his head, went outside, and found a ninety-five-dollar parking ticket on his windshield.

CHAPTER 2

I HEAR YOU BROKE some guy's finger in the one-fourteen," said Tony Natale, walking into the tiny living room where Max had begun making up the Castro convertible.

Natale, a former longshoreman on the Brooklyn docks, had taken the police exam and become a uniformed cop, then studied nights for about a hundred years to become a police shrink, but he'd never lost his heavy Brooklyn accent. He had offered Max a place to crash while he was working out his separation, little realizing he was taking on a semipermanent roommate.

"How the hell'd you hear that?" Max asked.

"Hey, bubbeleh, you're the talk of Queens," said Natale, chuckling. "I must say it sounded like a tiff on the girls' playground, though. Did you scratch and pull hair too?"

"Shut up, Tony, will you?"

"What the hell'd he do to you, Max?"

"It's not important," said Max, pulling the bed part out of the frame and setting up the extended legs.

"No, c'mon, tell me," said Natale. "What'd he do to you?"

"Pushed me and disparaged the Jewish religion, okay?" said Max tiredly.

"My hero," said Natale. "If only you'd been around in Germany in the late thirties."

"Okay," said Max. "What would *you* have done? What if he'd said *dago* things to *you*?"

"He wouldn't have said dago things to me," said Natale. "DaVinci *is* a dago."

"You know what I mean," said Max.

"I know what you mean," said Natale gently. "If DaVinci had insulted me? If DaVinci had insulted me, I would've told him to fuck himself and then I would've walked away."

"Because you're a police shrink and you know how to handle these situations better than the rest of us," said Max.

"No, because I'm not a Jewish guy going through a divorce with a wife who's shtooping an Arab."

This stung. The problem with Tony was he was enough of a shrink to see stuff like that, and enough of a longshoreman to zap you with it. A deadly combination. Max shook out a fitted sheet and tried to fit it over the mattress, but realized he'd put it on the wrong way.

"What makes you think that's why I broke DaVinci's finger?" Max asked.

Natale shrugged.

"Call me crazy," he said.

———•—•—•———

It was true that Max's wife was having an affair with an Arab named Achmed. ACH-med. It sounded like a disagreeable Caribbean singles club. Although Max's ancestry was distinctly Hebraic and Zionist, his Christian wife claimed that her affair with Achmed had no political content.

Achmed was a disconcertingly likeable guy—handsome, educated, and gentle. He was also a detective at Manhattan Homicide North. Max had met him when they'd both worked up there and liked him well enough to bring him home for dinner one night, which was how Babette had met him. In some ways Max liked

Achmed more than he did Babette. If Achmed had not been his wife's lover, they might have become friends.

Achmed was not your stereotypical billionaire napkinhead who kept a harem and owned oil fields the size of Montana, but that was a reasonably accurate description of Achmed's father. Although Achmed was currently killing time as a homicide cop, everyone at Manhattan North knew he could quit at any point and slide right into the family business.

Achmed was more attentive to Max's wife than Max had ever been to her since their courtship. Achmed brought Max's son, Sam, presents every time he saw him. Expensive presents. Better presents than Max could afford to give Sam himself. Max had learned not to ask his son where the best new toys came from; they came from Achmed.

Not only did Achmed bring Sam better presents than Max did, Achmed also had a comradely ease with Sam that Max was unable to achieve. This may have been because Achmed was not also obliged to see to it that Sam ate sufficient protein at mealtimes or remembered to cleanse all bodily orifices during showers or to floss his teeth before bedtime, but it may also have been because comradely ease was not one of Max's greatest talents.

Sam liked Achmed a lot. "Achmed is my favorite adult friend," Sam announced to Max on one occasion. Sensing Max's jealousy of their relationship, Sam tried to reassure him: "Don't worry, Dad," he told Max, "I love you just as much as Achmed." It had been necessary for Max to leave the room for five minutes after that one.

Max thought about taking Achmed to lunch in a medium-priced midtown restaurant and saying to him over dessert in this really calm, reasonable voice, "Continue shtooping my wife if you must, but be any nicer to my son and I'll rip your head off."

When Max's wife Babette was in a good mood, there was no more charming female on the Eastern seaboard. When she was in an angry mood, there were several. Achmed had either not yet seen the angry Babette or else was too smitten with the other one to let it register.

Babette claimed to be quite sensitive to Max's feelings about her relationship with Achmed. She had also systematically taken Achmed to every restaurant she and Max had considered romantic and uniquely theirs, and just recently she'd allowed Achmed to take her on a five-day vacation to the small island in the French West Indies where she and Max had spent their honeymoon. Max didn't ask whether they'd booked the same room, out of a wish to spare her feelings.

The hot sexual relationship which Max and Babette had enjoyed for years fizzled when Sam was born. They separated briefly when Sam was three, then they patched it up. When Sam turned seven, shortly before the affair with Achmed began, Max and Babette finally decided to call it quits, their great love frozen in mutual hurt and anger like prehistoric insects in amber.

Unwilling to throw mother and child out into the street, Max moved out of the small apartment he'd lived in for years before meeting Babette, the apartment he'd gone into hock buying when his building went co-op. He moved in with Tony Natale. Tony had himself broken up a ninety-day marriage a short time before to a girl named Cheryl who was his junior by a quarter of a century.

———

"Dad," Sam asked, "when are you going to die?"

"I don't know," said Max. "Not for a long time, though. Don't worry."

"How old will you be when you die?"

"Oh, I don't know, ninety or a hundred," said Max carelessly.

Sam had dishwater blond hair like his father and wore summer-weight Winnie-the-Pooh pajamas. Max was putting Sam to bed in the small second bedroom of his old apartment, the one he owned and paid the mortgage and maintenance on but didn't live in anymore, going through the rituals which he and Sam had built up over the years, rituals which by now meant as much to Max as they did to Sam.

Max had sung Sam his going-to-sleep songs, played him his going-to-sleep tape, and was now lying next to him on the tiny bed along with two stuffed rabbits, five stuffed dogs, nine teddy bears, and a four-foot-high polar bear that had come from Achmed.

"Could you live to a hundred and fifty, do you think?" Sam asked.

"Uh, sure," said Max. "But don't worry, Sam, by the time I die you'll be a grown man with a family of your own."

"How old will *I* be when you die?"

"Oh, gosh, I don't know, hon," said Max. "Pretty old, though."

"I want to die before you and Mom do," said Sam.

"I hope that won't happen," said Max, shuddering at the thought.

Babette appeared in the doorway in silhouette. "Max?" she said quietly.

From her tone of voice Max deduced it was time to go. He got carefully up from the bed.

"Can't you stay and cuddle with me a while?" Sam asked.

"I've *been* cuddling," said Max, smoothing the boy's hair off his forehead. "I've been cuddling for almost twenty minutes, hon. Now I have to go home."

"Why can't you stay and cuddle just a little longer?" Sam asked.

"I wish I could," said Max, bending down to kiss Sam's damp forehead, inhaling the heady smell of the boy's freshly washed hair and skin, a pleasantly soapy smell. "I'll try and see you in a couple of days, okay, buddy?"

"Okay."

"I love you, buddy."

"I love you, too," said Sam. "You're the best dad a boy could have."

Max smiled. It was something that Sam began saying about a year ago. At first Max thought it was a put-on. Then he realized it was sincere.

"You're the best boy a dad could have," said Max, completing the ritual.

Babette led Max to the front door in the tiny entryway.

"Sam and I had a long talk at bedtime last night," she said in the tone she used to inform Max of his many failings.

"Yeah?" he said, unaware of what his latest crime might be, but already feeling guilty.

"Sam says he thinks you're jealous of his feelings for Achmed."

"Mmm," said Max. "Well, Sam could be right."

"I *know* he's right," said Babette. "But he feels guilty about it."

"So?"

"So it's not good for him to feel guilty."

"So what do you want me to do about it?" Max asked.

"Tell him you're not jealous of Achmed," said Babette.

"You want me to *lie* to him?"

Babette furrowed her brow. "No, I don't want you to lie to him," she said. "Why don't you just tell him that you're not jealous of Achmed because you know that you and Sam have a special relationship which nobody else can duplicate."

"Mmm."

"Does 'mmm' mean you'll tell him?" she asked.

"'Mmm' means I'll think about it," said Max.

"Good," said Babette, opening the door for him. "Well, good night. Oh, one more thing."

"You need money," he said.

"I'm a month behind on both the phone bill and Con Ed."

"I'll put a check in the mail tonight," he said.

"Can't you give me a check now?"

"I don't have my checkbook on me," he said. "I'll drop it in the mail tonight, though, I swear to God. Listen, maybe we should talk about Sam and the jealousy thing."

"Maybe we should," said Babette, "but not now."

"You seem anxious for me to leave," said Max. "Is Achmed coming over or what?"

"What makes you think Achmed's coming over?" she asked.

"Why don't you just answer the question?" Max asked.

Babette's face was a stew of feelings. "I don't see why I should have to be defensive about who comes over here to see me," she said. "After all, this is *my* apartment now."

Whose apartment this was had yet to be determined by their attorneys and the court, but it was true that Max didn't relish the prospect of running into his wife's lover. On the other hand, he relished even less the prospect of fleeing what was, contrary to Babette's characterization of it, still at least *partly* his apartment, simply because her lover was on his way over.

"What time's old Achmed coming?" Max asked.

"What's the difference?"

"What time is he coming?"

Babette bit her bottom lip.

"Nine thirty. Why?"

"I think I might just stay and say hello," said Max.

"You're not serious."

"Sure I'm serious," said Max. "What makes you think I'm not serious?"

"What are you going to do?"

"Say hello," said Max. "I told you."

"I thought you told me you didn't want to see Achmed again," said Babette. "I thought you told me that."

"I did tell you that," said Max. "And at the time I said it that was what I felt. But now I feel differently. Now I want to say hello to him."

"What if he doesn't want to say hello to *you?*" she asked.

"Then I suppose he won't," said Max.

She cocked her head at him. "Why are you doing this, Max?"

"Because I feel like it."

"Why are you doing this?"

"Because I like Achmed."

"Why are you doing this?"

"Because, frankly, Babette," he said, "I'm tired of skulking around, avoiding Achmed, like you and I were having some sort of illicit affair or something."

"Max," she said, "you can't just be here when he arrives."

"Why the hell not?"

"Because I don't have any way of warning him about you."

"Nobody warned me about *him,*" said Max.

"Max, please don't do this."

"Why not?" said Max. "Hey, c'mon, Babette, it'll be great. You'll see. I'm really looking forward to it."

Shortly after nine thirty the doorbell rang. Nervous as hell, Babette buzzed Achmed in.

"Max is here!" she blurted as Achmed began running up the stairs, but Max was already standing behind her at the top of the flight.

Achmed looked wary, fight-or-flight hormones squirting into his system.

"Hi, Achmed, how ya doin'?" said Max.

"Hi, Max," replied Achmed.

"I was just about to leave," said Max, "but then I heard you were coming over and I thought, hey, I'll say hi to Achmed. I thought it was about time we had a chat anyway."

Achmed looked cloudy.

"You want to have a *chat*?" he asked.

"Yes," said Max. "A nice chat."

Anticipating a storm, Babette took shelter in a dry room. Max led the way into the living room. A cheap sofa with polyurethane cushions faced a small fireplace that actually worked. Achmed looked really jumpy.

Max liked Achmed. Achmed was nice. Achmed was smart and gentle and good to his son. Achmed was bigger than Max, but if Max struck him first he could inflict serious damage. It had truly never occurred to Max to strike Achmed, but now the thought flitted across his mind like summer lightning. But Max liked Achmed. Achmed was nice.

"Sit down, Achmed," said Max. "Please."

"That's okay," said Achmed.

"So. Achmed," said Max. "How ya been?"

"Okay," said Achmed, looking at the floor, perspiring heavily.

"What about this weather we've been having, huh, Achmed?"

"Yeah," said Achmed. "Look, Max, this is really awkward for me, you know?"

"I know," said Max, realizing suddenly that he felt less awkward than Achmed did, and relishing the realization. "You know, Achmed, I really like you."

"Thanks, Max, I like you too."

"I mean I'm not exactly thrilled that my wife has a lover," said Max. "But since she does, I'm glad it's somebody as nice as you."

"God," said Achmed, providing separation between his collar and his neck, then blotting his forehead with the sleeve of his right arm.

"As a matter of fact, Achmed," said Max, "the only thing that I find truly painful is your relationship with Sam."

"Sam is great," said Achmed.

"Yes, he is," said Max.

"I love Sam," said Achmed.

"Well, Sam loves you too, Achmed," said Max. "In fact, he told me 'My favorite adult friend is Achmed.'"

"Sam said that?" Achmed asked.

"Yeah," said Max. "I must tell you, though, that the picture of Babette and Sam and you together as a happy family in what used to be my home is so painful it's unbearable."

"I hate causing anybody pain," said Achmed. "I'm going through some pain of my own right now."

"Oh?" said Max a trifle petulantly. Max had thought this conversation was about *his* pain.

"Yeah," said Achmed.

"What pain are *you* going through?" asked Max dutifully.

Achmed shrugged.

"It . . . doesn't matter."

"No, what?" said Max, unable to use this disclaimer as permission to quit pursuing a trail he hadn't the slightest desire to pursue. "Tell me."

"Well . . ." Achmed puffed out his cheeks and then let the air out with a whoosh. "It seems that Babette has started . . . seeing somebody else."

"You're kidding me," said Max.

Achmed shook his head. "I'm serious."

"How do you know?" said Max. "She tell you?"

"More or less. I . . ." Achmed waved the rest of the thought away. "God, I'm sorry, Max. I shouldn't be telling you this."

"Maybe you shouldn't," Max agreed.

"No, I definitely shouldn't," said Achmed.

What was happening here? Was it conceivable that his wife's lover was hoping to have Max help him win her back? Was it conceivable Max *wanted* him to win her back? Was it conceivable that known Achmed was better than unknown rival?

Max *could* help Achmed win Babette back, he supposed, knowing her as well as he did, knowing what buttons to push and what circuits they engaged. He could also advise Achmed to do things which would pretty much ensure that he *wouldn't* win her back, in case that should prove to be the more interesting alternative.

"And then again," said Max, "perhaps you *should* tell me."

"What do you mean?"

"Well, Achmed," said Max, "my own relationship with Babette, the romantic one, is over. And I do like you. Perhaps if you told me the circumstances of your dilemma I might be of some help to you."

Achmed studied Max's face, trying to read whether Max was mocking him or truly offering his help.

"Is this a serious offer," said Achmed, "or are you making fun of me?"

"I would never make fun of you, Achmed," said Max. "Certainly not to your face. And the offer is serious. If you'd like to talk about your dilemma sometime, please give me a call. Here, let me give you my number."

Max jotted down the number of Tony Natale's apartment on an old parking lot receipt and handed it to him. Achmed looked at it quickly, as if to make sure there really was a number there, and then returned his gaze to Max's face and nodded solemnly.

"I might just take you up on this," said Achmed.

"I hope you do," said Max.

CHAPTER 3

"WHY ARE WE so hot to keep this death a suicide?" asked Buonarroti of his partner as they entered the lobby of Virginia Morales's building. "Because we don't want to get fucked out of overtime if Homicide comes into it or what?"

"I give a shit about overtime," said DaVinci. "I'm just trying not to invent a homicide we're never gonna solve. I just don't wanna get stuck with a loser and have it fuck up our clearance rate, so I'm not making this a homicide unless I got somebody in handcuffs, okay?"

The doorman was nowhere in sight. The coolness of the air-conditioned lobby was a relief from the sauna outside.

"What if the ME makes it a homicide after the autopsy?" asked Buonarroti.

"We'll cross that bridge when we come to it," said DaVinci.

Detective squads used two clearance rate numbers—the clearance rate for the current year and the clearance rate overall. If you arrested someone this year for last year's homicide, you were allowed to credit that clearance to this year's statistics. Your squad might have a clearance rate of only 10 percent, but if you cleared enough homicides from previous years you could end up with an overall clearance rate of over 100 percent, and the overall clearance rate was what mattered to the NYPD.

DaVinci and Buonarroti found Surtees, the porter, in the little room off the lobby where they kept large packages. Surtees was sitting on a UPS delivery, drinking a Dr Pepper, and reading a copy of a girlie magazine called *Bodacious Ta-Tas*.

"Mr. Surtees?" said DaVinci.

"Yais?" said Surtees guiltily, in a heavy but unidentifiable accent, quickly stowing the girlie magazine under a package.

DaVinci took out his shield with his good left hand and flashed it faster than a pervert in a raincoat at Saks Fifth Avenue.

"Police Department, Mr. Surtees."

A look of panic crossed the little porter's face.

"I'm Detective DaVinci, this is Detective Buonarroti. We understand you were on duty at the front desk on the night of the Morales suicide."

"Please?" said Surtees with a grin so forced it looked like his face might crack under the strain.

"I said were you on duty on the evening that Virginia Morales committed suicide?" asked DaVinci.

"Ah, no," said Surtees. "I am only de porter."

"We understand that, Mr. Surtees," said Buonarroti, "but the doorman, Mr. Khatchatoorian, told us that he went on a break shortly before Miss Morales jumped off the roof, and you took his place for about twenty minutes or so prior to the jump. Is that true?"

"No," said Surtees.

"It's not true that you took Mr. Khatchatoorian's place while he was on his break?" asked DaVinci.

"No no, ees not true was twenty minutes," said Surtees. "Was maybe thirty."

"I see," said DaVinci.

With the three taped fingers of his right hand he motioned to his partner to take notes. Buonarroti withdrew a stenographer's pad from his sport coat pocket and began taking notes with a Bic.

"And during that thirty minutes—" said DaVinci.

"Could be maybe thirty-*five* minutes, I dunno," said Surtees.

"And during that thirty-*five* minutes—" said DaVinci.

"Could be only *twenty*-five minutes, I dunno," said Surtees.

"And during that twenty-five or thirty-five minutes, Mr. Surtees," asked DaVinci, keeping his voice calm, "did Miss Morales have any visitors that you recall?"

"Eef Mees Morales have any veeseetors during thees period?" said Surtees.

"Yes," said DaVinci.

Surtees scratched his head reflectively. "Was only de one guy dat I remember."

"Miss Morales did have one visitor prior to her suicide?" asked DaVinci. "A male?"

"Yais."

DaVinci and Buonarroti exchanged glances.

"You're sure of this, Mr. Surtees?" asked DaVinci.

"Yais," said Surtees happily. "I sure."

"Mr. Surtees," asked DaVinci, "would you recall what this individual looked like?"

"Eef I know what he look like?"

"Yes."

"Pootty good, yais," said Surtees.

"How would you describe him?" asked Buonarroti, pen poised.

"Just some guy," said Surtees frankly. "You know."

"He meant was this individual Caucasian, black, Asian, or what?" asked DaVinci.

"What means Cowcayshun?" asked Surtees.

"Was he white? Black? Yellow? What color was his skin?"

"Was white."

"He was white?" repeated DaVinci.

"Yais, white."

Buonarroti made a scribble. "Short? Tall? Fat? Skinny?" asked Buonarroti.

Surtees cocked his head to think.

"No."

"No?" said DaVinci. "*What* no?"

"Was not short, tall, fat, or skinny," said Surtees. "Was just regular guy."

"What color hair did he have, Mr. Surtees—blond, brunette, red?"

"What means broonet?"

"Brown," said DaVinci. "Was his hair brown?"

"Was kinda brownish."

"Kinda brownish?" said DaVinci.

"Brownish blond."

"Brownish blond," said DaVinci.

"Brownish reddish blond."

"Brownish reddish blond," said DaVinci. "Right. Any tattoos or other identifying marks?"

"What means tatuse?" asked Surtees.

"Tattoos," said Buonarroti. "Any, you know, names or pictures or other stuff drawn on his skin in ink."

"What means identifying?" asked Surtees.

DaVinci covered his face with both his hands and shook his head.

"Mr. Surtees," said Buonarroti, "if we brought you a police artist, do you think you could work with him on a sketch of the visitor?"

Surtees laughed uproariously and shook his head.

"You couldn't do that, Mr. Surtees?" asked DaVinci. "Why couldn't you?"

"I lousy drawer," said Surtees. "He hov to do eet all by heemself."

CHAPTER 4

MAX WATCHED HIS partner in amazement. The big detective with the thick neck, the pockmarked but agreeably masculine face, and the massive beer belly stuffed the rest of his third cheeseburger into his face and continued chewing.

"Sal," said Max, returning his gaze to his driving, "I've got to ask you something, and whichever way you answer will be fine, I swear to God, but I really have to ask you, okay?"

Caruso grunted, his mouth fully dedicated to the ingestion of chopped meat and cheese and not to speech.

"As you're no doubt aware," Max continued, "I am currently facing a severe economic crisis, the consequence of trying to maintain a wife, a kid, and two matrimonial attorneys on the salary of a detective second grade. I am behind on my wife's rent, behind on my own rent, behind on both attorneys' fees, I am maxed out on all my credit cards, and I need cash. I wonder if you could possibly see your way clear to—"

Still chewing, Caruso closed his eyes and shook his head from side to side.

"Okay, okay," said Max, continuing to scan the street for a parking place. "I know you're strapped yourself, but Natale's almost as broke as me and I'm getting desperate, so I really had to ask. How the hell can you eat that crap, by the way?"

"What, cheeseburgers, you mean?" said Caruso, swallowing the last bite and emitting a magnificent belch.

"Yeah, how can you eat three cheeseburgers for lunch?"

Max spotted a place, eased the new unmarked Chevy Caprice into it, and turned off the ignition. The NYPD had gotten a good buy on Caprices. They weren't bad cars, but the name embarrassed Max. The last car the NYPD had gotten a fleet rate on was the Plymouth Fury. Fury sounded like a real cop car, justifiably angry and tough. Caprice sounded like transportation for ballet dancers.

"What's wrong with cheeseburgers?" Caruso asked.

"What's *wrong* with them?" said Max. "They're crap, that's what's wrong with them. Do you even know what goes into cheeseburgers?"

Max got out the driver's side, locked the door from the inside, and slammed it. Caruso hefted himself heavily out of the passenger's side.

"Beef, cheese, and bread," said Caruso. "Three healthy things. What the hell's unhealthy about beef, cheese, and bread?"

"Do you know what parts of the cow go into ground hamburger, Sal?"

"What parts?" Caruso asked.

"Fat, internal organs, hair, bones, hooves . . ." said Max, checking the address on the building and leading the way inside.

"Hoofs!" said Caruso. "Get serious, Max."

"I *am* serious, Sal. It so happens that hamburger meat contains a high concentration of cow fat, cow organs, cow hair, and cow hooves, plus a federally regulated amount of rat shit which—"

"Rat shit!" said Caruso. "Jesus, Max, for a minute there you almost had me going."

Max checked the names on the mailboxes and pressed a buzzer.

"You don't believe there's rat shit in hamburgers?" said Max. "You really don't believe it? They've *proven* it."

"Give it a rest, Max," said Caruso. "Rat shit. You think our government would let them put rat shit in hamburgers? Jesus, you almost had me going there."

"Yes?" said a tinny voice.

"Detective Segal from Homicide, Mrs. Morales," said Max.

The buzzer buzzed. Max opened the door and gallantly allowed Caruso to precede him.

"Okay, don't believe me," said Max. "What's your cholesterol count, Sal. You happen to know?"

"How the fuck would I know that?"

They stopped at the elevators. Max pressed the UP button.

"From your last physical," said Max. "They give you your cholesterol count with the results of your physicals. When was your last one?"

"I don't know," said Caruso.

"You don't know when your last physical was? Have you had one in the past year?"

"I don't know," said Caruso.

The elevator door opened. Max and Caruso entered. The elevator was too small, too brightly lit, and it smelled like rotting vegetables. He pressed the button marked six. The elevator lurched into motion.

"You don't know if you had a physical in the past year?" Max asked. "How could you not know?"

"I don't know, okay?"

"How about in the past *two* years?"

"I don't know, okay?"

"The past five?"

"Max . . ."

"The past ten?"

"Gimme a break here, would ya?"

The elevator jolted to a stop. The door shuddered open. The two men got out. Max looked in both directions, then headed left.

"Jesus, Sal, you mean you aren't even sure you had a physical in the past ten years?" Max asked. "At your age? With the weight you're carrying? With the crap you eat? Let me ask you something: Are you trying to kill yourself?"

"Give it a fucking rest, Max, for Christ's sake. What the fuck do *you* care how often I have physicals or what I eat? Are you my fucking mother or what?"

Max found a door with the name Morales on it and knocked.

"Okay, forget it, Sal," said Max. "Forget I even said a word."

"Fine," said Caruso.

"Kill yourself, if that's what you want to do."

"Fine," said Caruso.

"I'm not saying another fucking word."

"Fine," said Caruso.

The door opened. A haggard-looking middle-aged Hispanic woman looked up at them.

"Mrs. Morales?" said Max.

The woman nodded, her face impassive.

"Detectives Segal and Caruso, Mrs. Morales. I wonder if we could come in and have a word with you?"

The woman beckoned them inside. They entered.

The apartment was small and stank of cat urine. Although there were no cats in evidence, it smelled as though a dozen of them were using the apartment as a public lavatory.

The apartment was also amazingly cluttered. Every available inch of horizontal surface was taken up with collections of one sort or another. Collections of plaster religious figures—kneeling crèche figurines, upright saints. Collections of porcelain dancing girls. Of tiny teacups. Of little colored glass bottles. Of tiny metal toy cars. Of ceramic bunny rabbits. Of ceramic pussy cats.

"You want to sit down?" asked Mrs. Morales. "Sit, sit."

Max looked around for a place to sit, but other than the floor, saw none. Every chair was covered with stacks of old magazines, old newspapers, piles of linens, piles of tea towels. He wondered if she were in the process of moving.

"That's okay," said Max. "We'll stand."

The woman shrugged.

"Mrs. Morales," said Max, "I'm sorry to be coming here on a day when I'm sure you'd rather not be talking to anybody, but if you could just answer a few questions, perhaps it would help us to understand better how your daughter died."

She nodded soberly. Her eyes seemed dry. She had apparently done her crying before they'd come. Both Max and Caruso took out spiral notebooks and writing implements.

"Mrs. Morales," asked Caruso, "has your daughter ever tried to kill herself in the past?"

Max glared at him.

"Mrs. Morales," asked Max, "did you talk to your daughter in the past few days before her death?"

The woman nodded. "Of course," she said. "Many times."

"And did she seem at all depressed?" Max asked. "Unhappy?"

The woman shook her head.

"She didn't seem unhappy?" asked Caruso.

"No," said Mrs. Morales. "Virginia is happy girl. Very happy girl."

"Tell me," asked Max softly, "what do you suppose she was doing on the roof of her apartment building the night she died?"

Mrs. Morales shook her head, her eyes flat and dead in her face.

"You don't have any idea what she was doing up there?" Caruso asked.

The woman shook her head again. "She don't go to the roof," she said. "Not Virginia."

"Why not?" Max asked.

"Virginia is scared."

"Scared?" said Caruso. "Scared of who?"

"Not who," said the woman. "Virginia scared of high places. So scared she never live higher than the second floor. Virginia never go to roof of *any*thing."

Max checked his watch. Eleven P.M. Was it too late to call the Queens ME at home? He took out his cell phone.

"How do you like that?" said Caruso, shaking his head in wonderment as Max punched out the number. "Morales was angoraphobic."

"Not angoraphobic," said Max, listening to it ring. "*Acro*phobic. *Acro*phobia is fear of heights. *Agora*phobia is fear of open spaces."

"Then what's angoraphobia?" asked Caruso.

"Fear of fuzzy sweaters."

"Hello?" said a voice at the other end of the line.

"Dr. Werner?"

"Who's this?" asked the voice.

"Max Segal at Queens Homicide. Sorry to bother you at this time of night, Doc, but my partner and I are working the Morales case and we've just come from interviewing the mother . . ."

"Yes?"

"The mother states that Virginia Morales was phobic about heights, Doc," said Max. "Would you consider that adequate basis for reclassifying to homicide?"

"That's why you're calling me?" asked the ME. "To get me to reclassify the Morales case to homicide?"

"Yeah."

"I already reclassified two days ago," he said. "I told the detective to tell you. Didn't he tell you?"

"What detective was that?" Max asked.

"DaVinci. Didn't he tell you?"

"No," said Max. "He never tells me anything."

CHAPTER 5

THE NORTHWEST STATE Correctional Facility, or St. Albans, was a maximum security prison in Vermont, situated about eight miles south of the Canadian border in the midst of rolling green farmland. In the winter the temperature here routinely plunged to thirty below zero, but now it was May and the smell of manure hung heavily in the air.

The series of crisp one-story redbrick buildings with the gently peaked black roofs looked less like a prison than a progressive elementary school, although progressive elementary schools are not surrounded by two sets of twelve-foot-high chain-link fences topped by rolls of razor wire.

Inside the Northwest State Correctional Facility lived 232 prisoners, all of whom were doing hard time for crimes like aggravated assault, sexual assault, armed robbery, manslaughter, and murder. The prisoners were classified as either violent offenders or sex offenders, but many of the violent offenders were sexually deviant, and most of the sex offenders were violent.

There were neither bars nor guns in evidence inside the Northwest Correctional Facility, and most of the cells looked more like rooms in an inexpensive but stylish motel than a prison, but guns were present and the previous summer an inmate had been shot to death going over the twelve-foot chain-link fence.

Dr. Grace Stevenson drove her red Honda into the prison parking lot and braked to a stop in the crushed gravel. The forty-two-year-old psychotherapist was more than a little apprehensive today. Although she had a strong private practice in Burlington and the Lake Champlain area, and although she had worked with prison inmates in the past, she knew that one of the characteristics of violent offenders was their utter unpredictability. She knew little about the man she was going to be evaluating, only that his name was Andy Woods and that he'd shot his stepfather through the head with a .38 Smith & Wesson.

Grace was dark, pretty, green eyed, shy, small boned, and petite—scarcely five foot four with shoes on. She had evaluated a few violent offenders before. She'd apparently done a good job, for she had begun to acquire something of a reputation in correctional circles. She was aware that her interest in violent offenders was connected to her father, who'd been a fairly violent man when he drank.

She got out of her car, locked it, walked to the little red brick portico that sheltered the entrance to the prison, and read the two metal signs attached to the wall. One read: ALL BEARERS OF FIREARMS ENTER THROUGH THE GARAGE DOOR. SECURE WEAPONS IN WEAPONS BOX. The other read: NOTICE: SEARCHES MAY BE CONDUCTED BY DRUG DETECTION K-9.

She went inside.

A uniformed security guard in a tan military shirt and olive-green trousers tucked into black combat boots directed her to the reception desk. She asked for Dr. Theodore Pearlman, the man who had hired her. She wrote her name, the date, the time, and purpose of her visit in a large logbook. Then she took her cell phone and all of the metal out of her pockets and stepped through a metal detector that stood in the middle of the lobby.

This metal detector was evidently far more sensitive than the ones she was used to in airline terminals, for although she dropped into the guard's wicker basket all of her loose change, keys, silver bracelets, earrings, and the delicate silver necklace that had been given to her by her second husband in the final year of their marriage, the metal detector continued to beep.

She felt oddly guilty and contrite before the guard, as though she harbored some secret and shameful cache of metal and was deliberately holding out on him. She began to worry that she'd have to be strip-searched and wondered whether there were female guards here for that purpose or if the man now facing her would take her into another room and require her to take off her brown pants suit and tan silk blouse. She tried to recall whether her underwear was clean and free of holes.

"Take off your belt," said the guard.

For a moment she feared that the strip-search had begun, but then she realized he was still trying to mollify the metal detector. She unbuckled her skinny leather belt with its tiny silver buckle, pulled it free of her belt loops, dropped it into the basket, and she finally stopped beeping.

She was issued a pressure-sensitive visitor's badge, which she applied to the lapel of her suit jacket. She was issued a locker key and directed to put into the small, colorful Formica lockers that adjoined the reception desk all valuables, keys, cigarette lighters, matches, photographic or recording devices, knives, and other weapons. As she was locking her locker, Ted Pearlman appeared.

"Good morning, Dr. Stevenson," he said, extending his hand.

"Grace," she said, grasping it.

"Grace," he said. "You can call me Ted. We're all pretty informal here."

He wore a white shirt open at the neck, a red tie, tan chinos, and wide red suspenders.

"I'd like you to sit in on the last half hour of a violent offender group that started about an hour ago," he said. "It'll give you a sense of what some of our groups are like in the VOP, and it'll give you an opportunity to see Andy Woods in a group setting."

"VOP?" she said.

"The Violent Offender Program," he said. "We have seventy-two men in the VOP and another fifty or so in the Sex Offender Program. Has anyone given you any explanation of what we're doing in the VOP?"

"Not really."

"The VOP is not a behavioral modification program, it's not an incentive program, it's not a typical corrections program. It's a cognitive restructuring program that works under the premise that in order to change behaviors you have to change the thinking that leads to the behaviors. That means you have to be able to identify the thinking, the attitudes, the beliefs, the mind-sets, and the cognitive structures that help justify or excuse violating or hurting another person.

"It's like doing reconstruction on a house. If you bought an old house in ill repair, you wouldn't just paint the outside so it looked good, because the plumbing might be bad, the wiring might be bad, and the building might rot from within. So restructuring would involve going into that house and identifying the bad wiring, the bad plumbing, the bad structural parts of the inside of the house—or, with an offender, getting into his cognitive structure.

"It's a very intrusive process. It requires that they come to accept the distortions of their cognitive structures that are destructive and that allow them to victimize other people. Look, the best way to understand it is to see it. So let's go sit in on the group now."

"And when will you brief me about Andy Woods?" she asked him.

"Right after the group," he replied.

He guided her down a short hallway to a heavy steel door with a large bulletproof glass window. A uniformed guard in a booth called the bubble on the other side of the steel door buzzed her in. The lock released with a resounding metallic *thock*. She and Pearlman walked through the door and up to the bubble. It looked like the control booth of a recording studio, with banks of lights and switches positioned around the guard on all sides—except that it was enclosed in thick bulletproof glass.

The guard was immense. He looked to be at least six and a half feet tall and must have weighed three hundred and fifty pounds. At no point was his neck narrower than his head. She smiled what she hoped was a reassuringly unthreatening smile. The guard pushed out a heavy steel drawer lined with carpeting.

"What's that for?" she asked.

"Keys," said a metallic voice from a speaker near her head. What was this fetish they had about keys?

"I put all my keys in my locker," she said. "Do you want my locker key too?"

"No, you hang onto that," said the metallic voice.

The guard in the bubble released the lock of the next heavy steel door with another loud *thock*, and she and Pearlman passed through it into a large foyer.

"They're meeting in the Visitors' Room," said Pearlman as he ushered her into a sunny room with large windows and rows of plastic bucket seats facing a large green blackboard.

Nine or ten seated men and a standing group leader. The seated men wore jeans or sweatpants, sneakers, T-shirts or sweatshirts, and ranged in age from twenty to perhaps sixty-five. One or two had beards, one had a shaved head and a forked beard at least a foot long. Almost everybody had muscular arms and elaborate tattoos.

The group leader, a handsome blond fellow in a white shirt with the sleeves rolled up and the collar unbuttoned, would have looked more at home running a corporate seminar in communications techniques.

"All right," said the leader. "Cycles. Cycles are a recipe for committing sexual assault. Remove any part of the recipe and it doesn't work. The first ingredient in our recipe is Beliefs About Women—

mind-sets that exist or the behavior wouldn't happen." He hastily scribbled BELIEFS ABOUT WOMEN on the blackboard in loose capital letters. "Give me some more examples of beliefs you have about women."

"All women like sex," volunteered a boyish-looking fellow with a red crew cut, freckles, and improbable Yale sweatpants. Grace figured him as a good candidate for Andy. With the crew cut and the freckles, Andy was a perfect name for him.

"Good," said the leader and hastily wrote this on the board. "Another one."

"If they're drinking, they want it," said a handsome-looking guy with straight, shoulder-length brown hair and pumped-up arms covered with tattoos right down to his wrists. *Another possible Andy*, she thought, although she still favored the one with the red crew cut.

"Thank you," said the leader and wrote this down as well. "Another one."

"She's not a virgin, so she wants to fuck," said the guy with the shaved head and the foot-long forked beard. Grace somehow didn't figure this one for an Andy. Maybe a Siegfried.

"Good," said the leader. "Another ingredient is the belief of Entitlement." He scribbled ENTITLEMENT. "Who can give me an example of Entitlement?"

"If I want it, I'll have it," said a dignified-looking middle-aged man with a military mustache. Definitely not an Andy. Maybe a Dwight.

"Yes," said the leader, scribbling this on the board. "Okay, who remembers another ingredient in the recipe?"

"Power," said an elderly man with long greasy hair and emaciated, tattooed arms. "Fantasy." Not an Andy. Maybe an Eddie.

"Right," said the leader, writing down POWER/FANTASY. "That's what goes through your mind as you contemplate the behavior. And remember we said that the first active step in the cycle is Antennae. Radar. Looking for opportunity. Looking for a victim." He wrote down ANTENNAE/RADAR. "And when you spot a possible victim, next comes . . . ?"

"Risk Assessment," said the fellow with the shaved head and the foot-long beard.

"Yes," said the leader, nodding and writing it down. "Risk Assessment is 'Do I have a good chance of getting away with it?' 'Is this one worth a shot or should I wait for a safer one?' Okay, what's next?"

"Grooming," said the chap with the pumped-up, tattooed arms.

"Alignment," said the dignified-looking middle-aged fellow with the military mustache.

"Okay, GROOMING," said the leader, writing it on the board. "Complimenting the potential victim, making nice to her, and so on. And ALIGNMENT, which is seeming to agree with her on a wide variety of topics so that you're *aligned* with her, in *sync* with her. Okay. Humor and masking are, as we've said before, very useful in this phase. And all of this, of course, is Contact Through Manipulation, and sets up our final ingredient, BEHAVIOR. Behavior—the Sexual Assault—which gives us satisfaction, control, power, and a temporary feeling of superiority."

He managed to squeeze all of this onto the board. Then he glanced at his watch, turned around, and looked at the group.

"All right, gentlemen," he said, "that's enough for today. Homework tonight is to work on your thinking reports. And this time, guys, please, let's try to cut the bullshit, okay?"

The men got up and shuffled out of the Visitors' Room. Pearlman took Grace over to the leader, who was now energetically erasing the blackboard.

"Dr. Stevenson," said Pearlman, turning to Grace, "I'd like to introduce you to the young man who's more or less taken over this group. This is Andy Woods."

"Delighted to meet you, Dr. Stevenson," said Andy Woods.

CHAPTER 6

S O WHAT DID you think of Andy?" asked Pearlman, when he and Grace had gone outside to the yard, striking a match and trying to set fire to the tobacco in his pipe.

Grace shook her head.

"He's quite impressive," she said. "But don't you think it was a tad hostile of you to spring him on me that way?"

Pearlman chuckled. He tried again without success, to suck the flame from a wooden match into the bowl of the pipe. "I knew you'd be looking over all the other inmates, trying to decide which one was Andy," he said. "I knew you'd never suspect he was leading the group."

"Why *is* he leading the group?" asked Grace, still a little piqued at the prank he'd played on her.

Pearlman sucked at his pipe and puffed out a cloud of smoke. "Partly because we're short of trained facilitators," he said. "Partly because Andy happens to be able to lead a group better than anyone here but me."

"How do his fellow inmates feel about his leading their group?" she asked.

"It doesn't make them like him much," he said. "But they didn't like him much to begin with."

"Why not?"

"He pretty much keeps to himself," said Pearlman. "He's a lot smarter than they are, and he doesn't try to hide it."

"And where did he learn to lead groups?" she asked.

Pearlman shook his head. "Going through the VOP himself, I guess. I don't know. He's extremely smart and a quick study. He took to psychotherapy the moment he came in here. That's what turned him around. That's why we think he's ready to be released."

"If you think he's ready to be released," she said irritably, "then what the hell am *I* doing here?"

Pearlman shot her a surprised glance and chuckled again. "We think we may be a little too close to the subject," he said. "We want somebody who doesn't know him as well as we do to take a look and see what they see."

Pearlman led her along one of the chain-link fences that separated the outdoor recreational area from the garden and the sex offenders' quarters. Some of the men were jogging on the track that paralleled the fence. Some were doing improvised biceps curls by lifting buckets of sand. Their muscles and tattoos were equally impressive.

"You said you were going to give me some background," she reminded him.

They walked some more.

"Andy's mother, Cynthia Woods, was a Vegas showgirl," said Pearlman. "A stripper. She's six feet tall and still a knockout, even at her age. I've seen her."

"What *is* her age?" Grace asked.

"Oh, she must be about forty-one," he said.

"As old as that, eh?" said Grace dryly.

"Well, I only meant that she—"

"I'm forty-*two*, Ted."

He looked at her carefully.

"And pretty as a picture," he said lightly. "Anyway, Cynthia got knocked up when she was about eighteen. The father was a blackjack dealer who, needless to say, had no interest in marrying her. You'd have expected her to get an abortion, but she had some strong religious convictions at the time, so she took a year off from stripping and went to live with her sister out in the desert in Barstow. When she came back she said the baby was her sister's kid. Nobody doubted it, including Andy. He called her Aunt Cynthia for years. He didn't find out who she was till he was twelve."

"When did she begin abusing him?" she asked.

"How do you know she abused him?" he said.

She sighed. "A wild guess," she replied tiredly.

"He doesn't know when it began," said Pearlman. "He has some recollection that when he started getting up too much during the night she used to tie him to the bed. And whenever she had a date, she tied him up so he wouldn't get in trouble and left him, just like a little dog."

Grace nodded, trying to imagine why people did the things they did, thinking for the thousandth time that parents ought to be licensed like drivers.

"Did she beat him?"

"With belts, straps, that kind of thing," he said. "As her mother had done to her when *she* was a child."

"And as her mother's mother had done to her, and so on and so on forever," Grace said.

"Yes," he agreed. "One thing she did that was fairly original was scare him. She used to wake him in the middle of the night, dressed as a ghost or a ghoul, wearing some ghastly rubber mask. She thought this the height of humor. She was always dumbfounded at the kid's hysterical crying. 'What are you afraid of?' she'd yell at him. Not surprisingly, he still has night terrors and has to sleep with a night light on. It drives his cellmate crazy."

"Has he ever attempted suicide?" she asked.

"He tried to slash his wrists with a shank shortly after he arrived here," said Pearlman. "It wasn't a very serious attempt. There was another attempt before that."

"Did the mother ever have sex with him?" she asked.

"There were all sorts of inappropriate arousal games going on, so there was probably some early linkage between sex and fear," said Pearlman. "But I doubt that there was actual intercourse. But he does remember her practicing her striptease routines in front of him, and taking him with her when she worked, parking him in the dressing room with all the other showgirls. They seemed to like him, but they teased him unmercifully. Made him strip in front of them and then made fun of his little erections."

"He remembers this?" she asked.

"Yeah."

"And who was it he killed?"

"A rich investment banker from New York named Walter Woods," said Pearlman. "He saw Cynthia strip at Circus Circus and went bananas for her. He had old family money—an apartment on Park Avenue, a home in Southampton, horses, a boat, a chauffeured limousine—the works. He was about thirty years older than Cynthia. A gentle, weak man, but a very persistent one. He finally persuaded Cynthia to give up stripping—she was getting too old for it anyway—and they impulsively got married in one of those quickie wedding chapels that they have in Vegas. Then he took her and Andy back East to live with him."

"And he abused Andy, and Andy shot him," she said.

"No no, he was *great* to Andy," Pearlman answered. "Taught him all kinds of things. Bought a summer home up on Lake Champlain and taught Andy to sail. Bought a pistol and taught him to shoot. When Andy was sixteen, Walter took him to hunting camp, and—"

"What's hunting camp?" she asked.

"You live in Vermont and you don't know what hunting camp is?" he asked.

"What can I tell you?" she said.

"Hunting camp is a shack in the woods where Vermont males go in the fall for a couple of weeks to hunt deer, drink beer, fight, bond, tell dirty stories, and get rid of a lot of aggression. One night in hunting camp Andy turned his gun on Walter for no reason and blew his brains out. Pumped him full—not just one shot, but the whole magazine. It was pretty messy, I hear.

"If you kill a parent or a spouse, the courts tend to be very lenient. But this one was so brutal and so apparently unmotivated—Walter had been terribly sweet to Andy, and the kid repays him by making hamburger out of his head. The judge gave him twelve to twenty for manslaughter, and they sent him here."

"Does Andy understand why he shot his stepfather instead of his mother?" she asked.

Pearlman smiled. "I've scheduled your first one-on-one with him this afternoon at three," he said. "You can ask him then yourself."

CHAPTER 7

AT PRECISELY 3 P.M. he entered the sunny Visitors' Room in which he'd led the violent offenders group earlier that day. He still wore a white shirt open at the neck with the sleeves rolled up.

"Hello, Andy," she said.

"Hello, Dr. Stevenson."

They took seats opposite each other on the plastic bucket seats.

"That was quite an impressive job you did with the violent offenders group this morning," she said.

"Thank you," he said.

"Where did you learn to lead a group?" she asked.

He shrugged. "You watch, you pick it up."

"I can't believe it's as easy as all that," she said.

"You're free to believe whatever you like," he said.

"Well," she said brightly, choosing not to deal with his hostility yet, "I didn't come here to find out how you came to lead therapy groups."

"Why *did* you come here, Dr. Stevenson?" he asked.

"Why do you *think* I came here?" she asked.

He smiled. "Are you throwing the question back at me because you're a Freudian?" he asked.

"No, I'm throwing the question back at you because I think you already know the answer."

He smiled again. "You're here," he said, "because I've been a model prisoner for twelve years, and they've sent for an expert from the outside to see if I'm as rehabilitated as I seem."

"So you *do* know the answer," she said.

"So that was the right answer," he said.

"Yes," she said, "it was. Are you going to just give me answers you think I want to hear, or are you going to give me honest ones?"

"Both," he said.

"Both," she said.

"I *am* going to give you answers I think you want to hear. And they will also be honest ones."

"You know," she said, "I can't help feeling you're playing games with me."

"Well, Dr. Stevenson, I could just as easily believe you're playing games with *me*. People have been playing games with me for years."

"In here, you mean?"

"In here, out there, everywhere in between."

"And it seems to you that one of the games they've played with you in here is to see if you can come up with the right answers," she said.

"Oh, absolutely."

"Well, Andy, that may or may not be the way they work," she said. "But that's not the way *I* work."

"So you're telling me you're different from the others."

"That's my hope," she said.

"Well, I suppose we'll have to see about that, won't we?"

"Yes," she said, "we will."

Neither of them spoke for several moments.

"Tell me," she said, "how do the other inmates feel about your leading their groups?"

"Oh, didn't Dr. Pearlman tell you about that?" he asked.

She seemed momentarily thrown. "Yes," she said, "he did."

"Then pretending not to know would be playing the same sort of games they play with me, wouldn't it, Dr. Stevenson?"

"I didn't mean it to be a game," she said. "But I can see how you may have taken it that way. If you did, I'm sorry. I was just trying to make conversation."

He didn't speak for several moments, believing that his silence would force her to speak again. It didn't. The silence just hung there.

"Well, Dr. Stevenson," he said, glancing pointedly at his watch, "I'm afraid our time is up."

She smiled in spite of herself. "You have something else to do?"

"Yes," he said. "I have some Thinking Reports to evaluate."

"But we've barely spent five minutes together," she said.

"Closer to three, I'd say."

"You must be very angry with me," she said.

"Not at all, Dr. Stevenson. What makes you think I'm angry with you?"

"Well, for one thing, our session was supposed to last an hour, and you want to cut it to three minutes. For another, the words you used just now are a kind of parody of the way that therapists classically end sessions with patients."

"And why would I be angry with you?" he asked.

"I don't know," she said. "Why would you?"

"Please, Dr. Stevenson, don't keep throwing the questions back at me. I find it rather patronizing."

"I'm sorry you found it patronizing," she said. "That wasn't my intent."

"Why would I be angry with you?" he repeated.

"I don't know," she said. "Perhaps for being presumptuous enough to come here and, in just a few sessions, evaluate your degree of rehabilitation and your readiness to return to society."

He looked at her steadily for several moments before replying. "I *do* find that somewhat presumptuous, yes," he said.

"And you're angry about it," she said.

"Not angry," he said. "I don't know you well enough to be angry with you."

"You feel you have to know somebody to be angry with them," she said.

He smiled.

"Well, Andy," she said evenly, "it probably *is* presumptuous of me to try and evaluate your degree of rehabilitation in just a few sessions, but that's what I've been hired to do. And, assuming you want to make parole and leave this facility before you max out, what you're going to have to do is become a more active part of the process than you've been so far."

He inhaled deeply, looked at her, and smiled. Dr. Stevenson had what Cynthia called spunk. He liked that. He also liked the way she looked.

"May I tell you something of a personal nature?" he asked.

"That's why I'm here," she said guardedly.

"I find you extremely attractive," he said.

She was trying not to react, he noted, but her cheeks reddened slightly.

"Thank you," she said after a few moments.

"How old are you?" he asked. He figured she was forty-three.

The redness in her cheeks increased. "Why do you ask me that?" she asked.

"Thirty-seven?" he said. "Thirty-eight? No, thirty-seven. Am I right?"

"I'd like to know why you want to know my age," she said.

"Are you going to tell me how old you are, or shall I find out?" he asked. "It's not hard to find things out in here."

"I'd rather inquire what prompted you to ask me my age," she said.

"Oh, just idle curiosity," he said.

"I think it was more than idle curiosity," she said.

"Really?" he said. "What was it then, Dr. Stevenson?"

"I think you're being inappropriately flirtatious," she said. "Which would be the behavior of someone who was not yet ready to return to society."

"You think I'm being inappropriately flirtatious?"

"Yes," she said.

"Then tell me how to be *appropriately* flirtatious."

She met his gaze without speaking. She seemed angry. He could see the slight indentations of her bra straps in her shoulders. Judging by the shape of her blouse, her breasts were on the small side. He liked small breasts. He wondered if her nipples became erect when she was angry.

"Why are you doing this?" she asked. "Are you deliberately trying to sabotage your chances of getting out of here?"

"Why on earth would I want to sabotage my chances of getting out of here?" he asked.

"Why don't you tell me why?" she asked.

"Because I'm ambivalent about leaving the joint? Because, although it's restrictive and infantilizing and terminally boring in here, it's at least a familiar setting and far less threatening than the great unknown out on the street?"

"Is that what you think?" she said.

"No," he said, "that's what *you* think I think."

"I see," she said. "Tell me, Andy, why did you really ask me how old I am?"

"Because," he said, smiling, "I find you extremely attractive, Dr. Stevenson. And when I get out of here I'm going to date you."

CHAPTER 8

"SO HOW WAS your first session with Andy?" said Pearlman.

"The man is outrageous."

"He is," said Pearlman. "Did he flirt with you?"

"A lot," she said.

"Yeah, he does that with every woman he meets," said Pearlman. "I wouldn't pay too much attention to it."

"Well, thanks for the compliment, Ted, but I *have* to take it seriously. Flirting with the psychotherapist who's been sent to evaluate you isn't the behavior of someone who's ready to get out of here. It's indicative of an inability to be appropriate in social situations. It's also extremely hostile."

"Maybe, but that's just how he is," said Pearlman. "Grace, the guy may be outrageous, but he's fantastic. Have you ever seen an inmate lead a therapy group before?"

"No, I must admit I haven't."

"Well then, please try to suspend judgment on him for at least a little while, till you get to know him better. Do you think you can do that?"

"I suppose so," she said.

"Good. We're very proud of him here. He's not at all what he seems."

"I'd certainly be willing to believe *that*," she said.

CHAPTER 9

SO, ANDY," GRACE asked, "how are you feeling today?"

They were meeting again in the Visitors' Room. Today, though, it wasn't sunny. Dark cumulus clouds had bunched together like angry buffalo ready to stampede.

"I don't feel too bad," he said. "A little shaky, though."

"Oh?" she said. "Any particular reason?"

"Well, I had a rather perplexing dream last night."

"I see," she said. "Care to tell me about it?"

"I don't see why not," he said. "I was fairly young in this dream, I don't know how old. I was lying in bed, half asleep, and suddenly I realized that there was something in the room. Something not necessarily human. I slowly opened my eyes. At the foot of the bed stood a ghastly creature. A huge bald head. Protruding, bloodshot eyes. Rows of long, sharp, jagged teeth. Rotting cheeks with flesh hanging down in shreds. I screamed and it reached out for me. I became hysterical. Then the thing changed shape. It became a woman."

"A woman," said Grace. "Did you recognize her?"

"Yes," he said. "As a matter of fact I did."

"Who was it?"

"You," he said.

"Me."

"Yes," he said. "The arms that had reached out to me so menacingly suddenly became comforting. You drew me to your breast and tried to console me, but I couldn't stop sobbing. 'What are you afraid of?' you kept repeating over and over. You held me very closely. I gradually calmed down. You kissed me, and it was very sweet. But the kissing continued. You kissed me all over my face, and then you unbuttoned my pajama tops and began kissing me all over my chest and on my belly. You slipped down my pajama pants and you began kissing down toward my groin. Eventually, you kissed my penis. I knew it was wrong, that you shouldn't be doing this and I shouldn't be enjoying it, but it was the most excruciatingly delicious sensation I had ever experienced."

She watched his face, trying mightily not to react, trying not to give him the satisfaction of either embarrassment or anger.

"And then I woke up," he said. "It seems I ejaculated in my sleep."

"I see," she said.

"Well, what do you think?" he said.

"I think you're still so furious with me for having the audacity to come up here and evaluate you that you're willing to jeopardize your chances for getting out of here by continuing to provoke me sexually. But you know what, Andy? I get paid just as much whether I turn in a report that says you're ready to be released or whether I turn in a report that says you're not. So keep doing whatever you think you have to do. It's perfectly all right with me. It's your nickel. But be absolutely clear about one thing: you're the fool in this room, not I."

He smiled. He loved that she said "not I" rather than "not me." He loved that she could talk tough. He could see from the set of her mouth and the vein that stood out in her neck that he had gotten to her.

"Are you saying, Dr. Stevenson, that you don't believe the dream I just told you was one I really had?"

"I believe," she said evenly, "that your mother often woke you up while wearing hideous rubber masks, and that she often comforted you with kisses, and that her kisses were often sexually provocative. I even believe that you've had nightmares about it. Anybody would. And no, I don't believe that the dream you just told me was one you really had."

He nodded. "I owe you an apology," he said.

"No, you don't," she said. "The person you owe an apology to is yourself. For wasting your own time. Because, although I'm being well paid to hear this shit, *you* have to hear it for free."

He chuckled. "All right," he said. "You were absolutely right about everything you said. That wasn't a real dream. And I am still angry at you for coming up here to evaluate me. Very angry. So angry, in fact, that I'd like to kill you."

She shuddered inwardly but held his gaze.

"*That* I believe," she said quietly.

She suddenly felt very small and very frightened. If he were to come at her now, there'd be little she could do to prevent his attack. She could visualize him springing across the desk, grabbing her in a stranglehold. Would he also try and rape her? The thought left her weak. *Please don't let him see how frightened I am,* she prayed, *please don't. Perhaps, like a wild animal, he'll only attack if he thinks I'm frightened. Perhaps he's only trying to frighten me.*

"I would also like to make love to you," he said.

He watched her face.

"I don't know if I'd be any good at it, though," he said.

She thought she ought to respond to this. "Why not?" she was somehow able to say.

"Because I've never had sex with a woman," he said.

She continued looking at him. Showing, she hoped, nothing.

"You didn't know that, did you?" he said.

"I hadn't been told that, no," she said truthfully.

"That's because nobody knows it," he said. "Nobody but me. Does what I just told you surprise you?"

She nodded.

"I know that I'm considered to be extremely good looking," he said. "I'm not saying that to be conceited or because I even believe it myself, I'm saying it because that's the feedback I've gotten all my life, from women and from men. It's not something I had anything to do with, it's just what's so. I've had plenty of chances to have sex with girls and women as I was growing up, and I never took them, because I was absolutely terrified of what might happen. Are you listening to me now, Dr. Stevenson? Are you hearing me?"

"Yes," she said.

"I was absolutely terrified of sex with women, thanks to Cynthia. Terrified of the intimacy, I suppose. And so I never attempted to make love to any woman, even though they wanted to, and even though I've wanted to. Even though it's mostly all I ever think about. I'm being quite vulnerable with you now, in case you hadn't noticed."

"Are you?" she asked mildly.

"Yes."

"Why?"

"As a peace offering," he said. "For having been obnoxious to you. For having been inappropriately and inexcusably obnoxious to you."

She listened, saying nothing.

"You didn't deserve my being obnoxious to you," he said. "You're just doing your job. So I wanted to give you something to make up for it."

She continued to listen.

"I don't have anything left to give in here but pieces of myself," he said. "So that was a piece nobody'd gotten before. I'm sorry but it's all I have."

She studied him awhile and decided there was a chance that this had been genuine.

"Do you believe me now?" he asked.

"Let's say I do," she said, "and go from there."

Very tentatively, he reached out his hand. Very tentatively, she took it.

CHAPTER 10

GRACE CAME INTO the Visitors' Room about halfway into the first hour of the group session. Andy was once more up at the blackboard, his white shirt open at the collar, his tie loosened, his sleeves rolled up.

"Today," said Andy, "we're going to talk a little about The Code. But first I want to ask: how many of you guys plan your crimes and how many of you just go ahead and do them without planning?"

"I never planned nothing," said the man with the shaved head and the forked beard.

"You never did B&E?" said Andy.

"Well, sure."

"You ever put on gloves?" said Andy.

"Sure."

"Well, that's planning," said Andy.

"I never wore gloves," said the freckle-faced kid with the red crew cut. "I never worried about fingerprints, because whatever I touched, I took."

"I don't get outta bed without planning every single thing I'm gonna do the whole day," said the guy with the pumped-up arms and the tattoos all the way down to his wrists.

"Frank," Andy asked, "what's the history of your tattoos?"

"I was real young when I first got in the joint," said Frank. "So I decided to pump up and get tattoos. I wanted to look tough, and like 'Don't fuck with me.' But that becomes a problem, because then you have to live up to the image. You have to do what people think you're going to do. You have to kick some ass and break some heads. Even if you're a good guy and you don't enjoy hurting people."

"What are the beliefs we're getting here from Frank?" Andy asked the group.

"A real struggle between good guy and bad guy," said the dignified-looking middle-aged man with the military mustache. "Between good and evil."

"What's his image?" said Andy.

"He wants to be the man," said the guy with the shaved head and the forked beard.

"Nobody fucks with him," said the freckle-faced kid with the red crew cut.

"But he wants to be your friend," said the dignified middle-aged man.

"Good," said Andy. "So let me tell you something. Everything that Frank projects on the outside is the opposite of what's going on on the inside. Tell me, Frank, are you really a good guy? What's behind your wall?"

"I consider myself a good guy, yeah," said Frank.

"What makes you a good guy?" Andy asked.

"Well," said Frank, "I'm, you know, good to my old lady. And I'm a good father to my son."

"Bullshit," said Andy. "You're a bad father, Frank."

Frank looked stricken.

"To get out of prison and immediately do a crime to land you back in prison so you never get to see your son," said Andy, "that's being a bad father. It's not nice to think of yourself as a bad father, is it, Frank? Tell me, what do you look for in a friend?"

"Someone who's not a whine-ass," said Frank. "Someone who stands up for himself."

"The Code," said Andy. "Okay, Frank, that's what I wanted to talk about. What is The Code?"

"Well," said Frank, "one thing is you take care of yourself. Another is you never snitch."

"So what you're telling me, Frank, is that you'd never snitch?"

"Never," said Frank proudly.

"Okay, Frank, let's say you ask me to do an armed robbery with you," said Andy. "During the robbery I shoot somebody and they die, and you're not even carrying a gun. You go to the joint. You're on Death Row. Then one day they put you on the table and they're about to give you the lethal injection. They say, 'Frank, who pulled the trigger? Tell us and we won't give you the injection.' Do you seriously want us to believe that you wouldn't snitch me out?"

Frank looked very uncomfortable.

"Okay," said Andy, "The Code says don't snitch. What else does The Code do?"

"The Code defines real men," said the guy with the shaved head and the forked beard.

"You're full of shit," said Andy. "Let me tell you about real men. Real men do the most amazing things. Real men ask for help. Real men have feelings. Real men cry. Real men go to other men and say 'I'm afraid.' The Code is only armor. But the bigger the armor, the smaller the person inside it feels. The bigger the front, the bigger the lie, and the more energy it takes to maintain it. If you have real courage, gentlemen, we'll find out who the little person is who's *inside* the armor."

CHAPTER 11

I T WAS ANOTHER day and this time, since the Visitors' Room was otherwise occupied, they were meeting in Andy's office, a tiny room with stacks of papers all over the desk and floor. Andy was wearing a pink oxford cloth button-down shirt with a dark gray tie. They sat facing each other across his desk.

"Andy, you've told me that you've never, as an adult, had sex with a woman," said Grace. "Have you ever had sex with a man?"

Andy regarded her thoughtfully for several moments before replying.

"When I came into the prison system," he said, "I was a teenager. A rather good-looking sixteen-year-old virgin. What do you honestly think my chances were of not getting raped?"

She sighed. "So you were raped."

"One night five guys came into my cell. Five very big guys. They gang-raped me that night and every single night for the first week. By the end of the week I had gotten to the point where I said enough's enough, this is not going to keep happening to me, even if I have to kill somebody."

"So what did you do?" Grace asked.

"An old con said to me, 'Kid, you're gonna have to protect yourself.' He gave me my first shank. He put it in my hands and he said, 'You're gonna have to cut somebody, son.'"

"And you did?" she asked.

He nodded.

"How many people did you cut?"

"Just one," he said. "Five came in, one got cut. That's all. The other four didn't want any part of it."

"And that was the end of it?"

"That was the end of it," he said. "That was the acceptance: 'The kid's okay, leave him alone.' And next thing I know I'm getting bags of groceries and cartons of cigarettes and slaps on the back from the prisoners: 'The kid's okay.' I'm now one of the boys."

"Weren't you afraid that the man you cut was going to take revenge on you?" she asked.

"I was scared to death," he said. "Every day I went into my cell I had to hide my face behind a pillow to turn on the light."

"Why?"

"Because somebody could have put a syringe full of lighter fluid into the lightbulb. You take out the lightbulb and insert a syringe into the lead, and you fill the bulb with gasoline or lighter fluid and screw it back in again, so when somebody turns on the light . . ."

"It explodes?"

"Absolutely. And you never knew who was going to do it to you or when it was going to happen."

"Did he ever take revenge on you?"

"No. He had more respect for me for cutting him than anything else. I said to him, 'Aren't you angry with me?' 'Oh, sure,' he said. 'If I get the chance I'm going to cut your fuckin' *head* off, but now I'm just going to tell you that I respect what you did.' I was playing basketball one day out on the court. I went up for a lay-up, and I felt a hand go around my belly. I came down and looked and there he was, walking away from me, shaking his finger: 'See?' he said."

"I was very intrigued by what you said in group about The Code and real men," said Grace. "Do you really believe what you told them?"

"I believe that when we're frightened we hide behind a wall," he said. "And the bigger the wall, the smaller the guy behind it.

Growing up with Cynthia, I had to hide behind a wall all the time—still do, to some extent, because she still has the power to terrorize me. And I also realize that the wall cuts me off from the things I most need to get from my fellow human beings."

"From what you tell me now, and from what I heard you say in the group," she said, "you're in better shape than I suspected. It seems to me that you have a good chance of—"

"—getting out of here," said Andy.

"Getting out," said Grace. "And *staying* out. I think you might have the tools you need to make it on the street. And maybe even the understanding to have a real relationship with somebody, a relationship that's intimate and caring."

"Thank you. That's high praise coming from *you*, Dr. Stevenson."

"You know, Andy," she said, "you still have a lot of anger. When you get out of here, you're going to encounter many things to set you off. What are you going to do to manage that anger?"

"What they taught me in here, Dr. Stevenson," he said. "And what I've been teaching in the groups: cognitive control. Identification of the steps in my cycle, and then stopping the cycle. Remove any part of the recipe and it doesn't work."

CHAPTER 12

LOVELY TO SEE you, Grace," said a clipped British accent, as the tall man with the thinning white crew cut ushered her into the cheery, plant-filled office.

The small office was, in fact, overrun with flowering plants of all descriptions: African violets, hibiscus, miniature rosebushes, tiger lilies, rubrum lilies, anemones, even morning glories climbing up strings to the ceiling. This, in a climate which featured thirty-degree-below-zero temperatures for much of the winter, was a testament to Dr. Harry Lake, the tall man with the white crew cut, who seemed to have the same effect on people as he did on plants.

Once Harry had been Grace's psychiatrist. In the last few years she'd gotten to know him socially through committee work in the local psychoanalytic institute, but she still felt the need to pop into his plant-filled office every few months for a tuneup.

"Good to see you, too, Harry," she said.

"Well," he said, "working in prisons must agree with you, Grace. You look fresher and prettier than I've seen you in years."

"Harry," she said with mock exasperation, "they're not *prisons*, they're—"

"—correctional facilities," he said. "I know. And the guards aren't guards anymore, they're correctional officers. And the wardens are . . . what?"

"Superintendents of the facilities," she said.

"Quite," said Harry. "Last time we spoke on the phone, you were having a bit of difficulty penetrating young Mr. Woods's defenses. Is he still so tough to get through to?"

"No, as a matter of fact," she said, "he's not. I may actually be getting somewhere with him, finally. He confided a couple of things to me that he hadn't told anyone before."

"Mmm," said Harry. "I understand he's quite a handsome chap."

"Handsome would be an understatement," she said.

"Uh-oh," said Harry. "Do I detect a countertransference there already?"

"You bet," she said. "But don't worry, it's solidly in check. I haven't given him the slightest inkling I find him even mildly attractive."

"Mind that you don't," he said seriously. "Tell me, what sort of response to his violence have you noticed in yourself?"

"Good question," she said. "Well. In one of our first sessions he confided that he'd like very much to kill me."

"Yes."

"I could visualize it happening, of course. His grabbing me in a stranglehold. Maybe even ravishing me—isn't that a much nicer word than rape? Ravishing. 'My dear, tonight you look ravishing, simply ravishing.' I'm sorry to say that the possibility of being ravished by young Mr. Woods was not without a certain small element of . . . excitement."

"You're joking about it," he said, "to cover your discomfort?"

"Well, yeah," she said. "Being turned on by the prospect of rape by a criminal isn't exactly comfortable. It's frightening. It's also not politically correct."

Harry regarded her thoughtfully for a moment, compressing his lips.

"I don't believe the rape fantasy comes from wanting to be hurt by Mr. Woods," he said. "I believe it comes from not wanting to be responsible for your sexual feelings toward him. Your feelings for him are embarrassing to you, just as you were embarrassed by those same feelings for your father. Your father, as I recall, was alternately abusive to you when he drank and needful of rescue?"

"Yes."

"So you're unconsciously trying to repeat that pattern," he said. "I would imagine you're considerably less motivated by your masochistic tendencies than by your rescue fantasies."

"Well, that's a relief," she said.

"Tell me, Grace," Harry asked, "are you currently involved with anyone romantically?"

"Not really," she said. "Why?"

"I think you ought to be," he said. "I think you ought to, as they say, get a life."

"C'mon, Harry," she said. "Give me a break. I've not only got my work at the clinic now, and my private practice, I also have patients like Andy Woods at the prison. Where am I going to get time for a social life?"

"Listen to me, Grace. Not getting a life and being turned on by patients like Mr. Woods is a form of regression. It most definitely pulls you back to the earlier relationship you had with your father."

She nodded soberly. As a therapist, she knew that the unfinished business with her dad had always played a part in her failed relationships with men.

"Tell me," he said, "do you think this chap is ready to return to society?"

"Probably not," she said. "But he's got them so charmed at the prison, there's no way they're not going to let him out of there when he reaches his minimum next month. Unless I put up some pretty violent objections, the parole board is definitely going to spring him."

"And is your putting up some pretty violent objections a real possibility?" he said.

She mulled this over before replying. "If you'd asked me that a few weeks ago, Harry, I would have said definitely. I don't really think so anymore."

"You've got to be able to make an objective assessment of this man, Grace. You can't recommend his release simply because of your own eagerness to rescue him. Neither can you allow embarrassment at your wish to rescue him to make you feel he's not ready to be released. It's a thin line you'll have to tread, a very thin line."

CHAPTER 13

THE THIRD THURSDAY of the month. Nine A.M.

By the time he walked in, all six of them were already seated.

"Good morning, Andy."

Dark blue metal folding chairs. Four brown trestle tables, arranged in a modified U, topped by chipped, imitation wood grain Formica.

"Good morning."

A green blackboard on the far wall, flanked by American and Vermont state flags. A faint smell of lemony wood polish.

"Please, Andy. Sit down."

Framed prints on the wall by Van Gogh, Seurat, Gauguin, and a couple of artists he couldn't place.

"Thank you."

The carpeting was bluish gray. Two walls were cream-colored concrete block, the third a bilious yellow.

"As you know, we've been reviewing your progress here . . ."

Had the same mind that chose to hang prints by Van Gogh and Seurat chosen bluish gray carpeting, cream-colored and yellow concrete block walls?

". . . your participation in the Violent Offenders Program, your work in the computer center, your leading of the VOP groups, and of course, the detailed reports submitted to us by Dr. Stevenson and Dr. Pearlman . . ."

Six people. Three men and three women. Private citizens of this great state of Vermont. Dressed for church. Ready to decide his fate.

"Yes . . ."

What gave these six people the right to decide whether he was ready to leave here?

"We are, on the whole, quite impressed with your progress here at the facility . . ."

These six people who, although at present dressed in their Sunday best and looking so righteous and proper . . .

". . . and are considering ordering your release . . ."

. . . would later on in the day be sitting on toilets, urinating, defecating, copulating, fornicating, and secretly contemplating sexual fantasies so unspeakable that, were they to fulfill them, would cause them to become inmates here themselves . . .

". . . into the custody of your mother."

"Of my *mother*?"

"Yes."

"I see," he said. "Uh, pardon me, but . . ."

"Yes, Andy?"

"Why into the custody of my mother?"

"Well, we had an opportunity to meet her and to get to know her. She's a lovely woman, and so obviously fond of you . . ."

. . . that she tied you to beds, strapped your ass till it bled, terrorized you at night, flaunted her tits and ass in your face, and—here is the salient point—endowed the new computer center here at the Northwest State Correctional Facility.

"We just felt that she'd be most likely to assist you in a smooth transition back into the community."

The program has been set in motion. Do not do anything to upset the program.

"With the board's permission, I would like to ask that I not be released into the custody of my mother," he said. "I have made that request in the past and I believe that Dr. Stevenson has stated in her report her own opinion that I should not be released into the custody of my mother. I really feel strongly that if I were to be released into the custody of my mother—"

"We have read Dr. Stevenson's report, Andy, and you may rest assured that we have duly considered all of her recommendations."

"Yes . . ."

"And we will be making our decision sometime later today. You will be informed of that decision in the next day or so . . ."

"Yes . . ."

"It has been a pleasure to review your record here at the Northwest State Correctional Facility, Andy, and to see you in person here this morning."

"Thank you."

CHAPTER 14

TWELVE YEARS. ONE hundred and forty-four months. Six hundred twenty-four weeks. Four thousand three hundred eighty days. Enough time to go to high school, college, graduate school, and obtain a PhD in most professions. And he had spent it in this prison, which was not even called a prison anymore but a correctional facility. He had entered this correctional facility twelve years ago as a murderer and emerged today . . . corrected. He stood corrected. He was now Correct. He stood in the warden's office, wearing a soft cashmere Armani sport coat, pleatless Armani slacks, Armani loafers made from the skins of baby lambs.

"Well, Andy, this must be a very proud day for you," said Will.

"It is, Will, it certainly is," said Andy.

"We're all proud of you, Andy," said Ted. "Of the work that you've done here. Of the growth that you've achieved."

"Thanks, Ted," said Andy.

Will and Ted. Not the warden and the chief psychologist, but just a couple of guys named Will and Ted. What a friendly, happy place. Why would I ever want to leave such a friendly, happy place?

"Your mom didn't come to pick you up?" Will asked.

"No no, Will," Andy answered. "Cynthia had . . . a long-standing luncheon engagement. It's quite all right. She sent me my airline ticket, and her chauffeur will be picking me up at LaGuardia. She's been more than kind."

"How are you getting to Burlington?" asked Ted.

"Well, Dr. Stevenson has graciously offered to drive me to the airport. She's picking me up outside in the parking lot any minute now, in fact."

"Splendid. Well, Andy, good-bye. And good luck."

"Thank you, Ted."

"Oh, and Andy?"

"Yes, Will?"

"Don't come back."

All three men laughed and shook hands. Then Andy walked out of the prison through the front entrance, which he had never done before, because when they come into the facility to begin their sentences, prisoners entered through the garage directly into Intake and Booking, and now he was outside, with no double twelve-foot-high chain-ink fences topped with razor wire separating him from the rest of the world.

"How does it feel to be a free man?" asked a familiar female voice.

She had materialized at his side, unnoticed.

"It feels . . . peculiar, to say the least," he said.

"Scary," she said.

"Terrifying," he said. "But also kind of . . . loose and pleasant."

She smiled.

"That's a nice outfit," she said. "Did your mother send you those clothes?"

"Yes," he said. "Everything was made by Armani—the slacks, the shirt, the jacket. Even the underwear and socks. Cynthia has exquisite taste."

"Where is your suitcase?"

"I don't have one," he said. "I'm leaving everything here. I'm starting over completely."

"Good for you," she said. "Well, my car is in the lot. Follow me."

"No, Dr. Stevenson," he said, "follow *me*."

"You know what kind of car I drive?"

"Not yet," he said. "But let's see if I can guess."

He walked slowly from one car to the next, crunching the gravel, scratching his chin.

"All right, let me see," he said. "It wouldn't be anything as ostentatious as this Mercedes, would it? No, I don't think so. Or even this Jaguar sedan . . . No no, not at all. You're not at all ostentatious, you're very tasteful. And it wouldn't be anything as plain as this Chevy or this Ford or this Plymouth. Absolutely not. But maybe it would be . . . this Jeep Wrangler. Yes. No, on second thought, a Jeep would be a little too adventurous."

"You don't think I'm adventurous?" she asked, aware that this entire exercise was probably inappropriate, but fascinated by it nonetheless.

"Psychically, perhaps, but not physically," he said. "No, you're definitely not the off-road four-by-four type. And it wouldn't be . . . this Corvette. No no. Too sporty. You're not sporty. You'd *like* to be sporty, but you're not. No, you'd be more inclined to drive a car that's economical, sturdy, and yet has a tiny bit of dash to it. Like . . . like this red Honda here. Yes, a sturdy, practical, economical car like a Honda, but in red, to give it a bit of dash. Well, how close did I come?"

"You think this red Honda is my car," she said.

"That would be my guess, yes."

"Well . . . you're right," she said.

"I am? Really? You're kidding me!"

"No, that's my car," she said. "Did you really figure it out just now?"

He nodded and then he began to laugh. "I knew what kind of car you drove the first day you came here," he said. "It's not hard to find things out in the joint; I told you that when I met you."

She sighed and shook her head. "Get in the car," she said, embarrassed at having been so gullible.

They drove off and he turned around in his seat and looked back at the sprawling complex of low redbrick buildings surrounded by the twelve-foot-high chain-link fences topped by razor wire as they got smaller and smaller in the green fields until he couldn't see them anymore. He knew that he would never see them again. He felt relieved and unaccountably sad.

"You love to play with people, don't you?" she said.

"I do," he said. "The feeling of control, of power, is very satisfying."

She flashed him a look. "You're not really ready to leave here, are you?" she asked.

He considered this awhile before replying. "I'm as ready as I'll ever be," he said truthfully.

Neither of them spoke much again until they reached Burlington, parked in the airport lot, and entered the terminal.

"You know how monstrous I think it is that they released you into your mother's custody, don't you?" she asked.

He nodded.

"I tried everything I could to get them to change their minds," she said. "They like your mother. They think she's a terrific gal. Maybe a little eccentric, but otherwise harmless."

He nodded. "The fact that she endowed the computer center probably had no effect on their decision, either," he said.

"Tell me," she asked, "what are you going to do when she starts in on you, Andy? How are you going to react to her manipulations?"

He shook his head. "I don't know," he said.

"You're a lot stronger now than when you were sixteen," she said. "You've had twelve years to mature, to grow, to get strong, and to construct workable strategies for defending yourself."

"I know," he said.

"Your mother's not as tough as she looks. Inside she's an abused, frightened little kid, just like you are. Just like we all are. Don't be afraid of her. Don't let her get to you."

He smiled sadly. "Thank you, Dr. Stevenson."

She looked at her watch. "Well, I guess you should get to your gate."

"Yes."

They looked at each other.

"How do you feel?" she asked quietly.

"Terrified," he answered just as quietly.

"I'll be pulling for you, Andy," she said.

She reached out to shake his hand. She thought she saw wetness in his eyes. He seemed suddenly so vulnerable and young. She felt torn. She wished she could have comforted him, hugged him, held him, but knew how wildly inappropriate that would have been.

He took her hand and shook it. Then he swiftly slid both of his arms around her body and hugged her to him. Before she could break the hug, he had ended it and was walking swiftly toward his gate and the plane that would take him to New York.

CHAPTER 15

"SORRY TO KEEP you waiting, Mr. Segal," said the woman on the phone. "I was having a little trouble bringing your account up on the screen."

"No problem," said Max. He was at his desk at Queens Homicide, filling out forms on Virginia Morales.

"So what may I help you with today?" asked the woman.

"Well," said Max, "I was wondering whether it might be possible for you to increase my credit line."

"Let me just take a look at your account here, Mr. Segal," she said.

"Okay," he said.

"Mr. Segal, I see that you have an overdue minimum payment of two hundred fifty-six dollars and thirty-seven cents," she said. "That amount should have been received by us twelve days ago."

"Yes," he said, "I know. I'm just now writing a check for that amount. I was wondering in the meantime, though, whether you could possibly increase my credit line."

"Not at this particular point in time, I'm afraid," she said.

"And why would that be?" he asked.

"Just glancing here at your overall indebtedness, Mr. Segal, we wouldn't feel comfortable increasing your credit line at this particular point in time."

"I see," he said. "Is there anybody else I could talk to you about this? Some supervisor or something?"

"You asked for the supervisor with the last person you talked to, didn't you?" she said.

"Yes," he said.

"Well, *I'm* the supervisor," she said, the friendliness melting out of her tone. "And what I'm telling you is that I cannot increase your credit line at this particular point in time."

"Okay," he said. "Okay."

CHAPTER 16

WHEN DAVINCI SAW Max Segal walk into the one-fourteen squad room and approach his desk, his first thought was that Segal had come to break more fingers. DaVinci got up swiftly, took a defensive position on the far side of the desk and, holding his injured right hand with the three taped fingers well out of harm's way, scanned the desktop for office implements that might be used as weapons.

"Yo, DaVinci," said Max by way of greeting.

DaVinci locked eyes with Max. The fingers of his good left hand crept across his desktop and wrapped themselves around a ruler.

Max regarded DaVinci for a moment with great ambivalence and sighed.

"Look, DaVinci," said Max, "the last time I saw you I might have overreacted a little, okay? I've been under a lot of pressure lately and I might have overreacted, okay? I'm not saying I'm sorry, I'm only saying I might have overreacted."

DaVinci said nothing, watching for a trick.

"The fact of the matter is," said Max, "that the Morales case has been reclassified to homicide, as I'm sure you're aware, and whether you or I like it or not, we have to work together on it. So what do you say we bury the hatchet and let bygones be bygones?"

DaVinci continued to say nothing.

"How's the finger doing?" Max asked, realizing this might not be the most diplomatic of questions.

DaVinci continued saying nothing.

"Okay, look," said Max, "I'm sorry for breaking your finger, okay? And I hope we can somehow work together on this case. I understand you interviewed Surtees, the porter who was on duty when Morales was killed. That true?"

"I interviewed him," said DaVinci.

"And did he remember Morales having any visitors?"

"Surtees said that the entire time he was on duty at the front desk Morales didn't have a single visitor," said DaVinci.

CHAPTER 17

"SO, BABETTE, ARE you going out with somebody besides Achmed?" asked Max in what he thought was a casual tone of voice. He was back at his old apartment, sitting on Sam's bed, in the putting-Sam-to-bed process, and Sam had stopped the countdown to go to the bathroom.

"Why do you ask?" said Babette.

"Oh, Achmed said you were."

"*Achmed* said I was?"

"Yeah," said Max. "So are you?"

"You know," said Babette, "I don't really think it's appropriate for us to be having this discussion."

"Why not?" Max asked.

"I just don't think it's appropriate."

"Okay," said Max.

Sam came out of the bathroom, Babette withdrew, and Max shepherded the boy back into the darkened bedroom. They rearranged themselves in bed within the herd of stuffed animals.

"So, Sam," said Max casually, "is Mom going out with anybody else besides Achmed?"

"Yeah," said Sam. "Dad, how do you make a baby?"

Max was momentarily thrown.

"Uh, well, how do you think?"

"The mom swallows a seed," said Sam.

"No," said Max, "the dad puts the seed into the mom."

"Oh," said Sam.

"So who's Mom going out with besides Achmed?" Max asked.

"Some guy," said Sam. "Where does the dad put the seed?"

"Where do you think?" Max asked.

"Up her tushy-hole," said Sam.

"No," said Max. "But close."

"Up her vagina," said Sam.

"That's right," said Max. The kid was eight years old. He had probably gotten the whole story in the school yard and was just checking it out.

"So tell me," said Max. "Who's the guy?"

"What?"

"Who's the guy that Mom's going out with?"

"Just some guy," said Sam. "How does the dad get the seed in the mom's vagina?"

"Through his penis," said Max, wondering just how graphic you were supposed to get. "He puts his penis into her vagina."

"He goes *weewee* in her vagina?" asked Sam incredulously.

"No no," said Max. "He puts his penis into her vagina and then the seed comes out. When the seed reaches the egg, then it can make a baby. What's the guy's name?"

"And the baby grows inside the egg?" asked Sam.

"Yep," said Max, "you got it. Do you know the guy's name?"

"Yeah," said Sam. "How does the baby get out of the shell, though? How does it hatch?"

"It's not a real egg," said Max, beginning to wonder about the quality of information being traded in the school yard. "Not an egg with a shell like a chicken egg. What's the name of the guy that Mom's going out with?"

"Dieter," said Sam. "If it's not an egg, then why do they *call* it an egg?"

"Dieter?" said Max.

"Yeah," said Sam. "Why do they?"

"It *is* an egg," said Max, "it's just a different kind of one. It's much much smaller than a chicken egg. It's so tiny you couldn't see it unless you look at it under a microscope. It's too tiny to break, so it doesn't need a shell. Is Dieter a German guy?"

"I don't know," said Sam.

"He doesn't talk with an accent, does he?" Max asked. "Like Arnold Schwarzenegger?"

"Uh, let me think," said Sam. "A little bit, yeah."

"He does?" said Max. "Dieter has an accent like Arnold Schwarzenegger?"

"A little bit, yeah."

Great. There was only one thing worse than his wife dating an Arab, thought Max, and that was her dating a Nazi. In case he needed one, he now had an incentive to help Achmed win her back.

CHAPTER 18

AT SEVEN IN the morning, Astoria Park was still deserted. The air was cool and smelled unaccountably like burned coffee beans. The gigantic outdoor public pool that lay at the bottom of the hill would not open till eleven.

Astoria Pool was larger than a football field. It measured 165 feet in width and 330 feet in length. It had been designed to hold 6,200 bathers.

To the immediate left of the swimming pool was a diving pool that was considerably smaller, but considerably deeper. It was round on the left end and flat on the right end that abutted the swimming area, and it featured a gracefully curving three-tiered diving tower that stood thirty-two feet high. The pool and diving tower had been constructed in 1936 and were used in 1939 for the Olympic tryouts of the U.S. diving team.

On the far side of Astoria Pool, two blocks away, was the Hell Gate channel of the East River, and beyond that Wards Island and the skyline of upper Manhattan. Looming up four blocks to the left was the Triborough Bridge, and five blocks to the right was the considerably smaller Hell Gate Bridge.

The attendant who opened Astoria Pool most mornings was Angel Hernandez, a cheerful, somewhat obese man of sixty-four with short white hair. When he got out of his Parks Department pickup truck this morning and saw what was in it, he nearly had a heart attack.

Floating facedown in the pool, feet slightly lower than the rest of her, was the scantily clad body of a young woman. At first Angel thought she might still be alive.

Beginning to pray aloud, he scurried downhill to the edge of the pool as fast as his sixty-four-year-old legs could carry him, slipping and sliding several times on the grass, staining his hands and the knees of his clean khakis, but when he got through the locked iron gate to the edge of the pool he could tell that she was already dead. Could tell that she had most likely been dead for several hours.

Puffing with exertion and fear, he scrambled back uphill as fast as he could. He staggered into his truck, took out his cell phone, and, although he was still puffing so loudly he was barely comprehensible, he called the police.

By the time the first radio car arrived a small crowd had gathered. While one of the uniformed officers strung up the yellow plastic crime scene tape, the other radioed in for an emergency service bus and a medical examiner. Because this was a city pool, the ME would almost certainly order an autopsy, for legal reasons.

Dr. Wolfgang Erhard, the one-legged sixty-five-year-old Queens ME, happened to be on his way to work when he heard the uniforms call for an ME on his police radio. He turned his car around and drove directly to Astoria Park.

"What have we got?" he asked the first uniform he saw.

"Drowned female, Doc," said the uniform.

"I can *see* it's a female, you idiot," said Erhard. "And I can *see* she's drowned. Haven't you been able to determine any more than that before my arrival?"

"Uh, no sir," said the uniform.

Erhard cursed under his breath and hobbled on down the hill.

CHAPTER 19

ON THE WALL of the Queens Homicide squad room was a sign that read: IF IT AIN'T FATAL, IT AIN'T RELEVANT. IF THEY AIN'T DROPPING, WE AIN'T HOPPING.

Caruso walked heavily into the squad room and sank loudly into an office chair. It creaked under his weight.

"How ya doin', Sal?" asked Max without bothering to look up.

"Fine," said Caruso unconvincingly.

Max bothered to look up. "What's wrong, Sal? You look like your mother died."

"I did it, Max," said Caruso grimly.

"Yeah?" said Max. "What did you do?"

"Took a fucking physical like you said."

"You did?" said Max. "Hey, no kidding. That's great, Sal!"

"Yeah? You think it's great?" asked Caruso. "Well, maybe after I tell you what they told me, you won't think it's so great."

"What do you mean? What did they tell you?"

"Never mind."

"No," said Max, "what did they tell you?"

"Never mind."

Max shrugged. "Okay. Hey, going to the doctor reminds me of a joke I just heard. A guy about eighty years old phones his buddy. 'How ya doin', Sol?' he says. 'Morris,' says his buddy, 'I have wonderful news.'"

"I'm not in the mood for jokes," said Caruso crossly.

"It'll pep you up, Sal," said Max. "You look like you could use a little pepping up. 'I have wonderful news,' says his buddy, 'the doctor cured me of Alzheimer's.'"

"I'm not in the mood for any goddam jokes, for Christ's sake," said Caruso.

"'He cured you of Alzheimer's?' says Morris. 'Sol, that's fantastic! What's your doctor's name?'"

"Not only am I not in the mood for jokes, I already heard it," said Caruso.

"You *couldn't* have heard it, *I* just heard it," said Max. "'He cured you of Alzheimer's?' says Morris. 'Sol, that's fantastic! What's your doctor's name?' Sol thinks a moment. 'What's the thing that grows in the ground?' says Sol. 'It has flowers and thorns on it.' 'A rose,' says Morris. Sol snaps his fingers, turns his head—"

"—and calls: 'Rose? What the hell is my doctor's name?' I fucking *heard* it," said Caruso irritably.

"How could you have heard it?" Max asked. "McCarty told it to me only ten minutes ago."

"McCarty told it to me *yesterday*," said Caruso. "And I didn't think it was funny then either. You know what my cholesterol is?"

"How the hell would I know what your cholesterol is?" Max asked.

"You want to hear or not?" Caruso asked.

"Sure, tell me," said Max.

"No, guess."

"Just tell me," said Max.

"Take a fucking guess."

"High or low?"

"High."

"Okay, let's see," said Max. "Two hundred and forty?"

Caruso grimly shook his head from side to side. "Four eighty, Max. Four eighty. My fucking cholesterol is *four hundred and fucking eighty*. Do you know what that means?"

"Uh, well, I guess it means you've been eating a whole lot of cheeseburgers, for one thing."

"It means I'm going to *die*, Max. It means I'm going to fucking *die*."

"C'mon, Sal . . ."

"The doctor said if I can't get my cholesterol down three hundred points immediately, I'm going to fucking *die*," said Caruso.

"I find it hard to believe your doctor actually said that."

"That's what he said, Max. As God is my witness. Guess what my blood pressure is."

"There are things you can do about a high cholesterol count, you know."

"Guess what my blood pressure is," said Caruso.

"You can give up junk food, fried food, rich desserts, butter—"

"Guess what my fucking blood pressure is," said Caruso.

"Tell me."

"I said *guess*, goddamn it!"

"Okay," said Max. "A hundred twenty over eighty."

Caruso permitted himself a sardonic laugh. "Try a hundred and *eighty* over a hundred and *ten*."

"Uh-oh."

"You sonofabitch!" hissed Caruso.

"Come again?"

"You heard me, you sonofabitch," said Caruso.

"Excuse me, Sal, but why am I a sonofabitch?"

"Why are you a sonofabitch?" said Caruso. "I'll tell you why you're a sonofabitch, you sonofabitch. Who was it told me to go get a goddam physical in the first place?"

Max exhaled a forced, joyless laugh. Somewhere a phone rang and was answered.

"Oh, that's beautiful," said Max. "It's *my* fault you've got high cholesterol and high blood pressure. It's *my* fault the doctor gave you bad news. What is this, Sal, ancient Rome?"

"What?"

"Kill the messenger, is that it?"

"I'm not following you," said Caruso.

"Segal? Caruso?" called a voice from the lieutenant's office. "You just caught a job!"

"Be right there, boss!" Max yelled over his shoulder, then turned back to Caruso. "I did you a *favor* by telling you to go get a physical, you asshole! I got you to go to a doctor to find out you've been killing yourself! And for that you're calling me a sonofabitch? For trying to save your life? That's fucking beautiful!"

"If you didn't tell me to go get a physical," said Caruso, "then—"

"—then you'd still have the same cholesterol count and you'd still have the same blood pressure that you've got now," said Max. "You just wouldn't know it."

"Right!"

"And you wouldn't have a chance to save yourself," said Max.

"You guys want this job or not?" yelled the lieutenant.

Max and Caruso got up and walked into the lieutenant's office.

Lieutenant William "Wild Bill" Hickock was the commander of the Queens Homicide task force. He was fifty years of age, stood six foot three, had a powerful build, a sizable beer belly, and wore two nickel-plated revolvers, one on each hip. Nailed to the wall behind his desk were a black cowboy hat and a Western-style gun belt with a Colt .45 Peacemaker in its holster. Hickock maintained the nickname that had reportedly been hung on him as a gag, but many felt he'd made it up himself.

"I hope I'm not interrupting anything *important*," said Hickock.

"Sorry, boss," said Max. "What's the job we caught?"

"A drowning."

"A *drowning*?"

"Young female named Masters was found floating facedown in a public pool yesterday morning," said Hickock. "They just got the results of the autopsy. Some aspects of the case sounded suspicious, so the ME is reclassifying to homicide."

"You happen to know offhand what pool the victim was found in?" Max asked.

"Astoria Pool," said Hickock.

"Astoria?" said Max. "That's the one-fourteen precinct."

"So?" said Hickock.

"So who caught this case in the one-fourteen?" Max asked, dreading the answer.

"Guy by the name of DaVinci," said Hickock.

CHAPTER 20

WELL, MR. SEGAL," said the elegant young black woman in the smartly tailored suit as they sat down at a table in the conference room, "so nice to finally meet you in person." The surface of the wooden conference table had a shell of glossy polyurethane that looked hard enough to deflect bullets.

"Thank you, Mrs. Yamamoto," he said. "It's nice to meet you, too."

Max noted the strong smell of cologne, a not unpleasant odor.

"And what can we do for you today?"

"Well," said Max, "I was wondering about the possibility of refinancing or increasing the size of my mortgage loan. I'm in the process of a divorce and I now have to pay not only the expenses on the apartment I own, which my wife and son are living in, but also the expenses on the apartment I'm living in myself, plus the expense of a couple of divorce lawyers, and so on."

"I see," she said. She scanned the papers in his file. "Tell me, Mr. Segal, are you still employed by the New York City Police Department in the same capacity as before?"

"Still a homicide detective second grade," he said.

"And do you have another source of income?"

"Another source of income?" he repeated. "No, I don't."

"Do you have other property that you own, income-producing or otherwise?"

"No," he said. "I don't."

"I see," she said. "Well then, in that case I'm afraid the bank wouldn't be able to either refinance or increase the size of your loan."

"Why not?" he said. "I'm good for it. I mean I've never missed a payment yet."

"The bank simply cannot increase the size of your loan unless you have another source of income."

"If I had another source of income," he said, "I wouldn't *need* the bank to increase the size of my loan."

She smiled. "You're not the first person to make that particular point to us," she said.

"I didn't imagine I was," he said.

CHAPTER 21

MARIAN MASTERS HAD no heart. She also had no stomach, lungs, liver, bladder, kidneys, intestines, or brain. All of these had been removed during her autopsy, examined, weighed, dissected, and then unceremoniously dumped into a garbage can labeled CAUTION: BIOLOGICAL HAZARD. Like a Thanksgiving turkey, the empty shells of the woman's torso and head had then been stuffed with oakum, a hemplike fiber derived from old ropes, and sewn back up again with heavy, off-white twine.

Marian lay naked in a sliding tray that resembled a gigantic filing cabinet drawer, her head toward the drawer handle. She looked as though she were asleep, but the deep Y-shaped incision in her torso, the arms of the Y reaching for her shoulders, the base of the Y plunging to her crotch, suggested that her sleep might be a long one. Her skin looked puffy and bluish. Her clothing lay in a ball at her feet. A large "ninety-five" ID tag had been tied to her right ankle.

"Gentlemen," said the ME, "meet Marian Masters."

"Hiya, Marian," murmured Max. He wasn't as fond of kidding the corpses as were the ME and the other ghouls who worked here.

"Was she wearing these when they found her?" asked Caruso, pointing to the ball of clothing, taking out his spiral notebook.

"No, just underwear," said the ME "The rest of her clothes were found in a pile at the edge of the pool."

"You don't think she just peeled down to her skivvies on a hot night and went for a swim?" Max asked, staring at her body.

"That's what I thought at first," said the ME. "Especially since I found a considerable amount of alcohol in her bloodstream. I also found water in her lungs which she'd inhaled, and diatoms in the bone marrow, which is evidence she was alive when she went into the pool. I figured she was inebriated, she gravely underestimated her swimming ability, she got a cramp, panicked, and drowned. If she was drinking, chances are somebody was with her. But why didn't he rescue her when he perceived that she was in trouble?"

"Maybe neither of them knew how to swim," said Caruso.

"Neither of them had to," said the ME. "Astoria Pool is uniformly four feet deep."

"How the hell do you drown in a pool that's four feet deep?" Max asked.

"You don't know how to swim and you panic," said Caruso.

"Then why the hell do you go swimming in the first place?" Max asked. "Unless somebody cons you into it."

"Somebody has to do more than con you into it," said the ME smugly, playing his trump card, "if you're phobic about water."

"Who told you she was phobic about water?" Max asked.

"The father," said the ME. "He came in to see me right after I posted the body."

"Sonofabitch," said Max.

"Yeah," said the ME.

"Pfhew," said Max and then he said, "Virginia Morales."

"What?" said Caruso.

"Virginia Morales," said Max. "She's phobic about heights, but she goes up to the roof of her apartment building and plunges to her death. Marian Masters, she's phobic about water, but she goes swimming in a pool and drowns. Both cases just happen to land in the one-fourteen. You see any linkage there, guys?"

———

"Yeah, Segal, what is it?" asked Lieutenant Hickock without looking up. He was hunched over his computer screen, intent on whatever he was researching on the Internet. Max took a step forward and peered at the screen. Photos of handguns. Hickock working on his private collection again.

"Boss, I want to ask the DA for phone dumps on both Virginia Morales and Marian Masters," said Max.

Hickock shook his head. "Save your breath," he said.

Phone dumps were notoriously expensive. Getting the telephone company to "dump your phone" meant to get a computer printout of every call you made in a twenty-four hour period, every call you received, even incoming and outgoing calls that weren't completed. But dumps had to go through the entire NYPD chain of command and be subpoenaed by the DA. Without a phone dump the printout would show only completed outgoing calls, no incoming ones. It would also take six weeks.

"Why should I save my breath?" Max asked.

"Do you know what it costs to do a phone dump?"

"Yeah," said Max. "Five hundred dollars per area code per phone for every twenty-four hour period."

"Right," said Hickock.

"So for two phones the phone company would charge us three thousand dollars," said Max.

"Exactly," said Hickock. "You really think the DA's gonna stand still for three thousand bucks worth of dumps, Segal? Get real."

"Boss, I'd be willing to bet money that the killer called at least one of these women on the day she died."

"Your *own* money?" said Hickock.

Max smiled wryly. "Boss," he said, "I don't *have* any money. I'm teetering on the brink of bankruptcy."

"Sorry to hear that," said Hickock.

"Speaking of which, would it be at all possible for you to loan me a hundred bucks till payday?"

"You got a better chance of hitting the DA up for the three grand," said Hickock.

CHAPTER 22

MAX'S CELL PHONE buzzed. The caller ID spelled out "Babette."

"Hi, Babette," he said, feeling awful.

"I'm sorry to be calling you at work," she said. "But the mail arrived and your check wasn't in it."

"Oh God," he said, sighing. He idly picked up a stack of glossy photos which happened to be from Marian Masters's autopsy.

"You didn't send it, did you?" she said.

"I didn't send it," he said. "I'm so sorry." The top shot showed the open chest cavity. Max stuck it on the bottom of the stack, but the one that took its place wasn't any better.

"Max, what am I supposed to do?" asked Babette. "New York Telephone and Con Ed are both threatening to disconnect if I don't pay them. I'm scared they'll really do it."

"I'll get you the money," said Max. "I swear to God I will."

"You swore to God you were going to *mail* the money," said Babette.

"I know," said Max. "I'm sorry, Babette. I'll drop it off tonight."

"Do you even have it?"

"No, of course I don't have it," he said irritably.

"Then how can you give it to me?"

"I'll write you a check," said Max. "Before it bounces, I'll have found something to deposit in the account."

"Isn't there a twenty-five dollar charge for bounced checks?"

"Babette, what the hell can I do? I've given you every cent I have. I owe Natale for the apartment, I'm trying to refinance the mortgage, I'm trying to get my credit line increased at Visa and MasterCard. I'm trying to borrow money from the guys at work. I don't know what else I can do. I give you whatever I make."

"I know you do, Max," she said. "Look, I wouldn't ask you for money if I wasn't scared out of my wits or if I could get it anywhere else, believe me."

"What about Achmed?"

"What about him?" she asked.

"Well, he's loaded," said Max. "Couldn't you ask old Achmed for a loan or something?"

"Achmed doesn't have as much money as you may think," she said.

"No?" said Max. "Then why doesn't he sell something—an oil company, say—to get a little cash?"

"Achmed has been extremely generous, Max," she said, frosting up, "in ways I can't even go into now. I cannot ask him for more."

Max decided not to dwell on the ways she couldn't even go into now.

"I'll drop it off at the apartment tonight," he said and hung up.

CHAPTER 23

WELL, WELL, WELL, if it isn't the prodigal son," she said, as the elevator door opened directly into the penthouse foyer. "Welcome home, Andy-Boy!"

"Thank you, Cynthia," he replied, walking inside.

She was a wretched excess of a woman, larger than life. Six feet tall in her stocking feet, six-four in spike heels. Long flowing hair, a pastel shade that had never been seen in nature. Pointed breasts that had been surgically enhanced more than once and were now equal in size to those of the most generously endowed of nursing mothers. She wore a beige silk blouse unbuttoned one button lower than propriety dictated and a tan silk miniskirt.

She engulfed him in a bear hug, her long arms crushing him to her torso. Her mammoth breasts pressed against him, leaving, it seemed to him, meteor-sized craters in his chest. Her perfume, though expensive, was too fragrant by half and overwhelmed him, leaving him vaguely nauseated. She loosened her bear hug, grasped his wrists with hands like handcuffs, and held him at arm's length.

"Let me look at you," she said. "My my, don't we look handsome in our Armanis. Don't we look fucking drop-dead-Mary handsome. Tell me, how do your new duds fit?"

"Remarkably well, thanks," he replied.

"Even the undies?"

"Even the undies," he said.

A frail young Irish housekeeper in a black uniform trimmed in white lace materialized at her side. Her face was that of someone who had seen many sad things.

"Annabelle, this is my son Andy-Boy," said Cynthia. "Andy-Boy Woods."

"How do you do, sir," said Annabelle.

"Glad to meet you, Annabelle," said Andy.

"How do those undies fit in the pouch, dear?" asked Cynthia.

"They're perfect," he said.

"They're not too snug around your little bundle?"

He looked at the housekeeper for a reaction, but she showed nothing.

"No, they're perfect," he said. "How did you know what size of everything to send?"

"Are you *serious*, darling?" she asked. "I know your body like the back of my hand. Better. I know you as well as I know myself. Now tell me, did you eat on the plane?"

"No, Cynthia, it was a rather small commuter plane. They do not serve meals."

"Annabelle, this poor boy is *famished*," said Cynthia. "He hasn't had a thing to eat in twelve years at prison. Nothing but swill for twelve years. Gruel and swill. Will you get him something to eat that is neither gruel nor swill?"

"What would you like, sir?" Annabelle asked.

"I don't really care, Annabelle," said Andy. "Do you have any yogurt?"

"Yogurt!" Cynthia shouted. "For Christ's sweet sake, don't bring him yogurt! We have to fatten him up. We have to put some flesh on those bones of his. Is there still that roast chicken in the fridge, Annabelle?"

"Yes ma'am."

"Make him a hero sandwich with the roast chicken, plenty of bacon, lettuce, tomato, and lots of mayonnaise," said Cynthia.

"Yes, ma'am."

While Annabelle was preparing his lunch, Andy went off to his old bedroom to wash up and to use the bathroom. There didn't seem to be any locks on any of the bedroom or bathroom doors, a fact which he asked Cynthia about when he came back to the kitchen for his lunch.

"I don't believe in locks," she said by way of explanation.

"Why don't you?"

"I just don't like to feel shut out of anybody's life," she said.

"You don't believe in privacy?" he asked.

"I believe everybody should be open and accessible," she said.

Immediately after his lunch Cynthia insisted that he have a hot shower. She went into his bathroom and got it started, selected just the right temperature, then left the room. No sooner had he taken off his clothes and stepped into the steaming stall than she barged back in.

"Have enough bath towels, dear?" she shouted above the torrent of water through the clear glass door.

"Yes, thank you," he replied, turning away, shielding his groin with a washcloth.

"Enough soap? Shampoo? Hand towels? Washcloths?"

"I have enough of everything," he yelled. "Everything but privacy!"

Dinner was promptly at eight, served formally by Annabelle and a male servant named Victor at the long chrome and glass table in the elegant dining room. She'd requested that they dress for it and presented Andy with a white Armani dinner jacket.

A hundred votive candles in clusters on the table provided the only source of illumination. It looked like a banquet in a church. Annabelle poured them sidecars on the rocks, and when Andy protested that he wasn't allowed to drink, Cynthia guilted him into the first one, browbeat him into the second, and by the third had to do little more than suggest.

With dinner Annabelle served Dom Pérignon. Dinner consisted of lobster stuffed with crabmeat, potato skins stuffed with sour cream and cheese, bell peppers stuffed with ground lamb. For dessert there was pecan pie topped with Heath Bar Crunch ice cream.

"So," said Cynthia, "what do you think?"

"It was magnificent, Cynthia," he said. "You really know how to put on the dog."

"As good as the chow in the joint?" she asked.

"Almost," he said.

She reached across the table and covered his hand with hers.

"It's good to have you home, baby."

"Thank you, Cynthia," he said. "It's good to be here."

"I've missed you."

"Have you?"

"Yes."

"Then tell me something," he said. "Why didn't you visit me in prison?"

"I *did* visit you, sweetheart," she said. "How can you ask me that? I visited you and I sent you all those things—the flat-screen TV, the stereo, all those CDs, all those books, all those boxes of food—"

"I know what you sent me," he said. "You visited me six times, Cynthia. Six times in twelve years. That's an average of once every two years."

She looked down at her plate.

"Oh, honey, I know," she whispered. "I'm sorry. What can I tell you?"

"You can tell me why you didn't visit me more than six times in twelve years."

A sigh. "I couldn't."

"You couldn't?"

"I couldn't," she said. "I hated going up there, baby. It was so painful for me. I hated seeing you in that place with all those . . . people."

"All *what* people?"

"All those criminals," she said.

"What do you think *I* am?" he asked. "I'm a criminal, Cynthia, a murderer. I murdered your husband. That's why I was in prison, don't you remember that?"

"Please don't be angry with me tonight, pussycat," she said. "Please don't spoil your homecoming dinner. I wanted it to be so special. I wanted it to be perfect."

She began to cry. He thought he ought to feel something.

"You know what I wish?" she asked.

"What?"

"I wish you'd call me Mother," she said.

"You know what I wish?" he asked.

"What?"

"I wish that either one of us could imagine you in that capacity."

He got up a bit unsteadily. "I'm sorry," he said. "I can't censor myself when I drink."

He turned on his heel and lurched off to bed.

She stayed at the table, mopping at her streaming eyes with balled-up Kleenexes, and finished off the bottle of Dom. Then she had Annabelle make another pitcher of sidecars, which she took down the hall into her bedroom.

She went into her bathroom, slipped off her clothes, and studied her naked body from the many angles reflected in the mirrored walls and ceiling. Not too horrid a body, although it had all begun to shift and realign like plates in the earth's crust. A little more work on the boobs was right around the corner, and perhaps a bun lift and a tummy tuck. If you had the money, there was nothing, nothing that couldn't be enlarged, reduced, reshaped, or relocated. She had always thought of her body less as a final creation than as a work in progress. But the day would soon arrive when no amount of surgery could forestall the body's inevitable decay, and this notion filled her with unspeakable dread.

When she first started work as a Vegas showgirl her boobs were so small she wore padded bras, but the foam rubber in them made her sweat, and when she sweated she lost weight, at least one full cup size. So the producer of the show she was in told her to get silicone shots, and she did—two under each boob and one up on top. She had the shots in the afternoon, and that evening, while doing a show with little Band-Aids over the shots, she suddenly felt the silicone begin dribbling out. What a mess.

The silicone eventually did drop, so next she had saline bags surgically installed. Saline bags looked more natural than silicone, plus they didn't feel so hard. The girls called them sea water bags because they sort of slooshed around inside you. Some saline jobs turned out terrible, with ugly scars under the nipples, but hers didn't look too bad at all.

But big boobs were a mixed blessing to an exotic dancer. When you danced they jiggled around so much it hurt. It also broke down the tissues and made them drop faster. She almost got a reduction job. On a reduction job they cut fat out from underneath each boob, then they slice off the nipples and sew them on again higher up. The sensitivity was gone for awhile, but it did return. If they didn't reset your nipples higher, then when they took the fat out from underneath, your nipples would end up down around your waist. A reduction job was a fairly common operation. Perhaps she'd get one now.

She pulled on a peach silk nightgown, poured herself a sidecar, and began to ruminate on Andy.

It wasn't fair. You knocked yourself out to raise a child as a single parent, loving him as only a mother could love something that had once been a growth in her innards, making sacrifices that only a mother could appreciate, and then that child grew up to hate you. If only she had known how to love him less, it wouldn't be so painful now.

She had loved him from the moment he'd been born, loved him fiercely as a baby, as a toddler, as a prepubescent boy—a prepubescent boy who thought he was her nephew and had no notion that once he'd lived inside her gut, tucked up tight like a little fist. Loved him as a difficult teenager with an attitude problem who hurt her every chance he got. Would have loved him no less if he'd been plain looking and not the drop-dead-handsome hunk he had become, but loved him for that as well.

Her love for him had not even diminished when he'd gone and, for no fathomable reason, blown poor old Walter's brains out. What an awful mess he'd made. But she'd also forgiven him for that, as she'd forgiven him for all the other awful messes he'd made as a teenager. Indeed, she was more forgiving toward him for killing Walter than were a bunch of total strangers in the state of Vermont.

What good had twelve years in a maximum security prison done him anyway? Had it been up to her, she would have punished him herself—a good strapping of his butt with a belt, confinement in his room for a week, and then get *on* with it. Instead they stuck him in a prison where he learned to have sex with men and to be bitter toward the mother who created him, the mother to whom he owed every breath he drew.

If only things had turned out differently. If only they could have been a happy family, sharing birthdays and Thanksgivings and Christmases together, a happy family like hers had been with her parents, her seven brothers and sisters—a big, noisy, dirt-poor, often starving family who drank together and fought together and loved together and broke one another's furniture and teeth and sometimes didn't sober up for days. Now she had money and nobody to spend it on but herself and a twenty-eight-year-old ingrate son who even now lay drunk as a lord, wrinkling up his Armanis.

She finished off her glass and, leaning occasionally on a wall for balance, made her way down the long carpeted hall to Andy's bedroom.

There he lay, mouth open, hair matted and moist on his forehead, snoring softly. He'd flung his new dinner jacket on the carpet and managed to take off one wingtip shoe, and then passed out on the bed, one leg hanging precariously over the edge of the mattress.

She shook her head and smiled. He looked so uncomfortable, asleep in his clothes. She carefully unlaced and removed the other shoe, put teak shoe trees in both and placed them side-by-side in the closet. She moved his hanging leg back onto the bed, then carefully unbuckled his belt, unzipped his trousers, and tugged them down his legs and off the ends of his feet. She removed the loose change from his pockets, stacked it on the dresser, and hung the pants by the cuffs from a pants hanger in the closet.

She returned to the bed, smoothed his damp hair back from his forehead, bent down and kissed it, inhaling the heady smell of his hair and skin. He was so beautiful, so unbearably beautiful. So much like her in so many ways. How had he come to hate her so? She longed to cuddle with him as she had when he was a little boy.

She lay down beside him on the still-made bed, her heavy body making the mattress sag. She ran her fingers through his hair and kissed his slack and sleeping face.

He stirred and groaned, swimming upward toward wakefulness.

"Shh," she said, not wanting the moment to end. His eyes fluttered open. "Go back to sleep," she soothed, "Mommy's here."

His eyes focused. He recoiled, screaming, from her touch and jackknifed into a sitting position.

"Shh," she soothed, "go back to sleep. Everything will be all right."

"Jesus Christ, what are you doing in my bed?" he shouted. "And what the hell happened to my pants?"

"I didn't want them to wrinkle, so I—"

"You were *touching* me, Cynthia," he shouted. "What were you going to do, fuck me in my sleep?"

The words smacked her in the face like a slap. What had she done to deserve such words?

"I *was* touching you," she cried, heating up quickly. "I was *not* going to fuck you. If I wanted to fuck you, my darling, I assure you I would. I *created* you. I *own* you. You were a part of my body and you came out of me and I allowed them to cut the cord that connected us, but you're an extension of my body. I could use you anytime I want and it wouldn't be incest, it would be masturbation!"

"I came out of your body," he said, "but that doesn't mean you *own* me. And you will never ever use me for sex!"

Shame and revulsion broke over him in waves, chased by fleeting shreds of memory. He reeled into the bathroom and retched up lobster stuffed with crabmeat, potato skins stuffed with sour cream and cheese, bell peppers stuffed with ground lamb.

He felt overwhelmed and powerless and out of control. He felt six years old. He stuffed his feelings into a closet and squeezed the door shut. He had learned to do that over the years, stuff his feelings into a closet, and when he did it made him feel better. Detached. Calm. Superior. A superior being. A superior being who wasn't answerable to other people's rules.

He calmly washed his face with soap and cold water and then he carefully brushed his teeth and combed his hair. When he reentered the bedroom she was still seated on his bed.

"What did they do to you in the joint?" she said. "Did the bad men take their bad wee wees and put them up little Andy's poo-poo hole? Did they make Andy-Boy a faggot? Is that why the thought of sex with a woman makes him puke?"

"Not with a woman," he said. "With *you*."

"You little creep," she said. "You know what you are? A loser. A hopeless little loser. You've never done anything in your miserable life and you never will, you worthless little piece of shit."

"Get out of my room," he said.

"*Your* room?" she said. "Everything around here is *mine*, sweet pants. And every*body* around here is mine. Let's get that straight right away, okay? And since you've been released into my custody, if you don't like the way I run things around here, you can go right back to the joint—because that, as I understand it, is your choice. Would you like to go back to the joint, my darling?"

He studied her face for several moments, sifting through a wide range of possible responses.

"No," was the one he finally selected to say aloud.

CHAPTER 24

BY THE TIME he finally got dressed again and got out of his
mother's apartment and down the elevator and out onto Park
Avenue, it was almost 1 A.M. He had never been able to stand up to
her. He was trying to stick with the VOP program, but she was pushing his buttons and he had no defenses against her. He had left one
prison for another. At the Northwest State Correctional Facility he at
least had dignity as a group leader. Here he had nothing.

He walked along Park Avenue for several blocks and then swung
east. When he hit First Avenue he spotted a singles bar and went
inside.

The noise level was a little high for his taste, but there were, as he
suspected, a number of rather interesting looking women standing,
chatting, drinking, looking for company. Looking to get laid. *Beliefs
About Women*, he remembered. *If they're drinking, they want it.*

He felt uncomfortable in the singles bar and was suddenly
drenched by a wave of awkwardness and helplessness. But then he
drew on a mental file of singles bar scenes from movies and TV
shows he'd studied in prison and realized he knew exactly what to
do and say. If he were playing a role rather than being himself,
there was far less at stake.

He ordered a sidecar on the rocks and, while sipping it, casually
surveyed the room. *Antennae/Radar: Looking for opportunity*, flashed
through his mind.

At the end of the bar was a very good-looking young woman
with soft brown hair and a tight pink T-shirt. He wondered what it

would be like to just walk over to the young woman, drop his hand onto her breast and squeeze it through that tight pink T-shirt. All right, that would be *Fantasy/Power*. He had inadvertently begun a Violent Offender cycle.

It would probably be wise to intervene in the cycle before it went any further, but he couldn't help wondering what the young woman would do if he dropped his hand onto her breast and squeezed it. She might scream and she might hit him, but she couldn't prevent him from dropping his hand onto her breast and squeezing it if he decided that was what he wanted to do.

Ah yes, he thought, *that would be Entitlement: If I want it, I'll have it.* With detached amusement he watched himself passing through the next stage of his cycle and not intervening. *Cycles: A recipe for committing sexual assault—remove any part of it and the recipe doesn't work.* Well, he could stop at any point he wanted.

He beckoned the bartender over.

"How you doin' this evening?" said the bartender.

"Great," he said, using dialogue from a movie he'd seen only last week. "Couldn't be better. See the girl at the end of the bar?"

"Pink T-shirt?" said the bartender.

"Right. Tell her I'd like to buy her a drink."

The bartender nodded and withdrew.

When her drink arrived, the young woman in the tight pink T-shirt looked in his direction and smiled. He moved down the bar and stood next to her.

"Thanks for the beer," she said.

"You're very welcome," he said. "My name is Steve."

"Susan."

"Are you a student, Susan?"

"Not anymore."

"Then what do you do?"

"I work at Sports Training Institute."

"As what?" he asked.

"A personal trainer."

"Ah," he said. "You do one-on-one training with clients on Cybex machines, that sort of thing?"

"Mmm."

"Do you enjoy it?"

"Very much."

"Good," he said. "What do you enjoy doing most?"

"At work, you mean?"

"No, anywhere."

"I don't know," she said. "Working out. Biking. Skiing. Swimming. Hiking. A lotta outdoor stuff."

"Really?" he said. "Me too."

"Oh yeah?" she said. "What do you do?"

"Hiking," he said. "Mountain climbing. Scuba diving. Downhill skiing." *Alignment*, he thought.

"That's great," she said. "Where do you ski?"

"Switzerland," he said, sensing he might have bitten off more than he could chew. He'd never skied in his life, and all he knew about Switzerland he'd gotten from *The Sound of Music*.

"I'm afraid I've never been to Europe," she said. "I mostly ski in Colorado. Steamboat Springs, Vail, Aspen. Like that."

"You must be in good shape," he said.

"I am," she said.

He took a step backward and looked her up and down.

"You have a really nice body," he said. "What I can see of it, that is." *Grooming.*

The woman laughed, seeing no need to thank him for the compliment.

Could I get away with it? he wondered. *Risk Assessment. Get away with what?* he thought, squeezing a breast? What good was squeezing a breast? He wanted to take her somewhere and have total access to her for as long as he pleased. Total access. Total freedom to peel off that tight pink T-shirt and touch her naked breasts and perhaps even bite them, if that's what he decided he wanted to do. What would that feel like, to bite her nipples? Or just run his hands over her ass and do whatever he chose. Just own her for a period of time, and then get rid of her. Maybe not even have sex with her. Maybe just look at her body and scare her. See what made her sweat.

He found these ideas exciting. *Cycles: A recipe for committing sexual assault—remove any part of it and the recipe doesn't work.*

"Tell me, Susan," he said, "would you consider yourself happy?"

"Yeah, as a matter of fact, I would."

"That's wonderful," he said. "So few people really do. What frightens you?"

"What *frightens* me?"

"Yes."

"Nothing," she said.

"Really?" he said.

"Really."

"I don't believe you," he said.

"I don't care if you believe me or not," she said. "I'm not frightened of anything."

"Is that so?" he said. "Not even of me?"

"Why should I be frightened of *you*?" she asked.

He raised his eyebrows. "I don't know," he said. "What if I were a murderer?"

This intrigued her. "Are you?" she asked.

"We're all murderers," he said.

She drank from her beer, watching him, not speaking.

"We're all capable of murder," he said. "Some of us seize the opportunity, some of us don't."

"Really," she said. "What about *you*, Steve? Have you seized the opportunity?"

"I have," he said.

"What do you mean, in a war?" she asked.

"No, not in a war," he said.

She studied his face, searching for a clue, clearly puzzled and uncomfortable. He found himself savoring her discomfort and puzzlement. *I can stop this at any point*, he thought.

"I murdered somebody and went to prison for it," he said finally.

"At first I thought you were trying to hit on me," she said. "Now I think you're trying to scare me."

"Why not both?" he asked pleasantly.

And then he knew he was finally ready to stop. But was it because he had made a conscious decision to halt his cycle before proceeding to the final step of assaulting her, or because she said she had no fear and that had made him lose interest in her? He truly didn't know.

CHAPTER 25

HE AWOKE AROUND 10:30 A.M. After showering, shaving, and dressing, he was starved. If he were still at the Northwest State Correctional Facility, it would be almost time for lunch. Was it worth drifting into the kitchen and foraging for food, even if it meant risking running into Cynthia? He decided it was.

He walked into the kitchen. Annabelle was at the sink, unloading the dishwasher. Cynthia was sitting at the table, reading *Weekly Variety*.

"Well," she said, "here's Andy-Boy. And how is Mommy's little faggot this morning?"

Neither Andy nor Annabelle gave any indication that she had spoken.

"Annabelle," she said, "did you know that when my son was in prison, he had sex with men? I'll bet you didn't know that."

He decided to eat breakfast out.

———

PANCAKES MAKE YOU HAPPY said the sign outside the Atlantic Pancake House on Lexington Avenue. Well, he thought, it's worth a try. He walked inside, more than willing to feel happy.

After ingesting two stacks of flapjacks and three cups of coffee, he didn't feel happy, but at least he no longer felt hungry. He paid his check, left a more than generous tip, then strolled down Lexington Avenue, looking in windows. He passed a bookstore, a hardware store, a women's clothing store, a toy store, an antique store. He enjoyed looking in the windows. He hadn't done any window shopping in twelve years.

In the window of a small shop called The Bridal Path were mannequins dressed as a bride and groom. The groom wore a traditional black tuxedo with a white tie, the bride a lacy white gown with high-buttoned neck and a long train. Cheesy-looking birds, suspended from the top of the window, held flowers in their beaks. As he gazed at the mannequins, the groom's face morphed into Andy's and the bride's into Grace's.

He felt momentarily breathless, dizzy, and happy, and then the mannequins' own faces returned. What in God's name was *that*? He shook off the feeling of momentary dizzy happiness and continued on down the block.

In the window of a novelty store something caught his eye. A .22 automatic. He had heard it was easy to buy handguns in New York, but this was ridiculous. He went inside. An elderly man with saggy cheeks and an obvious brunette rug stood behind the counter. He asked the man to show it to him.

The .22 automatic turned out to be only a cigarette lighter that *looked* like a .22 automatic, but Andy rather liked it. Impulsively, he bought it.

"What're you planning to do?" asked the man. "Light cigarettes or rob banks?"

"Think it looks real enough to rob banks?" Andy asked.

"If you pointed that thing in my face?" said the man. "I'd probably give you the money."

"Yeah, maybe," said Andy.

"You'll never know till you try," said the old man with a wink.

Andy put the lighter in his sport coat pocket and strolled along Lex, looking in more windows. Then he walked east to First Avenue and turned uptown. The shops weren't quite as interesting on

First as they were on Lex. In a Korean grocery that was open to the street he spotted a young woman buying tulips. *Antennae/Radar.*

She had boyishly short blond hair and she wore tight white short shorts and a white tank top through which he could see a swell of breast. She looked to be no more than twenty.

If she's dressed like that, he thought to himself, she must want it. *Beliefs About Women.*

When she paid for the bunch of red tulips he decided to follow her. Because there were so many people around them he was able to follow her fairly closely at first.

He liked the shape of her bare legs. Through her shorts he could easily make out her panty line. He visualized grasping her hips from behind and burying his face in her flesh. *Fantasy/Power.*

He could see himself doing it, actually see himself doing it. It would frighten her and it would be terribly exciting. It was exciting just to think about.

What would she do? Scream. Flail at him with her tiny fists. Run away. Would she report him to the police? Not likely. In a city as big as New York, where would they even begin to look for him? *Risk Assessment.*

Of course there wasn't much chance he'd ever do it, not much chance at all, but if he wanted to do it, really wanted to do it, he just might. He had the right. He gave himself the right. Do unto others as others have done unto you. *Entitlement.*

The more he thought about it, the more exciting the prospect became. *A recipe for sexual assault. Remove any part of it . . .* He could stop his cycle now if he wanted to, he really could. If he wanted to.

As the people on First Avenue thinned out, he dropped back as far as half a block. She turned west on Sixty-third Street. He let her go out of sight for a moment, let those lovely buttocks in those tight white shorts go out of sight. He could let her disappear from his life forever, or he could catch up with her. This was the moment of decision, the point of no return.

He jogged up to Sixty-third and turned west. There she was, more than half a block ahead. He could plainly make out her buttocks under her shorts, even at this distance. He followed her to Second Avenue, and then to Third. And then he saw his opportunity—nobody on the block between Third and Lex but the two of them.

He began to lope toward her, closing the gap between them with every stride. When he drew abreast of her he was breathing loudly. When he pulled past her, his breathing quietened. When he was half a block ahead of her, he suddenly grabbed his chest, staggered, and fell forward on the sidewalk, gasping for breath.

She was up to him in seconds.

"What's the matter?" she cried out. "Are you all right?"

He winced in pain and tried to speak.

"I . . . won't . . ." he whispered.

"You won't?" she said anxiously.

"I . . . won't . . ."

Clutching her tulips, she bent down closely to hear what he was trying to say.

"You won't *what*?" she asked.

He showed her the fake automatic.

"I won't shoot you through the heart if you do exactly as I tell you," he said.

The tulips slipped out of her grasp and hit the sidewalk. Her eyes grew so wide he thought they might roll out of her head and land beside the tulips.

He got slowly to his feet, putting the lighter back into his sport coat pocket, continuing to point it in her direction.

"Don't shoot me," she whispered. "Please don't shoot me and I'll do whatever you want me to do, I swear I will. Just tell me what you want me to do."

"Good," he said. "Just continue walking. Just walk next to me as if we're very good friends out for a stroll. Yes, that's it. Now tell me what you're feeling."

"What I'm *feeling*?" she said.

"Yes."

"I'm feeling . . . very frightened," she said.

"Yes," he said. "Frightened. That's good. What else, dear?"

"I'm feeling . . . that I might faint."

"Thank you," he said. "That's very nice."

He was breathing very rapidly, he noticed, and his heart was racing. It was not from his run.

"Tell me," he said, "have you ever thought of dying? Ever wondered what it might feel like to die? Ever wondered whether, when you leave this realm, you really do pass down a long tunnel toward incredibly bright light, as some say, and then find dead loved ones waiting for you at the other end?"

"Please," she said. "Don't hurt me. I stopped to help you. I thought you were hurt and I stopped to help you. Is that a reason to hurt me?"

He could feel the pulse in his throat, the perspiration at his hairline, the stiffness in his groin. He knew that he was making a terrible mistake, but he was unable to stop himself.

A hunter green Range Rover pulled up a few yards ahead of them and three businessmen in very narrow-lapelled suits and tight slacks got out of it.

"Help!" she screamed. "This guy's got a gun! He's trying to kidnap me!"

The three men turned to look at them, and the young woman broke into a run across Sixty-third Street. Andy opened his fingers and released the cigarette lighter, letting it slip down into his jacket pocket, letting his hand slide out into the open.

"What's going on?" called the bravest of the three men, though he remained close to the car.

Andy shrugged, raised his palms skyward, and smiled an ingenuous smile.

"Young lady's having a difficult day," he said, tapping his temple.

The three men broke into relieved laughter, four sane guys united against a daffy dame, and continued on their way. The young woman was by now across Lexington and running for her life.

His excitement fled as quickly as his prey, leaving him deflated, depressed, and ashamed, the emotional equivalent of post-copulatory remorse. What in the name of Christ had he just done? How had he, of all people, ever allowed his obsessions to go this far? To drag him through his VOP cycle into sexual assault, in broad daylight on the Upper East Side of Manhattan? To jeopardize his parole and his precious freedom? He couldn't believe he'd been stupid enough to assault her.

He couldn't believe he'd been stupid enough to let her get away.

CHAPTER 26

THE GOOD OLD Days, thought Cynthia, humming along with the tape of her old stripper music, doing a slow striptease for herself as an audience of one in front of the bathroom mirrors with one of her old breakaway stripper outfits.

What made the Good Old Days good, and why didn't we realize then that they were good so that we could appreciate them, instead of waiting till now and having to decide how good they were, compared with the crappy days we have now—days that, however crappy they might be, will at some point in the sorry future look like Good Old Days themselves?

Is this the profound insight I think it is, she wondered, pouring herself another sidecar from the pitcher on the bathroom counter, *or is it merely the drunken musings of an over-the-hill exotic dancer who never made it past the ninth grade?*

If only she'd continued her education. Gone on and finished high school. Maybe even enrolled in a junior college. There was no telling how far she might have gone, no telling what she might have become if she hadn't been a single mother who needed to work so hard to support a son. She might have become a somebody. A philosopher. A poet. A scientist. A somebody. Somebody more than a rich over-the-hill mother of a bitter little pansy of a son who'd fucked men in prison and shot his stepfather and loathed his mother, despite what she had given up on his behalf, despite the fact that he owed her his very life.

In the Good Old Days her son had loved her. And if he'd ever seemed a little distant, a little detached, a little disconnected, she would sometimes as a joke put on a funny mask and go into his room and wake him from a deep sleep, and then she would hug him and quiet his pitiful little sobs and rock him in her arms and kiss away his tears and then they would be close again.

She removed her G-string and flung it over her shoulder. The tape ended. She looked at herself in the mirror. She was forty-one years old. Okay, forty-six. She was an over-the-hill exotic dancer of forty-six whose breasts and buns had begun to sag, whose body had begun to decay, but she would never again look as good as she did right now, today.

Andy awoke from a confused, exhausting, and impenetrable dream to the realization that there was something there in the room with him. Something alive. Something less than human.

Terror clutched at his heart and squeezed. The night light was on, but the night light didn't make it better; the night light made it worse. Instead of a black void there were now vague shapes in the dimness, vague shapes that could be imagined into the worst of beings.

He wanted to get up and switch on the overhead light, but he was frozen in place, not daring to move, not daring to reveal to whatever it was that he was conscious, as though a conscious self was a more appealing target to whatever it was that lurked there with him.

Perhaps it was nothing. Perhaps it was his imagination. It was common for him to awake in terror, lie frozen in place, not daring to move till first light, only to discover in the morning that it had been nothing.

Night terrors were quite common in the psychoanalytic literature. Patients who suffered from night terrors often stayed up till daybreak to avoid them, or awoke gasping for breath, lips blue, choking, suffocating, shrieking, shaking with fear, stamping their feet, streaming with sweat, certain there was an ominous presence inhabiting the shadows.

There was a shadowy man now standing in Andy's closet. He was certain of it. He had seen it move, a faint rustling among the hanging clothing. No. It wasn't possible. He was in a twelve-room apartment on Park Avenue, in whose closets shadowy men dared not lurk.

Summoning all his courage, Andy raised himself to a sitting position and tentatively swung his legs over the side of the bed and onto the floor. He was just about to stand up, reach out, and turn on the light when the thing in the closet stepped out into the bedroom and revealed itself.

It towered over him. It was hideous. Cloaked in a dark shroud. A huge bald head. Protruding, bloodshot eyes. Rows of long, sharp, jagged teeth. Rotting cheeks with flesh hanging down in shreds. The very nightmare he had manufactured and fed to Dr. Stevenson in prison!

As it reached out for him he screamed so loud it nearly tore out his vocal cords. He became hysterical, shuddering with fright. The thing changed shape. Took off its head. Dropped the dark shroud. Revealed itself as a woman. A naked woman.

"What are you afraid of?" she cried out drunkenly, trying to enfold him in her arms.

CHAPTER 27

BUSTER KAMINSKY WAS tired. Nineteen years as a parole officer in New York had worn him down and aged him as much as if he'd been an inmate in a maximum security prison. He was only forty-eight, but he looked close to sixty, and although he could still handle himself in a fight with drug dealers and drive-by shooters less than half his age, by the end of every day he was too tired to do anything but slump down in front of the TV and stare at it until he fell asleep. He had 192 cases to ride herd on, and it was grinding him into the ground. In a year he'd retire from the Department of Corrections and then . . . and then he had absolutely no idea of what he was going to do with the remainder of his life.

He sat in his rat's nest of an office, contemplating stacks of papers whose order once had some meaning to him and a pile of unopened mail, which had been there for weeks and which he had not the slightest inclination to open.

His next appointment was with a new guy named Woods, a transfer from some country club in Vermont. The guy was a murderer, and normally New York State wouldn't have taken him, but he was also a model prisoner with a rich mother. Some judge who had the hots for her got the guy paroled to New York. Now the word from the district office director was handle this case with kid gloves. Don't get too closely involved. Which, for Buster, who had 191 other cases to worry about, was just dandy.

The kid came in promptly at 1 P.M., which was always a good sign.

"Just push a pile of papers off any chair and sit down," said Buster.

The Woods kid carefully lifted a stack of forms off a folding chair near the desk and sat down.

"So," said Buster, "how long you been out now?"

"Two days, sir," said the Woods kid. "Since July thirtieth."

Buster was impressed by the "sir." It had been a long time since he'd been called that.

"And how's it going?"

"Okay."

"You got a line on a job yet?"

"Yes, sir," said the Woods kid. "I'm starting a job tomorrow as a clerical at the Bergman Institute in Astoria."

"You're out two days and you've already got a job?" said Buster. "Not too shabby."

"Thank you, sir. Actually, it was arranged for me before I got here."

"And you're living where, with your mom?"

"Yes, sir," said Woods and then he did something funny with his face.

"Sir, I wonder if I can ask you something?"

"Shoot," said Buster, then realized that wasn't the best choice of words.

"I wonder whether it might be possible for me to change residences. To live somewhere else."

"That's a tough one," said Buster. "This is an approved placement. It's kind of hard to change that now."

"I can appreciate that it might be hard," said the Woods kid. "I just wanted to know whether it was possible."

"Not really," said Buster. "Why do you want to move?"

"Well, since I've been back, my mother and I have been having . . . difficulties."

"Everybody has difficulties with their mother, kid," said Buster. "That's life. You just gotta learn to adapt."

"She tells me that if I continue to have difficulties with her, she could have me returned to St. Albans. Is that true?"

"Uh, yeah," said Buster. "I would say that particularly in your case, that that's true, yeah."

"I see."

"You want my advice," said Buster, "find a way to work it out with your mom. Whatever it takes."

"Okay."

"Look," said Buster, getting up, "I got a hundred ninety-one other cases. It sounds to me like you're on the right track, though. Keep up the good work and come back and see me in a month."

"Okay."

CHAPTER 28

I N PRISON ANDY had learned five valuable skills: (1) how to use a computer; (2) how to fashion a pick out of anything sharp and use it to open any known lock within three seconds; (3) how to make a shank out of anything hard and use it to lay open the largest expanse of human flesh in the shortest amount of time; (4) how to hot-wire a car; (5) how to lead a therapy group. Although he was equally proficient in all five, the career opportunities of the fifth appealed to him the most.

Cynthia had pulled a few strings and landed him a clerical job at a full-service psychiatric outpatient clinic in Astoria. The Bergman Institute was in the process of transforming itself into a paperless office. Andy was hired to transfer clinicians' notes from patients' sessions into a computer. The office manager sat down with him in the clerical area and explained how patients' case folders were set up and how to transfer the data.

It was tedious work until he chanced upon the file of a young woman named Virginia Morales. Under "Reason for Referral" he read: "Miss Morales is a nurse's aide who is a dependent personality and complains of fear of heights." He read through Virginia Morales's chart with mounting excitement. She sounded vulnerable and afraid. He certainly knew what it was like to be both vulnerable and afraid. And a dependent personality would be easy to manipulate. Easier than the woman in the bar who professed to be afraid of nothing. Easier than the one on the street whom he'd tried to scare with the fake gun—if she'd been a dependent personality she wouldn't have shouted for help or run away.

He felt that he understood something about Virginia Morales. Without even meeting her, he sensed they had something in common, a mutual vulnerability that originated with an abusive parent—in her case, an alcoholic father. He tried to visualize Virginia Morales being afraid of heights, fantasizing what she'd say in the throes of her fear, what her face would look like, what her body language might be, and so forth.

There was a color snapshot of Virginia Morales in her file. She wasn't gorgeous, but she wasn't all that bad. A bit swarthy for his taste, but not a bad-looking face, and by the slenderness of her neck he guessed her body might not be all that bad either.

She'd been seeing a therapist named Marmur. According to her chart, Marmur didn't seem to be getting anywhere with her. Too bad. Without even meeting her, he probably understood her better than Marmur did.

He copied down Virginia's address and telephone number, then impulsively slipped her photo into his pocket.

That night he took his mother's Lexus and drove back out to Queens, to Virginia's address. He parked across the street from her building, a tall, yellow-brick apartment building about twenty stories high, and waited to catch a glimpse of her.

He tried to visualize her inside her apartment, what she might be doing, how she might be dressed. He imagined her in her bathroom, taking a bath, sensuously sudsing her arms and legs, rubbing a soapy washcloth over her breasts and down her belly into the mysterious crevices between her legs. He imagined her reading in bed, wearing a flimsy nightgown, one hand holding open a copy of a magazine, the other between her legs.

He imagined somebody forcing her to stand on a span of the Queensborough Bridge, the wind whipping at her clothing, her skirt flapping like flags in a windstorm, her heart whamming away in her chest with fright, adrenaline pumping through her veins, terror clutching at her heart.

He waited for two hours, but Virginia Morales never came out of her building. When the two hours were up, he drove back to Manhattan and put the Lexus in the garage.

CHAPTER 29

S HE WAS SHORTER than he thought she'd be. After studying her photograph and scrutinizing her chart and fantasizing about her for so many hours, Virginia Morales had become a sort of mini-celebrity to him, and celebrities are almost invariably shorter in person than in our imaginations.

He had carefully noted the time of her next appointment at the clinic with Marmur and positioned himself just far enough away from the door of Marmur's office to get a good look at her as she entered without risking her seeing him. She was wearing a dark green blouse that buttoned down the front, the top buttons undone, and a dark green skirt. She looked like she was in good shape physically. Probably worked out aerobically.

When Marmur's door opened at the end of her session at six o'clock and Virginia left, Andy was ready. He swiftly turned off his computer, closed the chart he was working on, and murmured goodnight to the other clericals. He put on his jacket and made his way to the front door.

Outside the clinic Virginia put on a pair of sunglasses and took off along Queens Boulevard, walking west. By keeping three-quarters of a block behind her when there weren't many pedestrians around, he was able to follow her fairly unobtrusively.

Two blocks from the clinic was a newsstand. She stopped and bought a *New York Post*. She leafed through it briefly, then folded it up, put it under her arm, and continued walking.

Five blocks from the clinic was a small movie theater. Virginia slowed as she passed the theater and read the marquee: *Diabolique*, the classic French horror film. She studied the show times, glanced at her watch, then went up to the ticket window and bought a ticket.

As soon as she entered the theater, he went up to the ticket window.

"Yes?" said the young Asian woman seated behind the window.
"One for *Diabolique*."

He slid a crisp twenty-dollar bill under the window and received his ticket and his change. He walked inside. She was at the candy counter, buying popcorn. He waited till she entered the theater. A moment later, he followed.

On screen was an animated invitation to buy treats at the candy counter and not to litter or smoke. The small darkened theater wasn't more than a third full. He spotted her immediately, picking her way along a short row of seats, sitting down and settling in. A moment later he found a seat in the row directly behind her.

The feature began. He was familiar with it, having seen it several times before: The somber atmosphere of the little French private school. The frail woman with the weak heart who owned the school. Her despotic, sexist, headmaster husband and his voluptuous mistress. The pact the wife and the mistress make to kill the husband.

He leaned forward in his seat as if to tie his shoe till his nose lightly brushed the hair on the back of Virginia's head, and he inhaled deeply. Her delicate scent filled his lungs—a pleasing fragrance, a mixture of natural skin oils and the faint whiff of cologne she must have dabbed on her throat after her morning shower. Satisfied at having come so close to the object of his recent fantasies, he leaned back to watch with pleasure as the wife and mistress on the screen drowned the headmaster in his bath.

CHAPTER 30

"I S VIRGINIA MORALES there?" he asked when the phone was answered.

"Who's calling please?" said the voice, a woman's.

"Dr. Baker at the Bergman Institute."

"This is Virginia Morales."

It was hours after closing, so Andy had the Bergman Institute entirely to himself. He leaned back in Dr. Marmur's luxurious leather office chair, the one that Marmur sat in when he had his therapy sessions with Virginia. There were photographs in little brass frames on the desk. Pictures of teenage children in tennis clothes, on horseback, on a large sailing vessel. The sunlight in all the photos was so bright it made everybody squint.

"Ah, Miss Morales," said Andy, putting his feet up on the desk. "I've been going over your chart here. There appears to be a problem about your health insurance coverage."

"A problem?" she said. "What kind of problem?"

"Well," he said, "I'd like to discuss it with you in person, if that would be possible. I'd like you to come into the clinic tomorrow morning to discuss it. Could you do that?"

"Tomorrow morning?" she said. "Gosh, I don't know. Tomorrow morning isn't really convenient. Can you tell me what this is about?"

"If tomorrow morning isn't convenient," he said, "then perhaps you could tell me when a better time would be?"

"Can you tell me what this is about?" she repeated.

"I'd prefer to tell you in person," he said. "When would you like to come in and talk about it?"

"Well, not till later on in the week," she said. "But I really don't want to wait that long to find out what this is all about."

"I suppose I could stop by your apartment and explain it to you," he said. "If that would help you any."

"You'd be willing to do that?" she asked.

"Oh, absolutely," he said.

"Well, I'd hate to inconvenience you," she said.

"Not at all, not at all."

"Well, I'd really appreciate that," she said. "When could you come by?"

"Well, let me see," he said. He paused, as if consulting his day planner. "I could actually even do it now, if that would be convenient."

"Now?" she said. "Can't you at least give me some idea of what the problem is?"

"Yes," he said, "I could. But I'd really prefer to explain it to you in person."

"That sounds so ominous," she said.

"It needn't be," he said. "Is now a good time?"

"Uh, no, I'm sorry. Dr. Baker?"

"Yes, Miss Morales?"

"Listen, I . . . I'm sorry, I know that you're really who you say you are and everything, it's just that I wonder if I could . . ."

"You'd like me to give you some proof?" he asked.

"Well, yeah," she said. "If you don't mind."

"Perfectly understandable, Miss Morales," he said. "I'm actually glad you brought it up. May I make a suggestion?"

"Yes?"

"You've got the number here. Call me back. Okay? Will you do that?"

"Okay," she said. "I'm really sorry that I—"

"Please, Miss Morales," he said. "Don't apologize. I'm gratified that some women take their security as seriously as you do. I wish more of them did."

"Thank you, Dr. Baker," she said.

"I'll talk to you in a little while then, Miss Morales."

"Thank you, Dr. Baker." She hung up.

He opened Marmur's desk drawer and sifted idly through the contents. Paper clips, rubber bands, a roll of first-class stamps, a roll of double-sided Scotch tape, a stain eraser stick, a little Ziploc bag of quarters for the parking meter, a pair of scissors, three AA batteries, a letter opener, a bottle of buffered aspirin—nothing remotely interesting.

The drawer below it was locked. He picked the lock and opened it. More boring stuff, but also a Victoria's Secret catalog whose lingerie ads amazed him. He began looking at the photos as the phone rang. He let it ring five times before he picked it up.

"Bergman Institute," said Andy in a heavy Queens accent.

"Oh, uh, Dr. Baker, please."

"One moment please," he said in the same accent, then put her on hold. He punched the lit up line again. "This is Dr. Baker," said Andy in his own voice.

"Oh, hi, Dr. Baker, it's me again. Virginia Morales."

"Yes, Miss Morales."

"I'm sorry I had to do that," she said.

"Not at all, not at all," he replied.

"If you're still willing to come over now," she said, "I'd really appreciate it."

"Good," he said. "I'll see you in a few minutes, then."

"Do you have the address?" she asked.

"Yes," he said, studying a Victoria's Secret model who stared provocatively at the camera and appeared to be seriously considering lowering the waistband of her panties. "It's right here in your chart."

"Okay," she said.

"See you in a few minutes then, Miss Morales."

"Good-bye."

CHAPTER 31

THE AIR INSIDE the lobby of Virginia Morales's building was a welcome change from the steaminess of outside. The lobby featured a bleak concierge desk and two potted trees that made no apologies for their obvious plasticity. A small dark-skinned man of indeterminate origin sat behind the desk.

"Yais?" said the small dark man, smiling a goofy smile.

"Dr. Baker to see Miss Morales," said Andy.

"Okay," said the man, continuing to smile.

"Do you want to ring her up and tell her I'm here?" Andy asked.

"No, thass okay," said the man, nodding and smiling. He pointed to the elevator. "2E," he said.

"Much obliged," said Andy.

He entered the self-service elevator and noted with satisfaction that the numbered floors went up to twenty. He got out at the second floor and easily found apartment 2E.

"Good evening, Miss Morales," he said when she opened the door.

"Come in, Dr. Baker," she said. "Thank you for coming."

"My pleasure," he said.

He entered a narrow hallway. On its walls hung pictures of religious figures with uniformly ecstatic expressions on their faces. How holy did you have to be to get that big a kick out of God?

"Would you like to sit down, Dr. Baker?"

"Oh, thanks," he said.

He sat down on a small sofa facing a large flat-screen TV. Alongside the TV was an exercise bike with a small towel on the handlebars. He wondered how much she sweated when she exercised and where she sweated.

"Well," she said expectantly.

"Well," he said. "Miss Morales . . . May I call you Virginia?"

"Sure."

"Virginia, I'm afraid I have some disappointing news. I'm afraid your insurance eligibility has expired."

"What do you mean?" she said. "I thought I was covered till the end of the year. I mean they said at the clinic I was covered till the end of the year."

Andy shook his head sadly. "Under your particular policy, Virginia, after the deductible you're covered for only twenty visits." He pointed to his clipboard. "And according to our records, you've just had your twentieth visit."

She looked stricken. She tried to peek at his clipboard, but he kept it just beyond her line of vision so she couldn't see what was written there.

"Dr. Baker, what can I do?" she asked, her voice breaking. "I'm not even working full time anymore. I'm on a very limited budget. I simply can't afford to continue treatment if I have to pay."

"I quite understand," he said, sighing. "And I sympathize too, believe me. But there's nothing I can do, because your insurance no longer covers your treatment."

Tears sprang to her eyes. He studied her face a moment, frowning, then said: "You know, I wouldn't want to raise false hopes, Virginia, but something just occurred to me . . ."

"Yes?"

"Well, there *is* an outside chance that you might just possibly qualify for a new experimental program we're putting together."

"Really?" she said. "What sort of program is it?"

"It's a program set up to work with phobics in the field," he said. "I was just thinking that, should you be interested, and should you be able to qualify for entry into the program . . ."

"Yes?"

"Well, in that case we might be able to bend the rules a little and arrange coverage. Assuming, of course, you'd have any interest in that sort of thing."

"Could you tell me a little more about this program?" she asked.

"Certainly, certainly," he said. "I see from your case folder that one of the things you've been working on with Dr. Marmur is acrophobia . . ."

"Yes . . ."

"And that he's had you try some techniques in systematic desensitization."

"Yes . . ."

"The chart indicates that he's had somewhat limited success with these techniques."

"Yes," she said guiltily.

"Well, the experimental program we're doing utilizes a behavioral technique which is far faster, far more dramatic, and far more effective than systematic desensitization. It's called flooding."

"Flooding."

"Yes," he said. "In flooding, the phobic client is thrust into the very real-life situation which she most dreads, but in an extremely safe context. The stimulus that creates the anxiety is found to be harmless, and then the anxiety—and, ultimately, the phobia—disappear."

"Mmm."

"Does this sound at all like something that might appeal to you?"

"Uh, well, I guess so," she said. "If it would be covered by my insurance, I guess it might. I mean, we'd be working on my same problems, but in another way, right?"

"Well, yes."

She smiled expectantly. "I'd be very pleased if you'd consider me for the experimental program in flooding, Dr. Baker."

"Well, fine, fine," he said. "Glad to hear it, Virginia. The only thing to be determined now, of course, is whether you could qualify for the program. A lot will depend on the severity of your symptomology, of course. If we find it's either too severe or not severe enough, you probably wouldn't qualify."

"I see." Losing heart.

"You know," he said, "we could save a lot of time if I were to give you a practical test. In the field, so to speak."

"A test?" she said. "What kind of test?"

"Actually try and gauge the severity of your phobia," he said. "Take you to the top of a building, for example, and try to quantify your reactions. If you'd be willing to do that, and you *did* qualify, we might be able to move you right into the program—get a jump on the others, so to speak."

He looked at her questioningly. She appeared to be weighing this.

"Gosh, I don't know," she said. "It sounds kind of . . . When would this test take place?"

"Well, the sooner the better. I mean"—he permitted himself a short, amused laugh—"we could even do it here in your own apartment building tonight, if that would be convenient."

"Tonight?" She looked alarmed.

"If you have conflicting plans tonight," he said hurriedly, "we could make an appointment for another time, of course."

"Yes, well, maybe that might be better," she said.

He nodded, regarding her seriously. "Keeping in mind, of course," he said, "that the longer we wait, the greater the likelihood that the program would fill up with other candidates."

She seemed to be in momentary turmoil.

"It's not that I have anything better to do tonight," she said. "It's just that . . ."

"Yes?"

"Well, it's just that it's a little, you know . . . scary."

"Of course it's scary, of course," he said. "I understand completely. And I'd quite understand if you'd prefer not to do it."

"But I also don't want to pass up this opportunity," she said. A pause. A sigh. "Look," she said, "we might as well give it a try."

"Splendid, Virginia, splendid," he said. "Tell me, is there access to the roof of this building?"

"I, uh, imagine so. Why?"

"Is it just a matter of taking the elevator up to the top floor and opening a door to the roof?"

"I suppose," she said. "I don't know. I mean"—she gave a sardonic laugh—"I don't exactly spend a lot of time up on the roof of my building. Why do you ask?"

"Well, if we were to take the elevator up there now, and I could record some of your reactions to being thrust into the phobic situation, it might help me determine whether or not you'd respond to the program."

"I see."

"Would you be willing to do that?"

She appeared to be mulling this over. "I guess I'd *better* be willing," she said.

"Excellent, Virginia," he said. "Well then, why don't we do it right now?"

"Now?"

"Get it out of the way immediately. Don't leave any time to contemplate it and build up any anxiety. Just do it right away and be done with it. What do you say?"

She looked a bit unsteady. "Whatever you say, Dr. Baker."

CHAPTER 32

THEY GOT INTO the self-service elevator and he pressed the button marked 20. The elevator jolted into motion. She smiled at him uncertainly.

"Will this take long, do you think?" she asked.

"No, not very long," he said.

They both watched the light on the panel overhead as it skipped from 14 to 15 to 16 to 17 to 18 to 19 to 20. When the button marked 20 lit up, the doors to the elevator opened, but Virginia Morales made no move to get out of the car.

"Virginia," he said gently. "This is the floor we want."

She started to say something, then sighed and got out of the elevator just as the doors began to close. He held them open so she could exit, then followed her.

"I'm really nervous," she said to him as they walked the length of the twentieth floor to the door at the end of the hall.

"Of course you're nervous, Virginia," he said. "Why wouldn't you be? But you know what?"

"What?" she said.

"This is the very last time you're going to be nervous."

She looked at him hopefully. "You mean that?" she said.

"I can almost guarantee it," he said.

They reached the door to the stairwell. He pushed it open and led the way up the last flight of cement stairs to the roof. She followed, her steps as heavy as those of a condemned prisoner on the way to the room where she was to receive a lethal injection.

"Look," she said with a mixture of disappointment and relief, pointing to the sign on the emergency exit door. "We're not even allowed out there."

He smiled. "What are they going to do, Virginia, arrest us?"

"I don't know," she said. "But we really can't go out there."

"Virginia," he said. "The other tenants in this building go out on this roof all the time."

"How do you know that?" she asked.

"Have you ever heard the expression 'tar beach'?"

"I guess so," she admitted.

"What does it refer to?"

"People who go up on the roof to sunbathe, I guess," she said.

"And have you ever heard of any of them getting arrested?"

"I guess not." She sighed in resignation.

He pushed open the heavy door and stepped out onto the roof. She took a deep breath and followed.

The air outside was muggy, but there was a breeze. The roof covered a much larger area than she'd imagined. It was unlit and surrounded by a parapet about four feet high. She could make out the hulks of air-conditioning ducts and huge, ominously whirring fans. "It's really creepy out here," she announced.

"It shouldn't be," he said. "There's nothing up here but machinery to run the building. Nothing here that could possibly harm you."

"I guess you're right," she said.

"Of course I'm right," he said. "And look at that parapet. How high would you say that was?"

"I don't know," she said. "Three or four feet, I suppose."

"Four feet, easily," he said. "Why, you couldn't accidentally fall off this roof if your *life* depended on it."

She tittered at his wording, not knowing why.

"No, Virginia," he said, "I would say that this particular roof is one of the safest places a person with your condition could possibly be."

She looked dubious. He took out his iPhone, selected the recording app, and put it down on the tar paper.

"Now I'd like to demonstrate something," he said. "And we'll just get this on record for your application to the experimental program. Okay?"

"Okay."

He pointed to a foot-high plywood skid that some workmen had left on the roof.

"See that platform?"

"Yes."

"Part one of our qualifying test is to mount that platform, and then give me both your hands."

"What are you going to do?" she asked nervously.

"You'll just have to trust me," he said. "Do you trust me?"

"I suppose so," she said.

"Good girl."

She stepped up onto the foot-high skid and held out both her hands. He took her hands in his and held them very tightly.

"Now then, Virginia," he said, "I would like you to close your eyes and try very hard to get out of my grasp."

She closed her eyes and tried to pull away, but he increased his pressure and she was unable to move.

"That's it," he said. "But you're not trying hard enough. This time really try to pull your hands out of mine. Really try. Give it all you've got. Go ahead."

The harder she pulled, the more tightly he held onto her. Soon she was inclined at a forty-five degree angle away from him.

"Can't you pull any harder than that?" he taunted.

"No!" she said.

"Good girl," he said. "All right, stop pulling. I'm going to let go."

She relaxed. He let go.

"Congratulations," he said. "You did it."

She was incredulous. "I did? I qualified for the experimental program?"

"Oh, no no no." He chuckled patronizingly. "You just passed phase one. There are still a few more to go."

"Oh," she said. "Well, what do I have to do next?"

"Next, come with me," he said.

He led her over to the parapet.

"Phase two is a little harder," he said. "In phase two we're going to actually begin to confront, in vivo, the actual phobic situation."

"I thought that was what we'd been doing," she said.

"That was merely the warm-up," he said. "In phase two, you're going to simply stand up and lean against the parapet, which will come to about chest level. You're going to close your eyes, reach behind you, and give me both of your hands again. Then, when I give you the signal, you're going to open your eyes and, keeping them open, look downward."

"I would never be able to do that," she said simply.

"Virginia," he said, "I know that you can. Now then, take a step forward, so that your chest is leaning against the wall of the parapet."

She took a hesitant step forward and stood with her chest against the parapet.

"Good," he said. "Now close your eyes and give me your hands."

"I'll close my eyes and give you my hands," she said. "But I won't open them and look down."

"Let's just take this one step at a time," he said. "Okay?"

"Okay," she said.

She closed her eyes and gave him her hands. He gripped them as tightly as before.

"Now try to get your hands out of my grip," he said.

She pulled, but his grip held fast.

"You call that trying, Virginia?" he taunted. "Come on now, really try. Really pull hard."

She pulled again, harder, but she was unable to release her hands from his grip.

"Do you realize that I have you?" he said. "That you can't get away from me to fall, even if you wanted to?"

She nodded.

"Good girl," he said. "Now open your eyes."

She opened her eyes, shuddered, and immediately closed them tighter than before.

"Okay," he said. "I'll count that as having completed phase two. I shouldn't, but I will."

"Thank you, Dr. Baker," she said.

"Now for phase three," he said. "In this phase, Virginia, you're going to face me. I'm going to grasp you by the waist and, as you face me, I'm going to raise you to a seated position."

"A seated position on *what*?" she said.

"On the parapet."

"No *way*," she said. "No *way* am I sitting on any parapet."

"Virginia," he said sternly, "do you want to qualify for the experimental group or do you not?"

"I do," she said, beginning to cry. "But not if I have to sit on the parapet."

"Stop crying, Virginia," he said, but she continued to cry.

"If you don't stop crying *immediately*," he said, anger flooding his voice, "you will fail the test and that will be the end of it—no experimental group, no more insurance coverage, no more treatment. Is that what you want, Virginia?"

She shook her head and began crying even harder. Her body was wracked with sobs.

"Shut up!" he shouted.

The suddenness of his outburst stunned her into silence. In one swift motion he grasped her by the waist with both hands, raised her four feet into the air, and deposited her onto the parapet. When she felt her buttocks come in contact with the parapet, she began to cry again and tried to wriggle out of his grasp, but years of prison workouts had made him very strong. He held her in place until she relaxed into a seated position.

He moved first one hand and then the other from her waist to her hands, until he once more had a viselike grip on both of them. Her legs were spread wide enough that he could see right up her skirt. There was enough ambient light on the roof from surrounding buildings for him to make out the white of her pantied crotch.

"Now, listen to me, Virginia," he said. "You have completed phase three. There is only one phase left. I am holding onto your hands so tightly that you cannot get out of my grip, no matter what you do. Do you realize that?"

She continued crying, and her body began to tremble.

"In phase four, our final phase," he said, "you will bring your feet up under your buttocks and raise yourself to a standing position. I will never let go of your hands, so you will never fall. Do you hear me, Virginia? Tell me if you hear me."

She shook her head violently, unable to speak.

"What are you afraid of?" he screamed at her. "If you can't do this, you little creep, you can't do anything! You're a wimp, Ginny, a loser, a hopeless little loser! You've never done anything in your life and you never will, you worthless piece of shit! Stand up, you little slut! Stand up!"

Howling now, sobbing so violently that her body shook, she brought her feet up under her buttocks and slowly, shudderingly, raised herself into a standing position. He had to raise his arms over his head to continue holding onto her hands.

"Now open your eyes!" he screamed at her. "Open your eyes and look down, you miserable little slut!"

The instant she opened her eyes, he let go of her hands. The thrill of it literally took his breath away.

It took her a moment to realize what had happened. She gaped downward in utter horror, hands still outstretched, mouth open, frozen in terror. Then, teetering off balance, windmilling her arms wildly in a futile attempt to regain her balance, she toppled backward and, screaming, stepped off into dead space and disappeared from view.

CHAPTER 33

HE WAS SO excited he couldn't breathe. He wondered if he were having cardiac arrest. He wondered if he had climaxed. Neither proved to be the case. He was vaguely aware that he had just passed a point of no return, that he had in one giddy act nullified years of cognitive therapy in the Violent Offenders Program, as both student and teacher. The years of cognitive therapy hadn't helped. The payoff had been that powerful.

How cleverly he'd slipped into psychodrama to force her to stand up on the parapet, becoming the abusive father he knew she'd had, using dialogue that had probably been used on her time and again. He wondered whether he felt any guilt, whether he felt anything at all, and realized that he didn't. He wondered why. All the insight in the world hadn't been enough to halt his cycle. All the king's horses and all the king's men couldn't put Andy Dumpty together again. He had attained enlightenment, but enlightenment hadn't been enough to stop him from killing again. "In life, enlightenment is the booby prize." Who'd said that?

It took him at least five minutes to get his breathing to return to normal and to compose himself sufficiently to leave the roof, walk down to the twentieth floor, and ride the elevator down to the lobby. He could hear the screams of people who had seen her fall, and then, within minutes, he heard the sound of sirens.

The lobby was empty, the fellow in the lobby having fled to the street. On the street itself, all was chaos. He grabbed a man who was running back in the opposite direction.

"What happened?" he shouted.

"Suicide!" said the man. "A jumper! Body parts all over the place!"

"My God," said Andy. "How horrible."

CHAPTER 34

MAX WAS WONDERING what he could have for dinner. He'd seen lemon sole on sale at the D'Agostino. He'd had a tough day. Maybe he'd treat himself to a piece of that with some rice. The phone on his desk rang.

"Homicide, Segal," said Max picking up the phone.

"Dad, I've got great news!" said Sam.

"Hi, honey," said Max. "What's your great news?"

"Jeremy in school has a LeBron James hologram card which he said he'd sell me for just five dollars—"

"Five dollars?" said Max.

"—plus a Kevin Durant and a Kobe Bryant gold card," said Sam.

"Uh-huh," said Max, knowing what was coming. "And is that a good deal?"

"Are you kidding me?" said Sam. "For a LeBron?"

Six months ago Sam didn't even understand how basketball was played, much less who LeBron was.

"I guess it's a good deal, huh?" said Max.

"So can I have the five dollars for the LeBron?" Sam asked. "Mom said I should ask you."

"Don't you have any money left in your piggy bank?" said Max.

"Uh-uh. I used it to buy the Kevin Durant and the Kobe Bryant gold card."

"Sam, uh . . ."

"Yeah?"

Max studied an ME's form on his desk. It described in great detail the condition of the body of Virginia Morales when it was found.

"I'll give you the money," said Max.

"Oh *thank you*, Dad!" screamed Sam. "You're the best dad a boy could have!"

"And you're the best boy a dad could have," said Max, completing the ritual.

Max hung up, wondering where he was going to get the five dollars for the LeBron James card. Maybe he'd have a peanut butter sandwich for dinner instead of the sole.

CHAPTER 35

PATTY BAILEY LOVED animals. The twenty-year-old zoology major kept and cared for seven cats, three dogs, two dozen tropical fish, and a cockatiel in the apartment she shared with three other girls. Her love of animals extended to every member of the animal kingdom including bats—even insects, which she captured live in the apartment and set free through the open windows.

Everything, that is, except snakes.

The sight of a snake made the hairs on her scalp undulate. So when she discovered, upon taking the job as a summer intern at the Central Park Zoo, that one of her duties would be to share in servicing the python cage, Patty almost quit right there on the spot. Only her profound love of all the other animals, her need for money, and the scarcity of jobs convinced her to take it anyway.

The curly-haired college junior didn't know why snakes gave her such creeps, and it didn't have anything to do with their being phallic symbols either, as her wise-ass psych major roommate Tammy Abraham suggested, because Patty Bailey was rather fond of men's phalluses and didn't find them the slightest bit creepy.

This morning was Patty Bailey's morning to clean out the python cage. Stepping inside the Tropic Zone building was like stepping into a steam room in a gym. The air was heavy, warm, and moist from the steam which sprayed at regular intervals from jets near the forty-foot domed and windowed ceiling. She noted the surprisingly agreeable smell of vaguely rotting tropical vegetation. Thirty species of small, chirping red and yellow and purple birds darted from tree to tree. The walls were covered with moss, orchids, and wrist-thick tropical vines. Waterfalls splashed into pools in the center of the structure where outcroppings of rock and immense forty-foot tree trunks gave the impression of an authentic rainforest.

Clad in a Parks Department khaki military shirt and olive trousers, she carried her long-handled zookeeper's tools: coal shovel, brush, snake hook, and Pillstrom tongs. She marched along a walkway made of narrow-planked yellow pine decking past a shoulder-high tank of piranhas, past a huge glass-encased exhibit in which bats swooped in a cavernous space, past an exhibit of leaf-cutting ants in which penlight-sized television cameras embedded in the exposed ant burrows threw continuous enlarged images of ant activities onto three color video monitors. Ahead of her lay the python exhibit.

Behind a window roughly six feet high and twelve feet wide were a huge dead tree trunk, several hanging vines, half a dozen large boulders, and out of sight somewhere toward the rear of the exhibit, the python itself.

As she approached the window of the python exhibit, she steeled herself as usual for her first sight of the twenty-five-foot reptile coiled up upon itself, asleep with its eyes open. So intent was Patty upon cushioning herself against the sight of the giant snake that when she arrived at the exhibit it took a moment for her brain to register the image being transmitted to it by her eyes: not that of a twenty-five-foot reptile but that of a dead woman—a nearly *naked* dead woman—her face pressed up against the glass, looking sightlessly out at Patty from the floor of the cage.

Patty Bailey dropped her long-handled shovel and brushes, and screaming a truly primal scream that began deep in her belly and resonated up through her body to the top of her head, she ran the entire length of the Tropic Zone building till she collided with the supervisor of animals, Shep Kraft, who had just arrived, carefully balancing a prune Danish, a container of freshly-squeezed organic orange juice, and a hot Starbuck's venti cappuccino.

When the two paramedics from Emergency Services arrived and saw where they'd have to go to retrieve the body, saw the snake coiled lazily back and forth upon itself—black and gold chevrons on a tan background, blunt nose, round orange eyes—they grew pensive. The one named Maury had sad, droopy eyes like a basset hound and chewed bubble gum unceasingly. The one named Vinnie kept sneezing and blowing his nose.

"Summer cold?" asked Kraft sympathetically.

Kraft was a tallish fellow in corduroy jeans, hiking boots, and a tan shirt with epaulettes and coffee stains. He had a close-cropped reddish-blond beard and deep scars on his right cheek and above his right eye. It was better than even money that the scars had been snake-induced.

"I wasn't even gonna come into work today," said Vinnie, studying the snake. "I coulda avoided this one entirely and heard about it after I got well."

A card outside the cage read: HEAT-SEEKING LIPS: WELL ADAPTED TO HUNTING IN DARKNESS, THE PYTHON FINDS WARM-BODIED PREY WITH HEAT-SENSITIVE PITS IN ITS UPPER LIP . . . A SPECIALLY HINGED LOWER JAW ENABLES THE PYTHON TO OPEN ITS MOUTH WIDER THAN THE BODY OF ITS PREY.

"I don't suppose snakes ever attack their keepers," said Maury hopefully, popping a bubble.

"Sure they do," said Kraft, chuckling darkly, enjoying the EMS men's discomfort. "They'll come right out and nail ya."

"That right?" asked Maury, chewing furiously.

"Yeah," said Kraft. "Pythons in particular have a nasty disposition. A large reticulated python like this one is a really nasty individual. When you go to service him, you open the back door to the cage, and if he's pissed at you he'll come out of the cage striking with his mouth wide open. A python bites your hand, he'll lay it wide open with a series of very deep cuts that would take longer to recover from than the bite of a venomous snake."

"I really needed to hear that," said Maury. "Thank you so very much."

"How far can this thing strike?" asked Vinnie.

"Pythons can throw a third of their body length," said Kraft. "So a twenty-five-foot snake could throw a strike about . . ."

"Eight feet," said Maury sadly.

"Eight to ten feet, yeah."

"That particular piece of information I could never have lived without either," said Maury.

"No way am I going in there," said Vinnie.

"Vinnie," said Maury morosely, "we *got* to go in there. It's the job."

"I don't know about you," said Vinnie, "but my job description didn't say nothin' about pythons."

"If it'll help," said Kraft, "I'll crawl in first and keep the snake occupied."

"So if he strikes, he'll hit you first, right?" Vinnie asked.

"That's the general idea," said Kraft dryly.

"Okay," said Vinnie. "What the hell."

Kraft unlocked the door to the exhibit service area. On the floor were a bucket and a hose. Next to these was a neat pile of folded clothing: penny loafers, a blue blazer, jeans, a denim shirt.

What in God's name had possessed the young woman who now lay dead on the floor of the python cage to go in there at all, much less to take off her clothes, Kraft could not possibly imagine. *There are eight million stories in the naked city,* he thought.

Unlocking the back door to the python exhibit, he pulled it slowly toward him.

"Okay," he said to the two paramedics, "as soon as I go in and distract him, you follow."

"We're right behind ya, Sheppy boy," said Vinnie, loudly blowing his nose.

Kraft boosted himself up onto the three-foot-high floor of the snake cage and crawled inside. The snake was fortunately at the far end of the exhibit. Its lidless eyes were open. At the near end of the exhibit, her face pressed up against the glass, was the woman. Her eyes were open, too. Kraft glanced back at the python. It wasn't wise to look away from the python even for a second when you were inside its cage, but he didn't hear the EMS men behind him.

"Are you guys coming in here or aren't you?" asked Kraft through clenched teeth as loudly as he dared.

He heard an intake of breath as one of them boosted himself up onto the exhibit floor. Out of the corner of his eye he could see Vinnie crawl over several slate-gray boulders to the woman's head, take a swift pulse at her carotid, and shake his head. Then Maury crawled into the exhibit and the two men began sliding the woman's body carefully toward the exhibit door.

The heat-sensitive pits in the upper lip of the python sensed three heat-radiating sources on its turf. The half-awake reptile tried to determine which, if any, might be food.

CHAPTER 36

BOOKSTORE EMPLOYEE FOUND DEAD IN PYTHON CAGE

NEW YORK, Aug.14—The scantily clad body of Nancy Blanchard, 28, an employee of the Barnes & Noble bookstore at Fifth Avenue and 48th St., was found this morning in the cage of a 25-foot reticulated python at the Central Park Zoo. The young woman's body was discovered by Patricia Bailey, 20, an undergraduate student at New York University and a summer intern at the zoo. It was not known what Miss Blanchard was doing in the python cage or why she was wearing only underwear. Police at the Central Park Precinct who responded to the death had no opinion on whether the death was accidental or whether foul play might have been involved.

Sgt. Patrick R. Downey of the Central Park Precinct detective squad stated, "We have no information at the present time as to whether the individual was involved in a prank or ritual or some bizarre suicide attempt. Right now we're ruling it a CUPPI (Cause Unknown, Pending Police Investigation)."

Dr. Horace Chernin, Chief Medical Examiner of the City of New York, stated, following Miss Blanchard's autopsy, "Oddly enough, the snake seems to have had no direct contact with the deceased, who apparently suffered from premature atherosclerosis and died of natural causes. As far as I can determine, Ms. Blanchard was literally scared to death."

They were cruising down Queens Boulevard, with Max at the wheel of their unmarked car. It was nearly 1 P.M. and Max was getting hungry.

"What do you say we stop for a bite of lunch?" he suggested.

"Whatever," said Caruso, scanning a folded up copy of the *New York Post*.

Max spotted a hamburger joint on the corner and pulled into a parking place at a meter that still had a little time on it.

"Here?" asked Caruso, outraged.

"Yeah," said Max.

"Are you trying to *kill* me?" asked Caruso.

"What do you mean?" said Max.

"There's nothing I could possibly order in this here restaurant that would not clog up my arteries with deadly plaque and load up my body with lethal levels of sodium," said Caruso. "For me to eat here would be the same as putting a gun in my mouth and pulling the trigger."

"Sal," said Max, "you've been eating three cheeseburgers for lunch for as long as I've known you."

"Well, not anymore," said Caruso. "Those days are behind me, Max."

"So where would you like to eat?" said Max.

"I dunno," said Caruso. "There's a nice little health food place right off Queens Boulevard near Yellowstone. If we went there I could get some tofu, a little brown rice, and maybe some bean sprouts."

"You're serious about this?" Max asked.

"Of course I'm serious," said Caruso. "Why wouldn't I be serious?"

Max pulled out of the parking place and headed downtown.

"Tofu, brown rice, and bean sprouts, huh?" said Max.

"Yeah," said Caruso, continuing to scan the news.

"What are you going to wash it down with?" asked Max. "A Bud?"

"No, no," said Caruso. "Maybe some carrot juice or wheat grass juice, something like that. Max, are you still a red meat eater?"

"Sure. Why?"

Caruso laughed a short, bitter laugh.

"You're killing yourself," said Caruso. "You're digging your own grave with a knife and fork. You know that, don't you?"

"Excuse me?" said Max.

"Eating red meat increases your risk of developing heart disease and diabetes, as well as lung, stomach, and pancreatic cancers."

"Who the hell told you that?" said Max.

"A new and trusted adviser."

"Who told you that?"

"Who told me that?" said Caruso. "My yoga instructor, that's who."

"I've created a fucking monster," said Max.

"When you develop pancreatic cancer," said Caruso, "don't say I didn't warn you."

"Okay, I won't," said Max.

"Hey, listen to this," said Caruso, pointing to a story in the paper. "A nearly naked chick was found dead in the python cage of the Central Park Zoo."

"That right?" said Max. "What the hell was she doing in the python cage?"

"They don't know," said Caruso.

"The snake crush her to death?"

"Nope," said Caruso. "The snake never touched her."

"Then how'd she die?" Max asked.

"Our old friend Chernin did the autopsy," said Caruso. "He said it was natural causes. She had athero . . . she had premature hardening of the arteries. Chernin said she was scared to death."

"Why the hell would somebody go into a python cage?" Max asked.

"Beats the shit out of me," said Caruso.

"Unless it was a college prank," said Max. "How old was she, does it say?"

"Twenty," said Caruso.

"Probably a college prank," said Max.

"No, wait," said Caruso, rereading the story. "The chick who *found* her was twenty. The deceased herself was twenty-*eight*."

"That's a little old for college pranks," said Max.

"They said maybe it was suicide," said Caruso.

"Oh, right," said Max. "If you wanted to commit suicide, would you climb into a python cage?"

"No," said Caruso. "I'd eat three cheeseburgers every day."

"Yeah," said Max. "Me, I'd jump off a roof."

Max frowned and pulled out his cell phone, then punched out a number with one hand while he drove with the other. It took a while, but finally Chernin got on the line.

"Hi, Doc, it's Max Segal."

"Max, how are you?" said Chernin. "How are things in Queens?"

"We're a little slow," said Max. "I'm actually starting to miss Manhattan North, but at least half the homicides here are real ones. Listen, Doc, I read in the paper about the woman in the python cage. What's the story?"

"CUPPI," said Chernin. "Why do you ask?"

"Did you interview next of kin following the post?"

"Yeah," said Chernin. "Both parents came in. They were pretty shaken up, as you can imagine."

"Did they know she had premature atherosclerosis?"

"It didn't seem to surprise them," said Chernin.

"Doc, you happen to know the detective who caught the case?"

"A chick named McCleary in the Central Park Precinct," said Chernin. "Why do you ask?"

"A chick?" said Max.

"Yeah," said Chernin. "Hey, that's right, Max, you're a free man now, aren't you?"

CHAPTER 37

THERE WAS A homeless man sitting on the pavement as Max came around the corner on Natale's block.

"Good evening, sir," said the homeless man, getting to his feet as Max passed him.

"How ya doin'," said Max, maintaining his pace.

The man had a week's growth of beard, good strong bones in his face, shaggy gray hair, and bushy black eyebrows. He wore a tweed sport coat with a huge rip in the material and a long silk scarf, one end thrown rakishly over his shoulder.

"I wonder if you'd care to invest fifty thousand dollars in a brewery I'm starting," said the homeless man, keeping pace with Max.

"Sorry," said Max, smiling at the pitch in spite of himself.

"Then how about thirty-four dollars so I can buy myself a salmon au poivre and a glass of chardonnay?"

"Sorry," said Max, walking a little faster. He had a sudden dread that the gulf between the homeless man and himself had narrowed to a creek and that prolonged exposure to him might accelerate that rate to the merest trickle.

"How about just six bucks for a Campari and soda with a twist of lime?"

"I'm really sorry," said Max, speeding up to almost a run. "You're asking the wrong guy for money."

"Is that right?" said the homeless man bitterly, now running even with Max, a little short of breath but matching him stride for stride. "Look at you—a nice suit and tie, probably have a co-op on the East Side with a wife and kid, maybe a weekend cottage in the Hamptons. Now look at *me*. I have nothing. I *am* nothing. God, how I envy you!"

"You picked the wrong guy to envy," said Max, shifting into a dead run. "I'm getting divorced, I'm losing my kid, my wife is having an affair with a friend of mine, my wife's attorney is destroying me in court but I have to pay her salary, I'm in debt up to my ears, and I can't even borrow any more money from the bank or the credit card companies or any of my friends!"

The homeless man ran even with him for several paces, then grabbed Max's hand and thrust something into it.

"Here," he said.

"Here what?" Max asked, but the homeless man was gone, loping back to his corner.

Max opened his hand. The man had put a quarter into it.

CHAPTER 38

LUCKY THIS BLANCHARD case came along," said the young female precinct detective, showing Max to a seat in the Central Park Precinct squad room. "We were in such a homicide slump here I was cruising wakes just to look at dead bodies."

Max permitted himself a chuckle. P. J. McCleary was short, skinny, and red-haired. She had freckles and a pug nose and looked about fourteen years old. She was far from being a knockout, but she was cute in a boyish kind of way if you liked that look, although Max was just coming out of a marriage with an Irish Catholic and wasn't eager to get involved with another one.

"You like looking at dead bodies?" Max asked.

"Sure, don't you?" said P. J.

"Not that much," said Max.

"Whenever I go to wakes," said P. J., "I swipe those little plastic cards you get with the name of the person whose wake it is on the back."

"Uh huh . . ."

"You wanna get into somebody's apartment but you don't wanna ring the bell and make a commotion in the lobby, you just wanna slip the lock on the lobby door and get up the stairs, you don't wanna ruin a good credit card, but wake cards from the funeral home work great. I find the Sacred Heart of Jesus ones do the best job on the door—they're good for the ones that lock when they close behind you. I'll go to a wake and I'll take as many as I can get away with. I guess that's the extent of my religious affiliation, swiping Sacred Heart of Jesus wake cards. You want a couple?"

"Thanks," said Max. "So the ME tells me Blanchard's parents knew she had premature atherosclerosis."

"True. Quite true," said P. J.

"Tell me something," said Max.

"Yeah?"

"Even if you didn't have a heart condition, is there any way you'd go into a python cage *voluntarily*?"

"Not unless I had the hots for snakes," she said. "You're thinking she was forced?"

"That's just my hunch," said Max.

"Sounds okay to *me*," she said.

"Would you be upset to have this case turn into a homicide?"

"Why would I give a shit if it turned into a homicide?" she asked.

"I don't know," said Max. "Some precinct detectives are more worried about their clearance rates than about doing their job."

"Some precinct detectives don't *love* their job," said P. J.

"You do?"

She nodded. "Nothing I'd rather be doing," she said.

"Really?"

"Nope," said P. J. "Except maybe what *you're* doing."

"Yeah?" he said. "You want to end up in Homicide, huh?"

"It's every girl's dream," she said. "Isn't it?"

"Your father a cop or what?" said Max.

She shook her head.

"Older brother? Grandfather? Uncle? Cousin?"

She shook her head to all of these. "I'm the only cop in the family," she said.

"So where'd this burning desire to serve come from?"

"It's the only thing I ever wanted to do," she said. "I remember as a kid running after the radio cars. I always thought being a cop must be the most fun thing in the world. That doesn't go over well with the nuns in Catholic school, you know, who want you to grow up to be a nurse or a mommy."

"So when did you decide it was fun?" Max asked.

"I think what it probably was was when I was real little my pop used to take me with him to the bars," she said. "I'd sit in the booth with my Rheingold tray and my pretzels and my ginger ale, and sometimes he'd kinda forget I was in the booth and go home. So I'd trek myself over to the local precinct and they'd take me home."

"How old were you at this point?" Max asked.

"Six or seven," she said.

"Six or seven, and he just forgot you were there?"

"Occasionally, yeah." She laughed.

"This is a forgetful guy or a drunk guy or a . . . ?"

"Yeah, yeah," she said, a sad smile on her face. "A well-meaning forgetful drunk guy. But I didn't mind. I'd go to the precinct and they'd make a fuss over me. Then they'd sit me in the radio car in the front seat and then they'd take me home. I thought they were so cool. That's probably where it started with the cops. What about you?"

"Oh, my folks wanted me to be a lawyer, but . . . I don't know," said Max. "I was in pre-law at CCNY and the prospect of being a lawyer was just so . . . passive. I guess I thought I could do more for humanity on the street than in a courtroom or something. Anyway," he said, suddenly self-conscious, "what have you got on the Blanchard case that I don't know?"

"How about this?" she said. "Nancy Blanchard had an ex-boyfriend named Eddie Battaglia who was a practical joker and a real pain in the ass."

"And?"

"And once he got drunk and beat the crap out of her. Nancy went to court and got an order of protection to keep him away."

"Very nice," said Max. "Do you have an address for this character?"

"He's a bouncer at a club in the East Village," she said. "Would you like to come with me when I pay him a visit?"

"Would I ever."

———

The Sewer was a club in the Village that appealed to people whose idea of a good time was to be insulted by members of the band and then get into fistfights. A lot of kids went there, mostly bridge-and-tunnel people.

When Max and P. J. arrived, there was already a long line waiting to gain entrance. Two very large young men guarded the velvet ropes that surrounded the door and decided who got to go into The Sewer and who did not.

Eddie Battaglia was one of these. He stood about six-six and weighed in the neighborhood of three hundred pounds. He had a trimmed goatee and wore several gold chains around his neck. Although the night was not particularly warm, his shirt was unbuttoned all the way down to reveal a chest so hairy it looked like a mohair sweater.

P. J. moved the velvet rope aside and strode right up to the guy.

"You Eddie Battaglia?" she said.

"That's right, honey," he said, shoving her rudely away from him. "Now get the fuck out of my face."

P. J. drove her fist into his belly so hard that someone standing behind him would have seen the shape of it in his back. Battaglia doubled over in pain, but sprang back at her reflexively, only to receive two nearly simultaneous blows to his Adam's apple and his groin. Battaglia crumpled to the pavement.

"Police, Eddie," said P. J. "Touch me again and I'll eat you for breakfast."

"What am I doing here?" asked Eddie Battaglia. The handcuffs hurt his wrists and the bright lighting in the small interrogation room hurt his eyes.

"What you're doing here," said P. J. McCleary, "is talking to me about Nancy Blanchard, you miserable piece of cow shit."

"Who's Nancy Blanchard?" asked Eddie Battaglia.

"What did you say, bunghole?" said P. J.

"I want to see my lawyer," said Eddie Battaglia.

"Yeah, well he doesn't want to see *you*, sweater-chest," said P. J.

Eddie looked at Max for commiseration. Max shrugged.

"You're violating my rights," said Eddie Battaglia plaintively.

"Detective Segal, am I violating this douchebag's rights?"

"I don't know," said Max truthfully.

"You came here voluntarily, Eddie," said P. J. "I did not arrest you. I did not show you my weapon. Is that true, Detective Segal, that I did not arrest this man nor did I show him my weapon?"

"That's true," said Max.

"What is this?" said Eddie Battaglia to Max. "You're the good cop and she's the bad one? Is that how it works?"

"No," said Max. "I think that whatever you're seeing here is pretty much the way she is."

"How big are you, rectum-mouth?" asked P. J. "About six-six? About three hundred pounds?"

"So?" said Eddie Battaglia.

"So I'm five-three and weigh a hundred and five," said P. J. "I want to hear you tell the court I brought you here by force."

"What do you want from me?" asked Eddie Battaglia with a gigantic sigh.

"Talk to me about Nancy Blanchard, sewer-breath."

"Nancy Blanchard was a chick I went out with for a while," he said. "Then we broke up. That's about it."

"And you beat her up, shit-for-brains," she added.

"I might have roughed her up a little," said Eddie Battaglia.

"And she got an order of protection to keep you away from her," said P. J.

"If you know so much, what the fuck are you asking me?" asked Eddie Battaglia and instantly regretted it, because P. J. sprang across the table at him and grabbed him by the throat.

"If you ever use the word 'fucking' in my presence again," she said matter-of-factly, "I will fucking make you eat all your teeth."

"But *you* use it," he whined.

"And if you ever get to be *me* you can use it too," she said. "But otherwise not. Why did you rough up Nancy Blanchard?"

"I forget."

"I'll help you remember," she said. "I'll come down to The Sewer every night like I did tonight and show everybody what a panty shield you are."

Eddie Battaglia sighed again. "I roughed her up," he said, "because she couldn't take a joke."

"You want to amplify that a little?" she asked.

Another huge sigh. "I bought this rubber snake at a novelty shop and put it in her bed, okay?" he said. "It was a *joke*. How was I supposed to know she had a thing about snakes? She got hysterical and I had to shut her up, and that's all."

"She had a thing about snakes?" Max asked. He looked at P. J.

"Yeah," said Eddie Battaglia. "Some big phobia or something. How the fu— How the heck was I supposed to know about that?"

"Yesterday morning," said P. J., "Nancy Blanchard was found dead in the python cage of the Central Park Zoo."

"I read about that," said Eddie Battaglia. "What a loss, huh? Hey, you don't think *I* had something to do with that?"

Max and P. J. just looked at him. It didn't seem likely that Eddie Battaglia had killed Nancy Blanchard, but Max had a gut feeling that whoever forced Nancy Blanchard, who was terrified of snakes, into the python cage at the Central Park Zoo probably also forced Virginia Morales, who was terrified of heights, off the roof of her apartment building, and Marian Masters, who was terrified of water, into Astoria Pool. Somebody who took a great deal of pleasure in scaring his or her victims to death. The term generally used for people who took pleasure in their victims' suffering was psychopath.

CHAPTER 39

DEPENDENT PERSONALITIES WITH phobias were extremely promising. Virginia Morales had been his first. He began to sift the charts to locate others.

Sadly, the others he found weren't nearly as interesting. The most widespread phobia in the charts appeared to be public speaking. He found two cases of agoraphobia and one of claustrophobia, but the phobics involved were either men or elderly women, and his subjects needed to be female and young enough to be sexually interesting to him.

In an inactive file he located the chart of a former patient named Marian Masters, a thirty-four-year-old single librarian. Marian the Librarian, he thought. Probably everyone who called her that believed he was the first.

Marian's phobia was water. Not quite as easy a phobic environment to set up as Virginia's, but he welcomed the challenge. Marian had left therapy at the clinic when her health insurance coverage ran out and joined a support group called Phobics Anonymous that met on alternate Wednesday nights at a church in Forest Hills. First, he had to meet her.

He entered the Astoria branch of the Queens Public Library and took a casual look around. It didn't take him long to locate Marian Masters. He recognized her from the picture in her chart. She was standing behind a long counter, checking in a tall pile of books and computing fines for those that were overdue. She had straight brown hair and rimless glasses, plain but not at all unattractive. Better looking than her picture.

He walked up and cleared his throat.

"Excuse me," he said.

She looked up and raised her eyebrows.

"I'm not familiar with this library, and I need to look up two books and an article," he said. "If I give you the titles, could you direct me to the proper areas?"

"I'll do my best," she said.

"The first book is *Abnormal Psychology and Modern Life*, by Coleman, Butcher, and Carson. The second is *Behavior Modification: Behavioral Approaches to Human Problems*, by Redd, Porterfield, and Andersen. The article is 'Flooding in Imagination vs. Flooding in Vivo, a Comparison with Agoraphobics,' by Emmelkamp and Wessels. It's in a professional journal called *Behavior Research and Therapy*, volume thirteen, number one."

She frowned. "*Behavior Therapy and . . .* what was that again?"

"*Behavior Research and Therapy*," he said.

"*Behavior Research and Therapy*," she said. "I'm almost positive we don't carry that one, but you could check with them over there at the Periodicals desk. The books would, of course, be listed under the authors' names in the psychology section, third aisle on the right." She pointed.

"Ah. Thank you," he said.

"If you don't mind my asking," she said, "what on earth is flooding?"

"It's a technique in behavior modification therapy," he said.

"Oh?"

"Yes. I'm doing my doctoral dissertation on flooding as a means of dealing with phobias."

"Is that right?" she said, intrigued. "How does it work?"

"You really want to know?"

"I wouldn't ask you if I didn't," she said.

"Well," he said, "it involves putting a phobic person in a real life anxiety-arousing situation, but making it a safe place for him. With continued and repeated exposure in the safe setting, the stimulus responsible for the phobia loses its power to elicit anxiety, and the neurotic avoidance behavior is extinguished."

"You don't say," she said.

"Yes," he said. "I do."

"And where did you say you were you doing your dissertation?"

"I didn't say," he said.

She looked at him, cocked her head, and smiled.

"Where are you doing your dissertation?" she asked.

"NYU."

"How about that."

"Yes," he said. "Phobias are much more widespread than you might imagine. I, for example, am afraid of the dark, would you believe that?"

"Are you serious?" she asked.

"Absolutely. I often have night terrors so bad I have to sleep with a night light in the room. Whew," he said shaking his head in wonderment. "I didn't intend to just blurt *that* out. I hope you don't think I'm a dork."

"Not at all," she said, taking a long serious look at him. She clearly wanted to say more, but didn't.

He felt he'd accomplished enough for the first contact.

"Well, thanks for the information," he said.

"Anytime," she said.

"Anytime?" he repeated.

She nodded and blushed.

That night in bed he had fantasies about Marian Masters. About taking her to dinner. About flirting with her the way he'd done with Dr. Stevenson in the joint. About finding out more about her fear of water. About seeing if he could maneuver her into actually going to a swimming pool and exposing her to her fear.

He wondered what she'd say if she knew he had chosen to meet her because she was phobic. He wondered what swimming pool he might be able to take her to. He decided to do a little research on swimming pools before he saw her next.

CHAPTER 40

ALTHOUGH LOGGING IN a pile of recently returned books, Marian had paused to add a few items to her after-work shopping list—toilet tissue, depilatory, tall kitchen garbage bags.

"Well, hello again," said a man's voice.

She looked up and blushed.

"Hello yourself," she said. "Hey, didn't you say you were in the doctoral program at NYU?" She quickly folded up the list and stuffed it into a pocket.

"I did," he said.

"Then what are you doing way the hell out here in Queens?"

"Well, I found there was something in this library that they just didn't have in the psych library at NYU."

"Oh yeah?" she said. "What was that?"

"*You.*"

"Oh, right," she said, her cheeks turning bright red.

"What—you don't think you're worth coming all the way to Queens to see?" he asked.

"Right," she said. "What did you *really* come back here for?"

"To ask you if you'd like to have dinner with me."

"Get out of here."

"You don't want to have dinner with me?" he said. "I'm shattered. Absolutely shattered."

"You didn't come here to ask me to dinner."

"I didn't?" he said. "That's odd. I could have sworn I did."

"You mean you're serious?"

"Absolutely serious," he said.

"When did you have in mind?"

"How about tonight?"

"Tonight?"

"Yes," he said. "I realize that's awfully short notice, but I figured I'd take a shot. If you're busy, that's all right. I'll just kill myself."

"I don't even know your name," she said.

"Ted," he said. "Ted Pearlman."

"Would you like to know mine?"

"More than anything," he said.

"It's Marian," she said. "Marian Masters."

"Glad to meet you, Marian Masters," he said, reaching out and taking her hand. It was unexpectedly warm.

"If you're really serious about having dinner with me tonight," she said. "You're on."

"Hey, great. Now I don't have to kill myself," he said. "I'll pick you up at eight."

He started toward the door.

"Hey, Ted!" she called.

He turned around.

"You don't even know where I live." She laughed.

CHAPTER 41

MARIAN COULDN'T DECIDE what to wear. Couldn't believe that a man as handsome, charming, and young as Ted Pearlman was interested in her. Why wasn't someone that good-looking married or engaged? Did he have intimacy issues? She didn't care.

Should she go dressy or casual? How about the green paisley dress with the bow at the neck? No, too dressy and too much the librarian. Besides, it was so muggy out. Maybe something cooler. And racier. The scoop-neck silk sweater and the black Lycra leggings? No. Not on their first date.

Their First Date. Would there be a second one? You never knew. If he was interested enough to ask her out once, maybe she had a chance. What on earth he saw in her she couldn't possibly imagine. But the black silk tunic and the short black skirt would be a good compromise.

The restaurant he chose may not have been memorable, but at least it was dark, quiet, and more or less romantic. Red glasses on the tables with lit candles inside and plastic netting on the outside were the major source of illumination. He'd gotten a booth in the back, and immediately begun ordering sidecars. To her surprise, he seemed a little awkward with the process of getting a table and ordering. Was it possible someone that good-looking was inexperienced at dating?

She talked about her work at the library, her problems with the head librarian, her aspirations to be a novelist. He talked about his work at NYU, his problems with his graduate adviser, his aspirations to teach psych at a small college in Northern California.

At first she acted a bit stiff and proper, but after the third round of sidecars she loosened up considerably and her speech began to slur.

"You know," he said, "I have to tell you something."

"What?" she said.

"I really enjoy talking to you."

"Well, thank you," she said.

"I mean it," he said. "You're really very nice. Very warm and smart and sensitive."

"Well, so are you," she said.

"Well, thank *you*," he said.

He glanced at the point where her brown hair softly curled over her ear and had a sudden urge to lean forward and tenderly kiss it. He wondered at this inclination. Knowing the fate that he had planned for her, he was able to separate out a strain of tenderness from the hopeless mix of other feelings.

"What are these things you've been ordering us, by the way?" she asked.

"Sidecars."

"*Side*cars?"

"Yes."

"What the hell's a sidecar?" she asked.

"Brandy, Cointreau, and lemon juice."

"Whew! No wonder."

"No wonder what?"

"No wonder I feel so . . . Brandy, lemon juice, and *what* did you say?"

"Cointreau. It's a French liqueur. No wonder you feel so . . . ?"

"Woozy," she said. "Is that a word?"

"I think so," he said. "But you're the librarian. Do you like feeling woozy?"

"Mmm."

"Good," he said. "Tell me, Marian, *where* do you feel woozy?"

"*Where* do I feel woozy?"

"Yes, where?"

"I don't know," she said. "In my . . . everywhere."

"Can you be any more precise than that?"

"Everywhere," she said. "In my mouth . . . in my lips . . . in my fingertips . . . in my . . . my . . ."

"Vagina?"

"Hey now . . ." she said.

"Are you feeling woozy in there, Marian?"

She snorted disapprovingly, a cackle got caught in her nose, and she erupted in embarrassed inebriated laughter.

"You are, aren't you?"

She continued to laugh embarrassedly.

"I thought so," he said. "Is it the word that embarrasses you, Marian, or the body part?"

She was blushing too furiously to respond.

"I'll bet it's both," he said. No response. "It's both, Marian, isn't it?" He shook his head. "Tsk tsk. Poor uptight Marian. Poor uptight Marian the Librarian."

"Don't call me that," she said.

"Why not?"

"Just don't call me that."

"But that's who you are, isn't it?" he said. "Marian the Librarian, who's embarrassed to even hear the word vagina?"

He was relishing her discomfort, the more so because it was clearly turning her on.

"What are you afraid of, Marian?" he asked quietly.

"What do you mean?"

"I mean what frightens you?" he said. "What terrifies you? What gives you the willies? The shivers? The shakes? The shudders? The heebie-jeebies?"

She continued to hold his gaze a moment, then exhaled a single word in a whisper: "Water."

He nodded approvingly. "Water. Good, Marian. Very nice."

He took her hand and held it compassionately.

"Have you ever learned to swim?" he asked.

"Never," she replied.

"But I thought learning to swim was a prerequisite for graduating high school."

She nodded, took a deep breath, slowly let it out. In a monotone: "My parents got our family doctor to write a letter excusing me from swimming lessons. I took it to the phys ed teacher, who took it to the principal, but the principal refused to honor it. He forced me to take swimming lessons after school. During the first one I passed out. During the second one I threw up in the pool—all this vomit, floating in the water, and the phys ed teacher had to scoop it out." She permitted herself a wry chuckle at the memory. "He was very upset with me, as you can imagine. My grades were exceptionally high, and the principal decided to make an exception in my case."

He nodded, studying her with great intensity.

"Tell me, Marian," he said. "Do you enjoy being terrified of water?"

"Do I *enjoy* being terrified of water?" she repeated. "Don't be an ass."

"Then would you be willing to give up your fear of it?"

"Would I be *willing*?" she asked.

"Yes, would you be willing?"

"What do you mean would I be willing? Of course I'd be *willing*."

"That is all I ask, Marian," he said.

"What do you want to do, give me swimming lessons?"

"No, Marian," he said. "I only want to take away your fear of water."

"Is that so?" she said. "And how do you propose to do that?"

"Do you recall my explaining the technique of flooding to you in the library?"

"Sort of," she said. "Tell me again."

"Okay. It's a technique in behavior modification therapy," he said.

"Uh-huh."

"And I'm doing my doctoral dissertation on flooding as a means of dealing with phobias."

"Uh-huh."

"It involves putting a phobic person into a real life anxiety-arousing situation, but first making it a safe place for them. With continued exposure in the safe setting, the stimulus that was causing the phobic behavior loses its power to produce anxiety, and the neurotic avoidance behavior disappears."

She had been unaccountably excited by his sexual provocations and was relieved now that he had switched to a more professorial role. Relieved and, frankly, somewhat disappointed.

"You say they use this to treat phobias?" she asked.

"That's right."

"Have they ever used it to treat a fear of water?"

He nodded. "There's a famous case in which a therapist named Stampfl described a young woman who couldn't swim and who was terrified of water."

"Oh?"

"Absolutely terrified," he said. "So terrified she used to take baths wearing a life preserver."

A giggle. "Like Wade the Duck on the *Garfield* cartoons," she said.

"Like that, yes. Stampfl told her to imagine, in excruciating detail, taking a bath without wearing the life preserver. In a tub that had no bottom to it. In water of infinite depth. He told her to imagine that she was slowly slipping under the surface of the water."

He studied her face. Her cheeks had paled. Her eyes had assumed a faraway look.

"Still with me, Marian?"

She nodded.

"Good girl. At first the patient displayed intense anxiety while imagining this scene. Stampfl told her to keep repeating the fantasy over and over again. Then he told her to imagine herself drowning—what it felt like, what the precise sensations were as her lungs filled with water and she suffocated."

"Oh my God."

"Yes," he said. "After a while, after imagining all of these frightening things and finding that nothing bad had happened to her, her anxiety eventually diminished. By the end of her fourteenth therapy session, she was able to take baths without her life preserver and without even feeling frightened. Her maladaptive behavior had been completely extinguished."

"And that's what they call flooding?" she asked.

"No no, that's what they call systematic desensitization," he said. "Flooding, or, more properly, flooding in vivo, would involve taking the patient into the actual, real life situation rather than merely fantasizing it. Exposing her to the feared stimulus and demonstrating that the dreaded consequences wouldn't follow. Flooding is a *far* more dramatic, far more powerful and effective means of behavior modification therapy than systematic desensitization. *Far* more."

"Uh-huh."

"You don't sound convinced," he said.

"Uh-uh."

"What if I could prove it to you?"

"How?"

"Come with me and I'll show you."

CHAPTER 42

ASTORIA PARK, BY the time they drove up, was dark and completely deserted. The monstrously large outdoor pool had closed at 7 P.M.

Towering above them four blocks to the left was the Triborough Bridge, frightening in its height, festooned with lights and supporting a steady stream of cars. Five blocks to the right was the Hell Gate Bridge, unlit and slightly sinister in silhouette against the night sky, deserted but for the freight trains that thundered by at irregular intervals.

"My God," said Marian, "Astoria Pool."

"Yes," said Andy. "Quite beautiful, isn't it?"

"You know, I've lived in Queens for twelve years and I've never even been here once."

"Well then," he said, "you should be very grateful to me."

He drove up over the low curb onto the short winding road that led to the pool and stopped the car. Checking to make sure his iPhone was in his jacket pocket, he got out of the car, came around to the passenger side, and opened the door.

"Want to take a closer look?" he asked.

"Do I have a choice?" she replied.

"No," he said, smiling.

He grasped her right hand and helped her out of the car, noting the coldness of her palm, not releasing it for several beats longer than the situation warranted. It was a warm, muggy night. As they picked their way down the incline to the edge of the pool, a tropical wind ruffled their hair. He was able to unlock the iron gate that led to the pool in three seconds flat.

The pool, up close, was overpowering in size.

A freight train rumbled and rattled across the Hell Gate Bridge and disappeared into the distance.

"This is such a momentous occasion," he said, "I'm going to record it for posterity." He hit the recording app on his iPhone. "So, Marian Masters, here we are poolside. How do you feel?"

"How do I feel?" she said. "How do you *think* I feel?"

"Apprehensive," he said.

"Yes."

"Scared shitless," he said.

A surprised giggle. "Yes."

"What else?"

"I don't know," she said. "Dizzy maybe?"

"Good," he said. "Take off your skirt."

"You've *got* to be kidding."

"No, I'm completely serious."

"Why should I?"

"So you won't get it wet," he said.

"But I don't plan on doing anything that might get it wet."

"Well, you might want to eventually."

"What might I want to do eventually?"

"I don't know," he said. "Any of a number of things. Learn to do a passable breast stroke, for example."

"Very funny."

"I'm quite serious."

"Yes, I suppose you are."

"Take off your skirt, Marian."

"Somebody could come along."

"That's possible," he said, "although highly unlikely. The pool closed at seven P.M. Nobody comes here after dark."

She considered this briefly, then snorted, shook her head, sighed, and unzipped. She dropped her skirt to the ground and stepped out of it.

He felt himself beginning to get aroused. Less from the prospect of a young woman about to disrobe than from the prospect of a young woman about to die. From his having taken control of her life and death like a superior being. Like God himself.

"And now your shirt."

She looked at him and smirked. "Is this about overcoming my fear of water, Professor, or about getting me out of my clothes?"

"Both."

She laughed, swept the tunic over her head, got it momentarily caught on her chin, then pulled it off and dropped it atop her skirt. She wore a fairly demure white bra.

He felt the heat on his upper back, the sweat above and below his eyes, the rush of warmth to his groin.

"So now you've got me down to my underwear," she said.

"Yes."

"What would you like me to do next?"

"Step to the edge of the pool."

"And then what?" she asked.

"And then just . . . dip the toes of one foot lightly into the water."

She regarded him thoughtfully for a full minute, then shook her head.

"No way," she said.

"You're afraid," he said.

"Of *course* I'm afraid," she said. "What the hell do you think?"

"What are you afraid of?" he said.

She took a deep breath.

"Falling in," she said. "Drowning. Gasping for breath. Having my lungs fill with water till they burst. Sinking like a stone to the bottom of the pool. Being dead. Having my flesh rot. That kind of thing."

He nodded. "And what's the feeling? Describe it if you can."

She closed her eyes. "Difficulty in breathing . . ."

"Yes . . ."

"Heart beating so fast and so loud I can hear it my ears . . ."

"Yes . . ."

His own breathing was labored, his own heart beating fast and loud, in sync with hers. It formed a secret bond between them. It occurred to him that he might actually love her.

"Would you feel less afraid if I stepped to the edge of the pool with you, and you held onto me while you did it?"

"Truthfully?"

"Yes."

"No."

"Why not?" he said. "Do you think I'd let go of you? Do you think I'd let you drown?"

"I don't know," she said. "Maybe. Maybe not. Probably not."

"Then what are you afraid of?"

"I already told you."

"Marian," he said. "If I held you, you wouldn't fall in the water."

"No . . ."

"And even if you did, I'd jump right in and pull you out."

"I liked it better before the 'and-even-if-you-did' part."

"I'm sorry," he said. "If I held you, you wouldn't fall in the water."

She considered this. "I can't believe it," she said.

"What?"

"You're really going to make me do this, aren't you?"

"Only if you want to," he said.

"Only if *I* want to."

"Yes."

A massive sigh. "Okay," she said. "Let's get it over with."

"Yes?"

"Yes."

He was overcome with feeling. He wanted to hug her. "Good girl," he said.

"And don't keep saying 'good girl.' I'm not a puppy learning tricks."

"Sorry. Okay, put your toes in the water."

"My toes?"

"The toes of your right foot. Hold onto me, lower your right leg to the level of the water, then just dip the toes of your right foot about an inch into it."

She stared into his eyes a full five seconds, then fastened both hands tightly onto his extended arm. She took a deep breath and slowly lowered her right foot over the edge of the pool until it grazed the surface of the water. She shuddered involuntarily.

Their hearts thundered in their ears.

"You touched the water?" he whispered.

She nodded, shivering.

"Good girl," he said.

"Cut it out."

"Sorry," he said. "You're still alive, though?"

"Uh-huh."

"You didn't drown?"

"Uh-uh."

"Excellent," he said, barely able to speak the words. "Now dip your entire foot into the water."

"My entire foot?" she said.

"You can do it," he coaxed hoarsely.

"Okay."

Gripping his arm so tightly he felt his circulation being cut off, she lowered her foot into the water up to the ankle. She was trembling so violently now that her teeth were chattering. His body was trembling too.

"You're doing it, Marian!" he said. "Congratulations! Your entire foot is submerged below the surface, have you noticed that?"

"Y-yes!"

"And you're still alive and you still haven't drowned, have you noticed that too?"

"Y-yes!"

"How is it possible you've been able to accomplish such a feat?" he asked.

"I t-t-t-trust you," she stammered.

"Do you?" he said.

"Y-y-yes."

"Thank you, my darling," he said. "And now, I think you're finally ready to take the plunge."

He suddenly twisted the arm she was gripping, yanked it free of her fingers, and gave her a violent shove. She sailed sideways and landed in the water at an awkward angle, the splash soaking his slacks.

The shock of hitting the cold water was so immense it took her a full second before she was able to scream, and by that time her head was sinking below the surface and the scream was cut short by the water that was rapidly filling her open mouth.

Watching her frenzied flailing in the water, his own breathing stopped.

Trying vainly to keep her head above the surface of the water, liquid filling her mouth and then her throat and then her lungs, Marian still couldn't grasp what had happened to her, only that her very worst fear in life had suddenly been realized—she was drowning.

Through her panicked thrashing she saw him kneel by the edge of the pool and extend his arm in her direction. She thought he was reaching out to save her and she tried to propel herself back in his direction. But he was merely extending his iPhone out over the water to capture her last sounds before she died.

CHAPTER 43

H E SCREENED PERHAPS 75 percent of the charts of patients at the Bergman Institute before he found his next target. Her name was Nancy Blanchard. She was a book clerk who was mildly claustrophobic, but her real problem was an acute phobia of snakes. If setting up a phobic environment for Marian had been a challenge, then constructing one for Nancy Blanchard would be a true test of his art.

The first step, as always, was to arrange a chance encounter.

After following Nancy Blanchard for only two days, Andy saw his chance. From a block away he saw her enter the A&P. He took his time about getting over there. He picked up a cart in the parking lot and walked it into the store.

The store had been recently redesigned to look rural and rustic. Freestanding displays of produce were now encased in raw wood with knotholes. Baguettes and other breads were now displayed in big straw baskets. The linoleum flooring had been replaced by what looked like wide wooden planks but wasn't. Practically everything had a little sticker on it that read "Organic."

At first he thought she'd disappeared. Then he spotted her. She had short, shiny black hair that sort of flipped up at the ends. She had a slim body and was dressed in faded blue jeans and white leather sneakers, the leisure uniform of the free world.

She was scanning aisle three in the daze that people enter when they cruise the aisles of supermarkets. He took down a carton of cake mix, pretended to scrutinize it, then looked up just as she pushed past him.

"Excuse me," he said, "but would you happen to know how many pints in a quart?"

"Pardon me?" she said, startled.

"I'm just reading the label on this box of cake mix and trying to figure out what I need," he said. "But I can't recall if a pint is half a quart or half a glass, or for that matter how much a half pint is. Do you remember any of that stuff or are you just as mixed up as I am?"

"A pint is half a quart. No, wait," she said, then giggled. "I'm sorry, I don't know either."

"I'm so embarrassed," he said. "Four years of high school, four years of college, four years of graduate school, and I don't even know how many pints in a quart. How am I ever going to learn to bake a cake?"

"You're baking a cake?" she asked.

"Yeah, assuming I can ever figure out how many pints in a quart," he said. "Well, thanks anyway."

"Yeah," she said. "Well, good luck with the cake."

She left the Barnes & Noble a little after noon and strolled east on Forty-eighth Street. He tailed her to Second Avenue where she found a salad bar and went inside. He entered a short while later, coming up behind her at the salad bar and watched as she filled the sectioned bottom of her clear plastic container with pesto, chick-peas, and pickled beets.

He reached for the serving spoon she was using to ladle out cherry tomatoes, then apologized and feigned a double-take.

"Well, look who's here," he said.

She looked up, surprised, and smiled in recognition.

"Well, hi there," she said. "How did the cake turn out?"

"A disaster," he said. "An unqualified disaster. Hey, you aren't following me, are you?"

She giggled. "No," she said. "Are you following *me*?"

"Absolutely," he said. "From the moment you left the A&P last night. I thought you lived in Queens."

"I do," she said. "But I work in Manhattan."

"What do you do?" he asked.

"Oh, nothing special," she said. "I'm just a clerk in a Barnes & Noble. What about you?"

"Nothing special," he said. "I'm completing a doctoral dissertation in abnormal psych at NYU."

"Wow," she said, "I'm impressed."

"I wish they were at NYU," he said.

"What's your dissertation on?"

"Behavior modification in the treatment of phobias," he said.

"Yeah?"

"Yeah," he said. "Phobias are much more widespread than you might imagine. I, for example, am afraid of the dark, would you believe that?"

"Are you serious?" she asked.

"Absolutely. I often have night terrors so bad I have to sleep with a night light in the room. Whew," he said shaking his head in wonderment, "I didn't intend to just blurt *that* out. I hope you don't think I'm a dork."

"No way," she said. "I'm a little claustrophobic myself."

"No kidding," he said. "Well, there you are."

"There you are," she said.

"Well," he said, "there are things you can do about that."

"Yeah," she said, "I know."

She seemed to be getting uncomfortable.

"Well," he said, "nice running into you again."

"Yeah," she said, surprised he was ending the conversation. "Nice running into you too."

She was going through a stack of novels, carefully peeling auto-graphed-by-the-author stickers off a roll of backing paper and positioning them carefully on the cover of each book.

"Is it true that once they're autographed you can't return them to the publisher?" he asked.

She looked up and blushed. "What are *you* doing here?" she asked.

"I wanted to see you again."

"Right," she said. "I'll bet."

"It's true," he said. "I couldn't stay away from you. But we really can't continue meeting like this. Your husband is beginning to suspect."

She giggled. "How did you know where I worked?"

"You said a Barnes & Noble."

"But there are lots of Barnes & Nobles."

"I know," he said. "I went to eight of them before I found you."

"You didn't go to eight Barnes & Nobles looking for me," she said, blushing furiously.

"Okay," he said, "I didn't."

"I mean why did you want to find me?"

"I hit a snag in the dissertation," he said, "and I thought you might be able to help. I thought maybe we could talk about it over dinner."

CHAPTER 44

ANDY MANAGED TO find a parking place on Fifth Avenue at Sixty-sixth Street and walked the two short blocks to the Arsenal building of the zoo at Sixty-fourth and Fifth. He climbed the old stone steps, noticing what held the iron railing in place: iron muskets, standing upright, painted white.

Inside the small, dimly-lit, high-ceilinged lobby he saw the walls had been painted with murals depicting the Arsenal as a storage place for guns and ammunition in the Colonial era. He approached the glass-enclosed reception desk, decorated with the incongruously new graphics and politically correct new name of the zoo, the Central Park Wildlife Conservation Center.

"May I help you?" asked the receptionist, a Hispanic woman with acne scars and improbably blue eyes.

"Yes," he said. "I'm here to see Sheppard Kraft? My name's Maguire."

"Just a moment, Mr. Maguire," said the receptionist.

He strolled over to the murals and tried to imagine the building he was now standing in during Colonial times, with the rutted dirt road predecessor of Fifth Avenue out in front, with no cabs or buses anywhere in sight.

"Mr. Maguire?" said a tallish fellow with a reddish-blond beard and deep scars on his face, extending his hand, "I'm Shep Kraft."

"Thanks for seeing me on such short notice," said Andy.

"No problem," said Kraft. "So tell me, what's this novel you're writing?"

"Oh, it's just a thriller."

"Oh yeah?"

"Yeah."

"And it involves snakes?"

"Yeah. I've been told you have a fairly large specimen here."

"Yeah, we've got a beaut," said Kraft. "A twenty-five footer."

"I just need to take a look at the cage and the setting," said Andy. "See how to describe it in the book."

"Uh-huh. Well, let's go right on over there now and I can show you," said Kraft.

"Great."

Kraft led the way out of the Arsenal to the zoo entrance, nodded to the ticket taker in the booth, and passed through the turnstile on the low iron gate. A short walk along the zoo pathway brought them to the Tropic Zone building.

It was an impressive transformation. Outside the building was midtown Manhattan. Inside the building was the tropical rain forest. There was the smell of faintly rotting vegetation, the splash of waterfalls. Thick tree trunks, choked with tropical vines, struggled toward the light of the domed ceiling forty feet above them. Multicolored birds chirped and darted across their path. It was not as though an environment had been created within a city, it was as though a city had been hacked out of the steaming jungle and this was what remained.

When they arrived at the python exhibit Andy took out his iPhone.

"Mind if I record this?" he asked.

Kraft lifted his eyebrows, shook his head.

Andy began recording. "How big would you say this cage is?" Andy asked.

"About fifteen feet long, maybe six feet deep," said Kraft. "The keeper's got to be able to clean from the back door to the front, to be safe."

Gazing at the twenty-five-foot snake in fascination, many thoughts raced through Andy's mind, but the first one that found its way to his lips was:

"What's a creature this long weigh?"

"Well over two hundred pounds," said Kraft.

"Could he eat a person?"

"Wellll," said Kraft helpfully, "for sure he could eat a dog or a child. And there are stories of large specimens eating hundred-pound pigs. But could this guy eat you? Probably not. He could certainly kill you, though."

"Would he kill me, knowing he couldn't eat me?"

Kraft shrugged. "He might try to swallow your head, but I don't think he could do it."

"Why not?"

"What would save you is the size of your shoulders. Once a python gets past the head and shoulders on any animal, he's home free. This guy eats rats."

"How wide are his jaws?"

"Well, the head on this guy is about eight inches long," said Kraft. "He opens that up, you've got a fourteen, fifteen-inch spread, easy."

Andy's eyes were oddly bright. "Tell me," he said, "does he have long teeth?"

"No," said Kraft. "They're only an eighth of an inch long, but there are four hundred of them."

"*Four hundred?*"

"Yep," said Kraft. "There are four sets of curved teeth in the upper jaw. They latch on and hold you like fishhooks. Then he quickly throws these concentric coils around you, starting with your head. The way they kill isn't by crushing bones but by stopping your inhaling. Every time you release a breath, the snake just tightens up around you more, so it restricts the amount of movement in your rib cage and eventually you suffocate for lack of breath. This snake coils around his prey and he'll eat from the head down. He'll swallow the whole animal. When the prey has traveled a third of the snake's body length, it reaches the stomach and begins to be digested. Depending on the bulk of the food, it may take anywhere from a few days to two weeks to become completely digested."

"What would he do if I strayed into his cage one night when it was dark?" Andy asked.

"If he was startled, he'd strike you, then constrict to kill."

"How would he sense me in the dark?"

"Well, after dark he'd probably be resting," said Kraft. "Snakes don't have eyelids. You can't tell if they're asleep—like I don't know if this guy's asleep now or daydreaming or what. All pythons are capable of sensing heat, though. They have specialized sensing pits along their lipline, so even in total darkness he'd react to the warmth of your body. It would excite him."

"Could he smell me?"

"Sure," said Kraft. "The tongue is a receptor. It's not an actual scent organ, but it's a receptor. It picks up particles of odor and deposits that chemical information through a gland located in the roof of the mouth called a Jacobson's organ. That's his olfactory organ."

"How sharp is his hearing?" Andy asked.

"Snakes can't hear at all," said Kraft. "They don't have ears. But they do feel sensation and vibration, so any number of sensory cues tell a snake something interesting's there, like food."

"Has a snake ever attacked *you*?" said Andy, looking at the scars on Kraft's face.

"Oh sure," said Kraft. "I've opened a cage door and had them strike at me. When they strike, it's purely a defensive posture—just get out of my space."

"Were you scared?" said Andy.

"Uh-huh," said Kraft. "But one of the neat things about our exhibits is the door. If it's a mammal exhibit, the door is hinged so you open the door *into* the exhibit. So if the animal threatens you, you pull the door with you and then he hits the door. In the snake exhibit, the door opens *out*. So if the snake is threatening you, you walk back with the door and the threat goes past you. You don't want to open a cage door into a big snake."

"Could you show me the door?" Andy asked.

"It's just a regular door."

"I'd like to see it, though," said Andy. "If it's not too much of a hassle."

"Oh, no hassle," said Kraft, and he moved to the left of the exhibit.

In the planked wall was a narrow door with a knob and an ordinary dead-bolt lock. Kraft took out a ring of keys, inserted one, and opened the door.

Inside was the animal holding area, a narrow corridor. On the floor were a bucket and a hose. A yard ahead of them was another narrow door—the exhibit door—also with an ordinary lock.

"See?" said Kraft. "It's just a regular door."

"Uh-huh."

"Snake exhibits are all designed with the floor elevated," said Kraft, "because you can't work down at a snake. If you opened this exhibit door here, you'd see the actual floor of the cage. It's up about a yard. In the more traditional reptile house the doors would only be about yay high, like half a door, because the cage floor is about three feet up."

"And the keeper would just climb up into the cage?" Andy asked.

"Oh, you don't climb in with the big snakes if you can help it," said Kraft. "You use long shovels, long tools to get the crap, the shed skins out. One of the arts of being a reptile keeper is the use of tools to work around a potentially dangerous animal. At the Bronx Zoo the protocol with a snake over ten feet is you don't work in a building by yourself."

"The locks on these two doors are just regular locks," said Andy, surprised.

"That's what I was telling you," said Kraft.

"So if a character in my book knew how to pick locks . . ."

"He could get right into the exhibit," said Kraft. "Piece of cake."

CHAPTER 45

HE LIKED WHAT she was wearing: fashionably cut navy blue blazer, faded blue denim workshirt, faded blue jeans, socks, and penny loafers. He wondered what she was wearing underneath. They were having steaks and sidecars in a little place with brick walls and candles on the tables and they were getting along nicely, he thought.

"So tell me about this dissertation of yours," she said. "If you could explain it to a layman, I mean."

"I'm developing an experimental program in behavior modification."

"A what?"

"An experimental program in behavior modification. To desensitize people to their phobias."

"Really? What kind of phobias?"

"Well, like claustrophobia," he said, watching her carefully. "Are you at all claustrophobic?"

"Oh, mildly."

"Are you?" he said, knowing what her much greater phobia was. "Because I'm currently working on a theory that a system of rewards might encourage phobics to actively confront their fears."

"What kind of rewards?"

"Well, monetary ones, among others," he said. "For example, knowing you're mildly claustrophobic, what if I were to tell you that you climb into a confined space and stay there for five minutes and I'll give you fifty dollars?"

"Fifty dollars?"

"That's right," he said. "How much of an inducement do you think that'd be?"

"Oh, I don't know. It would depend."

"On what?" he asked.

She giggled. "On whether or not I thought you were serious."

He looked at her and smiled. He took a roll of bills out of his front left trouser pocket, peeled off a fifty, and showed it to her.

"You're *serious*?" she said.

He nodded.

"You'd give me fifty dollars if I just stay in a confined space for . . . how long did you say?"

"Five minutes."

"But that sounds so *easy*."

"It might very well be," he said. "Are you game?"

"I don't know," she said. "I mean *what* confined space? Any one in particular?"

"Well, yes. I've already selected one I plan to use in the program."

"Where is it?"

"Would you like to go and try it out now?" he asked.

"I don't know. Probably not."

"Why not?"

She made a pouty face. "I don't know. I mean I'm not sure it sounds like something I'd want to do, you know?"

"I see," he said. "And you don't need the fifty dollars either, I suppose."

"Oh, I wouldn't go *that* far." She laughed.

"You just wouldn't be willing to spend five minutes in a confined space in order to get it," he said.

A sigh.

"Five minutes for fifty bucks, Nancy," he said. "That's ten bucks a minute."

DAN GREENBURG

"You're really serious about the fifty bucks?"

"Absolutely."

"Well, I don't know . . . if it's only for five minutes . . ."

"Yes?"

"Well, I don't guess anything very bad could happen to me in just five *minutes* . . ."

"I wouldn't think so, no."

"Where is this place?" she asked.

"Somewhere not far from here," he said. "You'll see."

She looked at him a moment, cocked her head, blew air out of her cheeks, and shook her head. "In your bedroom, I'll bet."

He chuckled. "No no, nothing like that."

"Yeah," she said, "I'll just bet."

"No no, I swear."

"Then where is it?"

"You'll see," he said. "You like adventures, Nancy?"

"Yeah. Sure. Sometimes."

"Well then, this will be a little adventure."

A sigh. "Oh, hell," she said. "Okay. I just hope I'm not going to regret this tomorrow morning."

"You won't regret it tomorrow morning," he said. "I guarantee it."

He signaled for the check, paid it, and escorted her out to the parking lot. Guided her to his car. Gallantly opened the passenger door and let her in. Took a red bandanna out of the glove compartment and showed it to her.

"What's that for?" she asked.

"A blindfold," he said. "I don't want you to know where we're going."

"Why not?"

"Because," he said. "It would ruin the surprise."

"Uh, look," she said, "I don't think this is such a good idea after all."

"Why not?"

"I just don't like the idea of a blindfold," she said.

"Why not?"

"I just don't," she said. "It's too creepy. I mean I want to be able to see where you're taking me."

"Perfectly understandable," he said.

"It is?" she said.

"Absolutely," he said.

"Good."

"Unfortunately, Nancy," he said, "the whole impact of this experiment has to do with surprise. If you know where we're going, it would completely destroy the element of surprise. So if you don't want to wear a blindfold, I would certainly understand. But that means we can't do the experiment."

She didn't reply.

"And it means I can't give you the fifty dollars."

She formed her lips into a little girl pout.

"What's the matter, Nancy?" he said gently. "Don't you trust me?"

"I don't know," she said. "I guess I do."

"Really?" he said. "Why do you? You just met me."

"That's true," she said. "But you seem really smart. And nice. And sensitive. I just don't think you'd let anything bad happen to me."

He smiled in reply, a wide, ingenuous smile.

She looked at him a moment longer, measuring him.

"Hey, if I end up dead in a ditch somewhere tomorrow morning," she said, "I'm going to be really pissed, you know that?"

He laughed and held out the bandanna. She leaned forward and allowed him to wrap it over her eyes and knot it behind her head.

"Can you see anything?" he asked.

"Nope."

"Sure?"

"Yep."

"Good."

He turned on the ignition. They began to drive.

CHAPTER 46

"CAN I ASK you where we're going?" she said.

"Of course you can ask me where we're going."

"Okay, where are we going?"

"I'm not telling you."

"I thought you said I could ask."

"Yes, and you asked. And I'm not telling you."

She sighed with mock exasperation, a cute little toss of her head, her clean hair swinging around. He found this charming. He continued to drive.

Cruising Fifth Avenue around Sixty-fourth Street, he spotted a parking place on the east side of the street. He pulled up ahead of it and backed deftly in. He turned off the motor, got out of the car, came around to her side, and gently but firmly guided her onto the street.

"Are we standing in the middle of a street?" she asked.

"Yes," he said. "Just start walking, Nancy. I'll guide you."

"I can't believe I'm letting you lead me across a street *blindfolded*," she said.

"You're very good at taking risks," he said. "I congratulate you."

"Thanks a lot," she said wryly.

He led her up to the high iron gate of the zoo, took out a lock pick, and swung the heavy gate open. He guided her through it, and pulled it shut behind him.

The lock on the turnstile at the low iron gate proved hard to pick, so he merely placed his hands in her armpits, lifted her up in the air, and set her down on the other side of it. She squealed, enjoying the adventure. The warm, slightly moist contact with her body made his palms tingle.

They walked to the door of the Tropic Zone building. This lock was pickable.

Entering the building, they were enveloped by the warm breath of the tropics. Once more there was the smell of faintly rotting vegetation and the splash of the waterfalls, but the birds were silent now, presumably tucked up in their nests, asleep. A few strategically placed lights had been left on. They threw eerie shadows into the trees, but it was bright enough to make navigation along the decked walkways possible.

"Hey," she said, "where have you taken me to, Bermuda?"

"Yes, to Bermuda," he said, guiding her carefully along the decking. "To the Bermuda Triangle."

They passed the exhibits of the bats and the leaf-cutting ants. He stopped her before the secondary door to the left of the python cage, took out the picks, and swiftly unlocked it.

"You mean we aren't there *yet*?" she asked.

"Ssshhh," he said. "Almost there."

They walked through the secondary door and now stood facing the exhibit door, the door to the python cage. "Here we are," he said brightly.

"Where?"

"This is it," he said. "This is the confined space I've selected for our experiment."

"What is that *smell*?"

"The smell is incidental," he said. "The claustrophobia is what should be concerning us now. Focus on that, if you can."

"Where are we?" she said.

"At the confined space," he said. "How are you feeling?"

"Grossed out by the smell."

"Outside of that, how are you feeling?"

"Good."

"Good," he said. "We're standing at the side entrance to a large glass case, Nancy. I'll just unlock it. There. All right, now I'll boost you up into it. It's on a platform about a yard up."

"And tell me again: How long do I have to stay inside it to get the fifty dollars, did you say?"

"Not long at all," he said. "Five minutes. Think you can do that?"

"I guess."

"Good girl. Hey, Nancy . . ."

"What?"

"Would you like to double the fifty?"

"What do you mean?"

"Would you like to make that fifty into a hundred?"

"How would I do that?"

He drew a deep breath. "Take off your clothes."

She giggled. "You serious?"

"Absolutely serious, Nancy," he said. He put his hand into his pants, took out two five-dollar bills. "Here are the two bills, Nancy. Feel them?"

He thrust a bill toward her right hand. She grasped it between her thumb and the first two fingers of her hand.

"Yes."

"This is the fifty," he said, then he handed her the other five. "This is the hundred. Go into that case with your clothes on, I'll give you the fifty. Go into it without them, I'll give you the hundred."

"You think I'd be more claustrophobic without clothes on, is that it?"

"Or better motivated," he said. "I don't really know. I'm willing to pay to find out."

"Strictly business, huh?" she said, smirking.

"Strictly business," he replied flatly.

She appeared to be thinking it over. Then, chuckling darkly, still blindfolded, she slowly began taking off her clothes. First her blazer. Then her loafers. Then, leaning on him for support, her socks. Then she unbuttoned her faded blue denim workshirt and handed it to him. Under the workshirt she was wearing a black bra with translucent nylon cups that made no pretense of shielding aureolas.

He was holding his breath, afraid to move, to jeopardize the process. Subliminal flashes of ancient scenes flicked before his eyes: Very large women undressing in very small rooms. A row of lightbulbs around a mirror. She unzipped her faded blue jeans. Pushed them down below her knees and stepped carefully out of them. He felt his throat tighten. Found it difficult to swallow. She possessed, he noted, a considerably better body than he'd suspected when she was clothed. More subliminal flashes: Shiny underthings. Soft pink flesh. Extremely large breasts with spangly things over the nipples. Tremendous round buttocks with silver string in the crack.

He momentarily reconsidered where he was going with this. He was strongly tempted to touch her, to clasp her to his chest and weep. No no, stay with the program.

"Stop staring," she teased.

"What makes you think I'm staring?" he replied, his neck and forehead prickling.

"You'd *better* be staring," she said.

"Oh," he said. "Well then, I am."

"Good," she said.

Wearing just the bra and panties now. The panties made of the same translucent black nylon material as the bra, revealing a dark thatch at the crotch. His eyes fixed on the thatch. He felt his heart beating in his neck.

She was smiling. Still enjoying the adventure. Obviously turned on by being obliged to undress while blindfolded in the unknown place.

He could not take his eyes off her muff. His heart boomed so loudly in his chest he was certain she could hear it. He felt dizzy and wondered if he would faint.

"Okay?" she asked.

"Okay," he said, willing his voice to sound natural, barely able to speak, still staring at her muff. Why did they call it a muff anyway? Something to keep your hands warm.

"What now?"

"Now I'm going to boost you up into the case, Nancy," he said. "It's about three feet up. Lean on me. I'll pick up your foot and place it on my knee, and from there you can step directly up into the case. I'll guide you. Okay?"

"Okay," she said.

He bent down to get her foot, his face in the process accidentally grazing her buttock. Obeying a sudden impulse, he pressed his lips swiftly to her gluteal cheek through her panties, experiencing an unbearably sweet rush of warmth to his chest and groin. He wanted to grab her, hug her to him, bury his face in her skin and sob and blurt foolish words of love and passion and surrender and . . . No no no, stay with the program, must stay with the program at all costs.

"Well, so much for strictly business," she said.

He was suddenly ashamed. "I'm sorry," he murmured, genuinely contrite. "I don't know what made me do that. I'm really, really sorry. It won't happen again."

"Well then, I'll forgive you," she said lightly.

Trembling, he lifted her up onto the platform, studying her buttocks at point-blank range and experienced an overwhelming urge to touch her there—blindfolded and balanced precariously like that, what could she do for God's sake?—but then he squelched it. No, don't improvise. Stay with the program, stay with the goddamned program.

He pushed her all the way inside and shut the door behind her, immensely relieved that the temptation had passed without yielding to it. Clicked the lock. Snapped on the lights in the case and walked through the secondary door to the front, breathing with difficulty.

"Can you hear me, Nancy?" he called.

"Yes," she said. "Where are you?"

"In front of the case," he said. "The front of it is glass. I can see you quite clearly."

"Good," she said. "How do I look?"

"Magnificent," he said, and he meant it.

"You can remove your blindfold now, Nancy."

She reached to the rear of her head and unknotted the bandanna he'd tied around her eyes.

At first she was blinded by the brightness. Then she could make out shapes. Large rocks—boulders, really. A dead tree with gnarled roots. Hanging vines. Some dead palm fronds. And . . . what? Looks like . . .

"OhmyGod. No. Ohno."

"Beauty, isn't he, Nancy?"

"This isn't funny! Let me out of here! Quick!"

He was so turgid with excitement he could barely form words to speak. This was it, the feeling he'd sought. The summit. The pinnacle. A peak experience, wasn't that what Maslow would call it? Beer commercials notwithstanding, it didn't get any better than this.

"What are you afraid of, Nancy?" he called.

"What am I *afraid* of? The *snake*, God damn you!"

"This isn't just any snake, Nancy, it's a reticulated python. Would you believe they've documented specimens of reticulated pythons up to thirty-three feet in length? Would you believe that?"

"Help!" she screamed. "Somebody *help* me!"

"This one is about twenty-five feet, Nancy. Weighs well over two hundred pounds, I'm told."

"PleaseletmeOUTofhere!"

She was hyperventilating now.

The giant snake, irritated by the light and all the noise, but intrigued by the blast furnace warmth of the prey animal that had just entered its territory, began slowly uncoiling.

"Pythons, as you know, Nancy, kill their prey by constriction," he said. "Attacks on man aren't as common in the wild as popularly supposed, although a few have been reported. Mostly on women and children."

"FOR THE LOVE OF GOD PLEASE LET ME OUT OF HERE PLEASE!"

She gagged and whooped up her dinner. It splattered on the rocks and on her bare feet. Her legs telescoped inward and she collapsed to a huddled squat on the floor of the exhibit.

The vomiting temporarily cooled his excitement. Vomiting hadn't figured in his fantasies.

"There are records of large specimens swallowing one-hundred-pound pigs, Nancy, but not humans," he said. "So I really think you'll be quite safe in there."

"HELPME!HELPME!HELPMEEEEEEEEEEEEEEEEEEEE!"

Still uncoiling, taking its time, the two-hundred-pound reptile slowly slid over the boulders toward the intriguing hot creature crouching and shuddering in the corner of the case.

CHAPTER 47

MR. KRAFT, HAD you ever seen the deceased before?" asked Max, Scripto pencil poised above his spiral notebook.

"Not alive, no," said Kraft. They had gone into Kraft's small, cluttered office for privacy, but there were stacks of books and papers on every horizontal surface and no space for Max to sit down, so Kraft stood as well.

"She never came into the zoo before?" Max asked.

"She could have," said Kraft, "but not that I'm aware of."

"Can you think of any reason why she might have wanted to gain access to the python exhibit?"

"I sure can't," said Kraft. "And I sure can't imagine why she went in there half naked either."

"Has this particular snake gotten any publicity in the press—either the media in general or the professional journals—that might have attracted someone to this animal?"

"Nope. No press has been done on this animal that I'm aware of. Although a novelist did come here just a couple days ago to do some research on him, now that you mention it."

"A novelist, you say?"

"Yeah. He's writing a thriller which has something to do with a giant snake."

Max stopped taking notes.

"You happen to recall this novelist's name?"

"McGowan, I think. No, wait. Maguire."

"Maguire?"

"Yeah, Maguire."

"You remember what he looked like?"

"Nice-looking guy. Young. Clean cut. Well dressed. Very polite."

"How old? What color hair?"

"How old? I don't know. I'd say about thirty. Brown hair, I seem to recall."

"What kind of questions did he ask you?"

"Lots of stuff about how snakes strike, how they devour their prey. One thing he asked I thought was kind of odd, though."

"What's that?"

"He asked me if a character in his book knew how to pick locks, could he get into the exhibit."

—————

Max and Caruso divided up the list of trade publishers in New York and placed calls to all the editorial offices. None of the editors they talked to were aware of any novels in the works that had to do with giant snakes. One of the editors was working with an author named Maguire, but he was an older man and he was writing a book on household repairs, and the only snake in it was a plumbing snake.

Max went back to Lieutenant Hickock and demanded dumps on the phones of Morales, Masters, and Blanchard. This time Hickock called the DA himself and got permission.

Max divided up the list of phone numbers among the detectives in the squad and P. J. McCleary. On the day that Nancy Blanchard died, she had made five calls and received seven that would have to be checked out. There had been no calls between her number and that of Eddie Battaglia. On the day Marian Masters died she had made four calls and received only two. Approximately forty minutes before Virginia Morales died, she received a call from and made a call to a Bergman Institute in Astoria.

Max and Caruso went to the Bergman Institute.

209

CHAPTER 48

MAX AND CARUSO entered the waiting room of the Bergman Institute. There were several molded plastic shell chairs on either side of a long Formica coffee table stacked with outdated copies of *Psychology Today*, *Reader's Digest*, *Parents*, *Consumer Reports*, and *Pumping Iron*. There was a large dollhouse made out of rather cheap-looking fiberboard in the corner, and on the floor there were an assortment of beat-up toys including a red polyethylene fire engine and a compact model kitchen on wheels.

"Hi," said Max to the impassive-looking Asian receptionist behind the sliding glass panel.

"Hi," said the receptionist.

"I'm Detective Segal and this is Detective Caruso. We're from Queens Homicide and we—"

"Oh, yes," said the receptionist. "Dr. Golden has been expecting you. Just a moment please."

The receptionist dialed a number on her console.

"Hattie, could you tell Dr. Golden that the homicide detectives are here now, please? Oh, okay. Thanks."

"You can go in now," said the receptionist, pointing to a door just off the waiting room. "Right through there."

"Thanks," said Max.

"Thanks, doll," said Caruso.

They entered Dr. Golden's office. It had two windows, although what they faced was hardly worth the view. On a shelf was a small and rather delicate dollhouse which didn't look as though a child had ever played with it.

Ruth Golden was a short, attractive white-haired woman in a gold linen suit. She wore a black patch over one eye. She shook hands with them and beckoned them into two chairs facing her desk.

"So," she said, smiling. "How may we assist you, gentlemen?"

"We're working on a homicide investigation," said Max. "The deceased's name was Morales. Virginia Morales."

"Yes," said Dr. Golden, smiling.

"In the record of the telephone calls made to and by Miss Morales on the day of her death, we find that a call was made *to* Miss Morales from this clinic approximately forty minutes before her death, and then, approximately two minutes afterward, one *from* Miss Morales to this clinic."

"Yes," said Dr. Golden, smiling.

"Do you have any idea what the nature of those calls might have been or who might have made them?" said Caruso.

"At this moment I couldn't tell you that," said Dr. Golden.

"Was Miss Morales a patient of this clinic?" said Max.

There was no immediate reply from Dr. Golden, who continued smiling politely at both detectives. Max had just about decided that she had a hearing loss and was about to repeat the question, when she responded.

"Yes," said Dr. Golden, "I believe that she was."

"She was?"

"Yes," said Dr. Golden, "I believe that she was."

"I see," said Max. "Tell me, Dr. Golden, just out of curiosity, were you going to volunteer that information if I didn't ask you about it?"

"I'm available to answer any questions that you have to ask," she said, smiling the same smile.

"And was Miss Morales being treated for acrophobia?"

"I believe that was one of her presenting problems," said Dr. Golden.

"I see," said Max.

"Was Marian Masters a patient at this clinic?" said Caruso.

"Marian Masters?" said Dr. Golden.

"Yes," said Caruso.

"I'm not familiar with the name."

"Does that mean she wasn't a patient here?" said Caruso.

"No, that means I'm not familiar with the name," said Dr. Golden, never changing the intensity of her smile. "I'm familiar with the names of most of our active patients, and I'm not familiar with that name."

"Is it possible that Marian Masters was a patient here, but not an active one?" said Max.

"Yes," said Dr. Golden. "That is entirely possible."

"What about Nancy Blanchard?" said Caruso. "Was she a patient here?"

"Nancy Blanchard?" said Dr. Golden.

"Yes."

"Yes," said Dr. Golden, "I believe that she was."

"I see," said Max.

He held her gaze for several moments. He wondered whether the reason she wore an eye patch was that someone had stabbed her in the eye.

"So at least two out of a possible three of the victims of these homicides were patients at this clinic," said Max. "And at least one member of your staff appears to have had two conversations with one of the victims approximately forty minutes before she died."

"What makes you assume that the individual at this number who spoke with an individual at Miss Morales's number was a member of my staff?" asked Dr. Golden with the same smile.

By the time Max and Caruso left Dr. Golden's office Max had stabbing pains behind both eyes. They met briefly with Valerie Sheffield, the office manager, who furnished them with a list of all staff members of the Bergman Institute and their home telephone numbers.

When the two detectives had first gone into the medical director's office, several members of the staff found tasks to do quite close to the door. Andy had been one of them. What he heard convinced him that when he left the clinic tonight it would be wisest not to return.

CHAPTER 49

WHEN ANDY CAME back to Cynthia's he was pleased to learn that she was not at home. He walked into her bedroom and looked around. Annabelle had obviously been in here and straightened up, because everything was very clean and put away. Cynthia, he was sure, would not have left it this way herself. Cynthia was a slob.

When he lived here as a teenager he recalled that there was a safe in the wall, behind a painting of a cat with large liquid eyes. Sure enough, there was the painting. He pulled the painting back, and there was the safe. Unfortunately, he didn't know the combination, and what he'd learned in the joint about picking locks did not extend to combination safes. He tried the handle, just on the chance that she hadn't locked it, but it wouldn't budge.

On an impulse he opened the top drawer of the blond wood dresser under the painting and looked around. It was filled with underwear. In the rear corner of the drawer was a reddish brown leather Mexican box decorated with the Aztec calendar. He opened the box. Inside it was some jewelry and a stack of hundred-dollar bills.

He took a gold ring and the stack of bills and put them in his pocket. He kept on looking. There was nothing of any value in the middle drawer or in the bottom one either. There was another dresser filled with nothing but underwear, most of it gimmicky stuff from her stripper days.

In the top drawer of the little night table next to the bed he found another stack of hundred-dollar bills and a stainless steel Smith & Wesson .38 caliber revolver. He swung out the cylinder. It was fully loaded. What the hell was Cynthia doing with a loaded .38 revolver in her night table? And if she had a revolver and jewelry and all this cash outside the safe, then what the hell did she have inside it?

He put the gun in his other pocket and walked out of the bedroom.

CHAPTER 50

THE ELEVATOR GLIDED to a stop at the penthouse floor and the door slid open. Max had expected to see a narrow hallway with a few tan metal doors. Instead, a tall voluptuous woman with unsubtle breasts was gazing back at him from what appeared to be the inside of her own apartment.

"Oh, uh, Mrs. Woods?" asked Max uncertainly.

"I am indeed Mrs. Woods," she said. "And you are most definitely Detective Segal, aren't you? Come in, dear."

Max stepped out of the elevator and the door *whooshed* closed behind him. The foyer was the size of Max's entire apartment. The floor and walls were Italian marble and there were tall mirrors everywhere flecked with gold.

"Thanks for seeing me, Mrs. Woods," said Max.

"No problem, Detective Segal. Can I have Victor fix you a drink?"

"Oh, no thanks."

"I'm sorry," she said. "I should have realized you policemen don't drink when you're on duty. Won't you come into the living room? We can be alone there without interruptions."

"Good."

Max followed Cynthia Woods through the marble foyer into her living room. It was the size of a hotel lobby. The wall-to-wall carpeting was so spongy it seemed there was nothing solid underneath it. Max was by no means a connoisseur of art, but he knew the paintings on the walls hadn't been painted by professional artists. There was one of a nude woman who looked a lot like his hostess and another of dogs playing poker.

He sat down on a soft leather sectional sofa that occupied a good third of the room and could have accommodated perhaps two dozen people. Mrs. Woods sat down opposite him and crossed her legs, in the process affording him an almost subliminal view up her skirt.

"Well now, what can I do for you?" she asked.

"This is just a routine investigation of employees at the Bergman Institute," said Max.

"Yes," said Cynthia Woods.

"Your son, Andrew," said Max. "Is he an employee of the Bergman Institute in Astoria?"

"Yes, as a matter of fact, he is," she said.

She crossed her legs again. Once more Max caught an almost subliminal view up her skirt. He felt embarrassed and wildly inappropriate even to have noticed this, but the woman was rather striking looking. At least six feet tall, with abnormally large mammaries.

"I see," said Max. "And how long has he been working there?"

"Oh, he's only been there about two weeks," she said. "Just since he got out of the joint."

"Excuse me?" said Max.

"Just since he came home from St. Albans."

"St. Albans," said Max.

She recrossed her legs and this time Max had no trouble whatsoever seeing all the way up her dress.

"Are you saying," said Max, beads of perspiration popping out on his skin in unexpected locations, "that your son has recently been released from the correctional facility in upstate Vermont?"

"That's right," said Mrs. Woods. "He was doing twelve to twenty for manslaughter."

"I see," said Max. "Tell me, when would I be able to speak with him?"

"Whenever he gets home," she said. "Would you care to wait for him?"

"Do you think he might be back soon?" Max asked.

"You never know," she said, and recrossed her legs again.

"You know," said Max, "I believe I'll have that drink after all."

CHAPTER 51

S HE HAD JUST gone into the small bathroom of the office
she used for private consultations when the phone began to
ring. Although she had voice mail, she knew some of her patients
got too flustered to deal with answering machines, so she hastily
got up from the toilet and raced back to the phone.

"Hello?" she said.

"Dr. Grace Stevenson, please," said a male voice.

"This is Dr. Stevenson," she said.

"Dr. Stevenson," said the voice, "this is Detective Max Segal of
Queens Homicide in New York. Dr. Theodore Pearlman up at the
Northwest State Correctional Facility gave me your name."

"Oh, yes?"

"Dr. Pearlman tells me you treated an inmate of the facility
named Andrew Woods. Is that correct?"

"I didn't treat Mr. Woods, Detective Segal," said Grace. "I evaluated him over a period of several weeks."

"I see. Well, in any case, Dr. Pearlman said you spent quite a long
time with him and feels that you and Mr. Woods had a certain . . .
rapport."

"I'm sorry, Detective Segal, but I'm about to go into a session
with a client. What is the purpose of your call?"

"Well, we just had some questions about Mr. Woods which
Dr. Pearlman thought you might be able to help us answer."

"Questions pertaining to . . . ?"

"A homicide case we're working on. Three homicide cases we're working on, as a matter of fact."

"What cases are these?" she asked.

"Well, three females have had suspicious deaths recently in New York—I don't know if you read about them up there. One fell from a roof, one drowned in a pool, one was found in the cage of a large snake. Did you hear anything about these cases up there?"

"Yes, I think I did," she said. "We're not totally out of contact with civilization up here, you know."

"No, no, I didn't mean to imply that you were. I just didn't know if it was more than a local story, that's all."

"Is Mr. Woods a suspect in these cases?" she asked. "Is that the purpose of this call?"

"No, no, not necessarily, we just wanted to find out a couple of things and Dr. Pearlman thought you might be able to help. I thought maybe I could fly up there to Burlington and talk to you about him. Listen, may I call you after you finish your session?"

"Let me call *you*, Detective Segal," she said.

"Oh, okay. Let me give you the number here."

Grace hung up the phone and realized she was having a very peculiar reaction to the detective's call. For one thing, how she felt now. Dizzy. Full of dread. Why had she been so defensive with the detective? She was almost hostile to him. And why had she lied about going into a session with a client?

It was the idea of Andy being a murder suspect that had unhinged her. She did recall reading something about the cases, although she had only skimmed the story. She walked around the office, trying to find the copy of today's *New York Times*—despite what that patronizing idiot of a detective had implied, she *did* read the *New York Times*—but she couldn't find it anywhere. Then she remembered she had thrown it away. She went to the wastebasket and fished it out. There it was.

Deaths of 3 May Be Linked to Single Killer

NEW YORK, Aug. 16—Police now suspect that the deaths of three New York women, originally thought to be accidental, were due to foul play and may even be linked to a single killer.

Authorities have learned that Nancy Blanchard, 28, the bookstore employee whose partially clothed body was discovered in the python exhibit at the Central Park Zoo on the morning of Aug. 14, was deathly afraid of snakes. Similarly, the fall of Virginia Morales, 25, a nurse's aide, from the 20th floor roof of her apartment building in Queens on Aug. 6, originally thought to be a suicide, was reclassified as homicide when it was discovered that Ms. Morales had an acute case of acrophobia. And the seemingly accidental death by drowning of librarian Marian Masters, 34, in Astoria Pool on the evening of Aug. 9 was also reclassified as homicide when it was discovered that she was a non-swimmer terrified of water.

Det. Max Segal of Queens Homicide told a reporter: "We now believe that all three deaths were caused by a single individual, somebody who apparently takes delight in scaring people to death." Det. Segal stated that a number of leads were being actively pursued, but declined to say whether police yet had any suspects.

Grace read the story in the *New York Times* and reread it and then went back into the bathroom and took three Bufferins with a glass of water to ease the tension headache which had begun tightening up the upper half of her skull.

A killer who scared his victims to death. She recalled the fascination which Andy had displayed toward the anatomy of various phobias. Given his history, if Andy were ever to get into trouble and become a violent offender again, then frightening his victims to death would be a fairly plausible MO for him. In which case, Grace had to assume a good deal of responsibility for his victims' deaths, since her recommendation was a major factor in his being granted an early release from St. Albans. Hell, it wasn't just her recommendation, it was Pearlman's and the whole goddamn Andy Woods Fan Club parole board's. But she had certainly recommended his release, there was no getting away from that.

It was, of course, possible that Andy had killed these three women, but it was even more possible that he had not. Even before meeting Andy she knew how hard it was to predict aggression. Of course, he did have a history of being abused as a child and that was a risk factor, but he wasn't a substance abuser, he wasn't given to sudden angry outbursts, and his only prior act of aggression had been against a male. No, it was highly unlikely that Andy was the killer.

She had said she would call back this Detective Segal. What should she tell him? What could she tell him that would not compromise the confidentiality of the therapeutic relationship with Andy? What Andy had told her of his fascination with people's phobias was protected information.

Do the duty-to-warn laws apply here? she wondered. In *Tarasoff v. Regents of University of California*, a mentally ill patient revealed in therapy his intention to kill a girl named Tarasoff. Although police briefly detained the patient at the psychologist's request, the chief of the psychiatry department denied the psychologist's recommendation that the patient be involuntarily admitted to a psychiatric hospital, and no attempt was made to warn Tarasoff herself. When the patient killed Tarasoff, her family sued and the court ruled that a therapist bears a duty to protect potential victims from danger.

Well, Andy hadn't threatened to kill any of these women, so *Tarasoff* didn't apply here. All Andy had done was express a fascination about people's phobias.

If Andy *wasn't* the killer, then implicating him would be a staggering blow to a guy who already had two strikes against him. If Andy *was* the killer and she didn't assist the police in capturing him, other innocent women might die. What should she do?

CHAPTER 52

"COME IN, GRACE, come in."

"Thanks for seeing me on such short notice, Harry."

"Not at all, my dear. Sit down."

"Thank you."

Grace settled herself into a couch opposite the cheerful British psychotherapist and again marveled at how he managed to keep such a profusion of flowering plants alive in an area whose winter temperatures plummeted to Antarctic depths.

"Now tell me," he said. "What is this about?"

"Harry, I just got a phone call from a homicide detective in New York. He's investigating the three homicides of women who—I don't know if you read about it, but three women they thought died of natural causes were actually found to be—"

"—phobic in the areas in which they died. Yes, I do recall reading something about that. Why do they think your Mr. Woods may be involved in these cases?"

"First of all, he's not *my* Mr. Woods . . ."

"I'm sorry, Grace, that was merely a figure of speech."

"They didn't say why they thought Andy may be involved. The detective who called me didn't even say that Andy was a suspect, but why else would they want to know about him unless he was?"

"Well, they don't like to say who's a suspect and who isn't, but I should imagine that he was. So what is your dilemma?"

"What makes you think I have a dilemma?" she asked.

Harry smiled. "Relax, Grace."

"I *am* relaxed," she said. "What makes you think I have a dilemma?"

"Because you had to see me immediately. Grace, are you aware of how defensive you're being with me?"

She took a deep breath and then sagged into the cushions of the couch.

"My God," she said. "I'm wound up tighter than a top. Okay, the thing is that, although everybody at St. Albans was one huge Andy Woods Fan Club before I even got there, I did recommend that he be given an early release, so if he *is* the killer, Harry, then I—"

"—then you are still a competent therapist and a fine person, Grace, but you are not a superior being. All you can do is the best professional job you are capable of doing, and that is exactly what you did."

"So why am I so . . . why am I jumping out of my skin?"

"First, I want you to relax," he said.

"Don't keep telling me to *relax*, Harry. There is nothing less relaxing when you're not relaxed than having somebody tell you you're not relaxed."

"Shh."

"I'm sorry."

"Don't apologize."

"So why am I jumping out of my goddamn skin, Harry?"

He rose from his desk, picked up a watering can and a turkey baster, and walked from plant to plant, gently transferring water from the can to the earth of every pot in the room with the turkey baster as he spoke.

"Because you have an attachment to Mr. Woods, an attachment that you're not comfortable with. You're transferring something to him from your own childhood, something that has to do not with him but with your father."

"A rescue fantasy," she said.

"This is not new, Grace. This has come up before in your analysis. We have discussed this before."

"Hundreds of times," she said dully. "Thousands of times."

"But still," he said, continuing to squirt water with the turkey baster, "it bears repeating: Your father was alcoholic. Your father was two people. When he was drunk he was abusive, when he was sober he was loving. You wanted to repair him. You wanted to rescue him. And now you're afraid your decision about whether to cooperate with the police will have to do less with ethics than with your desire to cover for young Mr. Woods."

"No," she said. "The danger is that I'll give in to my rescue fantasy and . . . and . . . bond with him."

"You don't need me anymore," he said. "You know everything I have to tell you."

"Right," she said. She walked to the door.

"Thanks, Harry."

"Don't mention it."

"Good-bye."

"Good-bye."

She walked out the door. She walked back in again.

"Okay, I have to tell you something."

"By all means."

"On the day that Andy was released, nobody came to take him to the airport—not his mother or anybody else . . ."

"Yes . . ."

"So I took him to the airport . . ."

"Yes . . ."

"And when we were standing at the gate, he told me he was scared. He had tears in his eyes, Harry. I wanted so much to comfort him, to . . . well, to hug him. But I knew how wildly inappropriate that would have been."

"I'm immensely reassured," he said mildly.

"But when I stuck out my hand to say good-bye, he suddenly swept me up in his arms and hugged me."

"Grace . . ."

"I tried to break the hug, Harry, but it was over as soon as it started, I swear to God."

"Grace, mark my words. You need to have other anchors, other relationships in your life, or you will get swept away. You must find a way to develop normal healthy romantic relationships. You must."

"Oh, Harry, Harry," she said, "why can't I find a relationship with a man like the analytic relationship I had with you? The one with you was neither abusive nor overly dependent. It was appreciative and it was healthy."

"Yes, but analytic relationships are not life, Grace. We've discussed this. You need a real life relationship."

"I'll remember that."

"Do."

"Thanks again, Harry. I mean it."

"Get out of here."

"Good-bye," she said.

"Good-bye, Grace."

CHAPTER 53

"THAT PUTZ DAVINCI," said Caruso, coming into the squad room. "You know what he did?"

"What did he do?" Max asked.

The phone on Max's desk rang. He picked it up. "Homicide, Segal."

"Snuck Surtees down to One Police Plaza to work with a police sketch artist," said Caruso.

"Detective Segal," said the voice in the receiver, "this is Grace Stevenson."

"Oh, hi, Dr. Stevenson," said Max into the receiver, then covered the mouthpiece and said to Caruso "Who the fuck is Surtees?"

"Surtees?" said Caruso. "The porter in Virginia Morales's building? Who was on duty in the lobby when she died? While the doorman was on a break?"

"I'm sorry it took a while to get back to you," said the voice in the receiver.

"Oh, *Surtees*," said Max to Caruso, then to the phone he said, "Oh, no problem, Dr. Stevenson."

"So DaVinci snuck Surtees down to One Police Plaza to work with a sketch artist," said Caruso. "To get a likeness on the visitor that Virginia Morales had before she died."

"Virginia Morales had a visitor before she died?" said Max to Caruso. "That putz DaVinci told me Surtees said Virginia Morales didn't *have* any visitors before she died."

"Detective Segal?" said the voice in the receiver.

"That's what I'm saying," said Caruso. "That's why that putz is a putz."

"I'm sorry, Dr. Stevenson," said Max. "Thank you for calling me back."

"What is that putz doing withholding vital information on a case?" asked Caruso.

"Oh, he must still be pissed at me for breaking his finger," said Max.

"Am I calling at a bad time?" asked the voice in the receiver.

"Oh, no, sorry, Dr. Stevenson," said Max. "When would it be convenient for me to fly up and talk to you about Andy Woods?"

"Well, it's been a while since my last visit to New York," she said. "I was thinking I might fly down there for a couple of days, talk to you, and maybe take in a couple of plays."

"That's no reason to withhold vital information on a case," said Caruso.

"Great," said Max into the receiver, holding up a hand to silence his partner. "Would you be coming down here soon? The reason I ask is that time is a factor."

"Would tomorrow in the late afternoon be soon enough?" she asked.

"I wouldn't withhold vital information on a case if he broke *my* finger," said Caruso.

"Tomorrow in the late afternoon would be great," said Max. "If you tell me when your plane gets in, we'll even pick you up."

"Thank you," she said. "Have you had an opportunity to talk to Mr. Woods yet?"

"No, ma'am, I haven't."

"Would you withhold vital information on a case if he broke *your* finger?" asked Caruso.

"You know," she said, "it might be an idea for you to talk to him before I come. Meeting him may change whatever opinion of him you may now hold."

"Well, meeting him may take a bit of doing," said Max. "Andy Woods seems to have disappeared."

CHAPTER 54

SCORES OF ARRIVING passengers dragging black nylon rolling suitcases streamed past Max and Caruso in the Delta terminal at LaGuardia, bumping into them with their luggage, clutching more clothing and plastic bags than Max thought was allowed in the passenger cabin.

"What does she look like?" asked Caruso.

"Who?" Max asked.

"Who?" Caruso repeated. "Hillary Rodham Clinton. What does this Dr. Stevenson chick we're picking up look like?"

"Uh, I'm not sure," said Max.

"You're not sure?" said Caruso. "What do you mean you're not sure?"

"I'm not sure, okay?" said Max irritably.

"You told her we'd pick her up and you don't even know what she looks like?" said Caruso. "How the fuck are we supposed to pick her out of all these people, you don't know what she looks like?"

"Oh, I don't think it'll be that hard," said Max, scanning the crowd, silently cursing his own stupidity for not asking Dr. Stevenson on the phone what she looked like, for not telling her what he looked like, wondering why on this particular hot August afternoon the Delta terminal was as crowded as if it were the beginning of Thanksgiving weekend.

"We shoulda ate before we came here," said Caruso. "I'm starving."

"We'll grab a sandwich in the terminal as soon as we pick her up," said Max. "Then you won't be starving."

"What kinda sandwich could I get in the terminal that'd be healthy for me to eat?"

"Turkey," said Max.

"Turkey?" said Caruso. "Sliced turkey?"

"Turkey on whole wheat," said Max.

"Are you trying to kill me?" said Caruso. "You know how much sodium is in the sliced turkey they put in turkey sandwiches, Max? You got any idea how much sodium is in every slice of even whole wheat bread unless it specifically says 'low sodium' on the label?"

"Oh, Jesus," Max sighed. "Let's not get into another sodium discussion, okay, Sal?"

"Excuse me, are you Detective Segal?" asked a voice behind them.

"Dr. Stevenson?" said Max spinning around.

"Yes," said the green-eyed, small-boned woman in the tan silk dress.

"How did you know it was us?" Max asked.

"You're the only two men in the terminal wearing sport coats and ties on a warm day," she said.

———

Although on the drive back to the squad Caruso continued to rattle on about the high sodium content of almost everything edible in the world, Max was able to totally screen him out and laser in on every word that Dr. Stevenson was saying.

There was something about her that Max had not encountered before. For one thing, she really listened to you when you spoke. And she really looked at you with those great green eyes as if what you were saying was important and profound and entirely original. He did not recall responding to someone as immediately and as viscerally as this since the day he met Babette.

Dr. Stevenson told Max many things about Andy Woods, about watching him lead a therapy group and not realizing who he was, about his brilliance in the cognitive work in the Violent Offenders Program, about his early childhood and the abuse he had suffered from his mother, and from what she was telling him it was easy to see that she had a lot of feeling for Andy Woods. Max found to his surprise that he was even a little jealous of whatever relationship the two of them shared.

Dr. Stevenson came back to the squad room with them and met the lieutenant and the rest of the detectives and repeated some of what she had told Max in the car about Andy Woods. Some of the detectives asked her specific questions about Andy Woods and some of them just listened in fascination, and before they knew it it was 6 P.M. and the day tour had ended two hours ago.

Max offered to drive Dr. Stevenson back to her hotel, and on the way she said she was hungry and asked would he like to grab a bite with her.

Max was flattered that somebody as smart as a shrink had actually asked him to dinner and tried to think of someplace that was nice yet wouldn't cost an arm and a leg. He suggested the Oracle, a Greek diner where he and Babette used to take Sam when they had all been together, but Dr. Stevenson said she had always wanted to eat at the Loeb Boathouse in Central Park, right off Seventy-second Street, and as scared as Max was of what their prices might be, he was even more afraid to tell her he couldn't afford to go there.

CHAPTER 55

TO MAX'S SURPRISE, the Loeb Boathouse turned out to be this incredibly romantic-looking outdoor restaurant located at one end of a small lake in the park.

A bunch of rowboats were tied up at the dock, and then there was this open deck with a kind of peaked white tented ceiling held in place by a superstructure of white pipes. Little umbrella tables with red-and-white striped umbrellas lined the deck, and the minute they sat down Max's heart sank, because the waitress came over and brought them not normal rolls and butter but hunks of cakelike bread and little dishes of extra virgin olive oil to dip them in, and if that wasn't the mark of a place Max couldn't afford, he didn't know what was.

When the menu came he regretted that he hadn't held out for the Oracle. Dr. Stevenson ordered a glass of chardonnay, and Max ordered one too, and he must have drunk it too fast, because before he knew it he was a little dizzy.

Looking at the menu made him even dizzier. He thought maybe he could put a part of the tab on his expense account, although by no means all, because the NYPD did not approve of its employees going to places where you dipped pieces of cakelike bread into little dishes of extra virgin olive oil.

"Have you decided yet?" asked the waitress, a cute young girl with short blond hair and an overbite, "or do you need a little more time?"

"I think I know what *I* want," said Dr. Stevenson, turning to Max. "Do you?"

"Oh, yeah," said Max. "Sure."

"I'll have the seafood pasta and a small green salad," said Dr. Stevenson.

Max speedily calculated what that would cost, plus two glasses of chardonnay, plus tax, plus tip.

"And what about you, sir?" asked the waitress.

"Uh, well, I think I'll just have the, uh, small green salad. And a little more of this bread," added Max hastily. "It's *very* good bread."

"Aren't you having any entree?" said Dr. Stevenson.

"Uh, no, actually not," said Max. "I don't really feel too hungry right now."

"You told me in the car that you were starved," she said.

"Uh-huh," said Max. "Well, in the car I was, but not now."

"Okay," she said.

"Thank you," said the waitress and she withdrew.

Max was so hungry he could have eaten the tablecloth.

"Uh, Dr. Stevenson," he said, "can I speak frankly?"

"Only if you stop calling me Dr. Stevenson and start calling me Grace," she said.

"Okay, Grace," he said. "I happen to be going through an extremely costly divorce at present and I'm really strapped for cash. Would you mind very much if we went Dutch tonight?"

"Not at all," she said. "And I'm really sorry to hear about your divorce. It must be a very painful time for you."

"Is it ever," he said. "God."

"If you'd like to tell me about it, I'm a fairly good listener," she said.

And so he ordered the seafood pasta and some more chardonnay and he told her about his divorce. About little Sam and how he loved him and about how painful it was to not be living with him anymore. About Achmed and how painful it was to imagine him with

Babette and Sam in the apartment that used to be his. About Achmed being worried that he was losing Babette to a rival. About Max's financial situation and how terrifying it was.

He looked out on the lake which was bordered by trees and at the boats bobbing at the dock and at the big orange moon that had risen over the lake and he drank more wine. She asked gentle questions that elicited more from him than he thought he wanted to tell anyone, much less a complete stranger, and then he asked her about herself.

She told him about her private practice in Vermont and her committee work and about her work in the prison. She told him about growing up with a father who drank and about her two failed marriages. She told him about rescue fantasies and she told him that her former shrink had advised her to get a life.

Tied up at the side of the deck was what looked like a Venetian gondola with long, gracefully upcurved ends. It was painted black, so you could barely see it, and it was perhaps twenty feet long. When the waitress came with more wine he asked what it was.

"That?" said the waitress. "That's a real gondola from Venice, Italy. Some rich lady donated it to the Boathouse. We use it to give rides on the lake."

Between the orange moon and the chardonnay, Max was tempted to ask how much a ride on the gondola cost, but he knew he couldn't afford it whatever it was.

"How much does it cost for a ride in the gondola?" asked Grace.

"Thirty dollars a half hour," said the waitress.

Max shuddered.

"Would you like a ride on the gondola?" Grace asked. "It would be my treat."

"Really?" said Max. He couldn't believe it.

"Really."

"Okay," he said.

A kid in his twenties, wearing a striped shirt and the broad-brimmed, tasseled hat of a Venetian gondolier, seated them in the canoelike craft and then pushed off from the deck, navigating by means of a long Venetian oar.

It was beautiful out on the water. Max wondered whether Grace was interested in him romantically, and if she was, *why* she was. Perhaps she was as lonely as he. Perhaps he had presented himself so pitifully, with his divorce and financial problems, that she just felt horribly sorry for him. It didn't matter. Whatever the reason she'd suggested the gondola ride, he was willing to embrace it.

They reached a curve in the lake, and as they turned, the lights of the Loeb Boathouse disappeared and his eyes adjusted to the darker tones of the park at night. Central Park was what kept New York from being a total jungle. The people who'd laid it out and landscaped it and built it had preserved the sanity of millions of people over the years. Even though he knew how dangerous it was to walk through Central Park at night, to look at it from a Venetian gondola in the middle of a lake was to imagine that there was beauty and romance after all.

Ahead of them a little stone bridge arched out over the water. If he were to casually drape his arm around her shoulders just before they went under the bridge, he thought, and if she didn't shrink from his touch, he might just kiss her.

They approached the bridge. He casually draped his arm around her shoulders, which felt at once thinner and warmer than he had imagined, and as his arm settled upon them, she moved closer to him. As they passed underneath the bridge he reached out and cupped her chin in his free hand and brushed her lips with his own. Her arms slid around his neck and he felt giddy with pleasure.

As the gondola emerged on the other side of the bridge, somebody landed heavily on Max's back, knocking the wind out of him and throwing him into the bottom of the boat.

CHAPTER 56

MAX COULDN'T AT first figure out what had happened. All he knew was that three more people were now in the boat than before, and that these three people were punching and pummeling him. Three young men. Three muggers. Three muggers who must have been waiting for the gondola to pass and jumped off the bridge as it emerged on the other side.

Max smashed the closest one in the face, breaking teeth, and kicked at one who had grabbed Grace and was trying to take her purse.

The gondolier hit the third one, but got kicked in the groin and doubled up in pain.

Max grabbed the one who had Grace's purse and threw a choke hold around his neck, cutting off his air supply.

One of them kicked Max in the stomach and Max threw him into the water. A second one lunged at Max just as he reached inside his belt and drew his gun.

"Freeze, motherfuckers! Police!" shouted Max, but the mugger who'd lunged at him succeeded in throwing Max out of the boat.

Max landed in the lake. The surprisingly cold water was a shock to his system.

"Motherfuckers! Motherfuckers!" screamed Max. The three muggers took off toward the shore, arms and legs flailing like eggbeaters, scrambled up on the bank and disappeared into the foliage.

"Motherfuckers!" screamed Max again, but they were gone.

Grace and the gondolier pulled Max back into the boat.

"Max, are you all right?" cried Grace anxiously.

"I guess so," he said. "What about you?"

"I guess so," she said.

"What about you?" Max asked the gondolier.

"I guess so," said the gondolier.

Grace still had her purse.

"Boy, I love this town," said Max.

The gondolier was so grateful that Max had scared the muggers off he wouldn't let Grace pay for the ride. Grace insisted on paying the dinner check and Max put up no more than token resistance. They walked soggily to the car. When they reached Grace's hotel, she suggested he park and come upstairs and dry off. He didn't argue with her.

CHAPTER 57

GRACE TOLD MAX to go into the bathroom and remove his wet clothes and take a hot shower. She told him there was a big white terrycloth bathrobe in the bathroom with the emblem of the hotel on the pocket. She sensed she was being even more seductive than she'd been at the restaurant when she'd urged him to confide in her about his divorce and his financial problems. She sincerely liked him and found him attractive, but was her behavior the consequence of healthy horniness or of Harry Lake telling her to get a life?

Max came out of the bathroom, wrapped in the big terrycloth robe. With his wet hair slicked back he looked like a little boy. He was thirty-seven—five years younger than she. Why was that appealing to her? Andy Woods was twenty-eight—fourteen years younger than she. Why was that appealing? Did it mean she found younger men sexually less threatening or what?

"How do you feel now?" she asked.

"Better," he said. "A lot better."

"I want to thank you for what you did out there," she said.

"For what I did out there?" he said. "I screwed up a chance to collar three muggers, that's what I did out there."

"That's what you got out of what happened?" she said. "That you screwed up a chance to collar three muggers?"

"Isn't that what happened?" he asked.

"What happened," she said, "was that we were jumped by three

239

muggers, you saved us from them, and you scared them away. That is what happened."

"Really?" he said.

"Jesus," she said softly, taking him in her arms. "You sure are hard on yourself, aren't you?"

"I don't know," he said, kissing her on her forehead and then on her chin and then on her lips, "I guess maybe a little."

CHAPTER 58

THE BUILDING THAT housed Queens Homicide and the one-twelve precinct stood at the corner of Yellowstone and Austin in Forest Hills. Queens Homicide consisted of two rooms on the second floor. The larger one contained nine office desks, mostly paired and facing each other, with upholstered blue swivel chairs. The smaller adjoining room belonged to the lieutenant who ran the squad.

Max and Caruso were sitting at their desks, filling out forms, when the man walked in. Segal looked up first.

"Help you?" asked Max in a neutral tone.

"Oh, hi," said the man. "Are you Detective Segal?"

"Who are you?" Max asked.

"Mitch Morgenstern of the *New York Times*. I left a message earlier in the day, sir. I don't know if you got it."

"Look, Morgenstern," said Max, "we're very busy here. If we spent our time talking to the press, we wouldn't get any work done, okay?"

"Sure, I understand. I'm sorry to have come over without an appointment, sir. I'm on deadline and I just took the chance you'd be here and might have a minute to talk. I'm really sorry to have disturbed you, though."

He turned, walked out of the squad room, heard a sigh behind him, and then the word "Shit."

"Morgenstern?"

The man turned around. "Sir?"

"Come back here a second."

He walked back into the squad room.

"Look," said Max. "I'm sorry I snapped at you."

"Perfectly understandable."

"I know you're just doing your job," said Max.

"I guess the press can be pretty intrusive at times."

"Yeah," said Max. "Plus which I had a bad experience with a female reporter a few years ago, but that's not your fault. I can spare about sixty seconds, if that's of any use to you."

"Oh, absolutely," said the man as he took out the iPhone on which he'd recorded the death cries of Virginia Morales, Marian Masters, and Nancy Blanchard, and turned it on.

"You were quoted in the *Times* as saying you believed that the deaths of Virginia Morales, Marian Masters, and Nancy Blanchard were linked, and that one person had done all three killings."

"Right."

"I was just curious about how you'd made that assumption."

Max shrugged. "It was just a hunch."

"Is there anything else besides a hunch that links these three women?"

Max shook his head.

"Any suspects yet?"

"Not yet," said Max.

"Any leads at all?"

"Nothing that I'd care to talk about on the record at present," said Max.

"How about *off* the record?"

"What good would that do you?" Max asked.

"No good whatsoever," said the man with an ingenuous grin. "It would just satisfy personal curiosity."

"Well, I wish I could tell you something, but I can't," said Max. "I'm sorry to be so vague."

"That's okay," said the man. "Well, thanks for talking to me."

"That didn't help you much, did it?" Max asked.

"It's all right. Thanks anyway."

He walked back toward the door.

Another sigh and another "Shit."

"Morgenstern?"

"Yes sir?"

"Come back here a second."

The man came back into the squad room.

"I don't want you to leave empty-handed," said Max.

"Thank you." He turned his iPhone on again.

"You can say that we're looking into the possibility that the killer was somebody who worked in a psychiatric clinic in Astoria," said Max. "A clinic called the Bergman Institute."

"An employee at the Bergman Institute."

"Yeah," said Max. "A woman."

CHAPTER 59

A WOMAN? DID THEY really think that the killer was a woman or was Segal playing with him? He didn't know. Maybe they really didn't know anything. Maybe.

He'd sort of liked Segal. The guy was clearly ambivalent about talking to the press, but couldn't let him leave empty-handed, even if it meant making something up.

He went down in the elevator and walked out of the building and down Austin. He passed a Banana Republic. He went in and browsed. He wondered whether Segal would call the *Times* to check whether Mitch Morgenstern really worked there. If so, he'd find that he did.

Andy liked the name Mitch Morgenstern. Maybe he'd use it for a while. The name, the dark color he'd tinted his hair, the goatee, and the tan he'd applied with skin bronzer might distinguish him from pale Andy Woods, at least for a while.

So Segal had a hunch that Virginia, Marian, and Nancy had been killed by a woman who worked in the Bergman Institute? Well, he had a hunch that Segal knew more than he was saying. It might pay to follow him and see what leads he was pursuing.

There were two cars parked near the convergence of Austin and Yellowstone, an Audi and a Toyota. Andy selected the Audi, picked the lock, disarmed the alarm, and slipped inside the driver's seat. He hoped that Segal wouldn't spend his whole tour in the office today. He hoped the Audi didn't belong to Segal.

Andy's anxiety level had risen perceptibly since leaving the Bergman Institute, moving out of Cynthia's apartment, and moving into the Mayflower Hotel. He realized that it was only a matter of time now before he'd be reported to his parole officer as missing, only a matter of time till his disappearance would be linked to the homicide cases. Then all hell would break loose. The FBI would be called in and a nationwide manhunt would begin.

Eluding the authorities would be a challenge, but with the FBI currently estimating six thousand unsolved murders in the United States and anywhere from thirty to a hundred serial killers on the loose, the odds were certainly in his favor.

If eluding the authorities was not the major problem, then maintaining his emotional equilibrium was. Since the death of Nancy Blanchard, he'd sunk into a general low-grade depression. The part of him that was a VOP group leader felt ashamed at what he'd done. The part of him that was a serious violent offender missed the rush of stalking and killing victims.

He found his thoughts drifting back to Dr. Stevenson. She was the one person who seemed to understand how his mind worked. She not only understood him, she liked him. When he'd hugged her good-bye at the Burlington Airport, he thought he'd felt her shudder with pleasure. He sensed a certain animal attraction existed between them. If only he could talk to her. Call her up and, without telling her what he'd done, just generally discuss his state of mind. See what she might suggest. Maybe he'd even drive up to Burlington and pay her a surprise visit.

At 4:05, Segal emerged from the police building and walked halfway down Austin to a Chevy Caprice. He reached for what looked like a parking ticket on his windshield, tore it up, and punched the hood of the car. Then he massaged his fist, unlocked the door, and got inside.

When Segal pulled out, Andy hot-wired the Audi and followed him. In Segal's present state of mind, it was doubtful he would notice a tail, even if Andy were sitting on his trunk.

Segal drove to Manhattan over the Queensborough Bridge, then headed over to Fifty-ninth Street and began circling the blocks in the vicinity of Sixth Avenue. He appeared to be looking for a legal parking space and didn't seem to be having any luck. He finally pulled into a public garage.

When he emerged from the garage, Andy followed him back to a hotel facing the park. This Andy found somewhat encouraging. Whoever Segal was visiting there might be connected to the homicide cases. Andy double-parked across the street of the hotel and let his thoughts slide back to Dr. Stevenson.

He had a fantasy of walking with her through Central Park, perhaps along the reservoir, perhaps taking her rowing, perhaps slipping his arms around her as he had done at the Burlington Airport, but not letting go. Not letting go and kissing her hair and her lips and hugging her to his body. Telling her how much she'd been in his thoughts. Telling her that he was falling in love with her. Telling her that she'd been right about his need to form a meaningful relationship with a woman.

Scarcely twenty minutes after Segal had entered the hotel, he appeared again, this time with a woman. Judging by his body language, Segal's mood had improved dramatically. The woman was holding his hand. The woman was laughing. The woman was reaching up to kiss his neck. The woman looked oddly familiar to him. The woman was . . . The woman was Dr. Stevenson. *The woman was Dr. Stevenson!* Holy shit! THE WOMAN WAS DOCTOR FUCKING GRACE STEVENSON!

He felt as if he were going to pass out. He felt as though he were going to vomit. He began trembling uncontrollably, his breath burning his nostrils, something seeping into his eyes, possibly blood. His breath caught in his throat on something like a sob. The something seeping out of his eyes was clear: not blood but tears.

What in the name of fucking hell was Dr. Stevenson—his Dr. Stevenson—doing in fucking New York and kissing fucking Detective Segal! What was the woman he loved doing with the man who was trying to capture him!

He had a sudden urge to leap out of the car, pull out Cynthia's .38 and empty it into the two of them. He heard the shots, saw the bullets slam into their bodies, the blood splattering, the bodies pitching backward onto the pavement, passersby screaming, cars yerping to a stop on Fifty-ninth Street.

He had to calm down. He had to control himself. He had to get a grip. If he were going to kill either of them, he wanted to have some time to think about how he was going to do it. He wanted to do it on his own terms.

He walked unsteadily down Fifty-ninth Street, breathing hard, trying to formulate a plan of action. He was barely aware of other people on the sidewalk and narrowly missed bumping into a dignified woman with shellacked hair and a silver cane who glared at him, sighed audibly, and shook her head.

The tiny lingerie shop suddenly appeared before him. In its window were the usual ornate bras and gimmicky thongs, but there was also a demure-looking white silk nightgown. And suddenly, a plan began to take shape. He turned the doorknob, pushed open the door, and entered the shop.

The girl behind the counter, a pudgy nineteen-year-old with acne, looked at the man who'd just entered the shop and was suddenly sorry she'd come to work that day. He was movie-star handsome, but he had a deranged look in his eyes. Her first thought was that he was drunk or on some kind of drug, her second thought was that it was far worse than either of those.

"C-can I help you?" asked the girl, visualizing the under-the-counter panic button, wondering if he'd catch her reaching for it, afraid of what he'd do.

"I would like to see . . . the nightgown in the window," he said in a voice that he seemed to be controlling with great difficulty.

CHAPTER 60

TODAY WAS A wonderful day. Rain came down in torrents, soaking Grace, who'd neglected to hear the forecast of thundershowers before leaving the hotel, but she couldn't have cared less. She was in love, and when you're in love torrents of rain make you think not of ruined clothes and hairdos but of Gene Kelly and singing in it. And so she made her way along Fifty-ninth Street, heedless of the fact that she was now wetter than Max had been when he'd fallen into the lake.

Dear Max! How she adored him. Harry was right, she had needed to get a life. Well, now she had one. And Max appeared to care for her, too. It was too good to be true.

She was so deep in Gene Kelly–like ruminations that at first she thought the voice calling her name was one inside her reveries. And then she heard it louder. She turned. It was coming from a car over there. Somebody calling her name from a car parked at the curb not far from the entrance of the hotel. Who did she even know in New York besides Max? She walked up to the car. The somebody wasn't in the driver's seat, he was in the passenger's seat on the other side.

"Dr. Stevenson?"

"Yes?"

The window on the driver's side was open. She stuck her head half inside it.

"Hi, Dr. Stevenson! What a coincidence!"

He looked familiar, but . . .

"Andy?"

"Yeah, hey, come on inside the car, Dr. Stevenson, you're soaked!"

Andy! Oh my God.

"Get in, Dr. Stevenson. Get in the car."

He leaned across and opened the door.

"Uh, listen, Andy, I really don't know if I should . . ."

He was smiling that big infectious smile of his, and then she saw the revolver in his hand. It was pointed at her stomach.

"Get in the car, Dr. Stevenson," he said, still smiling the same tight smile.

She got into the car.

CHAPTER 61

"O H BOY," SAID Andy. "Am I ever glad to see *you*, Dr. Stevenson. How've you been?"

Time had slowed, slowed . . . slowed. Slowed. Down. Time was now running at half speed. A classic panic reaction, she thought automatically. She noticed that she was behaving rather well under the circumstances. Rather well under the circumstances that a convicted murderer had just forced her into his car and, although he was still smiling and talking in a friendly fashion, had placed the barrel of his revolver up against her carotid artery.

"So," he said in the same cheery tone, "what's new, slut?"

"What?" she said dully.

"I said what's new, whore? Isn't that what you are, Dr. Stevenson, a whore?"

Say something, she thought. *Feed back to him and interpret what he's presenting.*

"You sound . . . very angry with me," she whispered.

"Angry?" he said cheerily. "Why would you say that, whore?"

"You must . . . be . . . very very . . . angry . . . with me," she whispered.

"Why should I be angry with you, whore? Just because you're dropping your pants and spreading your legs for Detective Max Segal and letting him fuck you? Why should I be angry about that?"

She was going to die now, that much was certain. She had not known when or how she was going to die, had thought that it wouldn't happen for three or four more decades, but now that she

251

knew how it was going to happen and when, there was a certain resignation, a certain relief almost, a certain calming effect on the system.

"You must be . . . very angry to think that . . . Detective Segal and I are . . . friends," she said. "It must make you feel very . . . lonely and very . . . excluded."

"Friends?" he said. "*Friends*? Is that what you call it when you drop your pants for somebody and let him fuck you—*friends*?"

"Detective Segal and I *are* friends," she said. "Whatever else we may be . . ."

"Is that right?" he said. "Well, you may be *friends* with Detective Segal, but you *belong* to me." He placed the barrel of the gun in her ribs. "Now start the car and drive."

CHAPTER 62

MAX FOLDED HIS umbrella, shook off the rain, went through the revolving door, entered the marble lobby, and made a beeline for the house phone. He gave the operator Grace's room number and waited while she rang it. It rang and rang.

"I'm sorry, sir," said the operator. "There doesn't seem to be an answer."

"I'm sure she's there," said Max. "Are you sure you're ringing the right room?"

"Fourteen-eighteen," said the operator.

"She said to pick her up at eight," said Max, realizing the inanity of trying to convince the operator.

"Perhaps she's in the bathroom," said the operator. "Why don't you try again in a few minutes?"

"Thanks," said Max and hung up the house phone.

She wasn't in the bathroom. There was a phone in the bathroom. If she was in the bathroom she would have answered it.

Had he misunderstood her, that he was supposed to pick her up at eight? No, there was no misunderstanding. He was definitely supposed to pick her up at eight, and then he was going to take her to dinner at the Oracle, Dutch treat. Not that he could afford even Dutch treat at the Oracle, but she'd sprung for dinner last night and he sure couldn't expect her to pay two nights in a row. So if they'd agreed he'd pick her up at eight, then where was she? Maybe she was out shopping and got delayed. She did say she intended to go shopping down in SoHo and TriBeCa today. Maybe she got carried away shopping and forgot the time and would fall all over herself apologizing when she saw him, but he'd scold her and pretend to be cross with her, just enough to make her wonder, and then he'd kiss her to show he wasn't really mad and maybe it would heat up and they'd end up in the sack and say the hell with the Oracle and order room service. If they ordered room service, she'd sign for it and the dinner would go onto her hotel bill and he wouldn't even have to pay half of . . .

He was embarrassed at having such thoughts and began to consider other possibilities.

There was another possibility. She was in the bathroom taking a shower and couldn't hear the phone. When the water was on full blast in the shower stall, it was so noisy you could easily miss the ringing of a telephone. She'd get out of the shower and be drying herself off with those giant terrycloth towels when he called again, and if he could snag an elevator right away he'd find her still half undressed, they'd begin to make out, and before he knew it they'd be in the sack, making love, and end up ordering room service, which he honestly didn't see there was any way in hell she was going to agree to let him chip in on, because . . .

He picked up the house phone and had the operator ring her room again, but there was still no answer, although the phone continued ringing.

There was a third possibility, of course, the possibility that something bad had happened to her. That she was mugged or robbed or hit by a car. New York was, after all, a fairly dangerous city. And it had been raining all day. Cabs in New York always went through lights on the yellow if not on the red, and in the rain, when it was so easy to lose control of a vehicle on the slick streets and skid out of control, smashing into pedestrians, splintering bone and spattering blood and . . .

No, he didn't want to even think about that one.

There was a fourth possibility, and he didn't want to think about that one either. The possibility that she had simply stood him up. Simply come to her senses after two nights of animal lust and realized that the only thing a successful psychotherapist could be doing with a detective second grade who had giganto divorce problems and zero money was slumming. Simply decided that the fastest way to end it was just to end it, not show, stiff him, stand him up, hope he'd take the hint and go away.

Whew.

But she'd seemed so loving, so appreciative of him, so, frankly, needy herself. Was it likely she'd simply turned him off, just rotated the handle one full clockwise revolution and stopped the flow, just like the bank and the credit card companies and everybody else had done to him of late? If so, how pathetic of him to keep standing here at the house phone, having the operator continue to ring her number. Maybe she was even in her room now, not answering, and had told the operator when a man rang her room to pretend that she was . . .

The doors of one of the elevators opened and a well-dressed young couple got out, chattering away in a high octave. They glanced in Max's direction and erupted in laughter. Max walked quickly away from the house phone and headed for the revolving door.

CHAPTER 63

YOU'LL HAVE TO open the door for me, Dr. Stevenson," said Andy. "Between the suitcase and the gun I've quite run out of hands."

The rain had soaked through their clothing while parking the stolen car and walking across the street to the Hertz agency. Grace opened the door to the rental office.

"Please go in first," said Andy pleasantly. "And while we're in there, do hold in your mind the image of the gun in my jacket pocket."

Grace went through the heavy glass door and Andy followed. They walked up to the desk.

"And how are you folks this evening?" asked the perky young rental agent in the yellow-and-black uniform behind the desk. "A little wet?"

"Boy," said Andy, "you can say *that* again!"

"And what can I do for you?"

"Do you have a Jeep Cherokee or a Mustang convertible?" Andy asked.

"We don't have any Jeeps at all, but I think I can give you a Mustang in a hardtop."

"What color?"

"White."

Andy turned to Grace. "White sound okay to you, hon?"

Grace nodded woodenly.

"White will be great," said Andy.

"And how long will you be needing this?"

"Oh, about a week," said Andy.

"Okay, I'll need a driver's license and a major credit card."

"Dear," said Andy, "I seem to have left my wallet in my other jacket. Could you please put this on your card?"

CHAPTER 64

FOR THE NEXT hour Andy confined his communications to driving directions. By the time they left the outskirts of the city and were on the interstate the rain had slowed to a light drizzle and it finally got dark. There was no sound now but the muted whine of the engine, the continuous patter of rain on the windshield and roof, the hiss of tires on the wet pavement as faster cars passed them on the left, and the steady *flup flup flup* of the wiper blades.

She had no idea where he was taking her. She had no idea of what he planned to do with her once they got there. She knew only that she had to pee.

"If it's all right with you," she said, "I'd like to pull into a service station and use a restroom."

"It's not all right with me," he said.

"Well, I really have to urinate."

"Go in your pants."

"If I do it will soak into the car seat," she said. "That might not be very pleasant for either of us."

He didn't answer.

"Where are we going?" she asked.

"Somewhere."

"To do what?"

"To get married."

"What?" she said.

"To get married," he said.

It was not one of the first ten responses she'd expected.

"I've decided to marry you, slut," he said. "Even though you're a slut."

The level of his rage was so off-the-wall she didn't know how to play it.

"You feel you want to marry me . . ." she said.

"That's right, slut, and stop feeding back and interpreting everything I say."

"You must really have a lot of loving feelings toward me, in addition to your angry ones . . ." she said.

"I said *stop it*!"

"All right. Whatever you say."

"You're damned fucking *right* whatever I say."

It was clear he had kidnapped her to possess her, but she couldn't figure out the wanting to marry her. She wondered if it had anything to do with wives not being able to testify against their husbands, then realized his reasons were far darker than that.

"Why do you want to marry me, Andy?"

"You tell me."

"Because you've made a very strong transference? Because you'd like to live out some kind of Oedipal fantasy, and marrying your real mother is too dangerous? Because maybe you thought I was the good mother you never had?"

"If you like."

"Well, I'm not your mother, Andy."

"No, you're not," he said. "You're not even good."

"Okay."

"You're a slut," he said. "Just like she is. Even the windshield wipers think you're a slut. Hear them? Slut . . . slut . . . slut . . . slut . . . slut . . ."

"If I'm a slut," she said, "then why marry me?"

"So I can have sex with you."

"You don't think you could have sex with me unless you married me?"

"I know you'd let me," he said, "because you're a slut. But *I* wouldn't want to."

"I really have to urinate," she said. "Can't we please stop at a restroom now?"

"No."

"Why not?" she asked.

"You tell me."

"You think I'd try to escape. You think I'd try to get help. I wouldn't. I'd just go in and take a pee and come right out again, I promise you."

He laughed mirthlessly.

She didn't know what opportunity there might be at a service station to escape, but it was better than this. She felt that she was going to burst like a water balloon. The strain of holding her legs together was making her inner thighs ache.

"I really have to pee very badly," she said. "If you make me go in my pants it'll stink up the car and we'll have to travel like that to wherever you're taking me. If you let me go into a restroom to pee now, I promise you I'll come right back."

"Okay," he said. "Pull over."

"Pull off at the next turnoff and find a service station?" she asked hopefully.

"No, pull over now," he said. "Onto the shoulder."

She switched on her right turn signal, changed into the right-hand lane, then slowed to a stop, pulled onto the shoulder, and stopped the car.

"Now change seats with me," he said. "Slide over me."

She unbuckled her seat belt and slid over him, her back rubbing unavoidably up against his chest in the process, her buttocks and the bottoms of her thighs rubbing across his lap through the thickness of her dress and her undergarments as he slid beneath her. She was disappointed to find that this contact with his body did not repel her. Despite her overwhelming urge to pee, despite the fact that she was now very possibly in love with another man, despite the fact that this one was a dangerous killer who was kidnapping her at gunpoint and seemed prepared to shoot holes in her body if she disobeyed him, the contact with his body had mildly stimulated her. Nothing major, just a minor annoying tingle.

She reached for the door handle.

"Stop!" he shouted suddenly.

She stopped.

"Don't get out of the car," he said. "Pee off the edge of the seat. Your back will be toward me, so I won't be able to see you. You can use this Kleenex when you're done. If you try and escape, I'll shoot you. Do you understand me?"

"Yes."

"Okay, now you can open the door."

She opened the door, swung her legs out, moved her butt forward to the edge of the seat, and hiked her skirt just high enough to get it out of the way. If she ran now, would he shoot her in the back? It was more than possible. He'd already killed his stepfather and three innocent women. If she didn't run now, wouldn't he kill her sooner or later anyway? Maybe she should run for it now and take her chances. Maybe not. The prospect of taking off now, waiting for the shot to rip into her back at any moment, was too frightening. Maybe if she did things the way he wanted her to now, later she could find a way to reason with him.

She pulled her underwear down over her hips and forward to her knees and peed off the side of the car, a blessed relief, then used the tissue he had given her to wipe herself dry. She pulled up her underwear, pulled down her skirt, swung her legs back into the car, and closed the door.

"Feel better?" he asked indulgently.

"Yes, thanks," she replied. "Tell me the truth."

"What?"

"Would you really have shot me in the back if I'd tried to run away?"

He stuck the gun under his left leg, turned on the left signal, and pulled back onto the interstate.

"Absolutely," he said.

CHAPTER 65

"ANY TV DINNERS left in the fridge?" Max asked, closing and relocking the front door.

"I thought you had a date with the lady shrink tonight," said Natale, looking up from a stack of psychological evaluations of detectives in the Hostage Negotiation Unit.

"Yeah, so did I," said Max.

"So what happened?"

"I don't know," said Max. "Either she got unavoidably detained or I got stood up. I'm trying to decide."

"Stood up?" said Natale. "How the hell could you have got stood up?"

Max shrugged. "Hey," he said, "it's been known to happen."

"Uh-oh, self-pity alert!" said Natale, cupping his hands and speaking into them. "Wooop! Wooop! Wooop! Now hear this: You are entering an area containing dangerously low levels of self-esteem. Please proceed with caution."

"Are there any TV dinners left or aren't there?"

"No, but there's a giant slice of pepperoni pizza left over from a succulent repast I enjoyed scarcely a year ago. It was quick-frozen to lock in all of its savory goodness, and I'd be more than willing to sell to you for only half a buck."

"Tony," said Max, "your sensitivity is exceeded only by your generosity. I am deeply moved."

CHAPTER 66

AROUND 10 P.M. Andy told Dr. Stevenson that he was starving and turned off the interstate, looking for a place to eat. He followed a poorly lit two-lane blacktop for several miles until he saw something that looked promising, a roadhouse that served sandwiches and drinks. There were two cars and three pickup trucks in the parking lot. He pulled in and stopped, gravel crunching under the tires.

He opened the glove compartment and took something metallic out of it. It had two parts that clacked together and glinted in the reflected light from the parking lot. Handcuffs.

"Dr. Stevenson, would you prefer that I cuff you to the steering wheel and bring you something back here?" he asked. "Or would you like to come in there with me?"

"Come in there with you," she said.

"And do you understand what will happen to you if you ask anyone for help or try to escape?"

"Yes."

"Good girl," he said. "Let me come around the other side and let you out."

He was not doing this to be gallant; he was doing this to prevent her from running away if she got out of her side first. He came around the other side and gave her his hand. Maybe he *was* doing it to be gallant, she thought.

A swarm of moths and beetles was hovering and bumping around the light in the parking lot. A neon sign reading MICHELOB buzzed and snapped like a bug zapper. He opened the door and they went inside.

There was a line of booths along the windows and a counter with a row of uncomfortable-looking backless stools. There was the heavy aroma of frying food and the sound of grease popping and spitting on a griddle.

"So how are you guys doin' tonight?" asked a waitress cheerily, showing them to a booth.

"Couldn't possibly be better," said Andy. "How are *you* tonight?"

"Real good," she said. "You want me to tell you our specials?"

"Absolutely," said Andy.

They sat down in the red leatherette booth, facing each other. There were paper placemats with puzzles and games on them. A paper cup held crayons to use on the place mats.

"Well, the shrimp scampi is about all we got left," she said. "To be honest, I don't know I'd recommend it *personally*, but you look over these menus and I'm sure you'll find lotsa things to tempt you."

She handed them each a menu encased in heavy plastic.

"You guys care for something to drink?" asked the waitress. "We're world famous for our margaritas."

"Dear?" said Andy to Grace.

"I'll have a double vodka," said Grace.

"A sidecar on the rocks for me," said Andy.

"Be right back," said the waitress and withdrew.

Grace looked at her placemat. "What is wrong with this picture?" it asked. There were ten things you were supposed to find that were wrong with it. There was also a crossword puzzle and a maze. Somebody had already done the maze.

"Look at all the things you can do on this placemat," said Andy. "Mazes, puzzles, finding things that don't belong. This could keep me busy all night."

If she were clever about it, she might be able to write something on the placemat unobtrusive enough to get by him but obvious enough for the waitress to notice after they left the restaurant.

"Boy, will you look at all the dishes they have on this menu," he said. "Steaks, lamb chops, chicken, fish, clams, lobsters, pasta, sushi—how could a place this small have a kitchen big enough to serve all these dishes?"

"It's amazing," she said.

What could she write that would be short enough to escape detection by Andy, but informative enough to motivate whoever found it to help her?

"I mean, where could they even *keep* all that stuff?" he said.

"I know," she said.

How did you begin a plea for help? she wondered. What is the proper form here to (1) get somebody's attention and (2) make it believable? *Help me, I'm being kidnapped.* Would anybody in the world ever take that communication seriously? It sounded like the old joke about the message in the Chinese fortune cookie—Help, I'm a prisoner in a Chinese fortune cookie factory.

The waitress returned with their drinks.

"You guys decided what you want or you need more time?" she asked.

Grace was queasy with fear, but hadn't eaten in hours and didn't know when she'd get another chance. "I guess I'll have a steak sandwich," she said.

"Sounds good," said Andy. "Two steak sandwiches, medium rare."

"Good choice," said the waitress. "Fries, baked, or mashed?"

Maybe simply a plea to call the state police. Or, better yet, to phone Max at Queens Homicide. Not too likely, but it was all she had. If only she knew his number there. She took a crayon out of the paper cup.

"Dear?" said Andy.

"Yes?" said Grace, temporarily flustered.

"Fried, baked, or mashed?"

"Oh, baked," said Grace.

"Baked for the little woman," said Andy. "Fries for me."

"Thanks, guys," said the waitress, leaving the table again.

Grace looked for a place on the place mat where her message would be unobtrusive, yet prominent enough to be seen by the waitress when she cleared the table.

"I hope you remember," said Andy, without taking his gaze from his own place mat, "that I have a gun in my pocket, Dr. Stevenson, and that anything that appears on your placemat other than puzzle solving is going to win you a hole in your chest."

The steak sandwich was surprisingly tender and tasty. She hadn't had steak in about twelve years, having been worried about cholesterol. She was absolutely nostalgic now about cholesterol worries.

She'd been an idiot to think she could get away with something as obvious as a plea for help on a placemat. Lucky he'd warned her before she'd actually written anything. What could she do now? Try to get into the restroom and find some way to leave a message there? With what? A lipstick? A plea for help written with lipstick on a piece of toilet paper and tossed out the restroom window?

"May I go to the restroom?" she asked.

"I'm afraid I can't allow that, Dr. Stevenson."

"But I really have to go."

"You went when we were in the car."

"That was a while ago," she said. "I have to go again."

He didn't answer.

"I think my period is starting," she said. "I need to put in a tampon."

The tampon was a nice touch. Men were too grossed out to even talk about tampons.

"What happens if I don't let you go to the restroom?" he asked.

"It might get messy," she said. "I don't know how you feel about menstrual blood."

He got up from the booth. "Okay, let's *both* go to the restroom," he said.

"You're going to come inside with me?"

"Just to make sure it's safe for you in there."

He walked her back to the restrooms. Both doors had silhouettes of dogs on them. One had the word POINTERS on it, the other had the word SETTERS. He knocked on the one marked SETTERS, then swung it open and looked inside. There was a sink and a toilet, neither of which looked clean. To the left of the sink was a dispenser for liquid soap. Above the sink was a medicine cabinet with a cracked mirror on the front. There was a paper towel dispenser on the wall to the right of the sink, but it was empty. There was a wastebasket with a plastic bag inside of it. There was a window, but there were bars on it.

He opened the medicine cabinet and looked inside. Other than two glass shelves it was empty. He closed it. He looked in the wastebasket. There was nothing inside it.

"Well," he said, "I think you'll be safe in here, Dr. Stevenson. But you'd better leave your purse with me."

"But I need my purse," she said.

"Why?"

"My tampons are in there."

"Then take one out before you give it to me."

She took a tampon out of her purse, and also a lipstick and some mascara, figuring she might be able to use either of them to write with.

"What are those for?" he asked.

"I'd like to freshen up a little."

"You're fresh enough," he said. He took back the lipstick, the mascara, and her purse. "If you want to write messages, you'll have to use something else."

He left the bathroom. She closed the door and locked it. It was the first time she'd been away from him in hours. It was not a refuge but it was a breathing space.

What do I do now? she thought. *What the hell do I do now? What if I simply don't open the door? What if I scream and raise a fuss? Will the waitress or the bartender or a customer come to my aid or will he shoot me right through the door?* She wondered if his gun could shoot through a door. She looked at the barred window and wondered if she could compress herself flat enough to squeeze through it. Not a chance unless she left her head behind.

She took the wrapper off the tampon and looked at the white cardboard applicator. Her period wasn't starting, but the ruse had bought her a moment alone. If only she could think of a way to use it.

She studied the applicator. It looked like a writing implement. *Here is my pen*, she thought. *Now where is my ink?* She looked around the small restroom. Not much to work with.

He knocked on the door.

"How are you doing in there, Dr. Stevenson?"

"Fine," she said. "I'll just be a moment."

Where is my ink? she thought. Her eyes traveled to the liquid soap dispenser on the sink. She went to it and pushed on the lever. A pool of liquid pink soap squirted into her palm. *Here is my ink*, she thought. *Where is my paper?*

She flushed the toilet and used the sound to mask opening the door of the medicine cabinet. *Here is my paper*, she thought.

Working rapidly, she dipped the tampon applicator in the pool of pink liquid soap in her hand and began to write on the glass shelves of the medicine cabinet. On the first glass shelf she wrote:

HELP CALL DET. SEGAL

"Dr. Stevenson?" called Andy through the door. "Are you all right?"

"Yes," she said. "I'll be out soon."

On the next glass shelf she wrote:

QUEENS HOMICIDE NYC

"What's taking so long?"

"Female troubles," she said. "Nothing serious. Just a little blood."

On the bottom white metal shelf she wrote:

GRACE STEVENSON

She flushed again, using the sound to mask closing the medicine cabinet door. She threw the applicator into the waste paper basket, then visualized him taking it out and inspecting it, wondering why it had pink soap on the end of it and why the tampon with the string was still inside it.

She washed off the applicator, tossed it back into the trash and flushed the tampon down the toilet, just as she heard the sound of a lock being sprung and the door opening inward.

"I'm sorry to invade your privacy," he said, looking around, "but I was getting worried about you."

"I'm fine," she said.

"I'm relieved to hear that," he said. He looked around the room, peered into the wastebasket. He looked at the window for a long moment, then at the medicine cabinet. He took a step toward the medicine cabinet.

"I'd sure like some dessert if they have apple pie à la mode," she said. "You think they have apple pie à la mode? I *love* apple pie à la mode."

He looked at her thoughtfully, examining the remark for other meanings.

"Good idea," he said finally, guiding her out of the bathroom and back to the booth.

She realized that her bathroom expedition had been an exercise in futility. If anyone ever looked inside the medicine cabinet it wouldn't be for at least a week, they wouldn't know what to do with what she'd written on the shelves, and that it hardly mattered because by then she'd be dead.

***

"Well, night now," said the waitress, as the attractive couple got up from the booth and made their way to the door. "I hope you guys enjoyed your supper."

"We did," said the young man. "Everything was fantastic."

They went out to the parking lot and the waitress began stacking their dishes and silverware on her tray. When she picked up the placemats she noted that the man had completed his entire crossword puzzle in ink. The woman hadn't even touched hers. The man had left a rather large tip.

Cute couple, she thought, although the wife was twice as old as the husband. Pretty gorgeous guy, too. Wonder how somebody her age landed something that gorgeous. Probably had a ton of money is how. She envied the wife. Some people had all the damned luck.

CHAPTER 67

WHEN THEY EXITED the restaurant he led her around to the rear of the building where the restrooms were. He walked back and forth under the windows, looking at the ground in the dim light, then apparently decided that she had thrown nothing out of the window of the ladies' room.

"Well," he said, "you really behaved yourself in there, Dr. Stevenson. I'm proud of you."

"Thanks," she said.

"I wasn't going to risk it, but now I may just get us a motel room for tonight. Do you think you can behave yourself as well in a motel as you did in that diner?"

"Exactly as well," she said.

"That's what I like to hear," he said.

Two hours later they pulled into the parking lot of the Quality Courts Motel, which featured a TV, heated pool, a small playground with swings and teeter-totters for the kiddies, and XXX-rated features for the parents.

He took her into the office and registered. He gave their names as Mr. and Mrs. Will Emerson. Will Emerson was the warden at St. Albans.

"I am deeply sorry to inquire," said the short, diffident, dark-skinned man behind the desk, "but would your stay with us be limited to but a single night?"

Grace thought he sounded Pakistani. *How the hell does a man from Pakistan end up working in a tiny motel in the boondocks?* she wondered.

"Yes, just the one night," said Andy. "We're going to try and make New York tomorrow."

The possible Pakistani nodded seriously.

"I have the misfortune to inform you that this would be a long journey for a single day," he said, "yet I believe that it would be possible for you to be successful, notwithstanding."

The motel room was small but extremely clean and neatly kept. There were two queen-sized beds with a nightstand between them. There was a phone on the nightstand and an ashtray. There was a dresser facing the beds, and above it a flat-screen TV bolted to the wall. There were two landscapes, so ineptly painted it was hard to see why anyone thought they deserved to be framed, yet they were bolted to the wall in case a guest with unimaginably bad taste had an urge to steal them. There was a small desk with a chair next to it. There was a door to a bathroom on the far side of the bedroom.

He led her to the bathroom and looked inside it. No window in this one. A tub with a white plastic shower curtain around it. A toilet with a blue paper sanitary strip around the seat. A sink with a fake marble counter on which stood two thin plastic tumblers enclosed in sealed polyethylene wrappers. A stack of thin white towels—bath towels the size of hand towels, hand towels the size of washcloths. Two wrapped bars of soap—the bath bar the size of facial soap, the facial soap the size of a chocolate mint.

"Would you like to wash up for bed before I do?" he asked.

"Okay."

"Just a minute," he said.

He went to the bag on the bed that he'd brought in from the car. He unzipped it, took out a toothbrush in a cardboard container sealed in cellophane and handed it to her.

"Thank you," she said.

"Sealed for your protection," he said. Then he handed her a tube of toothpaste. "I chose a brand with extra whitening power," he said. "Original flavor rather than mint. Would you have preferred the mint?"

"I much prefer the original flavor," she said. "Shall I sleep in my clothes?"

"No," he said, once more fishing in the bag on the bed. He took out a flat package and handed it to her.

She tore it open. A nightgown, neatly folded. She took out the pins and let it fall open. A rather demure, old-fashioned, full length white silk nightgown. It was even her size. She looked at him oddly.

"You bought this for me?"

He nodded.

"How did you know my size?"

He shrugged.

"I know you, Dr. Stevenson," he said. "Do you think I'd be marrying somebody I didn't know?"

She studied his face. She wondered if it was possible he actually thought he knew her.

"Andy, preparing to marry somebody is a . . . a complex and time-consuming process," she said. "Apart from the terribly important emotional and psychological factors, which you seem to be ignoring, there are the somewhat banal procedural ones. As I'm sure you know, we'd need a blood test, a marriage license, a-a . . . We'd need to make a lot of other preparations in advance. Preparations that take a great deal of time. You can't just take someone somewhere and marry them on the spur of the moment."

"You can in Las Vegas," he said.

Las Vegas! So that's where he was taking them. He'd grown up in Las Vegas. His mother had married the man he'd killed, in a quickie wedding chapel in Las Vegas! And now he was taking her at gunpoint to get married there. Soon she would be legally married to a serial murderer.

"You killed those three women, didn't you?" she asked gently.

He didn't answer her.

"You can tell me if you like," she said. "You don't have to if you don't want to."

He sighed. He looked past her to the wall. A memory began to assemble.

"She started in on me the night I arrived," he said finally. "Trying to seduce me. Getting me drunk. Climbing into bed with me. She said I came out of her body and I was still an extension of it. She said she could use me for sex anytime she wanted and it wouldn't be incest, it would be masturbation."

He swallowed and stopped talking for a moment. "I threw up. She said it was because I was a fag. Another night she came into my room naked, wearing a mask." He stopped again, replaying the video in his head. "I tried using my VOP cycle to stop. It didn't work."

"And you're angry about that," she said.

"Fuck *yes*, I'm angry!" he replied. "Why didn't it work, Dr. Stevenson? And why didn't *you* heal me? Why didn't you heal me in the joint?"

"I wasn't there to heal you, Andy," she said. "I was there to evaluate you."

"Why didn't the fucking system heal me then? Why didn't the fucking VOP heal me?"

"Cognitive work alone can't heal you," she said. "You need to develop relationships. Trusting relationships."

He laughed bitterly. "I had one of those with you," he said. "But you betrayed me."

"How did I betray you?"

"You know."

"Tell me."

"You came down to New York to help them catch me."

"Andy, they called me in Vermont and told me that three women had been killed," she said. "They told me you were a suspect. If you weren't responsible for those deaths, I wanted to clear you. If you *were* responsible, I wanted to take you out of a situation where you were hurting others and put you back in one where you wouldn't be able to do that, where you could be helped."

"You even fucked the cop who brought you here," he said. "How could you do that to me?"

"Andy, what I do or don't do with my own body is my business and doesn't concern you."

"Yes it does."

"Why?"

"Because we meant something to each other."

"We did," she said. "We do. I have a lot of compassion for you."

"Bullshit."

"You don't think I have compassion for you?"

"I think part of you has compassion for me," he said. "And part of you wants to have my cock in your pussy."

"I think you're merely projecting your own fantasies onto me."

"Oh, you deny that you want to have my cock in your pussy?"

"I most certainly do deny it, yes. My feelings for you are purely professional and compassionate."

"We'll see about that," he said ominously, then changed his tone abruptly. "Okay, put on your nightgown."

"May I close the door while I change?" she asked.

"Oh, I would insist upon that," he said.

She closed the door and slowly took off her clothes. The past two nights she had spent in a luxurious hotel, making love to a gentle and loving homicide detective. Tonight she would spend in a cheap motel with a dangerous serial killer. She had no idea whether he would assault her sexually.

She washed her body and brushed her teeth and put on the white silk nightgown. It was, indeed, a perfect fit. She took one of the pins which had held the nightgown folded and looked at it. When Marie Antoinette was jailed by the French revolutionaries, they took away her writing implements but permitted her to keep her sewing. Marie used a needle to perforate a message into a piece of paper and managed to get it out of prison. It hadn't helped Marie, but it might help Grace.

There was a knock at the door.

"Leave your underwear in the sink and I'll wash it for you," he called.

She hid the pin in the rear of the drawer in the fake marble counter and opened the door.

"You look very beautiful," he said softly.

"Thank you," she said.

"Give me your left hand."

She extended her left hand. He took something out of his pocket and fit it around her left wrist. Something thin, made of black leather, with a buckle and a ring.

"What is that?" she asked.

"A dog collar," he said. "Size ten. Give me your right hand."

"What are you doing?" she asked uneasily.

"Give me your right hand," he said.

She gave him her right hand. He took a second dog collar out of his pocket and fit it around her right wrist.

"Why are you doing this?" she said.

He dropped to one knee, took a third dog collar out of his pocket and fit it around her left ankle. Then he took a fourth dog collar out of his pocket and fit it around her right ankle. Then he straightened up.

"Do you prefer to sleep on your back or on your stomach?" he asked.

"On my stomach. Why?"

"Your bed is the one farthest from the door," he said. "Go to it now and lie down on your stomach."

"What are you going to do?"

"Do as you're told," he said.

She did as she was told. She lay down on her stomach. He came up beside her and snapped a dog leash onto the collar of her left wrist and secured it to one side of the headboard. Then he snapped a second leash onto her right wrist and secured this to the other side of the headboard.

"Please don't do this," she said.

He didn't appear to have heard her, so intent was he on what he was doing. His breathing sounded labored. He attached a third leash to her left ankle and a fourth to her right and secured these to the foot of the bed.

"Why are you doing this?" she said.

"Because," he said, controlling his breathing, "I don't want to have to lie awake all night, waiting for you to do something cunning."

When he was satisfied that she couldn't move, he turned off the lights in the bedroom and went into the bathroom to wash up for bed. She heard him lock the door. Why in God's name had he locked the door? Did he imagine that she could get out of bed and invade his privacy in the bathroom? That she would *want* to invade his privacy in the bathroom?

She tried to find slack in the leashes which secured her arms. Surprisingly, there was a little. She thought there might be enough to bring either of her wrists in close enough to reach the buckle with her teeth. She was wrong. He had only allowed enough slack to permit her a very limited range of movement upon the mattress.

The realization that she couldn't move presented her with an uncomfortable mix of feelings: dread and stimulation. Which was the more uncomfortable of the two? "You have an attachment to Mr. Woods," Harry had told her, "an attachment that you're not comfortable with. You're transferring something to him from your own childhood . . ."

She imagined Andy emerging from the bathroom, coming to her bed, assaulting her sexually. She felt weak. She didn't want to be raped, by Andy or by anybody else, so why the fantasies? She wasn't masochistic, not really. She joked about it, but she truly didn't enjoy pain at all. "I don't believe the rape fantasy comes from wanting to be hurt by Mr. Woods," Harry had told her. "I believe it comes from not wanting to be responsible for your sexual feelings toward him."

She heard the door being unlocked and opened. The light from the bathroom spilled through the half-opened door. Heard him come into the bedroom and stop. Realized he was standing behind her at the foot of her bed. Looking at her. Thinking what he wanted to do. Thinking, perhaps, about his VOP cycle.

She heard the creak of knees. Then nothing. Then something brushed the sole of her right foot. Something soft and a trifle moist. Lips. Then a hand tentatively brushed her ankle, the fingers slipping around it in a loose grip. The grip tightening. The lips moving slowly up her ankle to her calf. Up her calf to the hem of her long silk nightgown and the concavity behind her knee. His lips lingered there. Then they withdrew.

He's stopping, she thought, not daring to breathe, not able to breathe. *He's stopping.*

Then she felt the hem of her nightgown being slowly lifted above the backs of her knees, slowly up the backs of her thighs. She felt his warm breath on the back of one thigh, and then his lips, warmer and moister than before. She felt the hem of her nightgown ascend to the base of her buttocks and stop. Then she felt it pulled up over her buttocks to her waist. She was very conscious of his eyes on her body. She could almost feel their caress.

She felt the tickle of his hair against the inside of her left thigh as he kissed the inside of her right thigh. And then, abruptly, she felt him withdraw, felt the hem of her nightgown being pulled smartly back down over her buttocks, over her thighs, over the backs of her knees, over her calves.

"I'm sorry, Dr. Stevenson," she heard him say, "I'm so sorry. Please forgive me."

A sheet was placed over her back and legs. The bathroom door was pulled slightly more closed, dimming the light in the room. She heard him sink down on his own mattress.

Out in the parking lot she heard a woman's drunken laughter.

CHAPTER 68

SHE DOZED FITFULLY, her limbs sore from being unable to move, waking often to listen to Andy moaning in his sleep.

When the dark blue outside turned to light blue she felt she couldn't take it anymore. She woke him and told him how sore she was. He got up and sat down on her bed, unsnapped the dog leashes and massaged her arms and legs for several minutes. His hands were strong and his touch was sure and tender. She wished it was Max.

She asked if she could go to the bathroom and he said yes. She went inside and locked the door behind her. She sat down on the toilet and reached into the wastebasket and took out some of the wrapping from the nightgown. Then she opened the drawer in the fake marble counter, took out the pin and began to perforate the paper, spelling out letters as best she could.

HELP CALL, she wrote. She flushed the toilet to make it seem that she was there for a purpose, then continued. DET. SEGAL QUEENS HOMICIDE NYC, she wrote and flushed a final time. She slid the message into the drawer, washed her hands, and reentered the bedroom.

Before they checked out she would somehow manage to transfer the message from inside the drawer to the inside of the pillowcase on her bed. When the chambermaid changed the sheets, perhaps it would fall out and be noticed.

CHAPTER 69

THIS MORNING AT 7 A.M. Max didn't even stop at the house phones, he walked right past them to the elevators. If one of the hotel security people had asked where he was going he would have simply flashed his shield. No one asked where he was going. He took the elevator up to the fourteenth floor and walked to room 1418.

After a friendly session of ego-pumping with Natale last night, he'd concluded that Grace hadn't stood him up after all. He'd phoned her at midnight, at 1 A.M., at 2 A.M., and then again at 6 A.M. and gotten no answer. The hotel insisted she hadn't checked out.

He'd thought of trying to get a warrant to search her room, but he hadn't thought about it for long. Search warrants were a damned waste of time. They were granted solely at the discretion of the judge, and judges were quirky. On this one a judge would doubtlessly turn him down on probable cause. What he had was a hunch, and a hunch wasn't enough for a search warrant.

He took out the Sacred Heart of Jesus mass card that P. J. McCleary had given him, slid it between door and jamb, and slipped the lock. The door opened easily. There were Grace's belongings still scattered about. And the bed was made. She hadn't been back to her room last night to sleep, just as he'd suspected.

He was getting a really bad feeling about this one. The fact that Grace had vanished just two days after Andy Woods couldn't be coincidence. He had a fairly strong hunch that Andy had grabbed her, but why would he grab her and where would he take her?

Grace said that Andy had developed a crush on her in the joint. If Andy had seen Max and Grace together in New York, it could have set him off. But how could he have seen them together? *Where* could he have seen them together? Well, Max and Grace had gone to dinner in Midtown Manhattan two nights in succession. Andy's mother's apartment was in Midtown Manhattan. It was possible that Andy had simply run into them by chance.

It was more likely that he'd been stalking either one of them. If that were the case, he could have seen them most easily just outside Grace's hotel. And if, when he spotted them, they were being affectionate . . .

Max let himself out of Grace's room and went back down to the lobby, thinking hard, moving mental furniture around, his forehead tight against his banging thoughts.

CHAPTER 70

ON THE ROAD again. It was shortly after one in the morning. Grace's turn to drive.

She passed two state police cars that were pulled up on the grass of the median to the left. They were parked alongside each other, facing opposite directions in the sixty-nine position that enabled the driver of one car to speak directly to the driver of the other.

She subtly increased her pressure on the accelerator and watched the speedometer needle creep past sixty-five toward seventy.

"Hey, slow down there, Dr. Stevenson," said Andy. "You're doing seventy."

"Am I?" she said. "Gosh, I'm sorry."

She released the pressure on the gas pedal. The car slowed gradually back to sixty.

"I sincerely hope you weren't exceeding the speed limit in order to have those two cop cars stop us."

She shook her head.

Grace kept her eye on the receding image of the two police cars on the grass, then saw first one and then the other one pull off the median and into the fast lane. She heard the first siren start up with a low growl and swiftly ascend the scale. The stuttering red-and-blue strobe lights on the roof racks of both cruisers began their erratic blinking.

"Shit!" said Andy.

"I'm sorry," said Grace.

"All right, pull over," he said.

"I'm so sorry," she said.

Grace clicked on her right turn signal, slowed way down, bounced up onto the shoulder and stopped. The first police cruiser pulled up behind them. The second one pulled up ahead of them.

"You are now going to be given a speeding ticket," he said. "When that happens, you may discover in yourself an almost overwhelming urge to give the arresting officers some inkling of your situation here."

He took out his revolver, checked the cylinder, and put it back in his pocket.

"Should you give in to that inclination and should they seem about to arrest us," he said, "please know that I will shoot them first and you second."

"I won't do anything to make them suspicious," said Grace.

"Even if you don't," he said, "if they seem about to arrest us, I will shoot them first and you second."

The officers in both cars remained in their vehicles.

"Why don't they get out of their cars and come over here?" Grace asked.

"Because they're running our plates through their computer system to see if this is a stolen vehicle," said Andy.

"Jesus, this is making me nervous," said Grace.

"It's making *you* nervous?" said Andy.

Her first inclination upon spotting the cop cars had indeed been to invite a speeding ticket and somehow alert them to her situation, but now she realized how naive she'd been. There was no way at all to tell them she was being kidnapped without creating horrific consequences.

At long last both officers got out of their vehicles. The one from the car in back came up on the passenger's side. The one from the car in front came up on the driver's side, one hand carrying a metal clipboard, the other hand on his weapon. He had a full mustache and, although it was quite dark out, he was wearing mirrored aviator sunglasses. Grace sensed a man with a shaky sense of his own masculinity and felt compassion for him.

"Would you please hand me your license and registration, ma'am?" said the officer with the mirrored sunglasses in a flat voice.

Grace took out her wallet, opened it to her driver's license, and handed it through the open window along with the contract from the rental agency.

"Would you please take your license out of your wallet and hand it to me, ma'am?" in the same flat voice.

"I'm sorry," said Grace.

She retrieved the wallet, took out the license, and handed it back to him. The officer looked at the license, the rental contract, and then at Grace.

"Are you aware of the speed limit in this area, ma'am?" he asked.

"Yes, officer," she said.

"And can you tell me what that speed limit is, ma'am?"

"Fifty-five?"

"Are you asking me or telling me?"

"Telling you," she said. "It's fifty-five."

"And are you aware that you were doing seventy-three miles per hour in an area zoned for fifty-five?"

"I'm sorry, officer," she said. "I wasn't aware I was speeding."

The officer copied down Grace's name and license number on his clipboard.

"What was your big hurry?" he asked.

She inhaled deeply and let the breath out slowly. She shook her head.

"I don't know," she said.

Two big tears, one in each eye, popped out and slid down her cheeks.

"Are you all right, ma'am?" he asked in another tone.

She shook her head. "No, I'm not," she said, aware that she was doing something dangerous.

"We're on our way to Nevada to be married, officer," said Andy brightly. "My fiancée is just beginning to get cold feet, that's all."

"Cold feet?" said the officer.

"That's right," said Andy.

"You're having second thoughts about the marriage, ma'am?" asked the officer.

She nodded her head.

"If you're having second thoughts about the marriage," he said, "then you ought to stop and think it over."

"Yes, sir."

"Marriage is a very important step, ma'am," said the officer. "It may not be what you really want to do."

"It may not be," she said.

"My advice to you is don't do anything you don't really want to do, so you won't be sorry later," said the officer, handing her the speeding ticket. "Will you remember that?"

She felt the officer was speaking not to her but to himself.

"Don't do anything I don't really want to do, so I won't be sorry later," she said. "Okay, I'll try to remember that."

When the officer had given Grace her speeding ticket and both policemen had gotten back into their vehicles and driven away, she put the car in gear and pulled shakily back onto the interstate.

"You did that deliberately," said Andy. "Didn't you?"

"No I didn't," she said. "I swear."

"You did it deliberately," he said. "And you're going to have to be taught a lesson. I'm going to make you feel as uncomfortable as you made me feel back there. Take the first exit you see."

"What are you going to do?" she asked.

"Something truly unpleasant," he said.

CHAPTER 71

"PLAY A GAME with me, Tony," said Max, standing in the bedroom doorway.

"Max, gimme a break, it's two A.M.," said Natale's voice from inside the darkened bedroom. "I gotta be up in four hours."

"Just give me two minutes, Tony. Please."

A gigantic sigh. "Two minutes, Max, but that's it."

"Thanks, Tony," said Max. He sat down on the floor near the doorway. "Okay, say you're Andy Woods."

"Yeah . . ."

"Say you develop a crush on the shrink who's sent to evaluate you in the joint. Say you're paroled, and your demons drive you to commit three homicides. You learn the cops are checking you out as a suspect. And then you run into your very own beloved shrink being affectionate with another guy. Not only with another guy, but with one of the very homicide cops you know considers you a suspect. What do you do?"

"Kill the cop, kill the bitch who betrayed me."

"Right," said Max. "And if you couldn't do that?"

"I don't know. Steal the bitch away from the other guy and keep her somewhere till I can win her back again."

"Right," said Max. "So you snatch her how? Off the street?"

"Off the street, yeah."

"Put a gun in her back, march her off down the avenue, and pull her into a vehicle?"

"Into a vehicle," said Natale. "Catch her unaware, then pull her into a vehicle, put a knife up against her throat, and convince her to accompany me."

"What kind of a vehicle?"

"Stolen," said Natale.

"Not stolen," said Max. "You get stopped in a stolen vehicle on a moving violation, they run your plates, then either you're collared or you have a shoot-out."

"Okay, a rented car."

"Yeah, a rented car, that's what I think," said Max. "And then you take her where?"

"I don't know."

"Somewhere in New York State?"

"Yeah," said Natale. "Somewhere in New York State. I know New York State. I'm going to take her somewhere I know."

"Okay, but say you decide that's too risky," said Max. "Somebody could spot you. The cops, a friend, whoever. You've got a rented car, where else could you go?"

"Somewhere else I know," said Natale. "Where else does he know?"

"Vermont," said Max.

"Yeah," said Natale, "Vermont. Back to wherever their summer house was in Vermont."

"Lake Champlain," said Max.

"Yeah," said Natale. "Back to Lake Champlain. Or maybe even back to where the prison is."

"St. Albans," said Max.

"Yeah," said Natale. "Back to St. Albans. Even though I don't want to go back inside the joint itself, there's something reassuring to me about the neighborhood. Something familiar. Hey, Max, that's it. I'm off to dreamland."

"Where else besides Vermont?"

"Max, my eyes are closed and I'm sleeping," said Natale.

"Would you go back to Vegas where you grew up?"

"No," said Natale. "Too many bad memories. Max, I'm seriously asleep."

"So Lake Champlain or St. Albans, right?"

"I'm not speaking another syllable," said Natale. "I can't even hear you anymore, that's how deep in delta I am."

CHAPTER 72

FOLLOWING HIS DIRECTIONS, she got off the highway at the next exit and followed the access road to the intersection. She turned right and drove till they came to a roadhouse with only three cars in the parking lot. She pulled in and turned off the motor.

"I've been thinking about what scares you," he said. "About what makes you really uncomfortable. Do you know what I came up with?"

"What?"

"Hurting other people," he said. "I think you hate hurting other people. I really think you'd rather be hurt yourself than hurt another human being."

"So?"

"So to punish you for your little stunt back there, we're going to play a game. We're going to go into this bar here and we're going to select a man drinking alone, preferably a drunkard, and then you're going to torment him."

"What do you mean torment him?" she asked.

"You'll tease him sexually, and then you'll humiliate him. You'll abuse him verbally. Finally, you'll take this out of your pocket and show it to him, and rob him of his wallet."

He put something small, heavy, and metallic into her hand. It looked like a gun.

"It's not a gun," he said. "It's a cigarette lighter. But you can convince him it's a gun. Once you do, he'll give you his wallet quite readily."

"And if I refuse to do this?" she asked. "What will you do, kill me?"

"No, Dr. Stevenson, if you refuse I won't kill you. I'll kill *him*. Because what's in my pocket isn't a cigarette lighter."

She nodded. She would try not to think of this as abusing a drunk. She would try to think of this as saving his life.

———

They entered the bar. There was the smell of stale cigarettes and the sweet heavy smell of putrefying beer. There were only three people in the bar. The bartender was talking to one man at the far end of the bar, next to the huge flat-screen TV on the wall. The other man was closer to the door than to the TV. On the TV was a rodeo with the sound turned down. Men trying to ride bulls and being flung into the air.

"Take the stool just to the left of the man nearest the door," said Andy in her ear.

Grace sat down on the stool to the man's left. Andy took the seat to Grace's left. The bartender was engrossed in his conversation with the man near the TV and didn't seem to notice he had more customers.

"Make friends with him," said Andy in Grace's left ear.

"Andy," she said, "don't do this. Please don't."

"Start making friends with him by the time I count to five," said Andy in her ear, "or he's a dead man."

She didn't reply. On the TV a rodeo clown was trying to distract a bull away from a man lying in the dirt.

"One," said Andy.

"Can we go back in the car and discuss this?" she said.

"Two," said Andy.

"I'm beginning to feel faint," she said.

"Three," said Andy.

"I mean it," she said. "I think I'm going to slide right off this stool onto the floor."

"Four," said Andy.

She shook her head and turned to the man on her right.

"What are you drinking?" she asked.

"Cutty and water, honey," he said, looking at her for the first time. "Howsabout you?"

He had watery blue eyes, oily white hair, and the ruddy complexion of a heavy drinker. Capillaries had exploded under his skin like roman candles in a Fourth of July sky. He was in his mid-sixties. She could smell his shaving lotion, something cheap and sweet, mixed with perspiration and whiskey.

"I haven't ordered yet," she said.

"Hey, bartender!" the man yelled. "Howsabout some service down at this end!"

The bartender didn't seem to have heard him.

"You want me to get you a drink, doll?" asked the man. "I'll get it for you personally."

"That would be lovely," said Grace. "A vodka martini, please."

"And what about your friend here?" He looked at Andy.

"A sidecar on the rocks for me," said Andy.

"A sidecar on the rocks and a vodka martooni coming up," said the man, lurching off the stool and making his way down the bar.

"Okay," said Andy, "end of Act One. You're off to a good start. The bartender isn't even going to notice what you're doing. Does this guy remind you at all of your father?"

"Of my father?"

"Yes, you told me your father was an alcoholic."

"He's . . . a little reminiscent of my father," she said. "He doesn't look like him physically, but he's a little reminiscent of him in other ways."

"Good," said Andy. "When he comes back, start being seductive. Tell him how sexy he is for an older guy. Put your arm around him. Kiss him."

"Andy, why are you doing this? What is the point of this?"

"To help you," he said. "To help you delve into your past and get in touch with the massive amount of buried rage you feel toward your alcoholic father. This will be terribly therapeutic for you, Dr. Stevenson, just wait and see."

At the other end of the bar she could see the bartender preparing their drinks. She felt an overwhelming anxiety about what he wanted her to do, an anxiety equal to her fear of death. Perhaps he could be distracted from this game. Perhaps an outright appeal to lust.

"Stop this now and let's go to a motel and make love," she said.

"Oho!" he said. "I *told* you you wanted to have my cock in your pussy."

"If you stop this game now you can take me to a motel and have sex with me. I give you my permission."

"I don't *need* to have your permission to have sex with you, Dr. Stevenson," he said. "You belong to me now. I'm gratified to learn that you want me, but when I make love to you it will be under my own terms. It will be as my wife."

The drunk came back down the bar, carrying their drinks precariously.

"All right, Dr. Stevenson," said Andy, "you're on again. Act Two."

"Well, here we are," said the drunk. "A vodka martooni and a . . . what?"

"A sidecar on the rocks," said Andy.

"Right, a sidecar on the rocks," said the drunk.

He gave Andy his drink, then placed Grace's in her hands and placed both of his hands around hers.

"Thank you," said Grace.

She put the drink to her lips and drank off half of it. It burned her mouth and her throat all the way down to her stomach. She didn't entirely dislike the sensation.

"So what's the story here?" said the drunk. "The two of you married or what?"

"No," said Grace, "he's my kid brother."

"Your kid *brother*," said the drunk. "That's good."

"Why is it good?" Grace asked.

"Because then maybe I got a shot at you."

"Would you like a shot at me?" Grace asked.

"You bet I would," said the drunk.

"Put your arm around him," said Andy sotto voce in her left ear. She made no move to comply.

"One," said Andy in her ear.

"What's your name?" Grace asked.

"Herb," said the drunk. "What's yours?"

"Two," said Andy in her ear.

"Esther," said Grace.

"Esther?" said the drunk. "Glad to meetcha, Esther."

"Three," said Andy in her ear.

"Glad to meet you, too, Herb," said Grace.

"You don't live around here, doya, Esther?" said the drunk.

"Four," said Andy in her ear.

"No," said Grace, "we're just passing through."

"Aw," said the drunk. "I kinda hoped you lived around here."

"He's a dead man," said Andy in her ear. "Kiss him good-bye."

Shuddering with revulsion, she put her arm around the drunk and kissed him on the forehead.

"Hey," said the drunk delightedly. "And to what do I owe this honor, young lady?"

"You just saved his life," whispered Andy in her ear.

"You remind me of somebody," she said.

295

"He must of been some guy," said the drunk.

"He was," she said.

"Well, allow me to return the favor," said the drunk and planted one on her lips. She was momentarily overwhelmed by his combination of sweat, sweet shaving lotion, scotch, and halitosis. She pushed him away and gulped down the rest of her drink.

"Hey," said the drunk, "there's a lady who can really put 'em away. You want me to get you another?"

Grace nodded.

"This time I'll make it a double," he said and lurched back down the bar.

"End of Act Two," said Andy. "So far so good. Your kid brother, eh?"

"I can't do this anymore," she said. "I'm going to be ill."

"You're doing a great job," said Andy. "I think you have a natural talent for this."

"If you keep forcing me to do this, I'm really going to vomit."

"Maybe so," he said, "but I think you're getting off on it. I think you get off on people forcing you to do things you wouldn't otherwise have the guts to do."

At the other end of the bar the drunk was getting her a double.

"If you stop this now," she said, "I promise you I'll do whatever you want me to."

"Thank you, Dr. Stevenson," he said. "You will anyway. When he comes back this time, I'd like you to be even more seductive with him. Run your fingers through his hair. Play with his belt buckle. Ask him about his sexual prowess. Ask him how big his cock is. Then begin making disparaging remarks. Really start humiliating him."

"I'm not doing any more of this."

"Then Herb will die a happy man," he said. "Do you know the Hemingway short story 'The Short Happy Life of Francis Macomber'? Well, this will be 'The Short Happy Life of Herb the Drunk'."

The drunk was coming back.

"Act Three," said Andy.

"Well, here we go," said the drunk. "A double vodka martooni."

Grace took it from him and drank off the top of it. It was considerably more than a double, but she welcomed the chance to turn off her mind. She felt the warmth spread throughout her body.

"Now," whispered Andy in her ear.

"So, Herb," said Grace, surprised to find her words slurring, "you a married guy?"

"Yeah," he said. "I been married a few times. I get married as often as I can, you know?"

"You have any kids?" Grace asked.

"Five that I know of," said the drunk with a chuckle.

"Run your fingers through his hair," whispered Andy in her ear.

"I can see why the women like you, Herb," she said, running her hand through his oily hair.

"Why does your brother keep whispering things in your ear?" asked the drunk.

"He's encouraging me," she said. "He thinks I need to have a love life."

"Good," whispered Andy in her ear.

"He's right," said the drunk. "You do need sex. We all do. People who have regular sex live eight years longer than the rest of us. They did a study."

"That so?" said Grace.

"Absolutely," said the drunk. "Eight years longer. You could Google it."

"Ask him about his sexual prowess," Andy whispered.

"So, Herb, how are you in the sack?" Grace asked. "You a pretty good lover?"

"I don't get many complaints," he said. "'Course, most of the women I fuck have passed out cold."

He cracked himself up with that one, wheezing with laughter.

"Ask him how big his cock is," said Andy.

"How big is your penis, Herb?" Grace asked.

"Big enough, honey," said the drunk. "Anyhoo, big enough to please you, don't worry."

"Is it more like a cucumber or more like a gherkin?" Grace asked, surprising herself.

"A gherkin?" said Andy delightedly in her ear.

"More like a cucumber," said the drunk. "A big fat ol' cucumber."

"Tell him you think it's more like a gherkin," said Andy.

"I'll bet it's more like a gherkin," said Grace, finding she didn't mind saying this, finding she didn't mind it at all. "I'll bet it's the size of a button mushroom. I'll bet it's so small I'd need a magnifying glass to even see it."

"Oho," said Andy in her ear.

"Hey," said the drunk, "what is this?"

"Tell him you think it's as limp as linguini," said Andy.

"I'll bet it's as limp as linguini," said Grace, beginning to feel a tightening in her chest, horrified to realize that abusing this man was actually beginning to excite her. "I'll bet after all the drinks you put away you couldn't get it harder than a marshmallow."

"You're cooking," Andy whispered. "Ask him if he ever abused his wives or kids when he was drunk."

"Tell me, Herb," she said, stroking his face, warming to her subject, drawing on old pictures, "when you were drunk, did you ever go home and act nasty to your wives or kids? Ever call them names, make them feel worthless, run down their self-esteem, smack them around—nothing serious, just open-handed slaps on the face or on the butt—then feel sorry as hell the next day when you sobered up? Apologize all over the place for the things you'd said and done, even though you couldn't even remember what they were? You ever do anything like that?"

"Good girl," whispered Andy.

"Hey, Esther," said Herb, "what is this? What's going on here? I mean I thought you liked me. I thought we were getting along fine."

"I do like you, Herb," she said, feeling her heart thumping in her chest. "I like you so much I want to help you to stop drinking and to stop abusing yourself and your wives and kids. I want to get you into a twelve-step program."

"Show him the gun," said Andy. "Get his wallet."

"The first step in the program," said Grace, "is to cut off the supply of liquor. To cut off the supply of liquor, first we have to cut off the supply of money. So give me your wallet, Herb."

"What?" he said. He looked like a large sheepdog who'd just been given an unfamiliar command.

"Give me your wallet," she said.

Grace brought out the fake gun and held it under his face.

"Oh my God," he said.

"Give me your wallet, Herb," she said. "I like you too much to shoot you."

He reached into his back pocket and brought out his wallet and gave it to her. His hand was shaking. She opened the wallet and took out a wad of damp bills. She put a twenty down on the bar.

"This is for our drinks," she said and gave him back the empty wallet.

Andy and Grace got up from their stools.

"Thanks for the drinks, Herb," said Andy. "It was good to meet you. Oh, and if you call out for help before we're gone, or if you report this to the police after we leave, we'll come back here and blow your fucking head off."

"Well, congratulations, Dr. Stevenson," said Andy out in the parking lot. "Your very first felony."

She was so drunk she could barely walk. She put her hand on the hood of a car to steady herself.

"I can't believe I did that," she said.

"*I* can," he said. "And not only did you do it, you enjoyed it."

"I can't believe I actually said those things to that poor man and then pulled a gun and took his money."

"And paid for the drinks," he said. "That was a nice touch. You know, I think we could be the new Bonnie and Clyde."

"I think I'm going to vomit," she said.

"That's what you said before all this began. I notice it didn't stop you from committing armed robbery. I'd say you had a real aptitude for crime, Dr. Stevenson. Hey, if the psychotherapy thing doesn't work out, now you've got something you could fall back on."

CHAPTER 73

FIRST THING THE following morning Max and Caruso phoned the head offices of all major car rental agencies and asked whether any vehicles had been rented in either New York, Connecticut, or New Jersey on August 20, the day that Grace had disappeared, or the day following, by anyone named Stevenson or Woods. Nobody had anything.

Although the NYPD normally avoided the feds like the plague, Caruso felt obliged to notify the FBI. There was a matter of an interstate compact between Vermont and New York, and there was a possible interstate kidnapping involved.

Caruso was not at all surprised when the special agent he contacted in the New York FBI office blew him off: What evidence did Caruso have that Dr. Stevenson had been kidnapped at all? Did he have a ransom note? A ransom demand? Did he have a witness who'd seen Dr. Stevenson abducted by the paroled suspect? Caruso said he had none of these, but his partner Max had a very good hunch. The special agent laughed in Caruso's face.

At first Max and Caruso felt they'd run up against a brick wall, but then a representative from Hertz called back to say that records showed a rental to a Grace Stevenson on August 20, the day in question, from a franchise in Yonkers.

Max put an alarm out on the car and then ran a DMV check for all states within a two-day drive of New York. By nightfall he received a report that a speeding ticket had been issued to one Grace Stevenson by a state trooper named Halloran at 1:10 A.M. on August 21, not far from Topeka, Kansas.

"Sonofabitch," said Max aloud. "He's taking her to Las Vegas!"

CHAPTER 74

FOR OUT-OF-STATE ARRESTS it is necessary to secure an accusatory instrument like an arrest warrant. The DA's office is as reluctant to grant accusatory instruments as it is to pay detectives' preindictment travel expenses. Sometimes the NYPD will pay a detective's expenses on the way there and the DA will pay his expenses on the way back. Expenses are twenty-three dollars a day for food and seventy-five dollars a day for lodging. The detective usually puts up all the money for his trip up front and then gets reimbursed, but trips always end up costing more than the reimbursements.

"Boss, you got a minute?"

"Sure, Segal, what's up?" said Lieutenant Hickock, looking up from his computer screen. Max thought he could see handguns displayed on the screen, Colt six-shooters, but he wasn't sure.

"Boss, we have good reason to believe that Andy Woods has apprehended Grace Stevenson and is taking her by car to Las Vegas."

"Really?" said Hickock. "What's your evidence?"

"Well, Dr. Stevenson has been missing from her hotel room for two days now, and Andy Woods has been missing from his place of employment and from his mother's apartment for four . . ."

"And?"

"And there's evidence that Dr. Stevenson rented a car from Hertz two days ago in Yonkers and got a speeding ticket yesterday in Kansas."

"Uh-huh," said Hickock. "So how does that implicate Woods?"

"Well, would Dr. Stevenson leave all her stuff in a hotel room in New York, rent a car, and drive all the way to Kansas unless somebody was forcing her to do it?"

"I don't know, Segal, maybe she would. I don't know the woman, but I've seen people do a lot weirder things than that. And I'm still not hearing how you think this implicates Woods."

"You aren't, huh?"

"No."

"Because what I was hoping was that you'd okay a request for me to get expense money from the DA to fly out to Las Vegas and collar him."

"Based on what?"

"Based on what I just told you."

"What you just told me is pure conjecture, Segal. Even if the city weren't broke, it wouldn't send you to Vegas on pure conjecture."

"Could you at least try to go up the steps on this one for me, boss?"

"No," said Hickock. "Because if I go to the Chief of the Borough with what you've given me, I'm going to be laughed out of his office. You guys are on a wild goose chase with this, Segal. Start looking somewhere else."

"Is there any way at all that I could go to Vegas to try and track him down?" Max asked.

"Yeah," said Hickock, returning to his computer screen. "On your own time and on your own money."

CHAPTER 75

HOW YA DOIN', P. J.?"

"Still cruising wakes and funeral parlors, Max," said the plucky female detective, walking him into the Central Park Precinct squad room and taking a seat on a steel chair. "How's about you?"

"Not too good, actually," said Max, sitting down.

"Yeah, I heard."

"Oh? What did you hear?"

"That you think Andy Woods apprehended Grace Stevenson and is driving her to Vegas, but your boss put the kibosh on it."

"How in hell did you hear that?" Max asked.

She shrugged. "Things are slow here at the Central Park Precinct. Lots of time to gossip."

"Did you hear why we think that?"

"Yep. Personally, I tend to agree with you."

"You do?"

"Yep."

"Listen," said Max, "would you be willing to come back to Queens and talk to Hickock with us and try to convince him?"

"Sure," said P. J. "But it won't do you any good."

"Why not?"

"Because the city won't send more than one detective to collar a perp, and somebody else has already put in for expense money to go get Andy Woods."

"What are you saying?"

"Somebody decided not to go through channels, went straight to the chief of detectives, and got expense money to apprehend Woods in Burlington, Vermont."

"You're kidding me."

"Nope."

"Do you happen to know who this person was?"

"Yep. Your old buddy in the one-fourteen, Dickface DaVinci."

CHAPTER 76

"DAD! GUESS WHAT!" said Sam breathlessly when Max arrived at the apartment. "The best news of my life!"

"Tell me," said Max.

"You know that pack of basketball cards you bought me on Tuesday? Guess what I found in it!"

"What?" said Max.

"A LeBron James card that LeBron himself actually autographed—and that's verified by Upper Deck!"

"Wow," said Max.

"You know what a Lebron James autographed card is worth on eBay?"

"Tell me," said Max.

"Two hundred and twenty bucks!" said Sam.

"Holy Toledo," said Max, genuinely impressed. "And that was in a pack of cards I got you, you say?"

"Can you believe it?" said Sam.

"I really can't," said Max. "Listen, Sam, when you say it's worth two hundred and twenty bucks, does that mean you or I could, you know, put it up on eBay and somebody would actually give us two hundred and twenty bucks for it? Is that what that means?"

"Yeah!"

"Mmm," said Max. "Sam, let me ask you something . . ."

"What, Dad?"

Max thought a moment, then sighed and shook his head, ashamed of the thought.

"Never mind," he said. There had to be better ways to get the money to go to Vegas than conning his eight-year-old son out of a basketball card, although at this point he was hard put to think what they might be.

On a sudden impulse, Max phoned the three frequent flier bonus plans he belonged to. All three said he didn't have sufficient mileage in his account for a trip to Vegas.

If he were to get any money to go to Vegas, it would have to be from someone rich. The only rich person he knew was Achmed. He could hardly ask Achmed for anything, much less a loan. No matter how desperate he might be, he would never stoop to something like that.

CHAPTER 77

"THIS IS ONE of my favorite spots in the world," said Max, looking out the window of the unmarked car at the corner of 175th Street and Edgecomb Avenue in Washington Heights.

"Yeah?" said Achmed. "Why's that?"

"Whatever time of day or night, they're always stripping cars here," said Max. "They'll have four or five guys take whatever they can off the car—fenders, doors, seats, interiors, radio—then they'll turn it up on its side and take the motor and the transmission. I mean there is absolutely nothing left when they get through. In two weeks there'll be a half a dozen cars like that, the Department of Sanitation will take them all away, and then it'll start all over again. It's the cycle of life, Achmed, the cycle of life. I love it."

"Uh-huh," said Achmed.

The General, a black homeless man wearing a military helmet, was currently directing another car-stripping operation. The shell of a car was turned on its side and two other homeless men were busily at work on it.

"I mean," said Max, "for example, what could possibly be left on that car that he could use?"

"I sure don't know," said Achmed.

"So," said Max, turning to face him for the first time. "How've you been, Achmed?"

"Pretty good, Max, pretty good. How've *you* been?"

"Pretty good, Achmed, pretty good. Yep. Pretty good. Yeah."

There was an awkward pause. This was not going as smoothly as it could have gone, Max thought to himself.

"So, Achmed," said Max. "Things, in the main, have been going well, would you say?"

"In the main, yeah, I would say. Uh-huh."

Another longish pause.

"Uh-huh," said Max. "So, Achmed, you're probably wondering why I came up here to Manhattan North to see you."

"Well, yeah, you know," said Achmed. "I mean I was, yeah."

"Well, you know, I recall your saying to me not so long ago that you were, uh, you know, experiencing some pain because . . ."

"Because, uh, Babette is . . ."

"Is going out with, uh, somebody else, yeah. So I was doing some thinking, and what I thought was that perhaps I could talk to you a little and, uh, you know, maybe figure out some things to, uh . . ."

"To, uh . . . ?"

"To maybe help you out a little, you know. To maybe help you . . ."

"Win her back?"

"Well, sort of, yeah, you know."

"Are you at all ambivalent about this, Max?"

"Ambivalent?" said Max. "Well, uh, yes and no. Not really. Sort of. Yeah, very ambivalent, Achmed, very ambivalent."

"Then why are you doing this?"

"Why am I doing this? Two reasons, Achmed. Actually, three reasons. No, actually two reasons. Well, either three reasons or two reasons."

"Uh-huh."

"One is that, as I told you before, I like you."

"Uh-huh . . ."

"And the second is I understand that the other guy she's seeing is, uh . . . Dieter . . . is that his name?"

"I didn't know he had a name," said Achmed. "I mean I didn't know what his name was, I only knew that she was seeing somebody else. His name is Dieter, you say?"

"Yeah, Dieter."

"And what else do you know about him?"

"Only that his name is Dieter and that he's, you know, German or Austrian or something . . ."

"Uh–huh . . ."

"And, apparently he speaks with an accent, kind of like Arnold Schwarzenegger or something," Max added.

"Babette told you this?" said Achmed.

"Babette? No. No, Sam. Sam told me."

"Sam told you. I see. And you figured it was, what, worse to have Babette going out with a Nazi than with an Arab, is that it?"

"No, no, no, nothing like that. Well, yeah, sort of, but not the way you're putting it. I mean I know you and I like you, and I don't know him and . . . you know."

"So you've got some ideas on how I can beat out the Nazi?" said Achmed. "What are they?"

"Well, they're not specific ideas, they're more a change in attitude. More a way of being, if you know what I mean."

"No."

"Oh, well, it's my impression that you are incredibly nice to Babette, incredibly generous, and incredibly . . ."

"Yes . . . ?"

"Don't get me wrong, I'm not saying you shouldn't be nice to her. I'm only saying that maybe you shouldn't be quite so . . . vulnerable with her."

"You think I'm too vulnerable with Babette?" said Achmed.

"That's just my impression, yeah. I think women like guys to be nice and to be generous and to be vulnerable, but I also think that after a while all that niceness and all that generosity and all that vulnerability gets a little . . . I mean I think they begin to find it a little boring."

"So you're saying don't be quite so nice to her."

"No, I'm saying be a little less available. Have a little more mystery. I'm not saying you should pretend you have somebody else that you're seeing or anything, although, come to think of it, that might not be such a bad idea after all."

"You think I should pretend that I'm seeing somebody else to make her jealous."

"Well, maybe, yeah," said Max. "Jesus, what grade are we in here—sophomore year of high school? I guess what I'm saying is that, the more things change and the older and wiser and more experienced and sophisticated we get, the more it looks like the guys who are really nice and really vulnerable and really totally available keep being aced out by the guys who are only intermittently nice and not very vulnerable and not at all available. In fact, the most intelligent and enlightened women I know have confessed to me that the guys they respect and feel comfortable with are not necessarily the ones that make them hot. That the nasty ones are the ones they fantasize about, and . . . You know, I really hate this discussion. Let's just end it here, okay?"

"Okay."

"Okay."

"Thanks, Max."

"Okay."

"Whatever your motives," said Achmed, "I appreciate the advice."

"Okay."

"If there's anything I can ever do for you, please don't hesitate to ask," said Achmed.

"Okay."

"*Is* there anything I can do for you?" Achmed asked.

"No. Not really. Well . . ."

"There is?"

"Well, now that you mention it, there is one thing," said Max. "But it doesn't have anything to do with my helping you out or anything like that."

"Okay," said Achmed. "What is it?"

"Well, I was just wondering . . ."

"Yes?"

"The thing is, Achmed, I don't know whether you're aware of it, but I've . . . we've . . . been having some rather severe financial problems of late . . ."

"Uh–huh . . ."

"I've tried increasing the size of my mortgage loan and refinancing it and trying to get my credit line increased and all the rest of it—without success, I might add. And then, to make matters worse, I suddenly find that I have a serial murderer who's kidnapped a friend of mine and fled to Las Vegas, and the NYPD won't give me expense money to fly out there and collar him . . ."

"So you thought that I could maybe lend you some money?" Achmed asked.

"Well, I don't know what your financial situation is right now, but if it'd be at all possible, yeah, I'd sure appreciate it. And, believe me, it has nothing at all to do with that other thing we discussed."

"No, I know that," said Achmed. "Well, Max, the thing is, normally I'd be only too happy to help you out, but at this precise moment in time, I'm afraid it just isn't going to be possible for me to do anything."

"Uh-huh. Oh, well, no, I understand. I'm sorry even to have asked you, Achmed, and I wouldn't have, believe me. It's just that I've kind of run out of people to ask."

"I understand."

"Yeah," said Max. "Just out of curiosity, why isn't it possible for you to do anything at this precise moment in time?"

"Confidentially?"

"Yeah."

"Confidentially, Max, I've just put down a million nine on a condo I've had my eye on for quite some time, and it kind of totally wiped out my liquidity, you know?"

"Yeah. I see."

"If you'd asked me last month, or even next month, I might have had a different answer for you."

"Uh-huh."

"But thanks for the advice about Babette," said Achmed. "I really appreciate it, man."

"Hey," said Max. "No problem."

CHAPTER 78

WELL WELL, DETECTIVE Segal," said Cynthia Woods. "How nice to see you again."

"It's nice to see you again, too, Mrs. Woods," said Max.

"Come in, come in," she said, ushering him into the penthouse apartment. "Would you like a drink?"

"No, no. No thanks. Well, maybe just some water."

She motioned for him to sit down on the sofa. It was made of cream-colored leather, it was very cushy, and it sighed when he sank down into it.

"Victor," she called to a man standing at the other end of the room. "Bring Detective Segal a glass of water and a very dry martini on the rocks."

"Mrs. Woods," said Max "I really—"

"You're under no obligation whatsoever to drink it, Detective Segal. May I call you Max?"

"I suppose so."

"You're under no obligation to drink it, Max. It'll just be there if you change your mind."

"Thanks."

"So what can I do for you today?"

"Well, I don't know if you're aware of it, Mrs. Woods, but—"

"Cynthia."

"—Cynthia, but we have reason to believe that your son has kidnapped the psychotherapist who evaluated him up at St. Albans—"

"Grace Stevenson, yes."

"—and is taking her across the country, possibly to Las Vegas."

"I see," she said. "And do you plan to fly out there and bring him back?"

"Well, we do feel it necessary to try and ensure her safety—and his, as a matter of fact—and the only way to do that would be to apprehend him, yes."

"So why have you come to me?" she asked. "To try and find out where he might go in Vegas?"

"Well, partly, yes. You could be very helpful to us in that regard."

"And what else?"

"Well, partly also, what I wanted to talk to you about was . . . Well, it seems that the NYPD is . . . Uh, it seems that the expense money generally available to homicide detectives to travel out of state and bring back suspects for questioning is, in this case—"

"You can't get the police department to send you, so you've come to see if I'd give you the money to fly to Vegas and capture my son?" she asked.

"Well . . . not *give* us the money, because, once the DA can be convinced that this isn't a wild goose chase, I'm sure we can reimburse you, but . . ." Max sighed. "I'm sorry, Mrs. Woods."

"Cynthia."

"I'm sorry, Cynthia, I realize it was an absurd request. I'm sorry to have bothered you."

Max stood up and headed back toward the door.

"Did I say it was an absurd request?" she asked.

"What?" he said.

"I don't think it's an absurd request."

"You don't?"

"No, Max, I don't. If Andy has killed those women, he has to be brought back here and punished. He's my son and my responsibility, so it makes perfect sense for me to finance his return to New York."

"You're serious about this?" he asked. "You're really serious? You'd actually lend me the money to go to Las Vegas and look for him?"

"Of course I'm serious."

"Well, I must say that's a really . . . incredibly enlightened point of view."

"Now how much money would you need?" she asked.

"Well, I don't know," he said. "I mean the NYPD generally gives us airfare, plus twenty-three a day for food and seventy-five a day for lodging, so that's about a hundred a day . . ."

"A hundred a *day*?" she said, shocked.

"Well, if you think that's too much . . ."

"Too *much*? My dear, a hundred a day will barely buy you decent food, much less lodging."

"I see," said Max. "Uh, how much do you think I ought to spend?"

"Well, three hundred a day would be more like it. But I have an idea. You want to hear my idea?"

"Sure."

"I'll go with you to Vegas. That way I'll also be able to—"

"That's ridiculous," said Max. "I can't have you—"

"Just let me finish, Max, will you please?"

"Sure."

"I'll take you with me to Vegas. That way I'll also be able to show you around and help you figure out all the places Andy would be likely to go. I'll pay all our expenses, and we'll go first class, which is the only way I travel."

"I can't have you coming with me to apprehend your son, Cynthia. It's ridiculous."

"It's not ridiculous, Max, it's the only way you'd have any notion of where to look for him. I'll have my secretary make reservations. When would you like to go?"

"As soon as possible. Tomorrow. Today."

"You're kidding me," said Caruso. "You're telling me the mother of a homicide suspect is bankrolling you to go to Vegas to collar her son?"

Max had raced into the squad and started grabbing all papers on his desk relevant to Andy Woods or the three homicide cases that he thought might be useful in Vegas.

"I'm dead serious," said Max, scooping papers off his desk and stuffing them into a nine-by-twelve manila envelope. "Cynthia Woods has offered to lend me the money to go to Vegas, and she's the only person in the entire city of New York who's willing to do that. I had to accept her offer, despite the terms."

"Terms?" said Caruso. "There are terms? What terms?"

"That she's, uh, coming with me," said Max.

Caruso stared at Max openmouthed, then burst out laughing.

"Good one, Max!" he said, still chortling. "Boy, you almost had me there. Coming with you, right? I love it! Jesus!"

"Sal, it's the only way she'd lend me the money. I had to agree. I had no choice. Now I don't have much time before I leave, so I'd appreciate if you'd help me by trying to contact the Kansas State trooper who ticketed Grace Stevenson for speeding on August 21. The cop's name is Halloran . . ."

Max scribbled a phone number on a Post-it and thrust it at his partner.

"Here's his number," said Max. "We need to find out everything he remembers about the stop—who Grace was with in the vehicle, how she seemed, whether there was any indication that she wasn't there of her own free will—you know the drill. Call me on my cell with anything you get."

Max grabbed some autopsy photos out of a case folder, realized there was no earthly reason he'd need those in Vegas, and jammed them back in the case folder.

Caruso stopped laughing. His face transformed into a sly, frowning smile.

"Oh, I get it now," said Caruso.

"What do you get?" said Max.

"You said Mrs. Woods is a cock tease. So you two are going to Vegas to play hide-the-pepperoni—what happens in Vegas stays in Vegas, right? And to think I bought it when you said you were falling in love with the lady shrink."

Max stopped shuffling papers and stared at Caruso in disgust.

"Sal, I am *definitely* falling in love with the lady shrink, okay? Which is just one of *many* reasons I'm not going to Vegas to play hide-the-pepperoni with the mother of the accused. The others are that I'm a professional, that I'm on the job, that Mrs. Woods is a sleaze, that I'm not at all attracted to her, and that I wouldn't play hide-the-pepperoni with her if she were the last living woman in the entire continental United States, okay?"

Caruso closed his eyes and sighed.

"Just don't come back from Vegas with the crabs," he said.

CHAPTER 79

S O YOU'RE GOING to Las Vegas after all," said Natale. He was making pasta from scratch in his tiny kitchen.

"Yeah," said Max. "I convinced Hickock to let me take my vacation now."

"Fascinating place, Vegas," said Natale, rolling out the dough. "They've stopped time in the casinos. They operate twenty-four hours a day, and there are no windows and no clocks, so you have no sense of the passage of time. They also operate on an enormous psychological advantage."

"Which is what?" said Max.

"Well, if you're winning," said Natale, "you're going to play till you're broke. And when you're broke, you're going to leave town."

"What if you quit when you're ahead and you leave town with your winnings?" said Max.

"Only one out of every seventy players leaves Vegas a winner," said Natale. "So not a lot of money leaves town. But if you leave town with your winnings, the fact that you were in a place where you won all that money will keep you from being satisfied with a life where you don't make that kind of money, so eventually you'll come back to Las Vegas with the money you won, and you'll lose it. The only people who don't come back to Vegas are people with no money. Do you have a theory about gambling?"

"Do I have a theory?" Max asked.

"When a machine or a dealer isn't paying off, do you believe they're Cold or do you believe they're Ready?"

"I really hadn't thought about it," said Max.

"Well, there are two schools of thought on gambling," said Natale. "Two theologies, actually. Fifty percent of people who gamble believe a machine can be Hot or Cold: As long as they're winning they think it's Hot and they'll stay with it—they'll hold the same machine if they go to bathroom. Even when they leave Vegas, they'll come back to the same machine. When a machine turns Cold, they'll transfer to another one. The other fifty percent believe machines or dealers or tables are Ready. They look for one that hasn't paid off in a while. When one pays off, they move to another one, because they believe that one is no longer Ready. They call it the law of averages, but the flaw is they're really betting that the dice or the reels of the slot machines remember what number came up last."

"I see what you mean," said Max.

"People don't switch from one theology to another, they're almost born believing one or the other. You going to play the slots when you're there?"

"No, no," said Max. "Sam gave me four quarters to play for him, I mean, but that's all I'm playing."

"Yeah," said Natale with a knowing smile. "I'll bet."

CHAPTER 80

"CHAMPAGNE OR ORANGE juice?"

Max had been staring out the window at the plane's wing as it flexed its dozen flaps and spoilers like a gigantic bird ruffling and preening its feathers. He was still grousing about having had to surrender his revolver to security, to be held in the cockpit by the captain for the duration of the flight, and the flight attendant had to repeat her question. He looked up, startled.

"I'm sorry," he said, "were you talking to me?"

"Yes," said the flight attendant. "What would you prefer before takeoff, sir, champagne or orange juice?"

"Oh, uh, I'll have the orange juice," he said.

"That's your problem," said Cynthia. "You never choose the champagne."

"What makes you think I *never* choose the champagne?" Max asked.

"I can tell," she said. "You're just an orange juice kind of guy."

"And you, I suppose, always choose champagne?"

"No, first I ask if it's Dom Pérignon."

"And if it isn't?"

"If it isn't I choose a sidecar on the rocks."

"What if they only have orange juice?"

"If they only have orange juice, it wouldn't be first class, and then I wouldn't be on it."

Max had never flown first class before. He loved the wider seats, the greater legroom, and the idea that he could get served free champagne before takeoff while the rabble in the back had to wait till they were airborne before even being permitted to pay for drinks, although such thoughts filled him with guilt and he never drank champagne because it gave him headaches.

He thought it was fitting that in a crash the rabble in the back stood a far better chance of surviving than did the snobs in the front.

When they were finally cleared for takeoff and the huge plane lumbered down the runway, Max wondered, as he always did on takeoffs, how something as heavy as an airliner could actually lift off into something as light as air. He knew the principle of the air-foil and how it created lift, but that somehow didn't do it for him. He always felt that this time would be the one time the principle wouldn't work.

But it did work and the big plane was soon six miles above the earth, hurtling through the air toward Las Vegas at half the speed of sound. Grace was also headed toward Las Vegas, he thought, might even be there already. What had the kidnapping done to her physically? Psychically? How had Woods brutalized her and how had she, as a shrink, defended against it? What was Woods planning to do to her once he got there? And how in God's name was Max supposed to find them in a city of more than a million people?

If only he had some inkling of what was going on between them. If only he could talk to somebody who had seen them. Like the cop in Kansas who'd given Grace the speeding ticket.

On a sudden impulse, Max picked up the Airfone and put through a call to the Kansas State Police. He was told that Officer Halloran, the cop who'd given Grace the ticket, wasn't available.

CHAPTER 81

IT SEEMED TO Grace that they had always been on the road, on this highway, driving in this car, although it had only been three days, or was it four?

After the first day the highway was relentless, uniformly straight, flat, hot, bright, and hard to look at, perfectly splitting the landscape below the horizon into two equal parts, with little mirrorlike pools shimmering in the distance that always kept well ahead of you as you drove, mirages to make you question your grip on reality, with nothing to break the monotony but the occasional roadside Native American curio shop or the museum featuring some oddity like a two-headed rattlesnake that nobody who wasn't driving in the desert and out of his mind with boredom would ever consider stopping to look at.

Luckily, the Mustang had a working air conditioner. Without that she felt she would have perished from the heat. Andy would listen to country and western music on the radio for hours, then abruptly grow moody and turn it off.

They had passed through Pennsylvania, Ohio, Indiana, Illinois, Missouri, Kansas, and were now somewhere in Colorado. Utah was next, and with any luck they'd make Arizona or Nevada by nightfall. Then it would be another steak sandwich in another diner and into another motel to be secured to the bed on her stomach for another night. To her chagrin, she was getting used to the routine. *If I can get used to this,* she thought, *I can get used to anything.*

She wondered what lay in store for her in Las Vegas. The fact that Andy felt he needed to marry her in order to have sex with her said nothing about what he planned to do with her once he'd consummated the marriage. The most likely scenario was that after consummation he'd either weary of the game and let her go or else he'd kill her. She didn't know which. She didn't think he did either.

CHAPTER 82

THE FIRST THING that threw Max when they landed at McCarran Airport in Las Vegas was getting off the plane and seeing all those slot machines right there in the terminal, and people playing them with all the seriousness and joylessness and determination that he had seen on the faces of slot machine players in Atlantic City, his only previous contact with this sort of depravity.

He wondered why these people couldn't at least wait until they got to their hotels to play the slots, and then he had the fantasy that these people hadn't even booked rooms in hotels, that they'd simply flown to McCarran Airport from wherever it was they lived and parked themselves at a machine in the terminal with their plastic cup full of quarters for the weekend, living off burritos and diet colas from the Taco Bell adjacent to the slot area, taking brief naps on the chairs adjoining the gates, returning to the slots till all their quarters were eaten up by the machines, and then flying back home.

The second thing that threw him was the heat. Although it was 9:30 P.M. Vegas time when they landed, stepping outside the terminal was like stepping into a kitchen where serious baking was in process. The temperature outside at nine-thirty was ninety-eight degrees Fahrenheit.

The third thing that threw him was the car that Cynthia chose to rent at the airport. It was from an outfit called Rent-A-Wreck. It was a robin's egg blue 1957 Thunderbird, the one with the fins and the continental kit on the back. He'd always considered the '55s and '56s more tasteful than the '57s, but the '57 had its own charm and, besides, questions of taste in Las Vegas were superfluous at best. She gave him the keys, got into the passenger's seat, and turned on the air conditioner. It spat hot air at them, then tried hard to cool down.

"Where are we going?" said Max, putting the car in gear and pulling out of the parking space, more pleased by the chance to drive the '57 T-Bird than he cared to admit.

"The Mirage," she said. "It's a five to seven-minute drive at most. Just take Paradise to the Strip. I'll direct you."

He was amazed to see that the airport was practically in the heart of town, the newer hotels so close to McCarran that being on the Strip could have referred to the landing strip as well as to the common nickname for Las Vegas Boulevard. The immense glass pyramid with the ominous sphinx guarding the airfield side of it had to be the Luxor Hotel.

A few weeks after the Luxor opened, the sun glaring off the side of the glass pyramid had blinded the pilot of a private aircraft. The plane crashed, killing all three passengers. There had been outraged demands to move either the pyramid or the airport. Not even the most naive resident of Las Vegas considered either of these a real possibility. What would probably happen instead was that the pyramid would be doused with the equivalent of dulling spray.

"What's the newest construction here?" Max asked Cynthia as the security guard waved them through the crossing gate.

"Hotels spring up here like mushrooms, Max, I swear to God," she said. "Since I was here a year ago, at least five have been built, and five more have gone out of business. The new ones all have at least five thousand rooms and some kind of gimmick like an erupting volcano."

When they pulled up at the Mirage, the volcano situated atop a waterfall in the lagoon outside had just begun erupting. It sounded like amplified indigestion and belched fire fifty to a hundred feet into the air every quarter hour. The original volcano and lagoon installation had cost the Mirage $185 million dollars—the 2008 redesign another $25 million—financed not by Mob money as some supposed, but by junk bonds. Vegas was becoming respectable.

Max and Cynthia surrendered the T-bird at valet parking and entered the hotel. On their left, in a glass-enclosed white habitat featuring white rocks, white palm trees, and a free-form swimming pool, were two snoozing white tigers. As Max and Cynthia passed, one of the tigers yawned, revealing a capacious mouth, a long pink tongue, and a yard of teeth.

Just past the tigers was a domed atrium with a rain forest inside it that cost $60 million dollars. Bougainvillea, hibiscus, orchids, ferns, waterfalls, rock-lined reflecting pools, and ninety-foot palm trees gave one more of a sense of being in the Caribbean than would being in the Caribbean itself.

The lobby was all marble with brass accents. The wall behind the registration desk was a salt water tropical fish tank fifty-two feet long. Prominent in the tank were several small spotted sharks. Directions to the dolphin habitat were prominently displayed.

"What do rooms cost here?" Max whispered to Cynthia as the clerk looked up their reservation.

"Oh, it depends," said Cynthia.

"On what?"

"On how booked they are. Regular rooms here go anywhere from seventy-nine dollars to two hundred seventy-nine. They're willing to lose on the room because they know they'll make it up on the gambling."

"How much was mine?" whispered Max.

Cynthia smiled patronizingly at him in reply. "I've taken the liberty of booking us a penthouse suite on D level," she said. "It's a locked floor. Very secure."

"Yes," said the clerk, bringing it up on the computer, "here it is, Mrs. Woods."

"A penthouse suite has how many bedrooms?" Max asked.

"Just the one," said Cynthia, handing the clerk her Platinum American Express card.

"Look," said Max, "I'm going to have to get myself a separate room."

"Really?" said Cynthia. "Can you afford it?"

The clerk took an imprint of Cynthia's card and handed it back to her.

"Not in *this* hotel, no," said Max.

The clerk gave Cynthia a registration card to fill out.

"In which hotel can you afford to stay?"

"I don't know," said Max. "I'll find something."

Cynthia scribbled illegibly on the registration card and returned it to the clerk.

"How much money do you have?" Cynthia asked.

"Uh, not too much," said Max.

"How much?"

"Oh, I don't know. Fifty, fifty-three dollars, something like that."

"Front, please!" called the clerk.

A bellman trotted over.

"Can I ask you a personal question?" Cynthia asked.

"What?" said Max.

"Will you need to eat anything while you're here? Because outside of those little crackers that come with the soup, I believe everything else here costs money."

"I'll manage."

"Mr. and Mrs. Woods," said the clerk. "The bellman will take you up to your suite now."

"Max, dear, don't be an ass," said Cynthia. "Stay with me."

"I'm sorry, Cynthia, but I don't think it's appropriate."

"Why not?"

"Oh, call me old-fashioned," said Max. "I just don't think it's appropriate for a cop to sleep with the mother of the man he's planning to arrest for murder."

"Mr. Woods? Mrs. Woods?" said the bellman, pointing the way to the elevators.

"Just a moment, dear," said Cynthia to the bellman. To Max she said, "Since I've paid for you to travel here, would you at least do me the courtesy of coming up to our suite to discuss this?"

Max looked past her to the wall of tropical fish. The largest of the sharks was looking wistfully at one of the smaller fish.

"I don't see the harm in discussing it," said Max.

———

The motif throughout the hotel was Caribbean elegance. Louvered doors, wicker, bamboo, brightly colored floral patterns, lots and lots of marble, brass, and mirrors. Opulence teetering on the brink of taste.

The bellman opened the double louvered doors of their suite and they went inside. The suite had its own lobby—settees, couches, coffee tables, upholstered chairs, lamps, marble floors with recessed carpet panels. It was not so much a suite of rooms as a suite of areas—a reception area, a living room area, a bar area, a kitchen area, a bedroom area, a dressing room area, another dressing room area, a shower area, a Jacuzzi bathtub area, a bidet area, a toilet area. The more private the area, the more mirrors it rated.

Cynthia slipped the bellman a tip and he withdrew.

"So, Max," she said, "what do you think?"

"How much is this all costing you?"

"What does it matter?"

"I just don't understand this kind of money."

"You don't have to understand it to enjoy it," she said. "And if you stay here with me tonight it won't cost you a penny."

Max looked out the window. From all the windows you could look down on the dome of the atrium and on the erupting volcano twenty-nine floors below.

"What'll it cost me to sleep on the couch?" he asked.

She considered this for a while before replying.

"To sleep on the couch it'll cost you a hug."

"A hug?"

"A hug."

"I guess there's nothing wrong with a hug," he said.

She smiled and walked over to him and put her arms around him. He hugged her for about twenty seconds. When he released his arms, to his surprise, she did too.

"I'm going out for a while," said Max. "Don't wait up."

"You're going to look for Andy?" she asked.

"Yeah," he said. "That's why I'm here."

"I'll come with you," she said. "Four eyes are better than two."

CHAPTER 83

I T WAS LATE.

Not late by Vegas standards. It was only midnight Vegas time, but Max, who'd arrived in Vegas only two and a half hours before, was on New York time and for him it was 3 A.M.

And for someone who had flown across the continent and then driven down a boulevard where hotels were not hotels but circus tents and glass pyramids and medieval castles and gargantuan sculptures of flowers and giant riverboats in undulating neon and where outside the hotels, volcanoes sent flames shooting a hundred feet into the air and where white tigers and miniature sharks lived in hotel lobbies, for someone such as that it was very late indeed, late enough to imagine that he had slid from wakefulness into a rather overproduced dream.

Cynthia told Max of Andy's childhood fascination with gambling as they wandered through the casinos, scanning the crowd for Andy and Grace, trying not to look at the carpets which were hideous floral patterns in magenta and chartreuse that made Hawaiian shirts look sedate by comparison.

Max was still smarting over the photo of Andy that Cynthia had shown him. He was about to ask what she was doing with a picture of reporter Mitch Morgenstern, then realized what happened. The previous pictures he'd seen of Andy Woods had obviously been prison mug shots, taken years ago. When Woods came to Queens Homicide, he'd darkened his hair and grown a goatee.

The thought that a perp had been able to interview him in his own squad room filled Max with self-loathing.

Before entering the Caesar's Palace casino, Cynthia took him downstairs to their shopping mall, a replica of two blocks in Rome. Behind authentic-looking Roman storefronts and under authentic-looking Roman balconies and roofs were franchises of Spago, Versace, Victoria's Secret, and shops selling sorbet, pricey ranch wear, and fifties memorabilia. Above this, on a smooth vaulted ceiling, stretched a painted blue sky with authentic-looking puffy white clouds, lit so the sky cycled through a full twenty-four-hours—sunset to sunrise—every hour.

At the ends of these indoor streets were full-blown Roman piazzas, complete with sidewalk cafes. One piazza was built around a full-sized replica of a Roman fountain, with splashing water and statues of snorting winged steeds. The other was built around an immense round platform upon which sat marble statues of three Roman gods. When Max passed by he thought he saw one of the gods nod to him. Then lightning flickered, thunder cracked, and the statues sprang to life, orating and gesticulating. Max feared he was hallucinating till he realized this was all part of an hourly show featuring laser graphics on an overhead dome.

If Andy and Grace were in the crush of people observing the laser light show, Max didn't see them. He and Cynthia proceeded to the Caesar's casino.

Passing hundreds of people, thousands of people, dropping coins into slot machines, hearing the electronic music of the machines burbling to the players and the madder music of machines paying off, rhythmically spitting quarters and dollar slugs into the metal pans at the base of each machine, Max had a sudden, almost mystical revelation:

THE REASON THAT HE, MAX SEGAL, HAD BEEN SUM-

MONED TO LAS VEGAS AT THIS PARTICULAR POINT IN TIME BY MEANS OF A SERIES OF SEEMINGLY RANDOM EVENTS WAS FOR ONE REASON AND ONE REASON ONLY: TO PUT A QUARTER INTO THE ONE SLOT MACHINE HE WAS SUPPOSED TO PUT A QUARTER INTO AND TO THEREBY REAP THE BOUNTY OF THE UNIVERSE WHICH HAD THUS FAR ELUDED HIM.

Yes, it was quite clear to him now. He had never been a mystic before, never been a fatalist, but he could now review his entire life up to the present moment and see how events had conspired to bring him to this place.

Andy's decision to kill Virginia Morales neither an hour earlier nor an hour later so that Max would be passing by the death scene and feel obliged to stop and volunteer his help, DaVinci's provocation in precisely the manner that would cause Max to become obsessed with proving a seeming suicide a homicide, the muggers jumping off the bridge onto Max and Grace's gondola and onto nobody else's so that Max would have to go back to Grace's hotel to dry out and end up in bed with her, Theodore Pearlman's having selected Grace rather than somebody else to evaluate Andy in prison, Andy's having been born in Vegas instead of someplace else so he'd come back here with Grace as his prisoner, and so on and so on.

It was clear that one of these machines had Max's name on it. The question was which one?

Over a bank of machines, in zany graphics, was the word QUARTERMANIA. Below it were two rapidly increasing dot-matrix dollar amounts—major and minor jackpots of some kind. The minor one was somewhere in the range of forty-eight thousand dollars. The major one was somewhere in the range of a million and a half.

"What's Quartermania?" Max asked.

"A pooled progressive jackpot," said Cynthia.

"Meaning what?"

"Meaning forty or forty-five casinos all over the state are pooling their money," said Cynthia. "As people lose quarters in Quartermania all over the state, the jackpot goes up. If four sevens come up for you, you win whatever amount the smaller jackpot is at that moment. If four of the Quartermania logos come up for you, you get the whole kit and caboodle."

It was clear that Quartermania was what he was supposed to play. Hadn't Sam given him four quarters and asked him to play them for him in the slots?

He looked at the Quartermania machines and zeroed in on one which was currently being played by a middle-aged woman in a wheelchair. The woman had lovely red hair in a hairnet. She held a large plastic cup of quarters and was systematically dropping them into the machine in front of her.

Max noticed that the woman had no legs. Then he had another mystical revelation: THIS MACHINE, THE ONE THAT THE WOMAN WITH NO LEGS WAS PLAYING, WAS THE ONE THAT MAX WAS SUPPOSED TO PLAY.

He didn't know how he knew that, he just knew it. He hated that he knew it. He could not see himself asking the woman with no legs to move to another machine. He knew that the machine would hit for him, but not for her.

"What're you looking at?" Cynthia asked.

"Shhhh," said Max.

He watched the woman play. She lost seven quarters in succession, got back two, lost twelve, got back three. It was clear that she was going to be playing this machine all night. IT WILL NOT HIT FOR HER, IT WILL HIT FOR YOU.

"Why are you watching that woman?" Cynthia asked.

"I just have a feeling about that machine," said Max.

She lost six quarters, got back one, lost eight, got back two. IT WILL NOT HIT FOR HER, IT WILL HIT FOR YOU. IT IS WAITING FOR YOU TO PLAY IT.

Max walked forward.

"Excuse me," Max said to the woman.

She looked up, alarmed.

"I didn't mean to startle you," said Max, flashing her a strained smile. "I just wanted to ask you a favor."

"What?"

"I wonder if I could play just one quarter in your machine," said Max. "Just one."

She looked at him as if he were mad.

"Why don't you play one of the other machines?" she asked. "Why don't you play that machine over there?"

"I don't *want* to play the machine over there," said Max, "I want to play the one you're playing. Just once."

"What if you win?" she asked. "What good is that to me?"

"If I win I'll give you ten percent of my earnings," he said. "How's that?"

"A fifty-fifty split or go to another machine," said the woman.

"Fifty-fifty!" said Cynthia.

"Stay out of this," he said to Cynthia. To the woman he said "Twenty percent is really about all I'm prepared to do here."

"Thirty-three percent is my final offer," said the woman. "Take it or leave it."

"You're getting screwed," said Cynthia.

"All right," said Max. "Thirty-three percent."

"Write it out," said the woman.

"What?"

She handed him a blank keno card and a ballpoint pen.

"Write out 'If I win I will pay Mary Ann Rasmussen thirty-three percent of my winnings,' and sign your name."

"You're certainly not going along with that, are you?" Cynthia asked.

Max sighed. He took the paper, wrote out what the woman had asked and handed it back to her. She read it, then moved her wheelchair smartly back and to the right.

His heart racing, Max stepped up to the machine. THIS IS THE ONE. THIS IS THE ONE AND THIS IS THE TIME. THE BOUNTY OF THE UNIVERSE, LESS THIRTY-THREE PERCENT, WILL SOON BE MINE.

He took out a quarter, wondered briefly if it had to be any particular one, and dropped it into the slot. He pulled the handle. The four reels spun.

A seven came up under the thin black line in the first window. SEVEN, YES, LUCKY SEVEN. A seven came up in the second window. TWO SEVENS, YES! AND NOW LET'S HAVE A THIRD. A bar came up in the third window and a lemon in the fourth. WHAT?

Max stared at the machine. He couldn't believe it. It hadn't hit. How was it possible that it hadn't hit? It hadn't hit because THIS WAS NOT THE RIGHT MACHINE.

Max walked away from the machine.

"What the hell was all that about?" Cynthia asked.

"I just had a feeling," said Max.

"A feeling," said Cynthia.

"Yeah."

"You're a helluva lot crazier than I thought," she said.

"Let's just continue looking for Andy and Grace," said Max, feeling foolish, beginning to scan the casino again.

CHAPTER 84

BY 2 A.M., which was 5 A.M. New York time, Max decided that Andy and Grace would no longer be out and about and that it was time to call it a day. He took Cynthia back to the Mirage, rode up in the elevator to D level, unlocked the floor, got out, unlocked the double louvered doors, and entered their suite.

"Boy, I'm bushed," said Cynthia.

"Me too," said Max, taking out his cell phone.

He checked the number he'd written down for the Kansas State Police and punched in the number.

"Kansas State Police Department," said a tired female voice. "How may I direct your call?"

"This is Detective Max Segal of the New York Police Department," said Max. "I'm trying to reach Officer Francis Halloran on official police business."

"You want a nightcap?" asked Cynthia, going to the bar area.

"No thanks," Max whispered.

"Officer Halloran is not available," said the Kansas police operator. "Do you wish to leave a message?"

"Yes, ma'am," said Max. "I'm calling with reference to a traffic stop Officer Halloran made on August 21, not far from Topeka, Kansas, and a speeding ticket issued to one Grace Stevenson."

"How'd you like to share a nice wide bed?" asked Cynthia.

"No thanks," Max whispered, then left his cell number with the Kansas police operator in his regular voice.

"Let me at least make up that couch for you," said Cynthia.

"Whatever," said Max.

Cynthia rummaged around in the closets till she found some extra sheets and, although they were the wrong size, managed to make up the couch into a passable bed. He thanked her and went into the bathroom to brush his teeth and wash up.

When he got out she was nowhere in sight. He turned off the light in the living room, stripped down to his shorts and T-shirt, and climbed under the sheets of the couch.

"Good night, Max," she said from somewhere in the dark.

"Good night, Cynthia," he said.

"How do you like my home town so far?"

"I don't know," he said. "It's been a really strange night."

"It could get stranger," she said.

<hr />

Max was walking down a street in Rome, but his fellow pedestrians were marble statues of Roman gods. It was raining. There was lightning and thunder. The marble statues walked calmly down the street as if the rain meant nothing to them. Bacchus, the god of wine, appeared in front of him, blocking his path. Bacchus was bald and paunchy and wore a garland of leaves atop his head and an outlaw mask over his eyes. He had but a single arm. Max tried to move past the one-armed Bacchus but he couldn't. A phalanx of masked, one-armed outlaws appeared behind Bacchus. Max yelled at the outlaws to get out of the way. Bacchus opened his mouth very wide and laughed unpleasantly. Bacchus had rows of very white, very sharp teeth. Bacchus began to vomit quarters. Waves of quarters cascaded from Bacchus's open mouth. With a low growl, Bacchus turned into a white tiger and lunged at Max. Max dodged and ran.

The white tiger pursued Max down the Roman street. A huge crack ripped down the middle of the street and molten lava poured out of it, shooting flames high into the air, building a cone higher and higher until it filled an entire piazza. Lava poured down the sides of the volcano, chasing him. The faster Max ran, the faster came the fiery fingers of lava. He tripped and sprawled headlong on the pavement, except that the pavement was now the magenta and chartreuse carpeting of a huge casino.

The tiger was upon him in a bound. It lifted a gigantic paw to his face. He expected to feel his cheeks being shredded by razor-sharp claws, but the touch of the tiger's paw was surprisingly gentle. It caressed his cheeks with the soft pads of its huge paw, its terrible claws safely sheathed.

Max woke gradually to the sensation of someone stroking his face in the still-dark living room.

"Wha'izzit?" Max croaked. "Who'zat?"

"Shh," whispered a voice in the darkness.

The soft stroking continued.

"Cynthia, izzat you?"

"Shh," whispered the voice. "Go back to sleep, dear. Everything will be all right. Mommy's here."

Max sat up sharply in bed and looked around. He saw nobody. He got slowly to his feet and examined the room in greater detail.

The draperies had been pulled over the windows which looked down on the erupting volcano and were billowing softly in the draft from the air conditioner. Neither Cynthia nor anybody else was in the room. Neither sound nor light emanated from the direction of her bedroom.

Had the stroking of his face and the accompanying conversation been part of the dream with the tiger? Was he asleep still? He had no idea. He went back to the couch, sank down, on it and collapsed.

CHAPTER 85

MAX AWOKE, TOTALLY unrefreshed and cranky, to sunlight invading the living room of the suite where he'd spent the night, or, more accurately, where he'd spent the last four hours of the night.

"Well," said a voice beyond his field of vision, "the sleeping giant wakes. Sleep well?"

"Not at all," he croaked.

Max watched with half an eye as Cynthia, in bra and panties, pranced across the living room to make coffee in the kitchen area.

"Like some fresh-brewed mountain roast coffee?"

"Not really," he said.

"Coming right up."

He heard the chortling sound of pouring coffee and before he knew it, there she was, standing in front of him in her underwear, offering him a steaming cup of java, among other things. He took the coffee, hoping it might excuse him from the other things.

Going outside the hotel into a typical August day in Vegas— blinding brightness, cloudless sky, air temperature forty-five degrees hotter than inside, car door handles too hot to touch—Max noted how different everything looked in the daylight. Without miles of neon, millions of bulbs, and erupting volcanoes, Las Vegas looked tacky, flat, and gray, a showgirl without her spangles, heels, and makeup.

When Max showed the Las Vegas police his shield and his NYPD credentials and when he told them why he was in town, they were extremely courteous. But when he confessed that he carried with him no accusatory instrument and that his mission was completely unofficial, he lost his audience.

Max figured the overhead video camera systems in the casinos would be an excellent way to look for Andy and Grace. He took photos of both Andy and Grace to the heads of security of the six largest casinos in Las Vegas and requested their help. Because Max was a policeman, the heads of security listened politely to his story and dutifully studied his photos. But since Andy was only wanted for kidnapping and murder and not defrauding the casinos, they found it hard to take his request seriously.

He returned to the Mirage and rejoined Cynthia, who was only too eager to resume the role of Watson.

The second time Max's mystical inner voices spoke to him, he and Cynthia were scanning the crowd at the Stardust casino. He was passing a Quartermania slot machine that wasn't occupied and he suddenly got the flash: THIS IS THE MACHINE. The voice was not as loud this time, not as clear, but it was definitely there. THIS IS THE MACHINE.

"Hang on a second," he said to Cynthia.

He fished through the pile of coins in his palm—pennies, nickels, dimes—but saw no quarters.

"Cynthia, you got a quarter?" he asked.

"I left my purse in the suite," she said.

A few paces off was a change girl. Max walked over and handed her a dollar.

"Four quarters, please," he said.

She gave him his change, he turned on his heel and went back to the machine, but now there was somebody standing in front of it, about to play. A huge guy in his maybe early fifties. A guy with a tremendous chest and arms. Not so much a tall guy as a wide-body guy.

"Excuse me," said Max, "but that's my machine."

"Uh, Max . . . ?" said Cynthia behind him.

The guy turned around and looked at Max. He appeared to have a seven-second delay on responses, like call-in talk shows.

"You talkin' ta me?" said the guy.

THIS IS THE MACHINE.

"Max, can I speak to you a moment?" said Cynthia.

"That's my machine you're standing in front of," said Max.

The guy was still processing this response. When the unified field theory was finally formulated, it would most likely not be formulated by this guy.

"*Your* machine?" he said.

"Yeah," said Max.

THIS IS DEFINITELY THE MACHINE.

"I din see your name on it," said the guy.

"Oh my God," said Cynthia. "Laverne?"

"What?" said Max.

"What?" said the wide-body guy.

"Laverne Paccione," said Cynthia.

The guy looked at her.

"Cynthia Morgan," said Cynthia.

The guy looked at her, processing the name.

"Shit," said the guy. "Cynthia? That you?"

"Yeah."

"Shit. How the hell ya been, Cynthia?"

"Good, Laverne, good. Max, this is Laverne Paccione, one of

the nicest guys I know. He used to look after me when I was a showgirl. Laverne, this is Max Segal from New York. A homicide cop."

The guy looked at Max, processing the data. Although he had the same first name as one of the Andrews Sisters, it was doubtful that people had ever teased him about it.

"A homicide cop," said Laverne.

"Yeah," said Cynthia. "We're traveling together."

Max flashed her a look.

"How's little Andy?" asked Laverne. "Still in the joint?"

"No, he's out," said Cynthia. "We're looking for him, as a matter of fact. You haven't seen him, by any chance, have you?"

Laverne frowned, processing this.

"Not since he was, what, twelve years old," said Laverne. "What's he doin' now he's out?"

"Well, he got into a little scrape in New York, which is why we're looking for him."

A little scrape, thought Max.

"Hey, Laverne, I'd love to catch up with you," said Cynthia. "Would you like to have a cup of coffee?"

Laverne ran this through the thought processor and nodded.

"Sure, Cynthia, sure. When would you like?"

"How about now?"

She looked at Max. Max nodded almost imperceptibly.

"Yeah, why not?" said Laverne. "I got nuthin' better to do."

"See you back at the suite in a couple of hours, hon," said Cynthia, giving Max a peck on the cheek.

Cynthia walked off with her arm around Laverne, and Max turned back to the machine.

THIS IS DEFINITELY THE MACHINE.

He put in a quarter. The reels spun. A Quartermania logo appeared in the first window. YES. A Quartermania logo appeared in the second window. YES! A double bar appeared in the third window and a lemon in the fourth.

Max's shoulders sagged. Not even close.

THIS WAS NOT THE RIGHT MACHINE.

CHAPTER 86

LIKE MANY CITY directories, Las Vegas combines its white and yellow page listings. Unlike many cities, the yellow pages of the Las Vegas telephone directory contain, under the heading "Entertainers," full-color ads for hookers. Also unlike many cities, the yellow pages in Las Vegas list wedding chapels.

At least two of the dozens of instant wedding chapels in town featured Elvis impersonators.

Andy didn't think he wanted to be married by an Elvis impersonator. And although the idea of a drive-up wedding ceremony didn't appeal to him on romantic or aesthetic grounds, being married in your car had the advantage of being able to conceal a weapon more easily than the fifteen-minute chapel service. Not that he wanted to kill her during the ceremony. There would be plenty of time for that after the marriage was consummated, if it became necessary.

Blood tests are not required in Nevada, nor are waiting periods. But marriage licenses costing sixty dollars have to be obtained at the Clark County Courthouse in downtown Las Vegas. The Marriage License Bureau is open from 8 A.M. to midnight Monday through Thursday, from Friday at 8 A.M. straight through till Sunday at midnight, and on all legal holidays. Getting married in Las Vegas has a dangerous, medical emergency feel about it.

At about 10 P.M., shortly after arriving in Vegas and checking into the Sahara Hotel, Andy and Grace drove down to the Clark County Courthouse to get a license. Andy helped Grace out of the

Mustang on Third Street. They walked up the steps of the court-house together.

"I really don't want to do this," she said as they reached the door.

"I know that, Dr. Stevenson," said Andy gently. "As it happens, that simply isn't a factor now."

They went inside.

The Marriage License Bureau was brightly lit and looked like most municipal buildings, only cleaner. Two clerks sat at desks be-hind a brown Formica counter, typing up marriage licenses on computer keyboards. Three couples were before them, two of them dressed in tuxedoes and bridal gowns.

"What do we do first?" asked Andy to an elderly guard at the door.

"Each of you fills out a form on the table there," he said, point-ing. "Then you bring your completed forms to that counter there and they type up the license."

"And about how long does it take?" Andy asked.

"Less time than it takes to get a hamburger at McDonald's," said the guard with a crinkly smile.

Andy led Grace to the table. The marriage license application form was quite brief and apparently designed by someone whose major source of income came from art directing placemats for children's fast food restaurants. Other than name, address, date, date of birth, state of birth, father's state of birth, mother's state of birth, father's name, mother's maiden name, male or female, it asked only NUMBER OF THIS MARRIAGE? SPOUSE DECEASED? DIVORCED? WHEN? WHERE? ANNULLED? WHEN? WHERE?

Andy gave their completed forms to a middle-aged female clerk with platinum hair and gimmicky gold glasses, who tapped the data from their placemats onto the keys of her computer in quarter-pounder time. She then printed out the license and handed it across the brown Formica counter to Andy.

"Good luck, you two," she said.

"Thank you," said Andy.

"Well," said the guard at the door with the crinkly smile, "was it fast enough for you?"

"It took the perfect amount of time," said Andy, throwing him a wink.

"You're really doing this," she said.

"Absolutely," he said. "And now we need to rent our wedding costumes."

CHAPTER 87

LACK OF SLEEP began to tell on him. By 8 P.M. Max began to fade. By nine he was a ghost. At ten he excused himself from casino-searching with Cynthia, went up to the suite, entered the bathroom, stripped off his clothes, and stepped into a hot shower with little needles that performed acupressure on his neck and back.

So absorbed was he in the sensation of hot needles of water on his neck and back that Cynthia's arrival in the stall was a complete surprise.

Her body was aggressively voluptuous, flamboyantly firm. In size and firmness her breasts rivaled children's heads. She began to soap her body in long, sensuous strokes.

"I thought you might like a little company," she said.

"You thought wrong," he said, lathering his hair.

"When I was a showgirl," she said, "men would hand me a hundred dollars just to stand next to them and look beautiful while they gambled."

"Yeah?"

"When I was a showgirl," she said, "men sent me bouquets of white long-stemmed roses, with a crisp hundred-dollar bill wrapped around every stem."

"Men like Laverne Paccione?" he asked with a smirk.

"Don't knock Laverne Paccione," she said. "Laverne happens to be a sweetie. In the old days the Mob used to pay him to break arms or legs of somebody who screwed up. It was twenty-five an arm, fifty a leg back then. Once they paid Laverne to break a guy's legs and by accident he went and did the wrong guy. But Laverne is such a sweetie, you know what? He went and did the right guy for free."

"Kind of makes your eyes fill up," said Max, rinsing his hair.

"Why have you been avoiding me, Max? Don't you like women? Is that what the problem is? Because I've been practically throwing myself at you since the moment we met. I mean, what is the problem?"

"The problem," said Max, "is that you've been practically throwing yourself at me since the moment we met. Aggressive women don't leave me much to do but react passively. Submit or withdraw. Usually I withdraw."

She tilted her head at him and shook it pityingly.

"You know what I think?" she asked.

"No, what do you think?"

"I don't think I've been too aggressive. I think I haven't been aggressive *enough*."

She stepped forward, put one soapy arm around his shoulders, drew him in close, and grabbed his genitals with her free hand. He found himself simultaneously repelled and aroused, a disconcerting combination.

Max's cell phone, which he'd left on the bathroom sink, began to buzz.

"Excuse me, Cynthia," he said. "I think that's for me."

He managed to disengage long enough to slide open the shower door and step out onto the tiled floor. Rivers ran down his body. He picked up the phone on the third buzz.

"Hello?" he said.

Cynthia followed him out of the shower.

"This is Officer Halloran of the Kansas State Police Department," said a male voice as deep as the ones on commercials for

Dodge pickup trucks. "I'm returning the call of Detective Max Segal."

"This is Detective Segal," said Max. "Thanks for calling me back, Officer Halloran."

Cynthia snaked her arms around him from the rear and began to lick the ear that wasn't covered by the receiver.

"I love your skin," said Cynthia in Max's free ear.

"I'm calling with reference to a vehicle stop you made on August 21," said Max. "The vehicle was a white Mustang rented from Hertz, and the speeding citation was issued to one Grace Stevenson. Do you recall the stop?"

"I particularly love the skin of your ass," said Cynthia.

"Uh, yes sir, I do," said Officer Halloran. "I'm getting another voice there. Do we have a bad connection or what?"

"The skin of your ass and the skin right here on your cock," said Cynthia.

"Yeah, I think it's a bad connection," said Max. "Grace Stevenson is believed to have been kidnapped by one Andrew Woods, a paroled murderer and a suspect in three homicide cases I'm working in New York."

"I see," said Officer Halloran.

Cynthia walked around to the front of Max, knelt down on the tiles and swallowed his member.

"I was . . . wondering whether Stevenson had a . . . male companion and, if so . . . whether you noticed anything about him that might . . . help me," said Max, trying to maintain his concentration.

"I did notice a male companion," said Officer Halloran. "It was too dark to provide you with a description, however."

"I see," said Max. Max was trying to push Cynthia away, although not very hard.

"I do remember that the female appeared to be crying . . ." said Halloran.

"She was crying, you say?" said Max.

"Affirmative. The male volunteered the information that they were about to be married, and that she was having second thoughts."

"They were going to get married, you say?" Max asked.

Cynthia coughed and nearly choked.

"Married?" she said when her mouth was free.

"Affirmative," said Officer Halloran. "I told them that if they were having doubts, they ought to think it over. Sorry, but that's about all I remember."

"Who's getting married?" Cynthia asked.

"You've been a tremendous help, Officer Halloran," said Max. "Thank you very much."

He turned off his cell phone.

"Who the hell is getting married?" Cynthia asked.

"Andy and Grace," said Max, grabbing a towel and beginning to dry off. "My guess is they're going to one of the quickie wedding chapels in town here. If you know where they're located, I suggest we start over there as soon as we can throw some clothes on."

CHAPTER 88

IT WAS ABOUT ten thirty when they went back to the Sahara to change into their rented wedding clothes. Andy slipped into his tuxedo while Grace was in the bathroom putting on the gown he'd selected for her. When she opened the bathroom door, Andy was not prepared for his reaction. The sight of Dr. Stevenson in a white wedding gown brought tears to his eyes.

"My God but you're a beautiful woman," he said.

She didn't reply.

"I know you aren't doing this voluntarily, Dr. Stevenson," he said, "but I really do believe that in time you'll adjust to our arrangement. Who knows, maybe one day you'll even learn to love me—Stockholm syndrome and all that—if nothing else."

She looked at him reproachfully, her eyes wet, and said nothing. He slipped the Smith & Wesson into his tuxedo jacket pocket

"Well," he said, "let's get me to the church on time."

A Little White Chapel was in the midst of Wedding Chapel Row on South Las Vegas Boulevard. It stood cheek by jowl with automotive parts stores, pawnshops, and adult bookstores. IT'S FAST, IT'S FUN, IT'S CHEAP! proclaimed a sign on its exterior.

The chapel itself sported a white brick front, a steeple framed in white neon, and a white wrought-iron archway done in a floral pattern. There was a large palm tree the height of the steeple. There were two beds of artificial flowers and a carpet of bright green artificial grass surrounded the building. A sign, taller than both palm tree and steeple, proclaimed that among the celebrities who'd been married there were Judy Garland, Mickey Rooney, Frank Sinatra, Paul Newman, Sylvester Stallone, Michael Jordan, and Bruce Willis. There was a twenty-four-hour Drive-Up Wedding Window.

At 11 P.M., when Andy pulled into the driveway and up to the drive-up window, Grace began to cry.

"Please, Andy," she said, "let's not do this."

"Too late for that, Dr. Stevenson," said Andy. "Wheels have been set in motion."

A middle-aged Korean woman slid open the drive-up window.

"How are you folks this evening?" she called out to them.

"Couldn't be better," Andy called back.

"Ready to do a little marrying?"

"Ready as we'll ever be," Andy replied.

"May I have the license and the forty dollars please?"

"Here you go," said Andy. He leaned across Grace and handed the papers and the money out the window.

"You may give the minister any donation you so choose after the ceremony is concluded," said the Korean woman.

"Thank you," said Andy.

"Just a minute, hon," said the Korean woman. "I'll go get Reverend Love."

"We're not going anywhere," said Andy.

She slid the window closed.

"What if I refuse to go through with this?" Grace asked through her tears.

"Well, the gun is in my tuxedo jacket pocket."

"You mean you'd actually shoot me, sitting right beside you in this white bridal gown?" she asked.

"Oh, Dr. Stevenson, of course not," said Andy. "I'd shoot the minister. Right through his heart. It would be such a pity."

The window slid open again.

"This is Reverend Love," said the Korean woman.

A round-faced man with a comb-over stuck his upper body through the drive-up window.

"Evening, folks," he said.

"Good evening, Reverend," said Andy.

"Are your hearts both brimful of blessed love tonight?" he asked.

"That they are, Reverend," said Andy. "That they are."

"And will you be wanting the religious service or the civil?"

"What's the difference?" Andy asked.

"We would either include the name of the deity or not," said Reverend Love. "As you prefer."

"I think we'll forego the deity," said Andy.

"As you wish," said the Reverend, a little disappointed. "How are you tonight, young lady? You seem kinda quiet."

"This is just such an emotional experience for us both," said Andy.

"It should be," said the reverend. "Well then, shall we begin?"

At the conclusion of the service Andy took out the gold wedding band that had been given to Cynthia by Walter Woods and slipped it onto Grace's finger. Then he kissed her lightly on the lips. It was the first time he'd ever kissed her and it made his back and shoulders tingle.

"Congratulations, folks," said Reverend Love.

"Thank you, Reverend," said Andy, slipping him another twenty-five dollars for a tip. "Can I ask you something?"

"Certainly, son."

"Well, the hotel we're staying in isn't very romantic," said Andy. "Are there any honeymoon hotels around here that you know of?"

"Not in Vegas proper," said Reverend Love. "But if you don't mind a little drive, there's a honey of a place about twenty miles from here called the Memory Motel."

"The Memory Motel?" said Andy. "Is it south of here?"

"Yep," said Reverend Love. "Just outside Boulder City. Just as you come around the bend there. It's the first view you get of Lake Mead and it's a knockout."

"And it's romantic?" said Andy.

"You better believe it," said Reverend Love.

"Well, thanks for the tip," said Andy.

CHAPTER 89

"GOOD EVENING," SAID the elderly lady with the light blue eyes and the sweet smile, opening the door of the wedding chapel. "You folks in a marrying mood?"

"No, no," said Max, flashing his shield. "We're looking for a couple who might have been here—Andrew Woods and Grace Stevenson? The man is twenty-eight, blond, on the slim side, and—"

"Extremely handsome," said Cynthia.

"Clean-cut looking," said Max. "The woman is forty-two, short, petite, and very pretty?"

"I'm sorry," said the elderly woman, "I don't recollect marrying nobody of that description recently."

"Thanks just the same," said Max.

CHAPTER 90

WHOEVER DESIGNED THE Memory Motel loved the heart shape and the color pink. The sign outside the Memory Motel was heart-shaped and pink. The lettering was done in pink neon script. The motel itself was a series of heart-shaped pink stucco cottages overlooking Lake Mead. On the registration desk, right next to the guest register, was a sign that said THINK PINK.

"Good evening, folks," said the gentleman with the immaculately groomed and waved white hair and the pink blazer who stood behind the desk. "Would you like a pink *casita*?"

Before entering their *casita*, Andy insisted on picking Grace up and carrying her across the threshold. She was surprised at how gracefully he accomplished it.

Their bedroom had a heart-shaped bed and their bathroom had a heart-shaped tub, and everything everywhere was pink—towels, washcloths, sheets, blankets, walls, ceilings, carpeting, wastebaskets, toilet paper. There was even a pink heart-shaped pad by the pink phone on the desk.

Andy took out a quart of brandy, a pint of Cointreau and a little bottle of lemon juice and mixed them two tumblers full of sidecars. They both drained their glasses silently.

Without a word, he took out the dog collars and began buckling them around her wrists and ankles. She offered no objections. He pulled back the pink bedspread and the pink sheets and fluffed up the pink pillows.

"Lie down on your back," he said.

"In my dress?"

"Yes. On your back."

She lay down on her back. It took him a while longer to attach the leashes to the legs of the bed because of the peculiar heart shape, but eventually she was secure.

She silently watched him take off his clothes. She did not ask why he had to be naked and she had to be wearing her bridal gown. She felt numb. She felt frozen. She felt like a voyeur about to witness a kinky sex scene. Andy stripped down to his undershorts. She had never seen him undressed before. Although they had lived together for four days, he'd seen to it that, apart from the first night when he'd lifted her nightgown and looked at her naked buttocks for a few moments, neither of them appeared undressed before the other. But now he was nearly naked, and Grace noted that she very much liked his lean and well-muscled body. It was not so very different from Max's. It was more muscular. It was nine years younger.

"Dr. Stevenson," he said, "I have to tell you something."

"I suppose, since we're married now," she said, "it would be all right for you to call me Grace."

"Thank you, Grace," he said.

"Now what did you want to tell me?"

He mixed himself another sidecar.

"I'm extremely nervous about having sex with you."

"I see," she said. "Well, if it's any consolation, I'm extremely nervous myself."

"I guess we're nervous for different reasons," he said.

"Yes."

He finished his drink and lay down beside her.

"I just want to tell you," he said, "that whatever happens, I would never hurt you. I would sooner kill myself than hurt you."

Slowly, shyly, tenderly, he began kissing her and caressing her. She felt his erection through her bridal outfit and she felt herself beginning to melt, to respond to his touch in spite of herself.

For somebody who hadn't done it before, he wasn't bad. He covered her face with kisses, teasing her lips, never quite coming in contact with her mouth until he had kissed every other square inch of exposed face and neck and hair. Then he kissed her lips. Licked them. Sucked them. Bit them, but not quite hard enough to draw blood.

"Andy," she whispered.

"Yes?"

"Release my wrists."

"Are they too tight?"

"Release them. Please."

He reached up and to the right and unbuckled her left wrist. Then he reached left and unbuckled her right wrist.. He ran his hands lightly over the upper part of her dress, over her shoulders and down over the tips of her breasts and then down over her belly and her pubic area so lightly and so swiftly that he barely touched it, except that she could trace the path that his fingertips had taken by the trail of fire that it left behind. He began to unbutton the long row of buttons that led from the high neck of her gown all the way down the front.

"May I have another drink?" she whispered.

"Of course," he said.

He got up and poured her an entire tumbler full of brandy, with just a splash of Cointreau and a few drops of lemon juice. She drank it off in about six gulps. Then she put down the glass and kissed him gently on the lips and then she slipped her arms around his neck and drew him down on top of her.

A sob caught in his throat. He held her very tightly and began to kiss her again around the face and neck and on her mouth. She shivered involuntarily.

CHAPTER 91

IT WAS ONLY half past midnight. The sign outside the wedding chapel said they were open twenty-four hours a day, but even after Max and Cynthia knocked on the door and rang the bell for several minutes, nobody appeared.

"I think they're asleep," said Cynthia.

"They probably went home," said Max, pounding on the door.

"No, I think they live here," said Cynthia. "When business is slow at night they just go to bed until more customers appear."

"Well, these people are either very deep sleepers or else they're dead," said Max. "Come on, let's go on to the next one."

At that moment someone appeared at the door. A middle-aged man with tousled hair and sleep in his eyes was buttoning up his shirt, trying to look cheerful.

"Well, well, good evening, folks," he said. "Or should I say good morning?"

"Hi," said Max. "Sorry to have awakened you."

"Not at all, not at all," said the man. "Well, you two seem mighty anxious to get married. I think that's a good way to start out a life of wedded bliss."

"We're not looking to get married," said Cynthia. "We're looking for a couple you might have married earlier tonight or maybe last night."

The man's face didn't fall but it did slip a notch. Not only had he been roused from a deep sleep, now he wasn't even going to get paid for it. He struggled to retain his cheerful manner.

Max took out his shield and showed it to him. "Andrew Woods and Grace Stevenson?" said Max. "The man is twenty-eight, blond, and clean-cut looking."

"Drop-dead handsome," said Cynthia.

"The woman is forty-two, short, petite, and very pretty," said Max.

"I'm sorry," said the man. "I've married quite a few lovely couples in the past few days, but nobody answering that description."

"Well, thanks anyway," said Max. "Sorry to have awakened you."

"No problem," said the man. "Just do me a favor."

"Yes?" said Max.

"If you two ever do decide to tie the knot, think about throwing the business my way?"

"We'll certainly keep you in mind," said Max.

"That's all I ask," said the man.

By the time they drove up to the next wedding chapel on the street, Max was beginning to lose heart. It was past one thirty in the morning. They'd already gone to two dozen chapels and found nothing.

"I just realized something," said Max.

"What's that?"

"We're just checking chapels on Wedding Chapel Row. What if they got married somewhere else, like downtown? There must be dozens of chapels we're not even thinking about."

"Why don't we go back to the hotel and do this by phone?" Cynthia suggested.

"They might not want to give us any information unless I show them my detective's shield," said Max, knocking and ringing again.

When the door finally opened, the Korean woman who appeared seemed less than pleased to see them.

"I hope you already have the license," she said, "because if you don't—"

"We're not getting married," said Max, flashing his shield, "we're looking for two fugitives you might have married tonight or the night before."

"Fugitives?" said the woman. "Fugitives from what?"

A round-faced man appeared, combing moist side-hair over his bald head.

"Good morning, folks," he said, a determined smile on his face. "I'm Reverend Love. Are your hearts brimful of blessed love this morning?"

"They're not here to get married, Otto," said the woman. "They're looking for fugitives."

"Fugitives?" said Reverend Love. "Fugitives from what?"

"The man is a paroled murderer and a suspect in three homicides," said Max. "His name is Andrew Woods. He's twenty-eight, blond, and clean-cut looking. The woman is Grace Stevenson. She's forty-two, short, petite, and extremely—"

"Oh, yes, the Woodses," said Reverend Love.

"You *remember* them?" said Cynthia.

"Of course I remember them," said Reverend Love. "I remember everyone I marry."

"Then you did marry them?" said Max.

"That I did," said Reverend Love, "that I did."

"About how long ago?" Max asked.

The Reverend looked at the Korean woman.

"About how long ago would you say, Emma?"

"Maybe a couple hours," she said. "Couldn't be much more than that."

"Did you notice anything unusual about them?" said Max. "Anything out of the ordinary?"

Reverend Love looked up and to the left, as though his replay screen was in that corner of his mind. "I recollect the missus was a bit on the quiet side," he said.

"Anything else?" Max asked.

"Not really," said the Reverend.

"Was there any indication of where they might be headed?" Max asked.

"Not really," said the Reverend.

"Didn't you say they asked for recommendations of places to stay?" asked the Korean woman.

"I'm sorry," said Reverend Love, "of course they did. Mr. Woods asked me whether I knew of any honeymoon hotels in town. I don't know how that slipped my mind. Getting senile, I suspect."

"And what did you tell him?" Max asked. "Did you give him any recommendations?"

"Just the one," said the Reverend.

"Are you going to tell us what it was," said Cynthia, "or is Vanna White going to come out here and help us guess?"

"Oh, I *am* sorry," chuckled Reverend Love. "It's the hour, I suspect. Yes, I told them about the Memory Motel down near Boulder City. Do you know where that is?"

"I know where Boulder City is," said Cynthia.

"Well, that's what I suggested to them," said the Reverend. "About twenty miles south of here on Route Ninety-five. Lovely place perched on a hill, overlooking Lake Mead. Don't know if they took my suggestion, but you might check it out. Mr. Woods is a murderer, you say?"

"That's right," said Max.

"A murder *suspect*," said Cynthia.

"And what is Mrs. Woods being sought for?"

"Cradle-robbing," said Cynthia.

———

"I can't believe it," said Cynthia when they got back into the car, "I simply can't believe it."

"What can't you believe?"

"That Andy would actually marry that woman. I'll bet she put him up to it."

"Put him up to it! Cynthia, Grace Stevenson is Andy's *prisoner,*" said Max. "He kidnapped her and brought her here by *force.* Almost certainly at gunpoint, if he still has the weapon he swiped from you."

"Nevertheless," said Cynthia, "I'll bet it was her idea. Andy's simply not the marrying kind."

Max shook his head, sighed, and kept his focus on his driving. The speedometer of the Thunderbird, he noted, was creeping up toward ninety.

He prayed that Andy had taken her to the Memory Motel, as Reverend Love suggested. He despaired of finding Grace untraumatized after all that she'd been through. He could only imagine the degradation and the suffering he must be putting her through at this very moment.

CHAPTER 92

THEY LAY IN each other's arms.

"I love you," he said.

She said nothing.

"You love me, too," he said. "You may not be ready to admit that yet, but it's okay, it doesn't matter. You do, that's the important thing. I can tell."

She continued saying nothing.

"Listen, Grace," he said. "Come with me to Mexico. I assure you they'll never find us there. Route Ninety-three goes all the way down to Nogales. I have friends in Acapulco. We'll be safe there and nobody will ever find us."

She sighed. "That's crazy, Andy," she said.

"It's not crazy," he said. "It's perfect. We'll be perfect together. Remember in the joint you told me you thought I might have the tools to make it on the outside? And the understanding to have a real relationship with somebody? A relationship that's intimate and caring?"

"I was crazy."

"What?"

"I was crazy," she said. "I was wrong, Andy. You've killed three women since I told you that."

"Yes, but that was before you and I became lovers. Now that we're lovers, everything is different, everything is changed, don't you see that? Now that we're lovers, I'm a changed man."

"Whatever you say," she said.

"Come on now," he said. "Get your things together. We're getting out of here."

"Now?"

"Yes, now."

"Andy, take a look at the time. It's two A.M. Why don't we at least wait till morning and think it over calmly and rationally in the light of day?"

"I don't *want* to think it over calmly and rationally in the light of day, Grace, I want to act precipitously and passionately in the dead of night. I've broken parole and I'm a suspect in three homicides. For all I know, the FBI is closing in on us at this very moment. Get your things. We're going to Mexico."

CHAPTER 93

A S THEY CAME around the corner, there it was below them, just as Reverend Love had said. Lake Mead. And there, perched on a hill overlooking Lake Mead, was the Memory Motel.

Max pulled into the parking lot and did a quick check of the cars.

"No white Mustangs," said Max.

"Maybe they decided not to come here after all," said Cynthia.

"Maybe, maybe not," said Max, opening the door. "Come on, let's see if they're registered."

They went into the motel office. No one seemed to be around. They rang the bellman's bell on the desk and waited.

In a few minutes they heard bustling, and a gentleman with white hair and a pink blazer stumbled into the office. His hair looked lopsided and there were pillow marks on his face.

"Good morning, folks," said the man. "Would you like a pink *casita*?"

"No thanks," said Max. "We're looking for a man and a woman named Andy Woods and Grace Stevenson. The man is twenty-eight, blond, and clean-cut looking. The woman is short, petite, forty-two and—"

"Ah, yes," said the white-haired gentleman, "Mr. and Mrs. Woods. A lovely couple. Checked in just a few hours ago."

"Then they *are* here," said Max excitedly. "What room are they in?"

"Well, first of all," said the man, "we don't call them *rooms* here at the Memory Motel, we call them *casitas*. And second of all, I'm not permitted to reveal that type of information."

Max showed him his shield. "This is police business," he said. "Mr. Woods is a suspect in three homicides."

"Oh, dear me," said the man. "He seemed so polite."

"Can you tell me what *casita* they're in and give me the key?"

"Well, I suppose so," said the man. "Dear me, this has never happened before."

He reached under the desk and brought out a key attached to a pink plastic heart with the number seven on it.

"Lucky number seven," said the man. "Just go out to the right and down the path."

"You stay here," he said to Cynthia, going out the door of the motel office.

"I'm coming with you," said Cynthia, trotting after him.

"There may be gunplay," said Max. "You could get your head blown off."

"It's my head," said Cynthia.

"I order you to remain here," said Max, irked.

"On whose authority?" she said.

"On the authority of the NYPD," he said.

"The NYPD didn't send you here," she said, "*I* did. I'm coming with you on *my* authority."

Max sighed mightily and counted *casitas* till he came to number seven.

"Stay away from the door," he whispered. "And don't make a sound."

He drew his gun, fit the key attached to the pink plastic heart into the door, flung it open, and stepped quickly away from the open doorway.

"Police, Andy!" he yelled. "Don't fuckin' move!"

There was no response. He stepped into the darkened *casita*. Gripping the gun with his right hand, he patted the wall near the door with his left. He found the light switch and turned it on.

There was no one in the bedroom. The bed was unmade, the closets empty. Gun extended, he entered the bathroom. No one. Cynthia had followed him into the *casita*.

"They flew the coop," she said.

Max reholstered his gun.

"On the way down here," said Max, "very few vehicles passed us going the other way. I counted two trucks and five passenger cars. None of them looked like a Mustang, and none of them were white."

"So?"

"So when Andy and Grace left here they were headed south. Once you leave Boulder City, Route Ninety-five and Route Ninety-three separate. They're following Ninety-three. They're going to Mexico."

CHAPTER 94

I'M CRAZY, SHE thought. *I am certifiably insane. I have let a serial killer believe I'm going to go and live with him in Mexico.*

They had left the Memory Motel in haste and were in the Mustang, heading south. Just outside of Boulder City the highway left the flat desert, ascended sharply, and snaked up into raw, craggy, mountainous terrain bereft of trees. A brutal lunar landscape that, in the moonlight, looked even more so.

"Hey," said Andy enthusiastically, "we're almost at Hoover Dam. Ever been to Hoover Dam?"

"Can't say I have," said Grace.

She knew that Andy had to be sent back to prison, to start serving time for his crimes and to get back into the Violent Offender Program. And in the eyes of the law she was quite probably his accomplice.

"This place used to scare the shit out of me when I was little," he said, chuckling. "Cynthia used to take me to the top of the dam and make me look down."

Having been his accomplice would have serious repercussions for her legally and professionally. She might have to go to prison. She would certainly have to go back into treatment. She would certainly have to discontinue her practice because of what she'd learned about herself that she hadn't known before—her inability to maintain boundaries, her own sadomasochistic tendencies, and so on.

"The top of this dam is as high as a seventy-story building," said Andy. "And the wall is curved, so when you look down there are no straight lines. You have no way of gauging the depth, and that really gives you vertigo."

She was tempted to excuse her odd behavior as a function of Stockholm syndrome, which caused prisoners to identify with their captors. Patty Hearst had been the most celebrated example of the Stockholm syndrome in the States, but Patty Hearst had been a young college girl at the time of her capture, and Grace was a middle-aged psychotherapist.

"Grace, you haven't said a word in the last twenty minutes."

"Just thinking, that's all."

"About what a great time we're going to have in Mexico?"

"Mmm."

Perhaps she really ought to go with him to Mexico. Her chances for a professional life in Mexico couldn't be any worse than they'd be in Vermont after a fiasco like this. And Andy was a good deal more interesting than any man she'd ever met in Vermont Psychoanalytic.

"Not chickening out on me, are you?" he asked.

Realistically, though, what the hell would she ever be able to do in Mexico? She didn't even like Mexican food. No, she had to get away from him. He was affectionate now, but she knew how quickly he could revert to violent behavior and hurt, maybe even kill, her.

"Andy, I was wondering," she said. "What would you think about going on ahead of me, kind of getting the lay of the land and then sending for me?"

His sunny tone vanished in an instant.

"I thought you were coming with me," he said.

"Well, this is a really important decision for me," she said. "I just think we ought to talk about it a little, that's all."

"You *are* chickening out on me," he said.

"I'm not chickening out on you," she said, "I'm just considering some of the more practical aspects of the situation. I need time to go back and get my affairs in order."

"Why?"

"Well, I left a lot of loose ends back there."

"Like what?"

"Well, for one thing, I have to go back to my hotel in New York, get my things, and check out. I have to go back to Vermont, select the things I want to take with me to Mexico, give the rest away or put them in storage. I just can't take off as impulsively as you can, Andy. Not at my age."

The road curved gently to the right, then twisted sharply back upon itself to the left. Coming around the turn, the dam itself suddenly hove into view.

It was an overwhelming sight. Between 1931 and 1935, 325 million cubic yards of concrete had been sculpted into an elegant Art Deco masterpiece. Bathed in floodlights from the bottom, the wall that held back the Colorado River and formed Lake Mead curved upward 726 feet. The wall at the base of the canyon was 660 feet thick. An army of spiky electrical towers marched out of the canyon at improbable angles, hauling power to three states.

"Good God," she said, "would you look at that."

"Yes," he said quietly. "Ninety-six people died building that thing. They fell."

"That's horrible," she said.

"Their bodies were smashed to pieces on the rocks below," he said. "What a way to go."

"Ghastly."

"Well," he said, "at least it's fast."

They were now on the upgrade to the dam itself. The road curved gently up over the top of the dam and then down again, a horseshoe tilted up off the horizontal axis. In the precise center of the horseshoe, U.S. 93 passed from Nevada to Arizona and the road began its descent into the red rocks. Four gigantic round intake towers behind the dam wall on the left rose eerily out of Lake Mead, sinister municipal buildings on an unfamiliar planet.

As they reached the center of the horseshoe, Andy turned to look at her.

"You have no intention of coming with me to Mexico, now or ever, do you?" he asked. "Tell me the truth."

"That's not it," she said, "I just need time to sort things out, that's all."

He pulled suddenly off the road and stopped the car.

"The *truth*," he said, his voice rising an octave in pitch. "The *truth*."

"Andy, I *am* telling you the truth. I really *do* intend to look into winding up my affairs as quickly as humanly possible and then—"

"In-*tend*? Look *in*-to? As quickly as humanly *poss*-ible?" he said. "Bullshit! Swear to me right now, right here, that you are coming with me now! Say right now 'I swear to God I am coming with you!'"

"Andy, I just told you I—"

"No," he said. "*Swear* it!"

"I can't swear it because I—"

He reached into his jacket and pulled out the gun, looked at it, jammed it back into his jacket, and threw open the door. He got out of the Mustang and ran toward the wall of the dam.

"Andy, what are you doing?" she cried, getting out of the door and running after him, suddenly recalling his attempts at suicide.

He had reached the wall. Placing his hands on either side of the chest-high parapet, he boosted himself into a standing position. He stared downward in morbid fascination.

"Andy, come down from there! What are you doing?"

He turned and looked down at her.

"I have no life without you, Grace," he said. "Are you coming with me or not?"

"Andy," she said, reaching out to him, trying to pull him to safety. "Please come down from there, please!"

"I love you, Grace! Do you love me? Tell me if you love me!"

"Yes!" she cried. "Now please come down from there!"

"Are you coming with me to Mexico or not?"

"Yes, I am! Please, Andy, you'll fall!"

She reached up frantically, but he eluded her.

"Swear it, Grace! Say 'As God is my witness, I love my husband, Andy Woods, and I will follow him anywhere, to Mexico or anywhere he chooses for us to go!' Say it!"

"I swear it, Andy, I—"

"Use the words I used: 'As God is my witness . . .'"

"'As God is my witness . . .'"

"'I love my husband, Andy Woods . . .'"

"'I love my husband, Andy Woods . . .'"

"'And I will follow him anywhere . . .'"

"'And I will follow him anywhere . . .'"

"'To Mexico, or anywhere else he chooses for us to go . . .'"

"'To Mexico, or anywhere else he chooses for us to go'—Andy, please!"

He suddenly grabbed her hand, yanked her up onto the parapet and hugged her to him.

CHAPTER 95

IF MAX AND Cynthia encountered few vehicles coming toward them on the way to Boulder City, they encountered fewer yet once they left the Memory Motel.

From flatness the road leapt into some of the harshest landscape Max had ever seen, twisting and turning back on itself like an angry serpent.

"What do you think the chances are we'll catch up with them?" Cynthia asked.

"If we drive all night and check out every truck stop and motel on the way for white Mustangs?"

"Yeah?"

"Not great," said Max. "But better than the needle-in-the-haystack situation we were working with in Vegas. And better than the much worse situation we're going to face once we get to Mexico."

"You'd actually follow them into Mexico?" asked Cynthia, impressed.

"I won't have any less jurisdiction in Mexico than I do here in Nevada," said Max.

CHAPTER 96

OH, ANDY, I'M scared," she said, trembling in his arms, trying not to look down at the yawning expanse of concrete curving more than seventy stories below her.

"I'm scared too," he said. "But fear is a rush, isn't it? It heightens all other sensations."

"Please let's get down before we fall," she said. "I don't want to die, do you?"

"I don't really know if I do or not," he said, continuing to stare downward.

"Well, I don't want to, and I don't want *you* to, so please, please let's get down."

"Do you really love me?" he asked.

"Yes," she said.

"And you'll really come with me to Mexico?"

"Yes, but please let's get down before we trip, or before the wind blows us off the wall."

"You promise you'll come with me? Cross your heart and hope to die?"

"Cross my heart and hope to die—please, Andy."

"All right then," he said. "In that case let's get down."

Slowly, carefully, they stooped down and held onto the parapet wall. He held her hand and guided her to jump the yard or so to the pavement.

"Come on, Andy," she said, looking up to him, reaching up her hand.

He smiled warmly at her. And then he jumped, just as a car came around the curve and onto the road at the crest of the dam. It was a 1957 T-Bird.

CHAPTER 97

THERE'S A CAR parked at the side of the road," said Cynthia. "A white Mustang!"

"And two people down there by the wall," said Max.

He pulled the Thunderbird to a stop. The two people were definitely a man and a woman. The woman was short and petite. Grace!

"Stay in the car," he said to Cynthia.

He opened his door, yanked his gun out of his shoulder holster, and put both feet on the pavement, crouching low behind the car door, using it as a shield.

"Don't move, Andy!" yelled Max. "Step away from Dr. Stevenson, drop your weapon, and put your hands where I can see them!"

"No, Max," said a voice at his back. "*You* drop *your* weapon and put your hands where I can see them!"

Keeping his gun pointed in Andy's direction, Max half turned and glanced over his shoulder.

Cynthia had a .45 automatic pointed at his back.

His first thought was where the hell had Cynthia gotten another gun? His second thought was Laverne Paccione.

"Stay out of this, Cynthia," said Max. "This is police business."

"I like you, Max," said Cynthia. "But if you don't drop your gun, I'll shoot you dead."

"Cynthia, you're making a dreadful mistake here," said Max. "Put away that gun before you get hurt."

"Max, I'm serious," said Cynthia in a steely voice he hadn't heard her use before. "Drop your gun or I'll kill you."

Very, very slowly Max turned away from Cynthia, showing her his back.

"Andy, drop your weapon and put your hands where I can see them!" yelled Max.

"Max, this is your last warning."

Would she actually shoot me? Max wondered. He doubted it.

"Don't do this with guns, Max!" yelled Grace. "Andy is willing to negotiate a peaceful solution!"

The automatic exploded behind Max, the round passing within an inch of his left ear.

Max dropped his weapon on the pavement, half deaf from the gunshot, his ears ringing, his back mercifully unpunctured.

"Andy, dear," called Cynthia. "Are you all right?"

"Quite all right, Cynthia," Andy called.

"Are you two really married?"

"Yes, Cynthia, we are."

Cynthia thought this over and sighed.

"Well, that's not irrevocable," she said. "Dr. Stevenson, step away from my son!"

"What?" said Grace.

"Step away from my son, Dr. Stevenson, and climb up on the parapet!"

Cynthia pointed the automatic in their direction.

"What the fuck are you saying?" yelled Andy.

"You belong to *me*, dear," said Cynthia. "Not to that slut of a shrink. Dr. Stevenson, step away from my son and get up on that parapet immediately or I'll shoot your fucking heart out!"

Andy stepped in front of Grace, shielding her with his body. He took his .38 out of his jacket and pointed it in Cynthia's direction.

"Don't do this, Cynthia!" yelled Andy. "I'll shoot you if I have to!"

A sudden wind came up, unexpectedly warm at this late hour of the night, smelling vaguely of sewage. It ruffled Cynthia's hair and she patted it in place with the hand that wasn't holding the automatic.

"Andy, dear, I love you more than life itself!" called Cynthia. "But if you don't step away from that slut shrink immediately, I'll shoot you both!"

"I mean it, Cynthia!" Andy shouted. "If I have to kill you to save her, I will!"

Cynthia considered this. She reached into her jacket pocket with the hand that wasn't holding the gun and withdrew a small brush and touched up her hair.

"Step away from her, Andy!" Cynthia called. "I'm not going to warn you again!"

"Please don't make me do this, Mother!" Andy pleaded, cocking his revolver. "I love her!"

Mother? How perfect that he'd chosen this moment to call her that. Well, nice try, kid, but years too late.

Aiming for Grace's face, Cynthia's automatic exploded three more times.

The first two bullets were wild, a foot over Andy's and Grace's heads.

The third bullet passed through Andy's left eye, the entry wound considerably smaller than the exit wound.

If the shot had been any lower or Grace any taller, it would have passed through Andy into Grace, killing them both. As it was, it killed only Andy.

Cynthia stared in horror at what she had done.

Max scooped his gun off the pavement and, in a single fluid motion borne of considerable practice on the range, whirled on Cynthia and got off a shot.

It caught her in the chest.

A second, third, fourth, fifth, and sixth shot came from the direction of the parapet, and one of these caught Cynthia in the neck.

Blood spattered all over the blue Thunderbird as Cynthia flew backward, dead before she hit the ground.

Max turned back and realized that Grace had picked up Andy's revolver and emptied it in Cynthia's general direction.

Max put his gun away and walked shakily toward Grace. By the time he got to her, she had dropped the .38 and was sobbing uncontrollably. He wrapped his arms around her so tightly she found it hard to breathe, but she never wanted him to let go.

CHAPTER 98

CYNTHIA'S SISTER IN Barstow had vanished into the California desert without a trace.

Since neither Cynthia nor Andy had any known next of kin, when their bodies had been autopsied and all police matters had been settled and all Nevada, Vermont, and New York State red tape had finally been cleared up, the Clark County coroner released the remains to Max, who was permitted to have both bodies cremated in Las Vegas.

The night of the cremations, about five minutes before midnight, Max and Grace stood at the edge of the three-acre artificial lagoon surrounding the volcano in front of the Mirage Hotel. Floodlights lit the fifty-four-foot high volcanic cone. Max and Grace each held a cheap-looking gray cardboard box.

Max's box held the ashes of the woman who had paid for his trip to Las Vegas, who had enabled him to clear the three homicides perpetrated by her son, and who had performed unsolicited fellatio on him in the shower. Grace's box held the ashes of the man who had killed three women in cold blood, who had kidnapped her, who had forced her to rob a drunk, who had forced her at gunpoint to marry him, and who had then more or less raped her, although sort of tenderly.

"What are you feeling?" asked Grace quietly.

"I don't know," said Max. "Relieved. Sick to my stomach. Terribly sad. Glad it's over. Horribly guilty you had to go through . . . everything you went through. What are *you* feeling?"

Grace didn't answer for a while.

"Nothing very appropriate," she said finally. "I'm usually pretty quick to come up with facile pop psych summations, but I can't do it here. I mean they were both horrible people, both psychopaths, and yet . . . I don't know. There was a certain . . . sweetness to Andy, you know?"

Max nodded.

"Yeah, and Hitler loved animals," he said. "Especially dogs. I mean he *adored* Blondi, his German shepherd. But before he committed suicide? He had some of the cyanide capsules he was planning to swallow tested on Blondi. And guess what, they worked. Well, poor Hitler was inconsolable. Oh, and then he had her puppies shot."

"Yeah," she said. "But still."

At precisely twelve o'clock the floodlights on the volcanic cone went off, and the music began, mostly drumming. Tom-toms, bongos, congas, tropical rhythms. Fiery blasts whooshed higher and higher, some more than sixty feet into the air. Fiery plumes, choreographed to the drumming, billowed up from over a hundred gas pipes at the surface of the lagoon.

Max nodded to Grace. Both of them opened their boxes and poured the contents into the water.

"Ashes to ashes," said Max. "Well, technically, ashes to the lagoon surrounding the volcano that *produces* the ashes."

"I think Andy and Cynthia would have approved," said Grace.

On the following morning, the day that Max and Grace were finally able to leave Las Vegas, the temperature hit 117, which was not even a record. Max burned his hand on the pitted chrome door handle of the blue Thunderbird when he got into it for the final trip to McCarran Airport.

When they turned in the Thunderbird at the Rent-A-Wreck counter, a chirpy young woman with bouncy blond hair greeted them, smiling irrationally.

"So, did you guys get lucky in Vegas?" she asked.

Max and Grace exchanged looks.

"Well, in the sense that we're still alive, I guess," said Max.

"Sounds lucky to *me*," said the chirpy young woman.

Shortly after the airline learned of Cynthia's demise and Grace's ordeal, they'd given Grace permission to fly first class back to New York on Cynthia's ticket. When their flight was called and first-class passengers were invited to board, at first neither Max nor Grace got up.

"Oh, hey, that's us," said Max.

They got up and moved to the gate.

In line at the entrance to the jetway, just as he was about to hand his boarding pass to the flight attendant, Max realized he had never played Sam's fourth quarter.

He turned and got out of line.

"Max? Where are you going?" Grace called after him.

"Just something I need to do," he said.

He walked five yards to the bank of slots nearest the gate and was pleased to see that they were part of the Quartermania jackpot pool.

He fished in his pocket and came up with Sam's last quarter.

He listened for the mystical voice, but it was finally silenced.

He dropped Sam's quarter in the slot anyway and pulled the handle down.

The three reels whirred, spun, and came to a stop, one by one by one by one. Four cherries.

It took Max several seconds to realize that the perky tune emanating from the machine meant that he had won a hundred thousand dollars.

ABOUT THE AUTHOR

Photo by Judith Greenburg

Dan Greenburg's 73 books have been translated into 24 languages and include the two previous bestsellers in the Max Segal series, *Love Kills* and *Exes*. Dan has also written the humor books *How to Be a Jewish Mother* and *How to Make Yourself Miserable*, as well as many movies, TV shows, Broadway shows, and he's been a stand-up comedian and a tiger tamer, among other things. To research *Fear Itself*, Dan spent two years with NYPD homicide cops, going to crime scenes and autopsies to check out corpses, accompanying detectives on high-speed car chases and door-busting arrests. Dan also spent several weeks doing research in maximum security prisons, interviewing convicted murderers in their cells.